the shadows behind her smile

Karen Millie-James

KING OF THE ROAD
PUBLISHING

King of the Road Publishing

First published in Great Britain by
King of the Road Publishing Limited in 2016

Copyright © Karen Millie-James 2016

A catalogue record for this book is available from the British Library

Hardback ISBN: 978-0-9935496-0-1
Paperback ISBN: 978-0-9935496-1-8
Ebook ISBN: 978-0-9935496-2-5

Set in 11.5/13.5pt Garamond by Geoff Fisher
geoff.fisher@yahoo.co.uk

Author photo by Rosanna Harris
Design by South Facing Geese Limited

Printed and bound in Great Britain by
CPI Group (UK) Ltd, Croydon, CR0 4YY

King of the Road Publishing Limited
Unit 2 Capital Business Park
Manor Way
Borehamwood
Herts WD6 1GW

www.kingoftheroadpublishing.com

For Mum and Dad
Their love, inspiration and guidance,
forever in my heart

Acknowledgements

What a wonderful writing journey this has been. I never thought it could be so rewarding or such an incredible experience but the more I wrote, the more my imagination expanded. The Shadows Behind Her Smile has been such a joy to write and I already miss it. I owe a debt of gratitude to so many people for their help and guidance without whom I would never have reached this point.

First of all my editor, the incomparable Elaine Denning. She has been tireless in her efforts to make my book the best it can be and her input has been invaluable. We have laughed together, almost cried together more than once, been up all night emailing and discussing options for the characters and their scenes. My book and I have taken over her life but it has been worthwhile. Elaine is an absolute gem and, I trust by now, a very good friend. I look forward to working with her on the sequel, Where in The Dark.

The research I have carried out over the last three years has been enhanced by a very good friend who has given me an insight into the army world. Thank you. Of course I could not forget my staff, nor my marketing team at King of the Road Publishing for getting the book out there. All of them have worked tirelessly and under pressure with enthusiasm and wit. Also, my sister in law, Deena Niren, for being as much like a sister as you could get and reading through one of the first drafts and liking it, Mark Iles for his input, Jim Sheehan at Signature Books for believing in me and Bill Norris at Central Books for all his help and advice.

A massive hug of thanks and appreciation goes to my daughter, Rosanna, for all her support during the last three years of this work in progress. She knew that writing a book was my lifetime dream and now it has come to fruition. I was nervous for her to read a draft but she ended up being an amazing critic, giving me feedback that I took on board. To quote her words, "Never in a million years did I think it would be this good nor get so hooked I would stay up until 3am because I couldn't put it down." I am glad she had confidence in me and am as proud of her as she is of me, more so, and love her up to the stars and back again.

Last, my husband, Peter, who has been my sounding board. He started reading the initial drafts but gave up when I changed things around. He helped me to analyse my characters, enacting scenes around the kitchen in his inimitable way and despite the fact, apparently, I never listen to him, on many occasions I do, and have listened. He is always there for me, making me laugh most of the time, and we make a spectacular team. You are appreciated and loved more than words can say.

Karen Millie-James
London, March 2016

Prologue

FOUR YEARS EARLIER

BLACK storm clouds gathered ominously overhead as if to signal that the day was destined to be catastrophic, as if it was waiting for the hand of God to reach down and fire the wrath of Hades. That was exactly how Cydney felt as an incredible sense of premonition washed over her and the terrible vision that had repeatedly inhabited her dreams, which she had chosen to banish from her mind, came flooding back.

The crunch of tyres on the driveway shook Cydney from her daydream. This was it. This was the time. It had happened as she knew it would beyond a shadow of a doubt.

She grabbed the sink in front of her with both hands as the blood drained from her head. Everything slowed down as if she was still in her dream and the world had stopped spinning. Cydney removed and folded her gloves and laid them carefully on the side of the sink, trying to delay the inevitable. Turning around, she pulled down the sleeves of her jumper, ran her hands through her hair and walked from the kitchen to the front of the house, her steps slow but sure.

Poised in the hallway, she waited for the doorbell to ring. She took one glance up the stairs towards the twins' bedroom, relieved to know they weren't there, and watched through the glass in the front door as a black saloon pulled up outside and two men in brown army uniform stepped out, one wearing captain's insignia, which she easily recognised. The men straightened down their jackets, placed their caps, glanced at each other and walked towards the house, their steps hesitant.

Opening the door, she said nothing. One held out a brown cardboard box towards her, willing her to take it and relieve him of his unwanted charge.

"Mrs Granger?" the other asked.

Cydney stood frozen to the spot. Her mouth wanted to work but if she spoke it would mean finality.

"I'm so sorry, ma'am..."

The words floated in the air as Cydney fell to the ground.

CHAPTER ONE

THE taxi was stuck in London traffic, which had come to a complete standstill. Cydney glanced at her watch again but no matter how often the second hand moved, it was not going to make the traffic disappear – nor was it going to get her to her meeting any quicker. The train had been an easier option to take that day, rather than asking Sean to drive her into London. Since he had work around the house to finish, he would have been so frustrated at not being able to get back to it.

When Steve died in the bombing in Afghanistan some four years ago, the retired Sean, who was a sergeant in her husband's battalion and with him at the time of his death, had stepped in to help, taking care of the house, the children, and tending to Cydney like a precious piece of crystal that could shatter at any moment. He had been her life-saver, her road to recovery. She wanted so much to know what had happened but Sean refused to answer any of her questions. All he told her was the captain had saved his life and in return he would always be there for her. Since then he had been living in the game-keeper's cottage with his daughter, Sophie, who was now housekeeper and nanny to the twins. Cydney trusted him with her life, knew she was in capable hands and that Steve would be happy he was around.

The honk of a horn pulled her from her thoughts and she watched as a driver manoeuvred his car purposefully in front of another. Lorries, vans and buses full of people surrounded her and the rising heat of the early Summer's day made her feel uncomfortable. The last place she wanted to be was dressed in her business suit, sitting in a stuffy, airless taxi in steamy London, with her toes already starting to pinch in her Manolo Blahnik shoes, but everyone on foot looked even more ill at ease than she felt. Men, unable to loosen their ties, strained their necks as perspiration slipped down the backs of their shirts, ladies wobbled on impossible heels and heavily laden tourists dragged suitcases along uneven pavements. However, once the cold air from the air conditioning began circulating around the taxi, her earlier mood evaporated.

London never ceased to amaze her. Cydney had travelled extensively around the world, especially with Steve when they were newly married, visiting many cities, but each time she returned to her place of birth it was always with a sense of awe at the constantly changing vista. An excitement went through her every time and brought back memories of her childhood, dressing in her best clothes and going to the pantomime with her family.

Cydney allowed her mind to wander to the day ahead. She had an appointment with her old friend and client, Rupert Van Der Hausen, Chairman of a large South African investment group, who was unexpectedly in town and had requested a meeting in Knightsbridge to discuss their future plans. The year before she had undertaken all the legal and corporate regulatory research, or due diligence as the lawyers called it now, and then overseen the purchase on their behalf of a sixty-five million pound commercial property in Central London. She knew they were still considering enhancing their portfolio. Cydney was looking forward to seeing Rupert again. He had always supported her, especially after Steve had been killed.

He had called her up the day before and told her he wanted her to look at a large corporation called Centurion Holdings but didn't tell her why. Centurion had interests in hotels, commercial buildings and large residential properties around Mayfair and Chelsea. She had spent most of the day delving into their history and it made interesting reading. While she had managed to obtain some details, who was the head of forensic investigations in her company, was good, but forty-eight hours would have been better notice even for him.

Cydney, excited at the prospect of the day ahead, tried not to get too stressed about the traffic situation, but thoughts of the morning's events at home did nothing to aid her. Getting Lauren and Jake off to school was not an easy task by any stretch of the imagination. There was always something forgotten in the rush and although she had Sophie to remember all the little things - packed lunches, washed sportswear and signed forms for the upcoming trip away - there was no time to just relax and get used to the day. Having fourteen year olds was wonderful and they were great kids, but oh... to be able to sit at the breakfast table and read the newspaper without the constant battles going on around her would be heavenly, just occasionally.

As the taxi snail-paced along the Euston Road from Kings Cross Station and up towards University College Hospital on the left, the traffic lights turned red and the taxi once again came to a standstill. The driver moaned, wiping the dripping sweat away from his forehead. The trip was interminable. Cydney sighed, glanced at her watch again, and became aware of a coldness along the length of her right side. She felt the hairs on her arms stand on end and recognised the feeling she knew so well. She waited, wondering who was there. Was it someone connected to the taxi driver? She really didn't have time for this today. Then she understood, because a middle-aged man in blue striped pyjamas jumped into the taxi and sat down next to her. The sense of him invaded her whole being, and even more goose bumps bristled along her arm. She looked ahead at the driver and could see he was still concentrating on the road. Were he to look in his mirror, he would undoubtedly see a smart, self-assured businesswoman, with an air of confidence and success, sitting alone in the back of his cab because Cydney chose to communicate with spirit telepathically.

"I was in that hospital over there." The man pointed it out to her to his left. *"The room up there on the fifth floor. I have no idea what I'm doing here with you."* He moved his head from side to side, as if trying to fathom things, and she picked up on his feeling of frustration and bewilderment.

"Last thing I knew I was in my bed, with my wife holding my hand and my kids sitting next to me. Now I seem to be going somewhere. What the hell's happening here?" The view of the busy and noisy London road changed to that of a quiet and sterile hospital room. By tuning into the man using her power of vision, Cydney was shown where he had lain in his bed with tubes in his arm and an oxygen mask over his face. Everyone was talking in whispers around him and his wife and three children were weeping. It was apparent that every breath was painful as his face contorted with the rise and fall of his chest, while nurses moved around him, checking he was comfortable. When Cydney saw the man's spirit rise above his body as he took his last breath, she understood exactly what had happened and the sense of sadness around him took her breath away. The love that came through to her from the man and his family was overwhelming and tears welled up in her eyes. She turned and looked at him, reaching out to hold his hand. Of course she had time for this.

"I know this is so difficult to understand," she said gently. "You must feel very strange."

"What am I doing here? Where are my wife and kids?"

"They were in the hospital room."

"That makes no sense — I'm here."

"Yes, you are, but your body isn't."

He looked down and saw he was in his pyjamas. It was as if he didn't recognise himself, sitting in a taxi in the middle of London. He was a man in his mid-fifties, his face pleasant with a sense of kindness that reached his eyes, slightly red rimmed against his paleness. His large hands were rough and leathered, used to manual work.

"I was in my factory. Plastics, mouldings. Always worked with my hands." He turned them over and back again, looking down helplessly.

"Can you tell me your name?" Cydney asked.

"Ray. I think I had a heart attack. I remember going in an ambulance from work." Suddenly the realisation hit him and his demeanour changed. "Oh my God! No! Sheila! My factory! My brother will take everything!"

A view of a large industrial unit came clearly into Cydney's vision where a few men dressed in blue overalls controlled the workings of a large conveyor belt, along which travelled empty plastic casings in varying colours. At the end of the belt, two women ensured the cases fell correctly into packing boxes. The sound of the machines was loud to her but it felt strange that nobody spoke, instead concentrating on their tasks, occasionally throwing sideways glances at each other. The atmosphere was tense and Cydney could feel everyone's apprehension.

Up from the ground floor was a walkway with metal safety railings, behind which she could see a row of glass fronted offices, one slightly wider. A man strolled out of the main office – he looked like a younger version of Ray. Approaching the railings, he placed his hands on them, rocking forward slightly as he viewed the factory floor, arms wide apart as if he were about to preach a sermon. A few of the workers stopped and glanced up at him but realised it was better to get on with their work. He had a look of 'the cat getting the cream'. His smile only reached his mouth, his eyes cold and calculating. He nodded to himself, shouted a quick instruction down, then turned around and walked back into the office.

"Your brother, is his name Charles? I just saw him leaning on the railing outside the office, looking down on the factory floor."

"So, he's there already. Well that didn't take long, did it? I knew he was up to something."

"Why do you say that?"

"He's had his eye on my business for years. I took him on to try to help *him make something of himself. I looked after him when our parents died and brought him up like a son and this is how he repays me. He got into trouble with the police, in with the wrong crowd. You see, he's fifteen years younger than me. We were on the brink of getting a huge order from the States. He wanted me out – said I was getting past it, time to move on and to hand over the reins but I've worked so hard and I know he'll run the business into the ground. He wants to sell off the building and make way for the huge supermarket that wants our land. All my old workers, my friends, would be made redundant. I can't let it happen."*

Cydney considered the scenario. Ray must have come through to her for reasons other than the fact she happened to have been passing the hospital. She knew having this gift of mediumship meant people reached out to her as if she were a beacon, but there was always a motive behind her visions.

"He won't help Sheila and the kids. My lovely children, they'll have nothing…all my money was tied up in the factory, you see. This order we were holding out for, it meant we could pay off the bank. Charles had shares in the company but I can't recall if I ever finalised my Will. I left it all to my solicitor. Now I think he has the whole lot. I never thought this would happen. I know I've been a complete fool when it comes to business, but I was a hard worker and loved nothing better than getting down on the shop floor with my men. Charles thinks all that's beneath him. He drew up all the paperwork with our lawyer and I trusted them both. What a complete idiot I've been."

"Ray, I will try to help you. Will you trust me?"

"What else can I do – who else do I have at the moment?"

"Ok. First thing, what's the name of your company?"

"Rayshel Plastics – me and Sheila, my wife, it's our names."

"I'm going to look into this for you, I promise. You know I can contact you and when this is sorted, you'll be able to move on."

"What do you mean?"

"Ray, you've died - you do understand that, don't you? And you can't stay with me all day."

"But…where will I go?"

"You'll be helped by others who've already passed over. This is a period of healing and recovery for you. In the meantime, I'll find out what's going on with your brother. You have my word I will come back to you."

As Ray left her, albeit reluctantly, his body melting out of the taxi, Cydney's skin returned to normal. She was now alone and the thoughts of the man faded to be replaced by the nose-to-tail traffic as the taxi driver turned south off the Marylebone Road and into Park Crescent, a beautiful area of London with elegant stuccoed terraced houses forming a semi-circle, which linked to Regents Park opposite. As they moved between the two halves of the crescent, Cydney looked into the private garden and saw between the railings the seven feet high statue of Queen Victoria's father, Prince Edward, wearing his field marshall uniform. Driving through brought pictures to her mind of old English gentry and peers of the realm visiting in their private carriages.

Turning her attention to the day ahead, Cydney took the opportunity to read through her papers once again. It was important nothing should go wrong and that the client maintained his faith in her. However, thoughts of Ray wouldn't leave her. She took out her mobile and dialled her assistant.

"Granger Associates – Jennifer Vere-Nicholson speaking."

Cydney never tired of hearing the sound of the phone answered so professionally by the staff of her own company. Jenny was her right-hand woman and had started work the day she and Steve had established the company. She had built up her own client base and always explained that she was learning from the master. Her father had been knighted several years ago for his contribution to industry and Cydney liked the fact she had such a good pedigree. Jenny was in her mid-twenties and had joined the company straight from university where she'd read law and criminology, deciding she didn't want to go into law itself but work in commerce. Cydney had taught her the business world she'd come to know and love and now she completely relied on her; she was worth her weight in gold. With no time for small talk she got straight to the point.

"I'm on the way to the meeting but I want you to do a complete check on a company for me called Rayshel Plastics. Get Richard to help you. I want everything by the time I come into the office tomorrow morning."

"Not much notice then…"

"This is important – full report, records, accounts, criminal stuff."

Cydney rang off. She knew they could trust Richard. Even though retired from CID he still had an 'in' to the powers that be. Now she could sit back and relax a bit whilst they did their work.

The taxi driver found a short cut around the back of Regent Street towards Park Lane and then around Hyde Park Corner that was thankfully clear and, as she gazed out of the window with the papers still spread over her knees, Cydney thought of how amazing it was to have got to this point in her life. Now, in her early forties, she was financially secure, completely besotted with her twins, loved the adrenalin rush she received from her work and wanted for nothing. The spiritual awareness that had been a part of her life since childhood was something that felt so special to her, and she loved the way it crept over into all aspects of her business life. However, the depth of her sorrow of being without Steve had never disappeared.

A feeling of satisfaction washed over her and she relaxed back into the seat. When they reached The Park Tower hotel in the heart of Knightsbridge, just a block from Harrods and across the street from Hyde Park, Cydney walked through the magnificent marbled entrance to the reception desk and asked for her client, who had taken one of the dedicated meeting rooms on the lower ground floor. Locating the stairway down the hall, she entered the room and was greeted by Rupert Van der Hausen, his financial director, Johann Andersen, and a third person she didn't recognise. Rupert rose from his position at the head of the board table to greet Cydney, leaning forward to kiss her on both cheeks. Distinguished and handsome, even in his early seventies, his full head of grey-white hair now extended into his beard. As normal, he was impeccably dressed in his trademark navy double-breasted suit with a coloured handkerchief poking out the top pocket to match his tie. With his chocolate brown eyes that always seemed to be smiling, it was hard to believe he was one of the wealthiest men in South Africa with companies and investments around the globe.

"How are you, Cyd?" Rupert used the familiar diminutive only allowed for her close friends and family. "You remember Johann, I am sure, and this is our counsel, George Edwards."

Cydney was again kissed, by Johann. She did remember him. A quiet guy but very astute when it came to Rupert's affairs. Turning to George, she received a firm handshake and was slightly taken aback by the way his eyes looked straight into hers.

"Pleasure to meet you, Mrs Granger. I've heard so much about you from Rupert - all good." He laughed and she noticed how his eyes crinkled at the corners as he did so.

"How are Lauren and Jake? They must be growing up," Rupert asked.

"They're fine. Fourteen now." He shook his head. "I can't believe it either."

"Well, come and sit down and let's see where we are with everything. Sorry about the short notice, Cyd. You know how I work though – when I see something I like, well, I need to get right to the bottom of things."

Cydney handed out the set of bound papers to each of the gentlemen and watched as they flipped through them, studying their faces to ascertain any reaction. From time to time George's concentration wavered and he looked intently at her, putting her slightly off kilter. She smoothed her hair and crossed her legs, his eyes following her every movement.

"Ok, so I've found some information you wanted. Centurion is a privately owned UK property investment and development company."

"Who are the current owners?" Johann interrupted.

"An offshore company located in the British Virgin Islands; Pegasus Group. Shall we call it the BVI for short. The directors, I assume, are nominees based there."

"What's this company, Northwest Holdings?" Johann asked. "Registered in Jersey, I see. Not a name I have come across."

"They own fifty percent of the shares in Pegasus," Cydney responded. "Then twenty-five percent of the shares are each held through two other BVI entities, called Whitfield International and New Cross International. I'm still using my resources to get the rest of the information on the ultimate shareholder information but nothing is on public record. Unfortunately, the jurisdiction provides anonymity for owners of companies but it doesn't help when you want to find out anything useful. I will get it though. Here, look at page three." She indicated the status report with the information detailed. They turned the pages simultaneously.

Rupert sat back in his chair and Cydney watched as he filtered through the information. "This is a heavy set up just for a UK company. What are they trying to hide?"

"Agreed, but at the moment I don't know. There could be a number of things. I have the financials if you look on page five. The entire portfolio is worth about five hundred and fifty million pounds. A private bank has a charge over some of their assets, which I've listed on page six," she added.

"You have been thorough. What do you think, George? Are you with us?"

"Yes, of course, sorry." George seemed to be lost in a space of his own.

And this is his counsel? Cydney thought. She caught Rupert giving the man some strange looks. Well, it was about time Mr Edwards took notice of what was happening around him, instead of looking her up and down.

"I'm interested in buying one of their properties in the docklands, but in all honesty I might be prepared to go for the whole portfolio if the price was right. Got plans for residential conversions. Could be really big for us, Cyd. I've been told by a reliable source it's for sale and that the company's in trouble, so they might do a quick deal. Can you get to the bottom of the shareholders for me, though? I need to know who I'm negotiating with and that if I'm going to be spending my hard-earned millions, the deal will go through without any hitches."

"Yes, of course. Can you give me a few days?" Cydney asked.

"Always, as it's you." He laughed. "We're flying off to Germany. I'll leave George here to work with you and will be back early next week. He'll keep me briefed, okay?"

George's smile never quite reached his eyes, which disturbed Cydney. For some reason she couldn't fathom, he didn't look happy at the prospect of spending time with her, despite his previous glances in her direction.

"Yes of course. He can come and work in our office. We'll set him up in the boardroom."

"Thanks for coming along today. It's been really lovely to see you. Give a big hug to the twins from me."

Leading Cydney to the door, Rupert bent to kiss her goodbye and she whispered, "Stop matchmaking."

His laughter followed her, even as she walked up the stairs to get a taxi back to Euston. She could always rely on her client and friend after all these years to make her feel good.

She rummaged in her bag for her mobile and dialled the office. Jenny answered and Cydney didn't give her a chance to speak this second time either.

"Me again. Can you put me through to Richard?" After a brief pause his voice came on the line.

"Hi Cydney," he said, "how's it going?"

"I met with Rupert and his minions. The legal guy is going to be at our offices for a few days from tomorrow. Can you ask Polly to sort him out in the boardroom, if it's not being used? You know the company we were looking at – I need more information. We need to find the actual beneficial owners, not just the shareholders who may be different, so see what you can do. Also, get Ash involved. We need access to all the records. Do we still have that guy on our payroll in the BVI?"

"Fortunately, yes. What about the plastics company?"

"That too."

"You don't ask a lot then."

"Which is why I pay you so much. I'll see you about nine-thirty tomorrow, after dropping the kids off at school." She put the phone down.

Richard had reminded her about Ray and his problems. As she passed by the hospital on the way back to the station, she glanced up towards the room that he'd pointed out. Her two worlds often crossed over and she found having a sixth sense helped her business, but this matter with Ray was something quite different and she couldn't get it out of her mind.

She caught the train to Bilhampstead where Sean was waiting for her and, as they entered the long tree-lined driveway to her house, she felt a calm wash over her. Before the storm probably, she thought, as she knew the twins – or rather Lauren – would be after her time as soon as she walked in.

The estate was at its most beautiful this time of year with all the trees in bloom, and her heart skipped a beat as it always did when she saw her house as if for the very first time. She and Steve had bought it together before the twins were born, spending a fortune renovating it exactly the way they wanted.

Every item had been purchased with thought and love. If only Steve was with her to share everything.

She shook away the thoughts as Sean brought the car round to the front of the house. As he opened the door for her, Lauren came bursting onto the driveway and ran into her arms.

"You'll never guess what happened, Mum!"

CHAPTER TWO

CYDNEY was woken by the sudden shrill of the phone next to her bed. She reached out her arm and picked up the receiver.

"Is that you, Cydney? I'm dressed and waiting. Why aren't you here?"

Cydney glanced at the clock next to her, rubbing her eyes to wake up properly. This wasn't the first time she had been woken in the middle of the night by her mum, and it certainly wouldn't be the last.

"It's three o'clock in the morning. You should be asleep."

"But you're picking me up. We're going shopping. I'm all ready."

"Mum, that's on Saturday, today is Wednesday. You need to get undressed and get back to bed."

"But I want to go shopping."

Inwardly sighing, Cydney moved and propped herself up against her pillow.

"Look out the window. It's dark. I'll come and see you tomorrow but shopping is in three days' time, okay?"

"Oh."

"Shall I call the nurse to come and put you back to bed?"

"No. I'm not five. I'll do it myself."

"Night night then. Love you, Mum."

"Love you too, sweetheart. I'll get undressed."

"Good. See you tomorrow."

As Cydney put the phone down, she sighed with the thought

of her mother being in the nursing home all alone in her room and trying to get herself back to bed. She decided to call the night staff anyway, just to make sure she was alright. No doubt she would phone again and they would have the same conversation. Her mum was slowly deteriorating and she knew that as the dementia progressed, it was going to be a downhill struggle.

"Nan?"

Cydney looked up to see a very sleepy-eyed Lauren peeping around the door.

"Yes – want to come in for a cuddle?"

Lauren padded across the room and jumped in next to her, curling herself around and into Cydney's arms. Thankfully, Lauren was not yet too old for this.

"I don't think she's well," Lauren mumbled.

"Why do you say that, baby?"

"I saw her the other night standing next to my bed. She said she had to leave us and wasn't feeling well."

"Are you sure you weren't dreaming?"

"Mum! I've told you before that I see things. Don't you believe me? I speak to Grandpa sometimes, too."

She had no reason at all to doubt her daughter. Why shouldn't Lauren have inherited her gift? However, her mum coming through worried her immensely. Something wasn't right. She understood the fact she could connect with spirit but normally it was with people who had passed over. If her mum was able to travel whilst sleeping so deeply, it would mean she was hovering between two worlds.

"Were you frightened?"

"No, it's nice to have them around. And Grandpa helped me find my locket, didn't he?" she said, reaching for it. She flicked it open and Cydney turned her head on the pillow to look at the tiny picture inside – her, Steve and the two children together.

"We looked everywhere, you remember. It used to be in the

little box with the ballet dancer that turned around to 'Twinkle Twinkle Little Star'."

"I know. And Grandpa told you it was behind the chest of drawers."

"I looked and there it was, as if by magic."

"Well, this time look after it."

"I'm never going to take it off. Mum, I'd never asked for anything before, but when I did, he helped me. Do you think he could help with my exams?"

Cydney laughed. "I'm not sure it works like that."

As Cydney thought back to her own childhood, she stroked Lauren's long dark hair and looked down at the face that bore so much of a resemblance to Steve. She knew sleep was not on the agenda for her now.

She recalled the first time she saw spirit, although she didn't realise it at the time, and how she used to sit and watch from her bed with some curiosity as two men in dirty grey clothing went about their work at the end of her bedroom. She couldn't quite see their faces as they wore peaked caps pulled down over their heads. They carried various sorts of tools, like shovels, and moved silently in and out of the wall between her room and the flat next door, where her best friend lived. One day they looked as if they were burying a big box in the wall where her old cot stood and one man, when he saw her looking, held his finger to his lips and said, "Shush," so she knew it had to be kept a secret. They were always around and sometimes they used to play with her, sending lovely balls of light around the room, like tiny bubbles, which she would try and catch. The sounds the bubbles made were like whispering fairies and she delighted in playing with them.

Cydney was only four at the time and dressed in a pretty pink flannelette nightie her mum had made for her, her hair tied up neatly in a ponytail to tame the curls that always managed to escape. She didn't need her cot any more as she was a big girl and it would soon be used by her new little brother or sister, who her mum told her she was having just for her. Cydney thought it strange that the men seemed to totally disregard the cot and move straight through it as if it wasn't there. She also wondered what was in the box.

One night she told her grandma about the fairy lights and the two men, when she came to sit on her bed to read her a story. She whispered into her grandma's ear in case the man who told her it was a secret could hear.

"Look, over there, that's where the men disappeared. I can't see them now, but shall I show you where they go?" Cydney climbed out of bed, took her grandma's hand and pulled her towards the side of the cot. "They buried secret treasure just here," she pointed, "and there are lots of fairies around."

"Yes my darling, I know. I've seen things like that, too. But I think we should keep our little secret and not tell anyone," she said, and tucked Cydney into bed with a kiss on her forehead.

"Shall we look for the treasure box?" Cydney asked.

"Maybe another time."

Cydney didn't know if her grandma ever told her mum and dad but it didn't really matter to her. She accepted what she saw and the important thing was that she was never frightened. Sometimes she used to stay awake on purpose to play. One morning, however, she decided to investigate for herself and try to find the treasure. She crawled down under the bottom of the cot and reached out her hand towards the corner of the wall. There was nothing there, so stretching further to feel right under the skirting board where there was a tiny gap, her hand made contact with some sort of rough edged paper, just as her dad entered the room.

"What are you doing? We're going out and you're going to get dirty lying there. Please get up."

"I want to find something special. I can feel it here and it's a present."

Pushing the cot out of the way, he pulled Cydney up and bent down to look. There was something poking out from under the skirting. He managed to clasp the corner of it and drew out a document of yellowed sheets of paper tied together with green ribbon and bearing a big red seal on the front.

"What's this? This isn't yours, Cyd."

Cydney couldn't explain at all. Her dad untied the ribbon and flicked through the pages, his eyes moving up and down the long sheets. He called out to Cydney's mum.

"Jan, come and see what we've found. I think it's someone's Will."

Cydney watched as her mum took the document from him.

"Gracious. It belongs to the man who lived here before us. I think he died in this house. Look, that's his name, Reginald Davies. How strange. How did you find it?"

"I didn't. Cydney did."

They both looked down at her and she just stood there, arms behind her back, and shrugged her shoulders, swaying from side to side.

"It was just there," she said.

"Ron, there's a solicitor's name here, we should contact him."

"What does the Will say?"

"I can't read that," she replied, "it's private." But then she snatched the document from him, turned through the pages and read it.

"It talks about some money he's left to his three children. He put it in a box, hated the thought of banks, and it's in a safe place behind the wardrobe, waiting for them."

"What wardrobe?"

"Well, there must have been one here before we moved in. This Will must have fallen down the back of something and somehow got pushed under the skirting."

Her dad got back down on his knees and felt around the back of the wall, knocking with his hand to feel any difference in the noise.

"It feels hollow here."

Cydney's mum got down next to him and felt around herself. Cydney stood there watching, knowing they would find something.

"We could be wasting our time, Jan. I've just decorated. I didn't notice anything before."

"We can't leave it. It may be important. Somebody might be waiting for money. Go and get a knife or something."

Cydney's dad left the room, muttering under his breath, but after a couple of minutes of banging drawers and cupboards he returned with a few tools. He sliced into the wall and revealed a large panel about twelve inches square, then took the knife along the other side and used a different tool to loosen around all four sides. After some jiggling it came away in his hands and there, sitting in the hollow of the wall, was a large black and gold-edged money box with a small lock attached. Her dad broke the lock easily and lifted the lid to reveal thousands of old banknotes.

"Good lord! What do we have here?"

"Ron, we have to take these to the solicitor. Are they still valuable do you think?"

"I believe they always retain their value, no matter how much time elapses. I'm sure we can check."

"I can't believe it." She turned to Cydney. "How did you know about this?"

"It's secret treasure. I told you it's secret," and she refused to say anything more on the subject. Her parents simply stared down at her in astonishment.

CHAPTER THREE

CYDNEY woke up with the sun streaming through the bedroom window and Lauren's long legs flopped over the top of hers. Carefully moving them, she eased herself out of bed, stretched her arms and headed to the bathroom to shower.

"Here we go again," she mumbled, as the water splashed over her.

Fifteen minutes later she applied her make-up, studying her face in the mirror to see if any wrinkles had appeared. Not yet, thankfully. Her roots needed touching up a little due to some grey appearing, but she could deal with that. Steve had always said her eyes were her best feature, he loved their greenness. Such a long time ago now, she thought. She shook her head as if to move on from the memory, walked to the wardrobe and slid her lime green suit from the hanger. Today was going to be busy for her; she had the wonderful Mr George Edwards joining her at the office all day, which would be amusing no doubt. She wanted to follow up on the offshore companies' situation, and of course she wanted to see what Richard had found out about Rayshel. That plagued her more than anything for some reason. Perhaps she simply hated injustices.

Sean drove the car to drop the kids off at school. Lauren gave Cydney a goodbye hug but Jake merely shrugged his shoulders and grunted. With them safely behind the school gates, Sean made his way to St John's Wood, near the centre of London where her offices were located.

"You're looking good!" Jenny said with a smile as Cydney

walked through to reception. "Your Mr Wonderful is in the boardroom. Arrived with the milk. He must be keen!"

"Very amusing. I'll go and see him first. Could you come in afterwards? I want a meeting with everyone at ten in my office. By the way, nice dress yourself."

"Okay boss," Jenny responded. "And thanks." Cydney blew her a kiss and walked down the corridor to the boardroom where she found George, who seemed to have made himself very much at home.

"Nice offices, Cyd." The use of her diminutive for some reason immediately annoyed her.

"Thank you. I see you're making yourself comfortable. Anything else I can get you?" She was almost ashamed as the note of sarcasm entered her voice.

She glanced around the boardroom. He had spread all his papers out on the board table, his laptop was open, the phone had been moved within his easy reach and he had a cup of tea and a half eaten croissant next to him. His jacket and tie were off. She avoided looking at his shirt, open to reveal a few dark, stray hairs she couldn't fail to notice.

"No. I'm fine thanks." He looked her up and down. "You look good. I like the suit."

She straightened her skirt, trying not to let his comments affect her. She hadn't dressed for him for goodness sake, so she ignored his words.

"I have my guys looking at the companies for you and I'll update you later, if there is anything. My office is next to reception."

She turned and walked out, aware his eyes were following her.

Jenny brought in the post and they spent a few minutes going through everything from the previous day, sharing out the workload. Richard and Ash put their heads around the door.

"Okay to come in?"

Richard Barrett was a bear of a man at well over six feet, a gentle giant in every respect and loyal to her completely. He'd worked his way up the ranks of the Metropolitan Police, taking early retirement as a Detective Superintendent, and Cydney felt blessed to have him on her team. Having been in the Fraud Squad for many years and moving into the business world with Cydney, his knowledge was invaluable. Also, he knew people, good and bad.

Ash Khattak was her IT specialist. He was a young man in his twenties, of Indian parentage but brought up in South London. He had been with her for about two years and was a graduate with intimate knowledge of computers and software, and an ability to gain access to even the securest of computer networks. Sometimes Cydney didn't want to know how he gained his information – it was all about results as far as she was concerned and the ends justifying the means, as long as she maintained the integrity and honesty instilled in her from a young age. It was never about breaking the law, as such, and in any case, she was confident in her belief that Richard would always keep her on the straight and narrow.

"Yes, come in. Have a seat. So, where shall we start? Richard, what did you get for me on Rayshel?"

"I found some information for you but who's the client?"

"Friend of mine. I said I'd do her a favour as her husband has just died. Non chargeable."

"So, now we're a charity?"

"Aren't we always?" She smiled at him. He was always watching her back.

"The Company was set up in 1979 by a guy called Raymond Gordon," Richard began. "He was sole director until 1993 when his brother, Charles came on board. Shareholders are the two of them. There was a transfer of shares dated August 1994 from Sheila to Charles. Strange that one, though. Raymond and his wife had fifty percent each until then. Anyway, the company is not doing particularly well. Here are the latest set of accounts from Companies House." He passed a stapled document to Cydney that Ash had downloaded. "The assets are there – building and land owned by the company, probably worth on the open market up to three and a quarter million, but it could be much more to the right buyer. I also checked the register of charges. Everything is mortgaged to Barclays. The plant and machinery are worth a bit, I'm sure, but totally written down in the balance sheet as capital allowances. Staff costs are quite high. It appears that regular dividends are paid out so there are no retained earnings left at all. Ash managed to get copies of the last tax returns." He glanced up. "No good looking like that, Cydney, and raising your eyebrows. Look…"

Cydney flicked through the accounts and tax returns. She should be used to surprises when it came to obtaining unavailable information.

"They're running on air. If the company doesn't improve, I wouldn't be surprised if the bank calls in the loan. Where has all the money gone?"

"Ah, well I have that answer. Here are the company's latest bank statements."

"The bank statements? How the hell…?"

Richard produced them with a flourish. "There's a lot of it going out to Charles every month, including car payments for a BMW and others to American Express. Not much is going to Raymond though, except a monthly salary, and certainly nothing to his wife."

"Well, maybe I shouldn't ask how you got this, but good work. What about the memorandum and articles of association, or a shareholders' agreement?" Cydney asked.

"I looked through the mem and arts. There are pre-emption rights in the articles – if either Raymond or Charles dies, the remaining person has the immediate right to buy the shares at nominal value and bypass the estate of the deceased. I don't believe Charles was thinking of his death first when this was drafted. Also, I doubt there's a written agreement in place but virtually impossible to check, even for us."

"Who on earth would allow that to happen?" Jenny asked. "It makes no sense to me. And surely that's not legal."

"Something very peculiar though, Cydney," Richard continued, acknowledging Jenny's remarks with a shake of his head. "I've managed to get my hands on the bank facility documents. Look here," and he passed her further papers. "The original facility was taken out in 1979, but has been extended a few times in the last few years. The signature at the bottom belongs to Charles Gordon but I wonder if Raymond knew about it."

"I had no idea you were so resourceful," Cydney said.

"Amazing who one knows! Also, I have Raymond's life insurance policies," Ash added, causing Cydney's eyebrows to rise further. "The sole beneficiary is Charles. However, look. The signatures on this and the bank papers are clearly different."

"So nothing to Sheila?" Cydney questioned.

"Nada."

"What about Charles himself?"

"Not a good boy. He got into trouble when he was a lad. Spent some time in a young offenders' institution – stealing cars, you know the score. Got out, no work, back inside for robbery with violence in 1985 and released after three years. He went abroad to Spain for a while, working in the nightclub business allegedly, then returned in 1993. He's been with Ray's company ever since."

"I'm very impressed you got all this, and in just a few hours. I'll remember this next time I ask you something and it takes forever."

"We aim to please."

"By the way, Ray may not have finalised his Will. That's something to bear in mind."

So Charles has been taking money out of the company, forging Ray's signature and somehow getting away with it, she thought.

Now she understood why Ray was so concerned for his wife and kids. At this rate, they would get absolutely nothing. She had to think through what she could do.

"Jenny, can you try and find Sheila's number for me. I want to go and see her."

"I thought she was a friend of yours?"

"She is, but I've lost it." A lame excuse, she knew.

Jenny knew all about Cydney's sixth sense so asked no more questions when Cydney gave her the look she recognised. Jenny knew she kept that part of her life very much under wraps.

"What about Centurion, Richard?"

"Can you give me another couple of hours? Just putting everything together for you."

"Yes of course, it'll give me a bit of time to catch up. Thanks everyone."

Cydney's mind was with Ray now and she felt him coming through to her again. She shivered as his presence appeared next to her, this time not in his pyjamas but in slacks and a shirt. He somehow looked younger and not so pained.

"I heard," he said.

"So now you know. Look, I'm going to go and see your wife, is that okay? I'll make some excuse about your engaging me to look at your affairs. Do you think she'll be up to it?"

"Yes. We discussed my passing, if it happened suddenly. Though we never thought it would. I said we would have a password, something that I could reach out to her with if needed. Just say 'Venice' to her. She will understand and will see you."

"Venice?"

"Yes. We went there on honeymoon. You have to put this right for me. I'm relying on you. Just don't let Charles get away with anything."

"Ray, as I said before, you can trust me. I'll do whatever's within my power."

Once again, he faded away into the air.

Cydney spent the next couple of hours going through emails

and dictating various letters to her secretary, Polly, a nice girl who had recently joined the company and was very keen to fit in. She heard a knock at her office door, and in walked George. Yes, he certainly was Mr Wonderful to look at. *Take your mind back to your work, girl,* she said to herself.

"How can I help you?"

"It's lunchtime, fancy a bite?" She ignored the innuendo, which he clearly meant by the look of the wry smile on his face.

"Actually, yes I do. There's a nice wine bar around the corner. I'll just get my bag." She turned to Jenny. "Back in an hour. We can go through the files then."

"Have a nice lunch you two. Together," Jenny called after them. Cydney glanced back at her as she walked out the office and got a thumb's up. Honestly.

"I fancy going to Covent Garden. I haven't been for years."

"I don't have all day, George."

Choosing to ignore her, George summoned a taxi. Cydney was keen to get on with her work, yet he wanted to go on a 'jolly' for the afternoon. Mustering all her powers of patience, she climbed into the taxi beside him and thirty minutes later they alighted by The Royal Opera House, right in the heart of Covent Garden. They strolled around the corner towards the central square with its street performers and George chose a rather busy bar where they could sit outside to watch the world go by. He obviously didn't want a quiet table for two somewhere, she thought. He disappeared inside to order their meal and returned with two glasses of Pinot Grigio.

"Thought you might like one of these. Nice warm day, cool wine."

"Thanks." Cydney took it with pleasure, needing a lift.

"Don't you just love everything going on here?" A man dressed in a colourful clown's costume rode by on his unicycle, holding out a hat to take donations from the crowd. Despite herself, Cydney had to laugh and threw in a pound coin. The clown doffed his hat in return and sounded his horn, which was more of a squeak than anything else.

"You see? This is fun. Perhaps you need to get out a bit more." What a cheek the man had. "Anyway, Rupert tells me he's known you for about fifteen years and was one of your first clients."

"Yes, we go back a long way. I think the world of him. He's been like a father to me."

"So I hear. He also said you lost your husband some time ago. I'm very sorry about that."

Cydney's eyes met his and she really felt he meant it. Perhaps he wasn't such a player after all. However, it was not something she was willing to talk about to anyone. This was too close to home and she certainly wasn't going to let down her guard under any circumstances.

"Yes. It was a long time ago."

"Sorry. That was insensitive of me. I shouldn't assume you want to talk about it."

"Nice wine," she said as a response.

"You know, I'm not such an ogre. But I respect you don't want me to ask you about him."

Instead, he began to tell her about himself. He was single, aged forty-three, and educated at Harvard. He had worked with a New York law firm for a few years before moving to Johannesburg, where he'd retrained and was eventually admitted to the Johannesburg Society of the Advocates in order to practice. A mutual acquaintance introduced him to Rupert, whereupon he joined the corporation. That explains his accent, Cydney thought to herself; a mixture of New York with a slight hint of South African, a rather intoxicating combination.

"I decided not to return to New York as there was nothing to go back for. My parents had died and I had no siblings and, well, Rupert looks after me. I travel the world and I'm happy with my lot. Are you happy, Cyd?"

27

"Yes, thank you. I lead a busy life and love my work. What more could I ask for?"

"What more indeed," but he looked at her as if he didn't believe a word she'd said.

They finished eating and walked to The Strand. George held her elbow as they crossed the road, exactly as Steve used to do. She felt a frisson of feeling, a shadow moving across her, a voice in her head. She was attracted to him, who wouldn't be? He was extremely good looking, smart, educated, and fun to be with – and he acted in a caring way. But was mixing business with pleasure a good thing? More to the point, was it too soon for her? She had a feeling he was going to ask her out for dinner. If he did, should she go? Would Steve mind? She grieved for her husband daily, hourly sometimes, and would never stop loving him. She felt regret at what they had lost but she was still young. Perhaps he wouldn't mind her going on the odd date or two.

"Cyd? Look, please don't think I am overstepping the mark but are you free for dinner one night?"

She smiled. "Actually, I believe I could be."

See? She had done it.

George stopped in the street and turned to her, looking straight into her eyes, a playful smile stretched across his mouth.

"I don't want to wait. Let's do this now. Take a chance. Let's not go back to the office."

"But, that's ridiculous. I have work to do. Everyone's waiting for me. Rupert is expecting answers from me."

"Just for once. Be spontaneous. When was the last time you played hookie?"

"Well… I just can't. Never actually."

"Exactly. Come on. Let's go out now."

"No, George. Really I can't." She saw the disappointment etched on his face and somehow felt really disappointed with herself for refusing him.

"But I'll come out with you tonight."

"Not a bad concession then. I'll take that, and gratefully. Now I shall get you back to your work."

The team were all assembled and waiting for her when she eventually returned. Richard waved some papers at her as they resumed back in her office. This time George joined them.

"Oh, by the way Cydney, here's Sheila's number, the one you lost." Jenny passed her a slip of paper, emphasising the word *lost* with a little smile.

"Thanks. Okay, so where are we...Richard?"

"Not so easy this one, as everything is well hidden. There are interconnecting companies, trusts, all in different jurisdictions. You name it, they've done it. It took me ages to try and piece this one together so I'm just going to start from the beginning and take you through it."

"Odd in itself then - why hide so much? Anyway, go for it."

Richard walked over to the flip chart standing against the wall. "I think I need to draw this one out for you. Easier to focus and see what fits where." He started to draw columns of boxes, with arrows pointing this way and that, and then filled in the names as he spoke.

"We start with Centurion, which is a UK company, as we know. It was set up in 1998 and owned one hundred percent by The Pegasus Group, a British Virgin Islands company set up in the same year. As you know already, Pegasus has three shareholders; fifty percent Northwest Holdings in Jersey, twenty-five percent Whitfield International, BVI, twenty-five percent New Cross International, also BVI."

The structure on the board was beginning to take shape.

"We found out Whitfield is owned in full by someone called Robert Crossley. New Cross one hundred percent by a Craig Benton. Northwest is owned by a BVI Trust called The Northwest Family Trust, settled by John Crossley."

"I presume you all understand how a Trust works?" Cydney

interjected, and as nobody responded, she continued. "Basically, it's a way of estate planning to mitigate any possible inheritance tax liability on the death of the settlor, so that assets go down the generations. In this case the settlor, or in other words, the person who set up the trust, was John Crossley, now deceased."

"Don't forget," added Richard, "it can also be used to hide assets. When you look at the ownership of a company you see the immediate shareholders, but you don't always look beyond them. The Trust gives another layer of confidentiality, especially when it's set up in a jurisdiction like the BVI, which is essentially a tax haven."

"And this is legitimate?" asked Jenny.

"Well, it can be if there is legitimate tax planning involved, and nobody is trying to evade tax. However, in this case I can't be sure. John Crossley was an American citizen and obviously subject to their tax rules. US citizens have to declare their worldwide income. We will need to look at that further because if he was trying to evade tax, and hide assets, then the whole structure is compromised."

Cydney glanced at George. He had muttered something under his breath and when he saw her eyes on his, he shrugged his shoulders. She tried to concentrate on what Richard was saying but George's complexion was changing and he looked slightly off colour and uncomfortable. Maybe the wine had been too much for him at lunchtime. Richard continued.

"John is Robert's father, as you may have realised. The beneficiaries are Robert and his wife and kids, plus any other legitimate children of John Crossley, but un-named, plus Craig and his family. It seems they're related. Robert married Craig's sister. Very incestuous, all this."

"But why go to all this trouble?" Cydney questioned, studying the wiper board.

"It doesn't make sense to me, although, of course, if they hold the portfolio here through an offshore holding company, they can no doubt get some tax breaks. Can we get some more detailed information on these brothers-in-law please?"

"I'll get right on it." Richard and Jenny left the room leaving George behind. He'd remained quiet throughout.

"Not sure how you've managed this, but I'm very impressed." He stood up and turned to Cydney. "But why am I surprised?" he said, before leaving the room.

Cydney remained alone in her office and pondered his reply for a moment before turning her thoughts to her other problems. She had planned to visit her mum tonight and felt guilty about seeing George instead, if that was still on the agenda, To be honest, for some reason after the meeting, she felt the moment with him was lost. Anyway, now she wanted to phone Sheila. She dialled the number Jenny had given her.

"Hi. Can I speak to Sheila Gordon please?"

"Speaking. Who is that?"

"My name's Cydney Granger. I'm so sorry to disturb you after your sad loss... please accept my condolences. Ray asked me to come and see you to offer my help."

"Ray asked you? When was that?" Sheila sounded as if she had been crying and was almost on the verge of tears again. Cydney could hear noise and voices in the background and someone shouting over whether she wanted a cup of tea.

"He asked me to give you something. Well, actually it's a word. Venice."

CHAPTER FOUR

TWELVE MONTHS EARLIER

THE man drove his truck into the Old City centre of Damascus. He parked and lost himself in the hubbub of people conglomerating around the Souk Medhat Pasha and the Saturday market. Despite the hour of the day, there was already a cacophony of noise from traders shouting out their wares, animals of every description crying out miserably in their pens while awaiting their fate, and stray dogs foraging in the gutters for scraps and barking viciously at anyone who approached them, if they were brave enough to do so. The smell of unwashed humans and animals in the steaming, relentless heat was overpowering. He sniffed at himself. No different, he thought wryly. The off-white slacks he wore and the once-white t-shirt had seen more than better days. He couldn't afford to look different, even if he wanted to.

Searching around to find a public telephone box where there was no risk of anyone tracing his call, and ensuring there were no security cameras trained on the area, he located a rundown hostel off Bab Sharqui Street, which led to the Old Christian quarter. Admittedly, it was near the Grand Mosque but sometimes there was safety in crowds, where he could lose himself quickly if required.

He strode purposefully into the building and told the man on reception, rather than asked him, that he needed to use his phone privately. It cost more than a week's wages to bribe the man but it was unavoidable. When he was certain he was alone, he dialled the number with some trepidation. He had remembered it only

32

recently and hoped he had it correct. After a few rings his call was answered with a simple hello.

"Dragonfly is ready to come home to roost."

"Please hold the line, sir."

The phone went dead for a few seconds until a man with a Scottish brogue took up the call.

"I'm sorry. I believe you have the wrong number."

"I shall say this again. Dragonfly is ready to come home to roost."

"Who is this?"

"For Christ's sake, man! Hear what I'm saying. I shall repeat it. Dragonfly. I don't have time to muck about. I'm going to put the phone down and I will call again tomorrow at the same time. Phone whoever you need to phone, then get me the fuck out of here."

He slammed down the receiver in frustration then remembered where he was and looked around him. The desk guy had gone upstairs so thankfully nobody had seen or heard him. He certainly didn't want to attract attention to himself for any odd behaviour. The secret was to blend, do nothing unusual to arouse suspicion. He had been waiting for this moment for so long and knew that after three years it was not going to be easy to get him out. Patience was not one of his best traits, and the fact he was desperate to return didn't help. But who was the idiot on the other end of the phone? The man should be briefed. That was his code name. Say it and they got you out, no questions asked, no matter what or when.

His memory, blank at first, had come back slowly and in patches, normally through flashbacks that woke him at night in a cold sweat and made him jolt upright in blind panic. His doctor and close friend, Salim, told him this was normal after the injuries he had sustained and that he should not try to remember, to let everything come back naturally and over time, and each time he remembered something, to compartmentalise it into a corner of his brain and retain it there until everything came together.

The headaches that came with trying to put the puzzle together brought him to his knees for days at a time. They attacked every fibre of his being, seemingly every brain cell, and it hurt even to blink. Salim administered as much pain relief as he was able but supplies were few and he had to be careful smuggling drugs out of the hospital where he worked. As the drugs took hold of him and the pain subsided, he would gratefully fall into a deep sleep, where no memories assaulted him.

Throughout this time, he had Mira with him, the daughter of Mohammad Bin Amadi, the village chief. She mopped his brow when he screamed at night, and sat holding his hand when he was in pain and Salim had not arrived with the relief. She was his rock and slowly he began to rely on her. She had small and delicate features, and there was a gentleness about her and in everything she did. Those eyes were bewitching, pools of dark looking out beyond the veil she wore. He could almost fall into them. She spoke little, out of respect for her father and the men in her family, but her actions said enough. He started to follow her with his eyes when he was recovering at the beginning and couldn't move. He looked forward to her administrations and spoke to her often, but all she would do was lower her eyes and not meet his.

As his legs recovered and he was able to walk again, Mira was always there for him. Then over time she began to look at him, a sideways glance and the odd word spoken quietly. Every day over the first year of his recovery, their quiet relationship grew. It would have been easy to marry her out of respect for her father when it became obvious her role as nurse had changed, as he had no recollection of already being married. However, for him there were many things missing. He felt sure there was another life for him somewhere but wherever that was, he had no idea.

He felt a concern and love for Mira, which was more a protectiveness as she was so fragile, but not a passion. At the back of his mind, that existed elsewhere.

More than two years passed quickly and he had fully integrated into the local community. He was a cousin of Bin Amadi to all who asked, had been in a serious accident and was now working in the family bakery. However, nobody asked questions and they lived a quiet existence. In the back of his mind, the life he'd had before the accident haunted him, but he just couldn't get the information from within himself, no matter how hard he tried. All that came to him were vague images that meant nothing. Sometimes, the anger from the frustration boiled over and he erupted like a volcano. Mira took it all in her stride. She continued to act as if this was normal behaviour and when he calmed down, as she knew he would, she was there for him - cooking his food and cleaning the house like a faithful partner.

"You must know how I came to be here. Can you not help me?" he had asked Salim when he came to the village, but the man was evasive and told him nothing.

"Your life is here now with our family and my cousin. I can't do anything at all. You have to be satisfied with what you have. Your memory needs to come back naturally. On the other hand, it may never come back. If I told you, you wouldn't believe me anyway."

"But I just can't bear the not knowing all the time. You have to help."

Salim ignored his pleas.

As the months passed, he began to recall little things that drifted in and out of his mind such as a patch of green grass, a tree, a road of houses that looked nothing like where he lived now, a park with children playing on the swings, or a chorus of a song. Each day brought something new to him but he still saw a reflection in the mirror of a face he didn't recognise, which bore little resemblance to anyone he knew. Who was the man with the beard looking back at him? Turning his face at different angles, baring his teeth, trying to peer through his eyes and into his head was a waste of time and gave him nothing. He examined his hands in minute detail, as if they could give him the answers he sought. All he noticed was that one finger on his left hand had a small indentation as if there was once a ring there.

He did file everything away just as Salim suggested until slowly, every piece started to fit together. It was a process he endured over several months but one day he woke up shouting Cydney's name and that was the catalyst. Memories and thoughts of his wife and the twins flooded back to him and then the desperation set in. He needed to get out and back to his home and family and there was no time to spare. It had to be immediate.

Salim recalled the night in the desert when Captain Granger was attacked and injured. They were trying to escape from the Syrian troops who had discovered their position. Someone had reported them. Salim had a feeling it was his 'friend' who had told him about the night-time activity in the desert, which was the reason they were there, photographing anything that could be useful to the combined American, Israeli and British governments. That man was dead and Salim had no reason to mourn him. Steve had taken the full force of the grenade explosion and was just lying on the ground. The sergeant ordered them to keep going and not look back, although every so often they stopped and returned fire, taking out as many Syrian troops as they could. The next day, Salim drove back to the point where they had left the captain. He knew the army would have decamped to another secret location as their current one was compromised. They would have been in a hurry and would not have bothered with the dead, leaving them to be taken by scavengers in the night, or more likely the vultures that hovered above, waiting for their prey.

His mind flew back to when he reached Steve. He knew he was hanging on by a thread. There was a mere flicker of a pulse but he dragged him onto the truck and drove to his uncle's village. Salim did the best he could with the limited means at his disposal. He cleaned the deep wounds, stitched the broken flesh together and splinted his broken ribs and leg. The Syrian army had not been kind to his body. There were boot marks over his torso and down his legs where they had tried to prove he was still alive. The bruising would heal, of course, but as the man started to wake up, Salim realised he had complete memory loss. He made the decision to keep things that way because it suited his purposes.

Now he was worried because his friend was beginning to regain his memory. Every day was something new and when Steve found out that he had kept everything from him, not sending him home when his wounds had healed, he knew there would be serious repercussions.

He could so easily have told Steve his history, of his life in the army, but he preferred to let sleeping dogs lie. He knew the army thought the man was dead and he wanted to keep it that way, because if they found out the consequences would be dire. They would try to get him out of the country, which would result in more bloodshed, compromise him and his family and cause heartache to Mira, the cousin he adored. Salim was doing so well living this double life as a revolutionary and a doctor. One day he knew it would all be worthwhile and the dreams he had of a new ruling class would come to fruition. Meanwhile, he was not going to rock any boats.

Lieutenant Jeremy Campbell felt the reverberation as the man slammed down the phone. Who was this Dragonfly? He had been in his current job for over a year and as far as he knew, there was no sleeper in the field of that code name. He called central headquarters and asked to speak directly to General

Bowles-Smith. He didn't want to risk getting this wrong in case there was something he should have known, and the man on the other end of the phone sounded desperate.

"Sir, sorry to trouble you. I have just received an extremely strange call. Someone calling himself Dragonfly. Do we have anybody of that name?"

"We did, but he's dead, over three years ago in Syria. Captain Steve Granger, Special Forces. Bloody good officer. Whole thing went horribly wrong. Did he say anything?"

"Said he was ready to come home. Sounded very agitated. Sir, should I call someone about this?"

"No, Campbell. Leave this to me. This is going straight to the top. Though how I'm going to get him out if he is still there is another story."

"Sir, Dragonfly is calling back tomorrow at the same time. What should I say?"

"I'll get back to you. Meanwhile, say nothing at all to anyone. Is that clear?"

"Completely, Sir."

The General held the phone in his hand for several seconds, staring at the receiver. He had never faced such a problem in his entire professional military career. The man was dead, killed in Syria, and he had attended his memorial service. Admittedly, there had been no body to bury, but what the hell? He shook his head as if he couldn't quite believe what was happening. The guy was alive and still in Syria? This really was a turn up for the books. The question was whether to get him out, and quick, but thinking it through in his mind, maybe the man could be of more use staying where he was. Either way, he needed to get that sergeant of his in - and straightaway.

CHAPTER FIVE

S EAN was ready and waiting when Cydney finished work the
following Tuesday and took her straight to the nursing home
to see her mother. It was set in ten acres of beautiful countryside
about a fifteen minute drive from where she lived, and the
grounds were a sea of colour and scent from the many flowers
planted throughout, sheltered amongst the aging trees.

Cydney had chosen it particularly for the location, but also
because of the history surrounding the actual building. It used
to be a hotel dating back to the previous century but American
developers had bought it up, and gutted and fitted it out as a
care home, making it as comfortable for the residents as possible.

The Americans certainly knew how to build and moreover
had the funds available. Lots of little corners to go and sit quietly
if the residents wanted, TV rooms, hairdressers, even a little cafe
and an activity room with various games stacked on shelves.
Books were everywhere and available for anyone to borrow and
it gave the whole place a lovely homely atmosphere. The decor
wasn't modern, because that would have spoilt the look the
developers were trying to create, but more in keeping with the
age of the property.

There were floor-length curtains in golds and reds, and
high-backed chairs and settees in similar matching colours, which
exuded comfort. Beautiful cushions in soft velvet added to the
decor along with wonderful pictures on the walls of country
scenes, picnics, and people enjoying themselves on the river.
They even had a communal dog roaming around called Brucie,

a beautiful and gentle golden retriever. Most importantly, it didn't have the smell of a nursing home. Cydney and her sister, Claire, had visited many similar places before deciding on this particular one. She hated the smell that lingered in many - that of hospitals, disinfectant, ill and old people. It reminded her of death and her childhood. When her dad was killed in the car accident, she was too young to see him and never quite believed he had gone. However, she had this image in her mind of him lying on his own on a marble slab, which was so vivid she could almost smell the formaldehyde.

On arriving, Cydney made her way to the huge reception area and greeted a few of the residents and staff, whom she knew quite well by now, and took the stairs to the first floor where her mum's room was situated, which overlooked the grounds. Her mum had always loved gardens, especially when all the colourful flowers were blooming.

She entered the room without knocking and found her mum sitting in front of the television, watching her favourite programme. Cydney and Claire had filled the room with all their mum's things from her old flat. There were photographs everywhere of their dad, themselves at varying ages, their graduations, Lauren and Jake, dogs and aunties, all full of memories for her. They had used her own furniture, where it fitted, to make it feel like home and there was even a little kitchenette where she could make a cup of tea using her favourite mugs and teacups. Familiarity and recognition were the key.

Cydney looked at her mum as if for the first time and saw a lady in her late seventies with hair white and thinning, although newly cut and styled. She had been so glamorous when younger, with her hair always coiffed, face made up, and long manicured nails. The early onset dementia was the result of years of taking tranquilisers for depression after her husband had died at such a young age and not being able to cope with such a traumatic loss. Now she looked so small sitting there, the jumper she wore seemingly oversized. Her feet rested on a little stool but her ankles looked very swollen today. Cydney took a deep breath, ready to face her fears. Her mum's face lit up when she saw her eldest daughter, and Cydney went over, bending to give her a big kiss and a hug.

"Hi. How are you today? You're wearing the new jumper I bought. It looks really pretty on you. A beautiful green, your favourite."

"What day is it?"

"Thursday."

"What's the time?"

"It's six o'clock in the evening. Have you eaten yet?"

"I don't know. Where are my keys?"

"You don't need them. We're looking after them for you."

"Where's my ring?"

"Everything is in your handbag, Mum." Cydney had actually taken all her mum's valuables home in case they got lost.

"What day is it? Is Claire coming?" So many questions, always repeated.

"No, Claire is coming at the weekend. How are you today? Is everything alright?"

"Is your dad coming?"

Cydney couldn't bear to repeat that he'd died nearly thirty years ago. Her mum's mind simply could not accept that her husband was dead and every reminder was heart breaking for her, so she just let the question remain unanswered.

"Have you got my keys? I don't know where my handbag is."

"Here's your handbag, right next to you."

Her mum picked up the bag and started rummaging about, looking for something, found nothing she wanted and then put the bag down on the floor. Three seconds later she grabbed the bag and went through it again, found a tissue, and put the bag back on the floor. Cydney's heart broke to see the person she loved so much like this and it brought tears to her eyes every time she went there. This wasn't the mother who'd brought her up; the dementia had taken over. Thankfully, she was in a good place with very caring staff.

"How are the twins?" She had a moment of lucidity, which was rare these days.

"They're great. Lauren's going to a party at the weekend. I'll bring her to see you before she goes so you can see her all dressed up. Jake is writing songs. He said he'll record one for you so you can listen to it on your DVD player."

"That will be good, dear."

"Shall I brush your hair to make you look nice?"

"Yes please. But do it softly. I have a bit of a headache today."

That was unusual in itself. Her mum never complained of any aches and pains. Cydney began to brush gently but suddenly her stomach dropped. What was that? Her mum's hair was shorter now and styled differently behind her ears so Cydney easily noticed the growth on the right side of her neck that hadn't been there before. She went cold. Not now, just when things were beginning to get straight in her life and she was learning to live without Steve. She couldn't face anything else.

"Mum, I'm just popping out for a moment. I'll be right back, okay?" Cydney almost ran down the corridor to find Gabrielle, a lovely Jamaican nurse with a huge heart, who had taken care of her mum since the start.

"Can you come and look at mum? There's a lump or something on her neck. I'm sure it wasn't there the other day."

The two went back to her mum who was sitting in the same place with all the contents of her handbag spewed untidily around her on the floor.

"I can't find my keys, Cydney, where are they?"

"I'll get them for you in a moment. We just want to check you over first. Is that okay?"

The nurse looked at her neck, feeling around it. Cydney's mum made no reaction except to grab one of Gabrielle's hands and put it to her lips with a kiss.

"Does this hurt, my love?"

"No. Is it supposed to? Are you looking at that lump on my neck? It's been there for ages. Please don't fuss. Now, where's my stupid purse?"

Gabrielle looked at Cydney and beckoned her outside.

"We'll call the doctor in to see her tomorrow. Don't worry. It's probably nothing but we'll get it checked out, just to be on the safe side."

Cydney sat with her mother for another hour, all the while holding her hand and stroking it. Sean was waiting for her when she returned to the car and he had the shock of his life when she promptly and unusually burst into tears. In between the sobs, she somehow managed to get out what was wrong.

"Let the doctor see what's what and then we'll take it from there. Sure it's probably nothing at all."

When they got home, Lauren and Jake were together for once in the same room, watching a film. She kissed them both and tried to hide her concern, but nothing escaped Lauren, who only had to take one look at her.

"What's wrong? Your eyes look red." That girl could see through a brick.

"Nothing. I'm fine, darling. I've just been to see Nan. She's okay - well, you know what it's like. Let me get changed and I'll come and join you."

"Was she looking for her keys again?" Jake said. "We should buy her a pretend set, so she doesn't have to ask."

Wise words from one so young.

Cydney eventually went to bed and fell into a deep sleep after tossing and turning and not being able to relax at all. She knew her mum had been losing weight but then she didn't eat much

43

anymore. And that lump? So her mother had known about it and hadn't said anything, or simply forgot to. Cydney hadn't noticed it at all, she just never looked. The guilt descended. Suppose it is...? She couldn't even think the word, never mind say it out loud.

Her dad stood in the middle of a ballroom. He looked about the same age as Cydney was now, so handsome in his black dinner suit. He was all alone until her mum walked into the room and stood in front of him, gazing into his eyes. She was dressed in the most beautiful, white, flowing off-the-shoulder gown that fell almost to her ankles. She took his hand and they started to dance a foxtrot to their favourite tune, turning around the dance floor with their eyes locked on each other. Their images reflected in the mirrors as they swirled round. Their movements were as one and the feeling of love and passion filled the entire room. Suddenly the music stopped, and Cydney saw her mother collapse into her dad's arms.

Cydney woke up with a start, breathing heavily, her heart thumping. It was always the same since these awful visions had started, shortly after they moved when she was seven, as if the new house had taken over her subconscious mind, breathing a life of its own into her sleeping world. They were so real, so vivid that she would wake up in terror, dripping with sweat, her heart beating so fast, and call out for her dad, never her mum, who would come to her bedside and attempt to comfort her and take the hurt and pain away.

"Don't worry, it wasn't real, sweetheart," he would tell her repeatedly until she could relax again. He always made sure she was fast asleep before he left her side, tucking the covers around her tightly to hold her in place so no harm could come to her, protecting her from whatever it was she was feeling.

She never told him or anyone else, but it was always the same dream about one of her parents dying. She never knew which, only that she could hear the screams of someone in the grip of unbearable grief. Every time she woke up afterwards she would feel such wretchedness and a huge sense of loss. It was something she lived with constantly but could not voice, and always there in the background.

Now there was no dad to comfort her and no Steve to hold her hand. The two most important men in her life were gone, and she was alone.

Cydney flicked her eyes to the clock. It was only five-twenty. With a sigh of resignation, she put on her dressing gown and crept downstairs to her study. She loved the room with its dark wood panelling and shelves full of books. This was her place to hide away and think. She logged onto her computer and began to trawl through the various emails she hadn't had time to look at yesterday.

There was one from George. *Looking forward to seeing you for dinner again.* She still hadn't decided whether to go, even though their date the previous week had gone well. Rupert had also emailed to say he would be arriving in London on Sunday, a bit earlier than expected, which was great news. The case was becoming increasingly more interesting and exactly the sort of work she loved to get her teeth into.

What else? There was some of the usual junk mail that always seemed to seep through, despite all Ash's attempts at control, and a few emails with new business enquiries that she would pass to Jenny to deal with. However, one email in particular drew her attention. She opened it and read an invite from one of the big city banks to a black-tie charity reception in two months' time. She was more than surprised to learn the guest speaker was none other than Robert Crossley. What a coincidence, and an occasion that she was definitely not going to miss. She would ask Richard to accompany her.

Around seven-thirty the twins emerged and burst into the study.

"Mum, I've entered a competition, or rather the school have entered me. 'Young Songwriter of the Year'. You will come, won't you?"

As if Cydney had ever missed anything.

45

"Wow, that's amazing Jake! When is it?"

"Next month. Well the first round is, anyway. Not sure where it's going to be though, but I'll find out."

Cydney had never seen him so animated. He was such a good-looking boy, olive skinned and already tall at fourteen. He had piercing blue eyes exactly like his dad and she noticed his more defined body. Where had that come from? Lauren also had the same colouring but she seemed such a child still in comparison, so young and vulnerable in her school uniform. Cydney worried about her more, especially as she so needed a male influence in her life. Sean was there but he worked for them, although in some respects he was a bit like an uncle, spoiling her outrageously whenever he had the chance.

"Come on kids. Sophie's got breakfast ready. I'm hungry and I can smell bacon."

Running ahead of Cydney, the twins hurtled into the kitchen, scraped back their chairs and sat down at the table where Sophie was waiting to serve them.

"Morning," Cydney said. "Any news from Dave?"

"Yes, I got a letter from him this morning. He's still out there, wherever *there* is, but should be back soon, I hope. He can't tell me anything, of course."

"Can I be your bridesmaid when you get married, Sophie?" Lauren asked, not for the first time.

"Course you can. Now eat up or you'll be late for school."

Sean appeared in the doorway and glanced at Cydney questioningly. She answered with a nod, indicating she was fine. Thank goodness she had him around. Sean knew that Sophie reminded her of the world in which she'd lived: the army, and always the secrets.

Cydney thought, but didn't know for certain, that Steve had been seconded out to military intelligence a few years before he was killed. No one ever told her the truth, not even Sean who had been with him at the time of the bombing, but had come out of it with no more than a broken arm and a few cuts and bruises, thankfully.

"Sean, I want to leave in about ten minutes. We can drop the kids off and then go straight to the office."

"Ready when you are, Mrs Granger."

Cydney couldn't stop Sean calling her that, although she had tried so many times. Mrs Granger it was and would remain, and it was certainly better than the *ma'am* he had called her originally. She had given up asking him to call her Cydney, she couldn't bear to see the look of absolute horror on his face at the mere suggestion.

Sean drove in silence and glanced in the mirror from time to time at Cydney in the back seat. She didn't look so good this morning, despite her immaculate make-up. Her eyes, a little dark and heavy, weren't concentrating on the documents spread out on her lap, but drifted constantly out of the window. She played with the wedding ring she still wore, twisting it around her finger. He knew she missed Steve badly, as he did.

Steve had asked him to look after Cydney should anything happen to him. He was doing his best but it was not always the easiest task in the world. A woman like her needed a partner, an equal, a father to her kids. He could ensure her safety, help around the house and deliver her from one place to the next, but he was not a husband. He couldn't see himself staying with Cydney until the day he died, but on the other hand he would be loath to leave her. Steve, his commanding officer, had run the battalion with a firm hand, but every man under him knew he was looking out for them. He demanded respect and received it in return. Sean had worshipped the man, for goodness sake. How could he possibly walk away?

A few miles before Sean made his way onto the motorway, Cydney interrupted his thoughts.

"I have another meeting, Sean. Can we go to High Wycombe first, please? I need to see a client. I won't be long, and then we can head back into London."

With a nod of the head and the address given, Sean moved the Mercedes smoothly onto the M25, no questions asked.

Forty-five minutes later he turned into a cul-de-sac of about twenty white-fronted bungalows with impeccable gardens. The road was quiet, with few cars parked, apart from a British Telecom van with a guy setting up his equipment alongside it.

"Sean, can you wait here for me please? I'll be as quick as I can."

He watched his boss, who was acting quite mysteriously, walk up to the door of one of the bungalows. Almost as soon as Cydney rang the bell the door opened, as if the woman had been sitting and waiting for her to arrive. For the first time, he asked himself what they were doing here.

As Cydney entered the house she felt the familiar, cold presence around her and realised Ray had followed her in. Sheila was an attractive woman, in her late forties with a welcoming smile, although Cydney got the impression that she felt the intrusion to her mourning quite strange. She was dressed in black, her skin pale in comparison.

The sitting room into which she was led was tastefully decorated in creams and beiges with a splash of dark-brown on the feature walls either side of the stone fireplace. Sheila invited her to sit on the leather sofa next to her. Ray stood by them and Cydney noticed him looking at the many photos on the walls of himself with his wife and children.

"You have a lovely home."

"*All Sheila's work,*" Ray said. "*She used to be an interior designer. She certainly married beneath her.*"

"Thank you. You must excuse my appearance. Everything has been such a shock. I simply can't believe what has happened.

One minute he was here, and the next..." Sheila's words hung in the air as she grabbed a tissue from the box on the glass coffee table in front of her and dabbed at her eyes.

"Oh Sheila, don't cry," Ray said. He moved around and knelt down in front of her.

"I'm so sorry to intrude, Sheila. As I mentioned on the phone, Ray asked me to come and see you. He was worried about the business and Charles, and of course you and the children. Are these their photos?" Cydney pointed to the mantelpiece.

"Yes. Henry, Freddie and Charlotte. They're with their auntie as I had to sort out the funeral. I didn't want them to be here when the man came."

"I understand. It must be a terrible shock for you."

Sheila nodded. "So, tell me, Mrs Granger, why Venice? How did you get that word? That was our special word. How do you know Ray?"

"Sheila, I remember our honeymoon, taking a gondola to see the sights, stopping at the Travatoria restaurant, just off the Piazza San Paulo. You looked so beautiful in that yellow polka-dot dress..."

"Please, call me Cydney. Listen, this is going to sound very strange to you, and I promise I would never approach anyone in this way if it wasn't for the fact Ray got in touch with me and asked me to help."

"What do you mean?"

"Ray came through to me the other day."

"Came through? What does that mean? He's dead."

"Yes I know. I have a gift, Sheila. I can communicate with people who have passed away."

Sheila looked up at her, her eyes widened, her lips parted ready to speak. Cydney waited but no words came. Sheila shook her head and lowered her eyes to her lap. "I'm not sure I believe in all that, but you've obviously found me for a reason. I said I would listen, so please, go on."

"Ray explained he was worried about you. He told me about

the business, the problems with Charles. He was in the hospital in Euston. He gave me your name, told me you were an interior designer, as I can see. He said you'd believe me if I mentioned the word Venice, and the taverna off the main square where you went on your honeymoon. Your yellow polka dot dress."

Sheila glared at her. "How can you know all this?"

"Make her believe you, Cydney. Talk about the dog we had called Scott. Had a red collar with a star disc around his neck," Ray prompted, and Cydney started to sense his frustration.

"Sheila, Ray is with us now. He asked me to tell you about Scott with the red collar. He wore a disc in the shape of a star. Ray's sitting right in front of you."

Sheila's head flicked straight ahead and Cydney watched as her eyes gazed into the empty space. "I'm sorry, Cydney is it?" She turned back to face her. "What you are telling me is absolutely ridiculous. You must have spoken to one of our friends."

"I don't blame you for thinking like that. It's hard, and just as difficult for me to come here and speak to you like this. I promise I am serious and not playing around with your feelings. Trust me when I say I just wouldn't do that. I do know what you're going through. Please, will you give me a few minutes and let me tell you what has happened? Do you know anything about the business, at all?"

"No, of course not. Ray was in charge there. I kept the house and looked after things here. He took Charles in a few years ago but I have no idea what went on. Except to say his brother was a complete waster. I had no time for him at all. I saw him under sufferance and never could stand the man. He was trouble, that's for sure. What has he done?"

"Good Cydney, you have to tell her. It will hurt her, but she's sensible, a strong woman. She'll understand."

"Can I just be completely straight with you?" Cydney asked. "Ray tells me you're strong and can take this."

She chuckled. "I would rather you were straight with me."

"Okay. We believe Charles may have forged certain papers of your husband's, and possibly your signature too, on share transfers to take the ownership of the business away from you. There are mortgage facilities with banks that Ray knows nothing about, insurances on Ray's life where the monies go direct to his brother, not to you, and Charles has been taking money out to fund his lifestyle. We also believe he's going to sell the land the factory is on to a supermarket chain. You'll get nothing, nor will the children. At the moment you have no rights to anything."

Cydney watched Sheila's face turn to one of shock as she tried to take in all the information. It was important she understood the situation and what she stood to lose.

"I really don't have the brain for this now. Ray loved that factory, and everyone there was his friend. I think, I do believe you, I'm trying to believe you, but this is all very difficult for me," she said.

"I know, he told me. Look, if I have your agreement, I'm going to look further into this and see where it takes me. Are you with me on this?"

"But why do you want to do this? What do you get out of it?"

"You know, sometimes you just have to do whatever you can to set things right."

Sheila turned to her. "Ok, I'm right behind you." She reached out to grab Cydney's hand and Cydney looked down at Ray, who was knelt beside his wife and nodding his head at her, mouthing 'thank you'.

"Sean, there's a man I want you to find out about," Cydney advised, as she climbed into the car. "His name is Charles Gordon. This is his home address and this is the business one, not far from the outskirts of Henley. I want you to see who he meets up with, what his movements are during the day and where he goes – you know, the usual information." She handed him a piece of paper with all the details hand-written in capitals. "Work on this over the next week. He drives a BMW, that's all I know."

"Well at least I won't need to wear a dishdasha this time," Sean said under his breath, referring to his tour in the Middle East.

"Well, you could try, but you may stand out in the middle of Henley."

"Thank you, Mrs Granger. I'll bear it in mind."

As they left, Cydney looked over her shoulder, saw Sheila at the window and gave her a small wave, just as the BT engineer stepped out from behind his van and raised both hands to his face. Before Cydney had time to register what was happening, Sean had turned the corner and was making his way to the main road. *Was that a camera?* Cydney thought, settling back in her seat. *What on earth would he be doing with...?*

Her mobile rang, making her jump, and as soon as she saw the care home's number flash on the screen she answered the call.

"Hi, my love. It's Gabrielle. I'll get straight to the point. The doctor has carried out his examination. Your mum's heart sounds fine and her blood pressure is good too, but he wants her to have a scan of her neck. He doesn't know what the lump is but we're taking her to the hospital this afternoon. We'll organise everything and one of the staff will go with her. You carry on with your day and come and see her tomorrow as normal. We won't have any results until next week anyway."

Carry on with her day? As if that could happen. Maybe she should accompany them to the hospital? she thought. But there were things at the office that required her attention; she couldn't put them off for another day. Her thoughts turned to George, who would also be there. They had arranged to go out for dinner together this evening but was she able to face it now when her mind was on her mum? Maybe it would take her mind off everything. But why were they sending her for a scan so quickly? Everything was happening too fast for her to think. She took a deep breath in an attempt to control her thoughts. Her mum was in safe hands and there was nothing she could do, even if she did tag along. No, it was best to get on with things and keep her mind occupied. For a brief moment she contemplated giving Claire a call, but instead sent her a text message. She wouldn't be able to bear her sister's usual rejection today.

George collected her in his hired car later that evening, despite her protestations that she really didn't want to go out, but he was having none of that. All eyes were on her through the windows when she left the house in the red dress Lauren insisted she wear, although her initial thoughts were to wear jeans. Of course, she was never going to let him completely into her life, but she could see her way to making him feel a bit more welcome, possibly. That was not going to include introducing him to her family though, so she made an extremely quick exit before he could even step inside.

He drove them to the Compleat Angler in Marlow where he had booked a table overlooking the River Thames. During the one hour journey, Cydney hardly spoke. Her mind was still on her mum and thankfully George must have sensed she needed silence so complied with her unspoken request.

They were taken to their table and after the Maitre'd had taken their order, he spoke.

"Why exactly are you here? You don't seem to want to be with me, so why bother?"

"I'm sorry. It's nothing to do with you."

"Really? You haven't said a word to me. I thought we were doing alright but somehow I can't get through to you. I'm beginning to wonder whether I should even bother."

"Just please bear with me. I have a lot on my mind." Cydney tried to avoid his intense gaze.

"Well, I am here, and a very good listener. How about sharing some of these things and see if I can help."

"I doubt you can, unless you're a cancer specialist."

"You're ill? Why…?"

"No, not me. My mother. I think, well I know almost, she is very ill. There's a lump on her neck."

"What do the doctors say?"

"They don't know yet. She's having a scan this week."

"Cyd, why on earth didn't you tell me this before? Do you really think I am that uncaring? I would have cancelled tonight, although from the look of you I think this outing might do you some good."

"I wanted to take my mind off things." She pondered for a second. "Yes, you're right. Plenty of time to worry later on. Let's have that drink you promised me and I'll try not to think of mum until tomorrow. Deal?"

"Sounds good to me."

She sat staring out across the gently lapping waters of the Thames as a few small cruisers went past.

Anything was possible.

CHAPTER SIX

As Cydney neared the office, George crept back into her mind. If she was honest with herself, she quite liked the attention he was giving her and enjoyed the banter between them and the competition that seemed to exist. His gentleness towards her after they'd had lunch, when he'd guided her across the road with his hand on her elbow, had felt protective and last night had been quite amazing, despite everything. She hadn't felt that way for a long time. Cydney was always in charge. She was the one to sort out problems, deal with any and every issue, and it was nice for a change to be looked after. Yes, she decided, she would go out for dinner with him again, and would wear the little black Gucci dress she had found recently, and get back her Chanel handbag from Lauren, who'd had her eye on it from the moment she had brought it home.

Cydney recalled with fondness the day they had moved into the office, several years previously. Steve had stood with his arm around her in the street and watched her face as she looked up at the sign mounted on the side of their new building. She had tears in the corner of her eyes and he squeezed her hand, aware of how emotional she felt. Seeing the words 'Granger Associates' in big black lettering with its red outline that had been especially designed for them filled her with more pride than she'd ever felt in her life. All their hard work had paid off. They'd decided to pool their resources and plan for when Steve would retire from the army. With Cydney's MBA in Business, and Steve being an expert in logistics, it was natural they would go into business together as corporate forensic specialists.

Cydney had been working a few years before for a large city bank in their corporate department but had felt so restricted in what she could do. The time was right to leave and do something on her own and there was a market for large companies who wanted external analysis and specific consultancy services. With her connections and experience, and Steve's expertise, their client base quickly expanded.

The building was an investment in a prime and highly desirable location of historical interest, just outside the centre of London and close to the tube station, enabling clients to reach them easily. They didn't have to spend too much on renovation as the original owner had gone into liquidation, leaving it with everything intact, and they had bought it for a really good sum. It was one of those turn-of-the-century villa-type houses in a tree-lined avenue, which were now being used for offices. It was beautiful to look at, with a white exterior opening into spacious rooms on each floor. The walls were painted in light greys and lemons, and the pale grey carpet gave it an expensive feel. They had bought numerous huge potted plants and placed them in every corner, and the decorative mirrors on the walls gave a further impression of space. Cydney had even located some prints from a local artist, which they had agreed to show for him.

Cydney had been quite nervous about the investment at first. It was important that her life was secure in every way, since her childhood had not been. Losing her dad so young had forced her mum to bring up two young children single-handedly with little money. Her mum had not been well for several years, always on anti-depressants and tranquilisers, certainly hating to leave her house or meet people. Everything Cydney had done since her dad had died had been to make her and her family's lives safe, by studying hard and working to gain the material things she had lacked growing up.

When she met Steve and he suggested going into business together and then buying a building, mentally she was torn. She wanted him to retire from the army, hating when he left her for long periods of time when he went to goodness knows where, but it meant resigning from her secure job at the bank with no guarantee that things would work out. There were no doubts in her mind about her capabilities, but there still remained a huge question mark.

"Your dad would be so proud of you, Cyd," Steve had said, wrapping his arm around her.

"I know. I wish he could be here now." And just as she'd spoken the words, a coldness came over her as her dad came forward to be at her side. She shivered, turning to her right, and Steve looked at her with a smile.

"I recognise that expression. Is he here?"

She nodded, wiping a tear from her cheek.

Cydney was used to this feeling. Although it was an everyday occurrence for her, it was one she usually kept to herself, not something she shared with the outside world. Apart from a few close friends and family members, it didn't sit well with most people. It certainly wasn't a gift people expected her to have, being so far removed from her life as a powerful businesswoman in a corporate world.

Cydney hadn't forgotten the time she had tentatively broached the subject with Steve not long after they had met, as she wanted to keep no secrets from him. Unsurprisingly, he was sceptical and couldn't quite grasp what she was saying, as it was not something he had encountered previously. He was a soldier who dealt in black and white and, to him, clairvoyants wore long gypsy skirts, blousy tops, shawls, and gold-looped earrings. However, when she gave him the names of his parents and grandparents and described his childhood home, including the colour of the swirled green-and-red sitting room carpet and the ormolu clock on the mantelpiece, he was astounded. Over time, he accepted her gift and felt comforted to know his family was around him.

"So, what has he got to say today?" Steve asked.

"You know, I think he just wants to be with us, and I'm happy about that."

It had taken Cydney many years to come to terms with the loss of her father and she'd been unable to connect with him at all, until she'd met Steve. It was just too painful. Then the blanket of security Steve gave her enabled her to accept her dad into her life and, from time to time, she felt his presence and was able to seek his advice when she needed it.

"Well, say thank you to him for me. I'm happy he's here with you, darling."

"I wish Mum was here too, but she's still getting over the flu. I told her she couldn't leave the house."

"Claire could have made the effort, though."

Cydney laughed. "What, and cut short her trip to Australia?"

"It's hardly 'cutting short'. She just talked you into paying for another six months!" He shook his head. "Your sister's always out for herself. But you know what? Let her enjoy herself. She'll settle down at some stage, I'm sure."

The door to the building opened, interrupting them, and Sean stepped out, dressed for a change in a dark suit and tie, which he'd worn especially for the launch of their new company.

"The telephones are now working, sir, ma'am," he confirmed, walking over to join them.

"Thank goodness for that. I can't believe we've had these problems with the systems, today of all days. Glad you could help out," Cydney said, kissing him on the cheek.

Sean was currently on two weeks' leave from the army. He had been a sergeant in Steve's battalion for the last few years and during their recent tour of Afghanistan. At thirty-seven, he was a few years older than her husband and slightly shorter, a couple of inches under six feet, with a receding hairline that he put down to the army headgear he was forced to wear. Irish by birth, and extremely strong with huge biceps noticeable even through the sleeves of his jacket, he held the battalion record for boxing. He was the most charming of men and respectful at all times, but you would not want to cross him. Cydney knew the story about how his wife had left him to bring up their daughter, Sophie on his own as she couldn't bear the army life. True, it wasn't for everyone but you got used to it, your husband being away for long periods of time. Sophie lived with Sean's mum in Dublin and at fourteen was a very pretty girl, judging by the photos.

"Sean, you're our friend now. You can call us Steve and Cydney, really you can," Cydney said.

"I couldn't possibly do that. No, you are Captain and Mrs Granger to me, and always will be." He turned to face the building. "Ma'am, I think the sign looks perfect. Congratulations to you both."

"Thanks, Sean. Please," Steve said, "come up and have some champagne; everyone's upstairs waiting for us."

They took the lift to the fourth floor where Richard and Jenny, recently recruited to expand the company, greeted them. There were a few partners from local law firms, some accountants and associates from the banking world whom Cydney knew, plus some prospective clients she hoped to bring in, all mingling in the reception area. They cheered as Steve and Cydney appeared, raising their glasses.

"You're missing yours," Jenny laughed, and passed them each a glass of Dom Perignon. "Sean, come on, you too."

"I'd rather have a beer, but okay, thank you ma'am."

Cydney laughed and started working the room, something that came so naturally to her. She was conscious of her husband watching her. He often told her how much he loved her every movement, the way she flicked back her hair over her shoulder and touched people as she talked to them, making them feel special. She knew she looked good today in her pink Chanel suit, the tight skirt that hugged her figure, her long legs in heels that made people wonder how she walked. She turned to watch Steve as he made his way round to a few of his friends, every so often looking over at her, as if he wanted to check she was fine, even though he knew she was. When she caught his glance she gave him that special smile of hers and the look he returned melted down to her very soul.

For Cydney, meeting Steve had been like something out of a movie. It was love at first sight. They met at a mutual friend's dinner party, quickly seeing through their matchmaking. They sat next to each other at the dinner table and were introduced as a young army captain and she as a professional, with very different backgrounds. They got on immediately, laughed at the same jokes, and discovered they loved the most obscure music, similar authors and even holiday destinations. After dinner, he asked to see her again and without hesitation she agreed. They met the next night, and the one after, and then he was back on duty.

The letters flowed back and forth over the few months he was away, Cydney worrying for his safety and he that she was working too hard. This was love, plain and simple, and after only six months he proposed. They married in an intimate ceremony at a London hotel with only close family and friends around them. With Steve by her side, now and forever, she was invincible.

Rupert Van der Hausen walked over to greet Cydney.

"I can't believe you flew in all the way from Johannesburg for this reception, just for me. I'm so grateful," she said, kissing him on both cheeks.

"Cydney, you have me in the palm of your hand. You know I wouldn't have missed this for the world. Oh, and here's the lucky man. Congrats! I am so very happy for you both. This is going to be the making of you."

"Good to see you again, Rupert. It's lovely to have you here. Do you like the office?"

"It's wonderful. Well done, great investment. Listen, I am here for a few days and have some work for you. Also, I want to introduce you to some colleagues of mine. They will be impressed with what you can do for them."

"Thanks Rupert, I'd be delighted to meet them. And thank you for helping us with the building, arranging the financing and everything. "

"My pleasure," he said, glancing at his watch. "I have to go now, last minute meeting arranged, but I will be back here tomorrow morning. Shall we say at eleven, to go through a few things?"

"Perfect," Steve replied, and they watched him leave the room, shaking hands and chatting with a few more people as he went.

"I so love him. He's been like a father to me."

"I know, my darling. Look around, this is going so well. Nothing can stop us."

"I really am happy, Steve. This is everything I could have wanted. I have you, the twins, our amazing house – once it gets finished. Life really couldn't be better."

Cydney brought her attention back to the work ahead of her and made her way to the office. Polly greeted her at reception and handed her a small envelope with her name written across the front in large letters. She opened it and began to read.

I really must apologise for the short notice, Cyd, but Rupert has asked me to fly to New York for a conference today so I'm heading out for the airport. I'll be back in about eight days, so can we take a rain check on our date tomorrow? I was so looking forward to having you all to myself for an evening again, but business seems to have got in the way as usual. Keep those pretty eyes of yours smiling. George xx

Cydney read it once more, noting the two kisses. The disappointment she felt took her completely by surprise. After not wanting to go, then realising how much she did and planning what she was going to wear, she now felt deprived. She had lived the evening in her mind before it had even happened, opening herself up once again for disappointment.

"Everything alright, Cydney?" Richard asked, as he strolled out of his office to meet her. He looked down into her hands. "What's in the letter?"

"Oh, not much. Nothing for you," she said, stuffing the note into her handbag. "Have you gathered the information for me on those two men yet? You know Rupert's back on Sunday and we have a meeting planned for Monday, so I want everything in place. By the way, George has had to leave for New York so we have our boardroom back."

Richard raised his eyebrows and Cydney waited for him to speak, but he said nothing.

"The information, Richard?"

"Yes, sorry, I have everything you want," he responded. Shall I give you five minutes to collect yourself?"

"I don't need any *collecting*, thank you. But give me fifteen minutes please."

Cydney entered her office and there, sitting on her desk, was the biggest bouquet of red roses she had ever seen – well, certainly for a long time. Richard followed her in regardless, looked at the flowers, looked at Cydney, and walked out without saying a single word. His face said it all. Cydney read the card.

Really sorry about tomorrow! G xx.

Perhaps, Cydney thought, she might just have to forgive him.

Fifteen minutes later, to the second almost, Richard and Jenny arrived. They looked at Cydney sitting in her black leather chair, and simultaneously said, "What's wrong?"

"Come in and take a seat. It's Mum, I'm worried about her. We found a lump on her neck and she's having a scan today. It could be ..." and she let the words fall away.

"Well, shall we wait for the scan before we come to any conclusions?" Jenny said. "You look done in, well, apart from the flowers that brought a smile to your face. From Mr Wonderful, I guess? Why don't you go home and rest up? Today can wait."

Cydney remained silent.

"Dare we mention Claire and whether she could be around?" Jenny went on, with a mere touch of sarcasm. Everyone knew about the 'unselfish' behaviour of Cydney's sister.

"No. I'm okay, but thanks for asking. Let's just get on, shall we? Richard, tell me what you have."

The look Richard and Jenny passed her didn't go unnoticed, but they knew there was no point in trying to get her to go home; she simply wouldn't go. Cydney was a complete workaholic and everyone was very protective of her because of it, not that it did any good. She loved the company, the work and the people around her, and since Steve had gone it had become the centre of her existence.

"And you can stop those looks! Come on Richard, what have you got?"

"Ok. So, let's start with Craig Benton," Richard began. "As Rupert told you, Benton was the Chairman of American Securities before it went into Chapter 11. This is a process a bit like our liquidation here in the UK, but with slight nuances as it allows the company to continue trading through its debt by restructuring its business. The company is under the jurisdiction of the courts, and protected against litigation during the process. In a sale, the value of the company is normally enhanced if it's sold as a going concern so that's why a Chapter 11 is preferred, rather than a straightforward bankruptcy."

"I understand, Richard," Jenny interrupted, "but how did this happen to American Securities? This was a huge case a couple of years ago, I thought."

"Wasn't the company sold to one of the big American banks?" Cydney asked.

"Yes, you're right. But let me explain. A mining magnate, Frederick B. Causwell, set up American Securities in the 1890s in New York. His family ran the bank for many years, generation after generation, and they were the real influence in providing small, long-term mortgages and loans to people who could not normally afford such things. It became the fourth biggest lending bank in the US with over three thousand branch offices in twenty States by the time it collapsed. It did this by buying up small banks and lending institutions to help it grow, plus credit card companies. It spent its money to expand."

"But surely it had sufficient assets to continue?"

"Well you would think so. Anyway, it went public in 1986 and Benton became chairman at that time. The founder's family were no longer involved as they had sold out their shareholding. Benton managed to double the bank's assets, mainly because of the rise in the use of credit cards and the fact people wanted bigger mortgages. Society changed from being one where you only bought what you could afford, to one where you wanted what everyone else had. However, interest rates rose but the bank kept lending and eventually the borrowers couldn't afford the repayments. These people wouldn't even be able to look at a credit card now, never mind be credit worthy enough to take out a mortgage. Nobody did any checks. It was all about making money, lending and not worrying about the future. It was completely insane and the market couldn't withstand it, so something was bound to happen. Then, in early 1999, the bank came into disrepute because it was foreclosing on the lending but couldn't afford to repay the deposits, so it borrowed from other institutions itself and, with all the bad press, the bank's credit rating was downgraded and huge assets were withdrawn, supposedly overnight, because people were running scared. The bank was insolvent."

"So where does Benton come into all this? He must have been fired?" Cydney said.

"Yes he was, eventually, but the circumstances leading up to the Chapter 11 are a bit of a mystery. Talk has it that before the downgrading, Benton secretly met with another bank with a view to their taking over everything. As he held huge shares in American Securities he stood to make many, many millions.

Nothing happened. However, when they eventually closed in late '99 and put it into Chapter 11, the bank he'd spoken to already bought American Securities at a knock down amount and the shareholders lost everything as the value of the shares disappeared. There were rumours of insider dealing by Benton and that he knew about the insolvency, so he sold his stock short before anything happened."

"How would that help him?" Jenny asked. "Sorry, I don't understand what you mean, Richard."

"In other words, one of the hedge funds negotiated the sale of Benton's shares before the Chapter 11 declaration. The hedge funder sold them so that when the shares were eventually wiped out, they were able to buy them back at a lower cost, pocketing the profit. They had to be quick and they had to have known. At least Benton was able to buy them back, but nobody could prove it, unfortunately. He was interviewed by the federal police and the Internal Revenue but they couldn't do anything, nor find out any information."

"Do you think he used an offshore vehicle for this purchase to keep his name out of it?" Cydney said.

"Probably, or rather more than likely. I haven't been able to get to the bottom of that as yet. However, Benton then went to live in Monaco initially, although he does spend his time between there and New York. He lives a very comfortable existence, judging by the size of his properties. Anyway, some of the investors tried to take action in a joint claim to recover their lost monies but the case was thrown out."

"Not a nice guy then," Cydney remarked, stating the obvious.
"Nope."

"And Robert Crossley's association"

"He owns the bank that bought American Securities."
"No!"

"Oh yes, indeed. He's behind Caxton Trust Bank, one of the big four. Used someone else, it seems, to front the deal. Again, his name appears nowhere at all, not even as a shareholder. This is all very clever. Obviously someone heads up the bank for him but he's the one pulling the strings."

"This is incredible. Surely it couldn't happen? And nobody put two and two together?"

"You would think, eh?"

"How did you find all this out?"

"Well, I have my sources. My brother-in-law works for one of the big hedge funders in New York. He's had his suspicions for a few years but couldn't prove anything."

"So, is this speculation?"

"I don't believe so. These two, brothers-in-law themselves, are making money hand-over-fist. It's how they managed to buy the assets in Centurion and build up the company and because it's all offshore, they are not paying anything in taxes, anywhere. Nice if you can get away with it."

"I'm sure. So now I'm wondering why they want to sell off Centurion's assets. What's gone wrong? Do I actually want Rupert involved in all this?"

"They must owe money somewhere. I'm still digging around but, Cydney, I think you should tell Rupert exactly what we have learnt so far and let him make up his own mind, don't you?"

"You're right. He'll be here in a couple of days. Thanks guys."

"What about Rayshel Plastics? What are we doing with that?" Richard asked.

"I have Sean researching our friend, Charles Gordon. Let him do that for a few days and then you can get more involved. Oh, and by the way, I completely forgot to tell you but I've received an invitation to a charity reception in a couple of months. Robert Crossley is the guest speaker."

"How come you're invited?"

"We work for the organisers but it's pure coincidence about Crossley. I'm going for sure. Richard, you'd better get your tux out of mothballs - you're coming with me."

CHAPTER SEVEN

TWELVE MONTHS EARLIER

S EAN plunged the sponge into the bucket and smeared the
suds over the bonnet of the Mercedes, whistling while he
worked and enjoying time away from the normal pressures of
his everyday life.

When the car approached he stopped what he was doing and
watched as two men got out and walked over to him. He
recognised who they were from the way they held themselves,
even though they were not in uniform. Stick an army man
amongst a thousand civilians and he would locate him quicker
than knocking back a pint of Guinness.

"Can I help you, gentlemen?"

"Sean O'Connell?"

"What can I do for you?"

"We'd like you to come with us, please."

He swilled the sponge in the water, squeezed it between his
hands and made a start on the windscreen. "Now why would I
want to do that?"

"Sir, I have orders to bring you in, if you refuse."

"From?"

"General Bowles-Smith."

He carried on cleaning. The general had been their
commanding officer in the Special Forces and military
intelligence, and the last time he had seen him had been at Steve's
remembrance service. Why the hell did he want to see him now,
when he had been out of action for the past few years?

"Now, Sir," one of the men insisted.

Sean knew he had no choice but to go. He dropped the sponge into the bucket and reached for a rag to dry his hands. Moments later he was escorted to the back seat of their car, where one of the men climbed in next to him. He felt grateful Cydney and the twins were out for the day and didn't see him leaving this way.

"I'm not running away, for Christ's sake."

"We know, Sir. Just following orders."

Sean was driven into London and directly to the Ministry of Defence headquarters, situated in Whitehall. The two men guided him through the front door and up the sweeping red-carpeted staircase to the first floor. He glanced briefly at the magnificent pictures of past army generals and famous admirals as he was led up the stairs, trying to get a grip on his anxiety. He had no idea what was happening or why. When he entered the office, all his years of service flooded back to him and he stood to attention, waiting for the man to speak.

"Please come and sit down, O'Connell."

Sean took a seat on the other side of the desk to the general, and said nothing. He was waiting to hear what this was all about.

"What I am going to say to you will come as a shock, as it has to me. Please remember this is governed under the Official Secrets Act."

Sean nodded.

"I want to cast your mind back to Syria and the last recce you were involved in. You were under Captain Steve Granger at the time. Can you tell me what happened there?"

"I can, Sir, but I was de-briefed after we got back. Everything is on record. Why is this coming up now? Captain Granger died as we tried to escape. He saved my life."

"Yes, O'Connell. Humour me though, I am asking for a reason."

Sean knew this to be true. Something important had come up or else he would not be sitting at HQ, so he recounted the whole story from beginning to end and left nothing out. Christ, he had gone through this often enough in his head.

"Yes, O'Connell, that's exactly what I read at the time, and what's in the file here." The man picked up an orange pack with the words 'Top Secret' written on the front in bold letters.

"Sir," Sean said, "Captain Granger was the best officer a man could have. If it wasn't for him I wouldn't be here now. He took the full force of the explosion and pushed me out of the line of fire. I wanted to go back for him but I had to save my men and the captain was dead. I live with that every single day of my life, Sir. I regret his death more than anything."

"Yes. I'm sure you do, O'Connell. However, the strangest thing happened. We got a call from Dragonfly."

"What?" Sean sat up in the chair, his heart racing. "Someone's impersonating him?"

"I don't know. Either we're all wrong and he's still alive or someone has got hold of his codename and is using it."

Sean sat in front of the general completely at a loss. Could Steve Granger still be alive? No. That was impossible. Christ almighty, alive?

"It must be an impostor, Sir. I saw the captain myself. He was dead. We had his funeral, or memorial service to be exact."

"Yes I know. I was there. Therefore, we have a dilemma here, Sergeant. I'm as bewildered as you are but we have to prove who this Dragonfly is or isn't, don't we?"

"Yes, Sir." Sean's thoughts immediately turned to Cydney. "Mrs Granger, Sir?"

"No, we say nothing at all until we know for sure. Is that clear, Sergeant?"

"Clear, Sir." Sean realised he was now being addressed as Sergeant and not O'Connell. That was quite ominous in the circumstances.

"Sergeant, would you say there was a particular way of sounding this Dragonfly out at all? Is there something that only you and he would know that we could put to him? A question, perhaps, that an impostor would not be able to answer?"

Sean sat there for a mere second as he knew, without a doubt, exactly what that was.

"Walnut Tree, Sir."

"What, Sergeant? Walnut Tree?"

"Yes, Sir. There's a walnut tree in his garden that he and his wife loved, and would watch coming into bloom. They sat under it through the summer; watched it through the winter from the window. That tree is very special to him."

"So, if we asked him to prove his identity, something from his past, you think he would say this?"

"Yes, Sir. We worked it out in advance, before the recce, in case a situation arose."

"Well done, Sergeant. Dragonfly is calling back tomorrow at midday. I want you to be here too. We will quarter you nearby. You don't need to go home for anything, do you?"

"It would seem not, Sir. But I do need to make a call to my daughter as she'll be worried where I am."

"Right, Sergeant. Off you go then. The officers who brought you here will stay with you and anything you need, just ask. They have my orders. In addition, Sergeant, in view of all this, please take this as my full authority for your reactivation. You may go, Sergeant."

Sean stood to attention, almost saluted then changed his mind, turned around and marched out the room as if he had never been out of the army. On the other side of the door, his two new friends were waiting for him. He had no time to think as they took him off to his overnight accommodation but he knew everything would sweep over him later like an avalanche. Steve alive? Impossible. Absolutely ridiculous.

CHAPTER EIGHT

THE day of those events a year ago went over in Sean's head so many times that he felt giddy. Keeping such a momentous secret was slowly eating away at his head and heart. It was almost impossible to live with but he had no choice, no matter what, because the alternative didn't bear thinking about. The consequences to people he loved were beyond imaginable.

He positioned himself not far from the open security gates of Rayshel Plastic's car park but near enough so he could see and not be seen. It was a beautiful summer's day once again, but thankfully with a slight breeze following the recent heat wave.

The factory and various outbuildings were set within acres of land that had probably been farmland years before, a couple of miles from the centre of town, something that would never be allowed nowadays with everyone worrying about Green Belt. There was not much activity about for an industrial unit, with only a few cars in the car park and some lorries with Rayshel emblazoned across them, not moving anywhere.

He had his binoculars trained on the large factory doors but there was nothing unusual, apart from a rather lovely black BMW Z3 convertible with the personal number plates, CG 500. That must be worth a bit, he surmised, so someone was doing very well.

He had been sitting in the same place for a couple of hours now and had seen the factory workers coming back from lunch. A few had mingled outside for a smoke and a couple of vans had come and gone. He wondered what he was actually doing there. Nothing untoward was happening but he knew Cydney would not have asked him without reason. He was used to reconnaissance work and could sit for hours if need be.

His mind wandered back to his last tour. He knew the captain had not told his wife what he was really up to in the army - that he was taking some time out until he started his new training for special assignments. Steve had told him how important it was for Granger Associates to be fully established before he had to leave, just in case, but duty and loyalty were the most important issues to him and he was and always had been a soldier, craving being in the heart of events and leading his men. The relationship Sean had with his commanding officer went beyond that of captain and sergeant, perhaps because their lives were always in danger. He knew Steve's heart had torn in two at the thought of leaving Cydney, aware of how insecure she would feel despite her outward appearance. However, neither of the two men could refuse their mission. He would never tell Cydney what had happened, he swore to the captain he wouldn't, but sometimes he came so close and really felt she should know what a brave guy her husband had been.

The story told was that they were in Afghanistan, while in reality they'd been in Syria under cover, along with eight others. They all spoke fluent Arabic, Steve due to his upbringing as his father had worked in the Middle East for so many years. He was chosen for that very reason as he could mix easily amongst the locals.

The team had entered Syria through Israel at the request of the combined British and American governments, and they worked in conjunction with the Israeli forces. The view was that Syria was a volcano waiting to erupt, what with all the diverse religions and ethnic groups. All the minorities thought they were going to be slaughtered by the others, there were gangs of militia in each sectarian division and the governments wanted to have an in-depth look into what was brewing. If anything happened, it could spark a major flare up in the Middle East which would have serious repercussions throughout the world.

Their purpose was to undertake a reconnaissance of the surrounding areas to Damascus and report any unusual activities such as the movements of troops and the build-up of weapons. It was nothing they hadn't done before. They were going to be in and out within a month, allegedly.

A movement took Sean away from his thoughts and he watched as a tall man in his mid-thirties strolled out of the Rayshel warehouse and headed towards the convertible. He was dressed rather too smartly for a factory, in a dark suit with a striped pink tie, and the ubiquitous sunglasses. He opened the car door with his remote, slid his briefcase into the boot and climbed into the car. Sean watched longingly as the roof glided back into its recess. He could watch that movement all day long. He longed for his own sports car but for now he had to be content with driving Cydney's. The gates opened and the car turned into the road at some speed. Sean followed, keeping a safe distance as it moved quickly along the country lanes away from the centre of Henley and towards the M4 motorway.

"Now where would he be going in such a hurry?" Sean said aloud.

The driver headed west once he turned onto the M4 and Sean followed, keeping pace. They moved along for about thirty minutes and then took the Reading turn off. At the main roundabout, the car headed towards the town centre and after a couple of miles signalled to turn into the car park of a large modern building with the name *Prestons* across its façade. Sean parked up again and wondered why this guy was going into the main headquarters of the biggest shopping supermarket owners in England. He called Cydney on her direct line and she picked up immediately. "Hi. Any news?"

"Yes. I went to the factory and the guy you wanted me to watch left about an hour ago. Now I'm sitting in the middle of

Reading outside the offices of Prestons, the supermarket people."

"So, he's moving in on them already."

"What do you mean?"

"Sean, this man's slippery. I believe he's fraudulently trying to sell Rayshel's factory and land to Prestons and pocket the money. My friend, who we visited earlier, owns the factory with her husband, Ray. He died recently and I'm trying to help her. Can you stay with him and see what he does next, please?"

"Of course. I may be back late though. Can you manage?"

"Yes. I'll call Sophie to pick me up with the kids and then take them all out for pizza. Don't worry. We'll save some for you."

"Grand. By the way, the factory site is practically empty. There are five other units but they've been vacated, so only Rayshel's operational. It's very odd."

He smiled as he put the phone down. It was impossible not to do whatever she asked of him. Sean got out of his car and walked across to Prestons' car park, making sure there was nobody about to see what he was doing. When he reached the BMW he dropped his keys and, as he bent down to pick them up, he placed something under the chassis and returned as if nothing had happened.

An hour and a half later, Charles Gordon emerged, talking animatedly on his mobile. Sean switched on the device that logged into the microphone come tracker he had placed surreptitiously under the car. He always carried a few toys with him, he never knew when they were going to come in handy.

"Don't be ridiculous, of course it went well. Who do you think I am, my brother? They fell for it, completely. No, I didn't give anything else away. Just leave me to do this will you, William? You stick to your side of the bargain, and you'll get your money. No, I'm not going to leave the country, not yet anyway. I want my share. We both do, don't we?" Sean noted the beginning of a rise in the man's voice.

"Christ. Just make sure you've done your bloody job right and that the land titles are properly registered in our names and we'll be laughing all the way to the bank. Yes, I know you will. Of course. Yes, I trust you." On that, Charles closed his phone, muttered an expletive, got into his car and drove off at high speed.

Sean didn't bother to follow him, after briefing Cydney on events. It was getting late and he wanted to get back to share the pizza. He was curious about what he had heard but it could be that Mrs Granger would know more about it when he played back the recording. Hopefully, she would let him into what this was all about at the same time.

CHAPTER NINE

CYDNEY'S immediate thoughts when she awoke on Saturday morning were of her mum and the coming weekend. She would be going to the nursing home of course, and hoped Claire would actually turn up for a change, if she could be bothered.

Claire lived a wonderfully charmed life and didn't have to work. Her husband was a top barrister in the City and they had no kids, and so she spent her time lunching, shopping, and holidaying - seemingly without a care in the world. Everything was down to Cydney where their mum was concerned, and just once in a while a little help wouldn't go amiss. Even a few words of comfort would be nice. How did someone become so selfish after they had been brought up the same?

"It's Saturday, it's party day! Can I get ready now? Will you do my hair? I'm so excited!" Lauren screamed as she ran full pelt into the bedroom, her words tumbling out in a torrent.

"Good morning, Lauren! Yes it is and no you can't – and yes, I will do later. Can I get up first, do you think?"

"Oh okay, but I can't wait to put on my new dress," she said, pulling at Cydney's covers to force her up.

"Lauren, at least let me wake up properly, get out of bed and go to the loo before we start getting ready for the palace ball."

"Mum, you're so funny. It's just that it's my first grown up party with boys!"

"There are going to be boys there? You never told me that. Well, I may have to change my mind now."

Lauren's face fell but then she saw her mum's broad smile.

Lauren leapt on top of her and Cydney pulled her over and started to tickle her tummy.

"Stop it, Mum, stop it! I can't bear it…" Lauren screeched, convulsed in laughter.

Jake, tousle-haired, appeared at the doorway wearing a t-shirt and sweatpants.

"Can't anyone get any sleep around here? Women!"

With that he turned round and sloped off, shaking his head, which caused Cydney and Lauren to laugh even harder.

Breakfast was ready for them when they got downstairs. Sophie always cooked the full works on Saturdays and she was there waiting to serve it, whilst the twins scrambled to sit down.

"Are you ready for your party then, Lauren? What are you taking your hostess?"

"Oh no! We didn't think of that. What shall I take, do you think? Maybe some wine?"

"Er, no I don't think so, do you? Nice try though," Cydney said.

"Well, definitely some chocolates. And I saw a lovely bracelet for Jamie I think she'd like for her birthday. Is that alright? Can we go and get it later, please?"

"Of course. We'll go into town, get the shopping and a few things, come home, get you ready, and go via Nan's so she can see you all dressed up. Is that a good plan?"

"Is Nan okay?"

Cydney turned to Jake. "Yes, darling. So, what's the man of the house up to today? Want to come with us?"

"Um, let me think about it. On a scale of one to ten, minus five."

"He's so rude, Mum. Ignore him."

"What are you going to do, then? It's a lovely day. You can't stay in your room all afternoon."

"Well, actually, that's the plan. I want to finish my song, record it, and get things ready for the competition."

"He thinks he's a famous rock star," Lauren groaned, and

started to sing at the top of her voice, mimicking her brother.

"That's enough, thank you, especially over breakfast. Okay, Jake, but I want you to come with us to Nan's later."

"Can I go tomorrow instead? And can you *shut up*, Lauren."

Lauren carried on regardless until she got the look from Sophie to be quiet.

"By the way, Mrs Granger, Dave should be back from his tour in the next couple of weeks. Is it okay if he stays with Dad and me in the cottage?"

"You know he's always welcome. You don't even have to ask. How long is he here for?"

"Not sure at the moment. It's all very secretive, as you know. But that's the army for you."

Cydney tended to hate Saturdays, apart from the fact she could spend time with the kids, but over the years she had become better with the day. Saturdays for her always meant sadness and took her back to the time when the officers had come to the house to tell her about Steve. She pushed the image out of her mind.

"Hello, Mum… you there?"

"Sorry darling, yes. Shall we go?"

"Maybe we should get dressed first. Just a thought," Lauren suggested.

"Oops. Good plan. Meet you down here in half an hour," she said, and they both rushed upstairs to get ready. Cydney could hear Jake in his room, sounds of piano and guitar invading the quietness of the landing.

Well as long as he's happy, Cydney thought to herself, making a mental note to buy some ear plugs of her own.

When they had finished their chores and returned home, Lauren raced upstairs to get ready. She'd been nagging Cydney all day and was so excited about the party. At the allotted hour of four o'clock on the dot, Cydney was at the bottom of the stairs with

Sean and Sophie, waiting for her to appear. She hadn't been allowed to see the finished article but only help with hair and make-up. Even Jake had managed to stumble out of his room and make an appearance.

When the door opened to Lauren's bedroom, out she came and stood at the top of the gallery, looking down at her admirers with the biggest smile on her face. Cydney's heart lurched as tears pricked at her eyes — this could not possibly be her fourteen-year-old daughter. This was a young woman. Steve would have been so proud to see his little girl all grown up. Lauren moved down the stairs towards her mum in silence. She had on her new blue dress and black shoes with a hint of a heel, and carried a matching handbag. There was a little bit of glitter around her eyes, and the mere touch of a pale pink lipstick.

"Wow, you look amazing my darling!"

"Actually, you scrub up quite well," Jake said, the king of under-statement.

"Now don't you look the pretty one," seconded Sean, also quite emotional.

Sophie clutched at Cydney's arm. "Where's our baby gone?"

"Do you like my dress? Sophie, look at my nails! Shall I do a twirl?" Without waiting for an answer, she twisted around a couple of times to show everyone the back of the dress.

"Let me take a few photos. I want this for the album. Your first party... with boys!" Sophie said.

"Boys?" Sean stared at her. "Is that allowed?"

"Mum and I have had that conversation," Lauren laughed.

When they arrived at the care home, Gabrielle caught them before they reached the room.

"Your mum hasn't been feeling too well today," she explained, "and wanted to stay in bed. I just thought I'd let you know."

Cydney nodded and opened the door quietly. As soon as she walked in, the first thing that struck her was how small her mum looked under the duvet. Her head was turned to the side and she was making little snoring noises.

"Should we stay, do you think?" Lauren whispered.

"We will for a moment, in case she wakes up. I know you wanted her to see you in your dress."

They both sat down on the chairs at the side of the bed and held hands, Lauren squeezing Cydney's every so often in support. Ten minutes passed before Cydney's mum woke up and turned her head to see them.

"Oh, I didn't know you were here, darlings. I would have got up," she said, trying to sit but not succeeding. Instead her head fell back on the pillow. "Sorry, I'm just not up to it today."

"Nan, look at my dress. I'm going to a party. Look!" she said, giving her a twirl.

"You look beautiful... so grown up." Her voice came out quietly, like a whisper, as if she was completely void of energy. Cydney took her hand.

"I'll make you a nice cup of tea, shall I? Then I'll help you up so you can see better." Cydney fetched some extra pillows and propped them up behind her mum. She weighed nothing at all. Then, locating her cardigan, she wrapped it snugly around her mum's shoulders to keep her warm, despite the fact it was summer.

"Can I have my handbag please? I need a tissue."

Lauren passed it to her nan, who fumbled around and eventually found what she was looking for.

"Where's Grandpa? I haven't seen him today. He was here last night before I went to sleep. He sat at the end of my bed and we had a little chat. He looked so young. Is he coming again today?"

Lauren's face fell. She blinked several times as she didn't want her newly applied mascara to run down her face. Cydney looked at her daughter and saw what was happening. She didn't want her to go off to the party upset in any way.

"Darling, why don't you go and wait with Sean while I see to Nan? She loves your dress. I won't be long and then we can set off."

"Grandpa's here," Lauren whispered. "Look!"

Cydney flicked her eyes to the corner of the room and saw her dad standing there, a look of pride on his face. She smiled, grateful for his presence. Lauren was certainly a surprise to her every single day of her life.

"It's okay, darling. You go. He's here to look after Nan."

Lauren kissed her nan and left the room, glancing back just as she got to the door. Cydney mouthed a 'don't worry' as she went, then turned back to her mother.

"He isn't coming today, Mum. Look, I have your keys here."

"He said he was waiting for me and would be back later."

"Have your cup of tea. I'll sit here a while and then I have to take Lauren to her party. How are you feeling?"

"Oh, much better. Better than yesterday, anyway. Lovely seeing Ron though. I do miss him."

Cydney didn't have the heart to break the spell so she let her mum carry on thinking of her husband, who she had lost so many years ago. The feeling her mum would soon be reunited with him was constantly in her thoughts and she wondered how long she could continue not remembering anything and feeling so tired all the time. This was no quality of life, yet the thought of losing her mum was so unbearable that she persuaded herself, albeit selfishly, that having her like this was better than the alternative. Hopefully the lump would prove benign and there would be nothing further to worry about.

Her mum looked lost against the pillows, a shadow of her former, vibrant self. All Cydney wanted to do was take her in her arms and cuddle her, pour life into her, and never let her go. She didn't want her mum to ever leave her like her dad and Steve had done. Tears prickled the backs of her eyes.

"Can you help me to the toilet?"

Cydney pulled the covers back and stared down at her mum's frail and tiny legs. Pulling her flowery nightie down to cover them, she lifted her out of bed and helped her to the bathroom, almost carrying her. So this was how it was, and this was how it would stay until the inevitable happened. She was almost reconciled to the sorrow that inevitably awaited her.

On the way back from dropping Lauren at the party, Sean and Cydney took the opportunity to talk about the events concerning Charles Gordon, and Sean played back the tape of the conversation he had recorded.

"So, who is this William, I wonder? Obviously they're doing something dodgy together."

"So it would seem. Do you want me to keep on the case for a few days longer?"

"Yes, I think so. Monitor his movements, see who he meets. Let me just make a quick call in case Sheila knows."

Cydney dialled Sheila's number from the car and after a few rings it was answered.

"Sheila, sorry to disturb you on a Saturday. How are you?"

"Hello Cydney. Yes, not bad, thank you. The funeral is on Monday. We want a quiet affair with close friends and family. Have you got any news for me?"

"Well, we're working on it. Just a quick call, but I was wondering if you know someone called William."

"William? No, I don't think so. No, we have no friends of that name. Why?"

"Oh, the name came up so I thought I'd ask. Thanks anyway. I hope Monday goes as well as can be expected. I'll be in touch," and with that Cydney ended the call.

"Damn. I was hoping she would know."

A few minutes later, the phone rang.

"Cydney, Sheila here. Sorry, I must have had a blank moment. Our solicitor who did all the documents. He used to be a friend of ours from way back. The name of his firm is William Harper & Co. I think he's in the local town now."

"Used to be?"

"We had a falling out over something stupid. I don't know all the details. Anyway, it's a long shot but it may be worth looking at. He's the only William I can think of."

"Thanks Sheila. Greatly appreciated. I'll look into this and let you know."

Sean glanced at her. "Sounds like I have my work cut out next week then, Mrs Granger."

"Yes. I think you should go along to the funeral on Monday. Not the actual service, but can you sort of hang around and see who comes along? See if anything unusual happens? You never know, something of interest might arise."

"Do you not think you could actually tell me what this is about now?"

Cydney proceeded to get Sean completely up to date. He was right. How could he help when he had no idea what he was looking for? In any case, Sean knew about Cydney and her special gift so it came as no surprise to him. He was part of the family and was involved in every aspect of her and the twins' lives, and her business. She was wrong to exclude him.

"This William, I'm interested to find out what he's up to. I'll ask Richard and Ash to have a look at him on Monday. With luck you'll have some news for me too."

By the time they got home, it was still quite light. Jake was in the kitchen and searching through the cupboards for food, leaving doors ajar, biscuit packets open on the worktop and crumbs on the floor in his wake.

"All right for some, going off to parties, but I have nothing to eat!"

"Jake, I'll make something for both of us – just hold on a bit and stop making a mess. Anyone would think I was starving you. Sean, do you want to join us?"

"No, it's ok. I want to watch a film. I'll see you tomorrow." Cydney loved the way he pronounced 'film' as if it had another vowel.

"How was Nan? Did you give her the keys we bought for her?"

Cydney sighed. "I did, love. Nan was very tired, but she was ok. Go on up to your room, I'll call you when dinner's ready."

Later that evening when the house was quiet, Cydney sat with a glass of her favourite Sauvignon in her hand. Dressed in her comfortable pyjamas and lazing in the armchair, she looked around at the lounge she and Steve had designed together. She remembered when they first saw the house and what a mess everything was, but still so beautiful in the summer sunlight with the wisteria climbing wildly and un-tamed over the door and up to the first floor. When she walked through the double wooden doors into the most magnificent hallway with the sweeping stairs leading up to the gallery around, Cydney knew the house was special. She felt the atmosphere as it invaded her whole being, as if someone was saying to her, *this is your house, it's waiting for you*, and it felt good and loved.

Cydney knew Steve would never deny her anything and goodness knows he had tried in the past. She knew she was the centre of his universe and he always told her that without her he was nothing, and he had felt like that since the moment they'd met about two years before.

The place was truly wonderful but dark and very cold, despite the summer sun, and there was that smell of damp of an un-lived in place. But it was the outside that sold it to Steve, the view of the walnut tree and the amazing garden just waiting for children to run and play around in. Now the house was restored to its former glory and the wooden floors under the aged carpet renovated and shiny. There were two large settees either side of the grand fireplace in heavy red velvet and between them sat a beautiful Turkish rug in blue, turquoise and red. Intricately knotted, it formed a pattern of swirls and flowers. They had found this on a holiday to Istanbul and imported it. They had also browsed around many antique shops looking for those special pieces of furniture to fit in the nooks and crannies of the room: a lovely inlaid coffee table, a Victorian bureau in one corner, and a large cabinet in another to house all their ornaments, plates and tea services they so enjoyed collecting. The heavy swag and tailed curtains in red and black were not drawn as Cydney loved to look out the window, and tonight was a full moon so she could still see the walnut tree.

Cydney had not really had time for any of that since she'd become a widow. All she had time for was the twins and she worked every hour available to be able to keep going financially. Steve had left her very well provided with a good pension from the army and there was some money left from his trust fund after the house renovations, but it was never enough and Cydney felt a constant need to prove herself and make her business more successful, to make him proud of her.

She sipped at the wine and thought she should make a move for bed when the phone rang, jarring into her thoughts. Not her mum. No, she wasn't ready for that. She'd only left her a couple of hours ago. She leapt up, almost spilling the wine down the front of her, and ran to pick up the receiver.

"Gabrielle, is that you? Is Mum okay?"

"Hi, Cyd," came a cheery voice. "It's me, George. How are you? Sorry to call you so late, but the time difference..."

"Oh, George, hi. Sorry, thought it was the nursing home. Yes, it's late. I'm fine thanks." She paused. "How did you get my number?"

"Hope you don't mind but Rupert gave it to me. I told him I had to speak to you about the current matter. I'm sure he thought otherwise, but really I wanted to speak to you and hear your voice. I know it sounds crazy as we've only recently met but I thought I would...well, you know."

Once Cydney got over the relief it was not her mum, she settled back into her armchair with her bare feet curled under her and warmed into the conversation with George. It was easy, she had to admit, and they ended up talking for well over an hour about what he'd been doing, what Cydney had been up to, Lauren's party and Jake's competition. The subject of Cydney's mum wasn't discussed, as that would have meant allowing him in a little too much.

"I'm back at the end of the week. Please have dinner with me again? I promise not to leave this time."

"That would be lovely," Cydney said, and when she put down the receiver it was with a smile on her face. Regardless of what was going on in her life, she was actually looking forward to the week ahead.

CHAPTER TEN

CYDNEY was at the office bright and early on Monday morning and working with Richard, who was briefing her on the Rayshel matter.

"I carried out a complete land registry check on the site where the factory is. Cydney, are you sure about this? We're spending an awful lot of time on something that we're not getting paid to do."

"Yes I know. These are friends of mine, I told you, so if you could just..."

"Right," he interrupted. He cleared his throat. "There are six units on the entire site and, as Sean told you, five of these are completely empty. Here's the interesting thing. Rayshel sold them all to one company over the last year for a song, and they were leased out short term to other companies. Then the ownership of the final unit, being Rayshel itself, was transferred to the same purchaser - Intervest Holdings Limited. The director and shareholder is Charles Gordon. Patricia Smith is the company secretary."

"Have we heard that name before?"

"Um. She's married to William Harper, the solicitor you mentioned. Smith is her maiden name. They've not been very clever here at all. Also, the businesses that took the short leases then either closed down or moved away. Very strange that, to be honest, and I never believe in coincidence. That's where I am with everything."

"So, hold on, let me get this right. From what you told me

before, Rayshel was owned jointly by Ray and Charles, but now solely by Charles. He must have hived off the actual building and land to Intervest Holdings, separating it from the company, so Charles effectively owns everything now. I just can't believe Ray Gordon knew anything about this. Why would he give away all his assets? It's too much of a coincidence to think Charles Gordon and this William Harper are not involved in this together. They clearly want the land but I wonder how they managed to get rid of five businesses and persuade Ray to hand everything over on a plate. There's definitely something very strange going on here."

"We may never find out about the other businesses. Do you really want to spend time chasing up the companies if they are no longer trading?"

"You may be right. Let's hold that thought. Anything else?"

"Well, I found out Harper was involved in a very messy case a few years ago. His partner in a previous law firm was struck off for playing with client funds. Harper got off scot-free and of course his indemnity paid out so he continued practicing. The partner died a couple of years ago. Anyway, if it's okay with you I'll meet up with Sean and see what we can dig up together."

"Yes, please do. I'll tell Sean you'll call him."

"I know William Harper from a long time ago."

Cydney felt the presence of Ray come forward to her as Richard left the room.

"Good morning, Ray. Please explain."

"William used to be my solicitor. When his partner got into trouble, William allegedly lost an awful lot of money and virtually started again. There was talk he was involved and to be honest I think it's true, because his lifestyle hardly changed despite everything; still the big house, holidays. I think the money was hidden somewhere, or Patricia had it. Anyway, I couldn't work with him but then he started to get friendly with Charles, and that's when the trouble really started."

"How do you mean, trouble?"

"Well. I think Charles found out somehow about what William had been up to and started to bribe him. Charles was pushing and pushing. William prepared all the documents that you have discovered. The false stock transfer forms, life insurance, everything."

"So are you saying now that William is involved, big time?"

"Without a doubt. I heard what your man was saying just now. You need to find out what they did. They obviously want to sell the land to the supermarket, but at what cost to the business and my employees?"

"We'll find out, you must trust me on that. I won't let you down."

"I'm beginning to realise that. Anyway, you have a guest so I'm going."

Ray faded away as Rupert put his head around the door and walked in.

"Cyd, my! You're a sight for sore eyes. Come and give me a hug."

Cydney stood up, shaking the presence of Ray from her and, laughing, walked towards Rupert to be swept into a huge bear hug. He pulled her away from him and gazed into her eyes.

"How are you, is everything okay? You look tired."

"Yes, all good thanks. Come and sit down. I'll get you a cup of tea and ask Richard to join us as well."

"I arrived back from Germany last night. Good trip, though. I decided to invest in some further iron and steel industries over there. No good looking at me like that, Cyd. I'm never going to retire."

"Yes. Clearly. As long as you're not over-doing things. But that's good news for you."

"How are you getting on with George?"

Richard appeared as George's name was mentioned. He passed Cydney a questioning glance with a suggestion of a raised eyebrow, but she ignored him and turned to Rupert.

"Fine. He's back at the end of the week I understand."

Rupert laughed. "He's a great guy. You two should get together, if you haven't already!"

"Yes, thank you for that."

"By the way, George has already briefed me on what you have found out about Centurion, so I'm fully up to speed. This Benton guy. I should tell you we know each other, and not under good circumstances. He's sharp, too much so. One of those men who shake your hand, look you in the eye and act friendly, but there's nothing behind it. I was interested in American Securities at the time, which Benton got into trouble, and then I'm sure he was behind the sale to Caxton Trust Bank. It was not doing too well. I spoke to my broker and he thought it would be a great investment. Build it up, take it to market. It had a good client base but small, localised branches. I wanted to get into investment internationally with the intention of expanding the bank into Europe."

"So what happened, Rupert? Why didn't you proceed?" Richard asked.

"Benton happened, and he screwed me out of the deal. He knew I wanted the bank. His brother-in-law, Crossley, obviously tipped him off about American Securities, or somebody did. Pure insider dealing and both of them made millions from it. I doubt the broker was snowy white either but I couldn't prove anything."

"So what do you want now? Is this why you want Centurion, to get back at them?"

Cydney asked.

"No. I didn't know they were involved, and they must never find out it's me looking at the company."

"No reason they would Rupert, is there?"

"Not that I can think of. However, I wouldn't want this to leak out. You know I like to maintain my privacy so, whilst you are investigating, let's keep things within these four walls. I don't trust these guys. If they get wind of our investigations they may take action detrimental to us and they may try to do a deal elsewhere just because it is me."

"So far we've not done anything to alert them. We'll watch what we're doing. So what's the next step for you?"

"I want Centurion and I am not prepared this time to have it taken from me. They're obviously in big trouble, and I think the Internal Revenue Service are after Crossley and Benton, probably the Inland Revenue here, too. I think we can get it cheap. The company is tainted with bad money and they cost me a huge chunk at the time. Cyd, this is very close to home for me. Watch yourselves. Benton is bad news, worse than his brother in law, and his back is against the wall so he could be even more dangerous. I wouldn't put anything past him."

"At the moment we're busy looking into the finances. We know what we're doing, don't worry."

"Which is why I always come to you for the big deals. I've another meeting now, for a change, and need to go. My plans are to be here for a few days and then go back to Johannesburg, but you know you can reach me any time. Look after George for me."

"I doubt he needs looking after," Cydney replied sarcastically.

"But as I said, watch what you do. I want this, but not to the extent anyone gets harmed. Pay-back is good, but sometimes it doesn't always leave a sweet taste in your mouth."

"I will get back to you Rupert, very soon."

"Don't forget, my door is always open, Cyd. Any time you fancy a holiday, come over with the kids and stay. Bring Sean as well. I like that guy - the way he looks after you, especially when I'm not around."

"Sounds perfect! Once we get through this deal, I may well take you up on the offer."

"Wonderful. Please report to me as soon as you can, before anyone else gets a chance at this. I don't want to lose the deal. Oh, and please send your invoice to me in the normal way. Don't pull a face! I want a weekly invoice from you and then if you get this for me it's big bonus time."

"Thanks, Rupert. I appreciate your trust. We'll do everything we can."

As Rupert left, Cydney turned to Richard.

"You know this isn't going to be easy, for a change?"

"I know, but we've had more difficult cases. Anyway, I'm going to call Sean and see what he's up to."

Sean, who was positioned outside the small eighteenth century church in Marlow, watched as people arrived for Ray's funeral, with his long-lens camera in hand. The sky looked ominous and overcast as if it was about to rain. Always at funerals, no matter what time of year, Sean thought. He hadn't bothered with Charles over the weekend but still had the tracker under his car so he knew his movements anyway, and there was nothing out of the ordinary going on.

He saw the widow arrive in a black limousine with her three children. The driver stopped, stepped out of the car and walked around to help her out, an umbrella at the ready. The teenagers followed. Sheila was dressed in a black suit with a matching hat and veil that covered her face. He could see a white handkerchief gripped tightly in her hand. Her children stood close, appearing lost, but with their arms linked in support as they sheltered from the rain. People approached them, kissing and patting the backs of the children and no doubt giving words of comfort. Sean could see the youngest girl crying uncontrollably. She looked about fifteen, slightly older than Cydney had been when she'd lost her dad, he thought, and it reminded him of Steve's funeral and little Lauren. The tallest of her two brothers put his arm around his sister and then guided the family through and into the church. Sheila glanced around to see who else was there, but then disappeared from Sean's view. From the crowd that had gathered, it was clear Ray was popular. Some people Sean recognised from his vigil outside the factory the previous week. Everyone had their photographs taken nevertheless.

Charles Gordon arrived noisily in his BMW. The man had no respect. He brought his car to a quick standstill, causing the stones on the ground to fly up around him. He got out and waited for the vehicle behind him to arrive. At least he had the decency to wear a black tie, Sean thought, disliking the man already, even after such a short time. A rather battered blue Rover pulled up next to Charles and out from the passenger side emerged a smartly dressed woman in her early forties looking decidedly unhappy, followed by a grossly overweight and much older man turned out in an ill-fitting suit with his tie askew. Sean's camera clicked away as he snapped lots of close-ups of this threesome. The woman watched as Charles and the man spoke for a short while and then marched off ahead of them impatiently. After walking a few yards, she turned around to face her two companions, gesticulating madly, whereupon all three walked up the path towards the church entrance. Charles strode ahead whilst the other two followed and Sean could see the woman arguing with the man. Sean guessed this was her husband, William Harper. At one stage they stopped, and Harper stood there with his head bent whilst she berated him, hitting out at his arm. Strange scenario, he thought. If only he could hear what the argument was about, but they were too far away from the microphone still hidden under Charles' car.

The cortege arrived. There were flowers along the side spelling out *Ray* and *Dad* in red, white and blue. A cold shiver ran through Sean. The four funeral directors slid the coffin from the back of the hearse and lifted it up onto their shoulders, shifting themselves to bear the weight, and then walked slowly into the church for the service.

Sean had nothing much else to do but sit and wait. He reached for his newspaper and flicked through to the sports pages, running his finger through the list of horses, looking for his winner. He swore under his breath as his mobile rang, looked at the screen and took the call. It was Richard from Mrs Granger's office. After all these years of working for the same boss they had become more like friends than work colleagues, especially as they had a similar background. They were very easy with each other and recognised their mutual and complementary abilities. Sean had a guess this was about the Gordons. This wasn't the first case they had worked on together and probably wouldn't be the last.

"Hiya, old man. How's it going?"

"Not so much of the old please, Sean. I only have a few years on you, and at least I still have my hair."

"Yeah sure you do, but for how long? Anyway, I'm outside the church. I presume that's why you're calling?"

"Yes, Cydney asked me to. She's tied up with another client matter but I believe we're both up to speed, unless anything else has happened since last week?"

Sean reported what he had seen at the funeral so far.

"I think they must be the Harpers. From what you're telling me, Patricia seems to be wearing the trousers. What do you reckon to Jenny and me paying Harper a little visit? Would be interesting to see him at work, see how he behaves, and maybe we could take a little look around his office."

"Grand. I want to steer clear in case they've seen my car. You never know. I'll keep my eye on Charles while you deal with the others. Richard, do you actually know what this is all about? I mean, how is Mrs Granger involved? Not exactly her usual type of client, is it? I'm a bit worried to be honest. She's really not quite herself at the moment."

"I know what you mean. But let's humour her. You know she likes to help people and get involved, sometimes more than necessary. I think she's over-doing things, though, and this business with her mum is getting to her."

"Well I suggest we both keep a close watch."

"Agreed. Let's speak later. Have a good one."

Cydney had a huge workload to get through but she was sitting at her desk and accomplishing nothing worthwhile. She was aware things were getting on top of her and recognised it was because she was so worried about her mum, and had no one with whom to share those worries. If only Claire would actually show up, answer her phone even and in some way step up to the mark, but there was little hope. Gabrielle had rung Cydney and asked her to meet with the doctor later in the week to discuss the results of the scan, and this concerned her even more. If it was serious and the lump was malignant, she knew her mum was far too weak to undergo any surgery or chemotherapy, but surely they wouldn't put her through all of that? Cydney's mind spun in circles as the knowledge that her mum wouldn't be able to cope sank her further into despair.

Thoughts of the day her dad had died tumbled into Cydney's mind. At only twelve, she'd felt as if her whole world had ended, as if she had been picked up and dropped into a parallel universe where her father didn't exist and life would never be the same again. Numbness, shock, fear, pain, rejection, anger, and thousands of other feelings she couldn't even describe enveloped her, Claire, and their mother. The grief was tangible, as if a knife could cut through it, and it became part of her existence from dawn until dusk for weeks. Months, even, and into years.

Her dad had understood her like no one else and he instilled in her a belief to be the best in everything she did. By the age of ten she had read all the classics and exhausted the children's section of the local library. He taught her French so she was speaking fluently from an early age, and gave her a love of music, especially jazz. There was nothing better, in her dad's eyes, than dancing around the room on his toes to Frank Sinatra. Their house, until he had died, had been filled with laughter and joy.

Cydney's dad had driven her to school each morning. He would pull up outside the gates and watch her skip up the driveway in her blue uniform, smiling at her and waving as she went. He would tell her to work hard and be top of the class. But then one day – a day she would always remember - he had to go away on business for a few days and she was to look after her mum and Claire for him. Cydney cried, clinging on to him in an attempt to prevent him from leaving because she knew, without a shadow of a doubt, that she'd never see him again. The dream she'd had the night before he had left played out now, like a film.

"Please don't go! We need you here. You have to stay with us. I'll do anything for you not to go." She held on to him as if by doing so she could stop the inevitable.

"Cydney, why are you being so silly? I've been away before on business and I'll be home in a few days. Just look after Claire for me, and make sure mum is okay."

She heard those words as she walked up to the school gates, so slowly, turning around at every step, and he smiled at her and mouthed the words, "I love you," and then, his last words, "Go on, it's okay."

Then, the following night, Cydney was woken from a deep sleep. It was almost midnight and she heard screaming. She recognised the sound, always the same noise from her dreams, and she ran out of her bedroom, knowing something awful had happened. It had to be her dad. She charged downstairs and her mum was standing in the hall motionless, the telephone still in her hand, her face fixed as if in a trance. Cydney had no idea who was on the other end of the phone, but whoever it was must have given bad news. She grabbed her mum's shoulders and shook her, but nothing worked. Without thinking, she slapped her around the face to bring her out of her shock, but the only words her mum spoke were, 'You do love me. Tell me you love me, promise me you love me.' Each time she heard the words, they drove deeper into Cydney's soul. Then the police turned up at the door and Cydney answered it, a twelve-year-old, still in her dressing gown and pink nightie. Her father had been in a motorway pile-up outside Manchester. Nothing could be done. It was too late and Cydney had to be a brave girl, grown up and responsible, but she wanted nothing more than to be a twelve-year-old girl without a care in the world.

Everything felt so surreal to Cydney, as if it was happening to another person. Her dad was the core of her existence, everything revolved around him. He was the hero she worshipped, the rock she relied upon, the person who protected and took care of the family. Their provider. And then it dawned on her. How would they survive? They had no money and there would be no income. How would she look after her mum and Claire? Could she possibly leave school now? Each night Cydney fell asleep with the whole weight of the world on her very young shoulders and each day came and nothing had changed, but everything had changed. Cydney was now on her own because the day her father died, she became a parent to Claire, and a carer to her mum. At still only twelve years' old a lifetime had come and gone. It was impossible to cry and she would not cry, for that would be giving in to her feelings and showing the world how she felt. Cydney vowed to be brave for everyone.

Her dad came to her the day after they lowered him into the cold, dark ground. Cydney was sitting in the lounge with her mum and went out to the kitchen to get a drink. She switched on the hall light and the crystal chandelier hanging from the ceiling exploded into a thousand pieces. Cydney felt the impact and shouted out for her mum and they both just stood in the hall looking at the shards of crystal all over the carpet. How could they even begin to pick up the pieces of glass, their lives? Cydney felt cold all over. Her mum was stunned into silence and then her dad appeared next to her as if nothing had happened to him, smiling at her, with so much love. Cydney needed to reach out and touch him but the shock was so intense, her body wouldn't move and no words would come out.

"What is it, Cyd?" asked her mum. "Why are you looking like that?"

Cydney shook her head, as her dad signalled for her not to say anything.

"Nothing Mum. I'm just in shock. You go and sit down, I'll clear up."

Her mum went back into the lounge, now only a trace of her former self remaining, moving like a robot. The high doses of Valium she took transported her into another world. Cydney didn't blame her for this but recognised she had to step up to the mark now.

"Was that you?"

"Yes, sorry. I didn't mean to scare you, Cyd. You know I will always be here, looking over you."

"Why did you leave us?"

"I had no control over it. You knew, and have always known since you were very small that it was just a matter of time. I know that now and understand. You have a gift and you must use it wisely. If ever you need me, just speak to me. I love you, my darling."

"Dad, please don't leave us! How will I manage without you?"

"You will, my darling, don't worry. I have every faith in you. This is your path in life. Mum needs you. Look after Claire. She thinks she's strong, but she isn't. You are."

"Dad, no! I can't do this."

"Yes, you can. I am here for you always. I will never leave your side."

Cydney felt the mere touch of a kiss on her forehead as he faded away. She could not believe her dad had spoken to her. Nobody would understand, except her grandma. However, she decided to keep everything to herself.

Every night, her dad and the life they used to have filled her dreams. She always woke up with such a sense of loss that he'd evaded her and she couldn't reach out to touch him. Although she knew he was around, it was not the same.

Bringing herself back to reality, Cydney looked around at her executive office. She had everything, yet nothing. She yearned to be free of the shadows of sadness and heartache surrounding her. All the phone calls, the knocks at the door, always the same scene, always bad news and always Cydney answering. Thank goodness for the twins, who really were her saviours. With those thoughts, Ray arrived, sensing her despair.

"Cydney, let me remind you that because you're helping me, I will help you. All is not lost so don't you believe for a second that it is."

"Oh, Ray. You're here," she said. "So now you're a mind reader?"

"Your mum is in good hands, and being watched over. Your dad is with her but she's not ready to go to him yet."

"Be there for her too, Ray. I don't want her in any pain."

"I will be when she needs me to be," he said, and left her to carry on with her day.

CHAPTER ELEVEN

A FEW days later a secretary showed Jenny and Richard into the offices of William Harper Solicitors. The practice was above a small gift shop in a sleepy village street of High Maldon, with not a lot of passing trade. The place was typically English and consisted of a couple of pubs, a quaint tea room with blue-checked table cloths, a grocery shop come post office and the gift shop, all set around the village pond. The stairs leading up to the office were narrow and damp, and Jenny noticed the carpet needed replacing and the walls were in need of a lick of paint.

"Not too impressive, Richard, is it?" Jenny whispered.

"No. Obviously he's not doing as well as he used to."

"Come in, please," Harper said, showing them into his office. "Mr and Miss Fothergill, is it?"

"Yes." Richard looked across at Jenny with an arched eyebrow.

"All I could think of," she mouthed back.

The office was in complete disarray. It was crammed with tired legal textbooks, stacked on shelves and piled on top of filing cabinets. Blue files covered every available dust-covered surface, some with pink ribbon tied around them. Harper's desk overflowed with even more files, documents and papers, and a couple of used coffee mugs sat in front of an ancient computer that had probably seen better days.

"Please excuse the mess – rather busy at the moment and not had time to put everything away," Harper said, as he hurriedly moved some lever-arch files off the chairs so they could sit down.

"Don't worry. We're here to see you."

"So, Miss Fothergill tells me I was recommended by the Watsons in Marlow. I can't actually recall the family to be honest."

"Yes, Nigel and Elena Watson. You did some conveyancing work for them a few years ago. They used to live on Urlingham Farm but moved away."

"Of course! So how can I help?"

"My daughter and I are thinking of buying a little antique business in the area," Richard explained. We need someone to take care of the purchase and all the formalities, and I need to make a Will." Richard turned to Jenny and took hold of her hand. Jenny gave him a big broad smile as he patted it.

"Let me make some notes," Harper said, and rattled around on his desk trying to find his notepad and a pen, moving papers from one side to the other.

This Harper was a strange guy and totally disorganised judging by the absolute chaos around them. Richard watched him closely. The man's shirt collar was too small for him, and he kept moving his head to shake his neck loose. He was sweating profusely, using a handkerchief to mop his forehead and around the back of his neck all the time they were talking. Was this because he was grossly overweight, as Sean had told them, or just extremely nervous, Richard wondered. The man's suit was also far too small, with old food stains down the front. He was a heart attack waiting to happen.

"Perhaps you could give me some details to start with."

Richard began to explain and Harper took everything down, twice changing his pens when they failed to write.

"Excuse me, Mr Harper. Do you mind if I use your ladies room?" Jenny said, rising from her seat.

"Not at all. It's along the corridor to the left. My secretary will show you."

Jenny walked to his secretary's desk and was pointed in the right direction.

"I'm just popping out to the post office. You'll be okay, I hope?" the secretary asked. "Please tell Mr Harper for me, would you?"

What a piece of luck, Jenny thought.

She found her way down the narrow corridor towards the ladies' room and as she was about to open the door, she heard the secretary's footsteps on the stairs, followed by the click of the front door closing. She tip-toed back, careful not to make a sound in case Harper appeared. This was her opportunity to look through all the documents on her desk.

She went through the first pile, scanning the names on the file covers. Nothing there. Every few seconds she glanced up to check nobody was coming, even though she was sure Richard would be regaling Harper with tales of goodness knows what to give her time. The second pile of documents also revealed nothing of interest. There were a few papers on a stand next to the computer but these were hand-written and she guessed the secretary was just copy typing. She turned to the filing cabinet and went straight to the Gs for Gordon. She flicked through but found nothing. Then she tried the Rs for Rayshel. Nothing also. Where could they have filed the papers?

She moved to some other sections, but again there was nothing. As she was closing the cabinet, she noticed an open file named 'Industrial Estate – CG' that was propped on top of a large, heavy-duty safe with an old-fashioned combination lock. Obviously, someone had opened the safe but hadn't had time to put the file away. Jenny opened it and started to read the pages when the phone next to her rang and she jumped out of her skin, dropping the file to the floor. The noise echoed around the office. She quickly bent down to retrieve the papers as the door to Harper's office opened, and she just had time to put the file back on top of the safe before he came into view.

"Your secretary went to the post office," Jenny said. "I was on my way back to you."

Richard, standing behind Harper, gave her a signal that it was time to leave.

"Thank you for telling me. Anyway, I think your father and I have finished. Please let me know how your business purchase comes along and in the meantime I shall have a draft of your Will prepared."

"Wonderful. Thank you so much, Mr Harper," she said. Richard shook hands with him and they made their way down the stairs. Outside, Jenny told him she had found a file but didn't manage to look through it properly. Richard, however, had picked up some keys he had seen poking out from under one of the piles of paper on Harper's desk. He dangled them in front of her.

"Well, I may have to get Sean to pay him another visit."

"Richard! Let's hope he doesn't notice them missing."

"In that mess? Doubtful."

"Anyway, what did you make of him?"

"I think he's running scared of something. I've never seen anyone sweat so much, and it wasn't just his weight. He was completely on edge. We'll see what Sean can find out."

Sean and Cydney turned up the driveway to the nursing home and saw Claire leant against a red Ferrari, waiting for them to arrive. She was certainly an impressive sight, tall and dark like Cydney, and expensively dressed. But something was missing from behind her eyes, a coldness that was in complete contrast to Cydney's soft and gentle nature.

"Hi," Claire said, as Cydney got out the car. They inclined their heads towards each other to air kiss. "Good morning, Sean."

"And to you, Mrs Armstrong-Lane."

"Lovely to see you," Cydney said. "Really pleased you could make it this time, as I need you here. I hope it isn't bad news."

"Let's wait and see. I don't have long as I'm catching a flight tonight to Bali. I've got two weeks with some of the girls at one of those spa and beach resorts for some pampering."

"How lovely you have the time at all. You know, Claire, she's your mum too. I've carried us for a long time and I could do with your support sometimes."

"But you do it so nicely, sis. Come on, let's not bicker. It's far too boring."

Claire took Cydney's arm and pulled her along into the entrance of the nursing home. Gabrielle was waiting for them in the reception and led them into her office.

"Have a seat. Dr. Stubbs will be with you shortly. He's just seeing another resident."

Left alone, the two sat in silence for a short while but Cydney was not in the most patient of moods.

"How long is he going to keep us waiting? This is ridiculous." She stood up and started to pace the small room.

"Just sit down. You're making my nerves jangle."

"Sorry, I can't. I hate sitting around. I just want to know what's wrong with Mum."

"We both do, but a few minutes isn't going to make any difference."

At that moment the door opened and Cydney turned to face the doctor.

"Alistair Stubbs. Pleased to meet you." He shook their hands and took a seat behind his desk. "Sorry to have kept you waiting. That always seems to be my opening line." He smiled at them both. "Anyway, I won't keep you waiting any longer. I know you're worried about your mum. I've looked at the scan, and read through the blood results and other tests we carried out."

He buried his head in their mother's file and started to read it, as if for the first time. Delaying tactics, Cydney thought. He looked uncomfortable and moved around in his seat, finally looking up at them.

"Look, there's no easy way of saying this, I'm afraid. The lump on your mum's neck - it's a cancer of the mandibular gland. That's where saliva is produced. I don't want to get too technical but I need to explain to give you a clearer picture. There are clusters of salivary glands in several places in the head and neck and under the jawbone, and also smaller clusters in parts of the upper digestive tract tissue lining, and the windpipe."

Claire seized Cydney's hand, squeezing it tightly. They looked at each other. For all of Claire's bravado, Cydney knew her sister was not immune to the news. Now she felt completely numb.

"I understand, but what are we going to do? What's the treatment? How much time do we have?"

"Let the doctor speak, Claire."

"Well, normally we would suggest removal of the lump followed by six weeks of radiotherapy. However…"

"However what?" Cydney interrupted.

"Unfortunately the cancer has spread down the windpipe and we've found some small tumours in your mother's stomach. You know she is nearly eighty and usually that wouldn't be a problem. We operate on much older ladies these days. However, she has dementia that will not get better. I would not want to put her through operations and rigorous treatment."

"Oh my God! Please no!" Claire cried out. Cydney sat there, not quite taking in the information.

"Sorry, I actually don't understand, Doctor. You mean you are refusing our mum treatment. Is that what you are saying?"

"No, Mrs Granger… Cydney. What I am saying is I think your mum is too weak and just wouldn't survive the treatment. My opinion is we should keep her comfortable, in her own bed, until we need to move her. I will write a prescription for some pain medication."

"Move her where? I don't want Mum moved anywhere. Comfortable? What does that mean? How long have we got with her?" Claire asked, her questions tumbling out in a torrent.

"She may have to move into a hospice at some stage. But let's take this one step at a time. I know it's hard for you both to take in."

"How long has she got, Doctor?" Cydney asked, sounding calmer than she felt.

"In all honesty I don't know, but I would think no more than a matter of months, possibly a bit longer. I am so sorry to give you this news. I know it can't be easy for you."

"Thank you for being so honest with us. It is appreciated, Doctor, but if you don't mind I think we will go and see Mum now, if that's okay. Perhaps Gabrielle can discuss it with us later." Cydney stood up, yanked at Claire's arm and they both left, holding hands.

Once again, Claire had stolen the limelight, even in these awful conditions, and Cydney was the one to put on the brave face. No tears allowed for her. It would be Claire who would get the pity, the 'there theres', the words of sorrow. Cydney would be the one to hold everything together, be strong, and look after Claire. Again. Sometimes she wanted to scream out loud at the injustice of it all, but instead she held it back and forced herself to keep everything inside her. It was in these awful times that she so badly needed Steve beside her, to help and guide her through. If only she could connect with him. But for some reason he never came through to her; his spirit evaded her. Oh, she had tried... many nights she had begged him to connect but all she ever got was a picture of the place where he had died, a desert and nothing else. She had pleaded with all her spirit guides to bring him through and sat countless times on her own in quiet meditation, but no answers came to her. It was as if he was nowhere in heaven or on earth and that made her despair even more.

They found their mum dressed and sitting up in one of her comfy chairs, waiting for them, although Cydney half expected to see her lying in bed again. She had a bright coloured tartan blanket over her legs to keep her warm, as she always felt the cold even on warm days, and Cydney was even more pleased to see she had put a little bit of lipstick on. She smiled as they entered and Cydney and Claire did the same as they'd both agreed not to let her see how upset they were, nor talk about anything the doctor had told them. After all, what would that accomplish? Cydney shivered as they entered the room and felt the presence of their dad around them, which did not surprise her at all, considering the circumstances.

"Hi, Mummy," Claire said, and leant forward to give her a kiss. Cydney had never understood why Claire still called her that. It seemed so odd to hear it come from an adult, so affected almost. She shook off her annoyance. Perhaps she was being a little unfair.

"You look well. All made up and sat in the chair," Cydney said, smiling gently.

"Well, I have to make myself look good, don't I? Ron told me he was coming to see me today. I have my things all ready, over there." Both girls looked to see all their mum's belongings taken from the drawers and set out in various piles on the bed, and her handbag full to the brim of everything she had collected from the bathroom. A mauve silk scarf hung over the edge, preventing the bag from closing, and there was a green comb stuck out on one side upon which chocolate had clearly melted and then hardened. Cydney took a proper look and discovered there were so many tissues stuffed inside plus tea bags, small sachets of sugar she must have been collecting from the communal dining room, old peppermints, and sticky toffees that had lost their paper covers, that the bag was fit to bursting.

"Do you really need all of this? Shall I put a few things back for you? You won't be able to carry everything."

"Well, I've decided not to live here anymore and go with Dad. Who's this with you? Is it a nurse?"

"No, it's me, Claire. I've come to see you."

Cydney saw tears were welling up in her sister's eyes.

"My sister? Is that you, Pam?"

"No, your daughter, Claire. It's me – see? I'm in those photos over there."

"Oh yes, I can see now. Silly me, aren't I? Forget everything. Where's Dad? What time is he coming?"

"Maybe later," Cydney said, feeling him standing next to her.

"I'm looking after her. I'm not ready to come and get her just yet. When she's ready, she will know."

"I know. My dream. I saw you both, dancing together," Cydney said, speaking to her dad telepathically whilst Claire took a chair next to their mum. Claire didn't have the same gift as Cydney and was extremely sceptical of her abilities so it was something never spoken about between them.

"It's very hard for you but you must never forget we'll both be looking over you when she joins me."

"I really can't imagine a life without her."

"She will slip away quietly. We're all here waiting for her, her parents, her sister and brother..." With those words he left Cydney and the room became still.

Claire looked across at her and Cydney went over to join them, and they both sat either side of their mum, each holding her hand. Cydney felt closer to Claire than she had for many years.

"I'm not going to Bali," Claire said. "I'll cancel – you need me here."

Those were the best words that Cydney could have hoped to hear, not to be left on her own again.

"I love you Claire," she mouthed.

"I love you too, big sis."

"And I love both of my girls," their mum said.

By the time Cydney left, said goodbye to Claire and arrived home, it was quite late. Sean was upset at the news of her mother and agreed with her to only tell Sophie in case the twins raised questions. They were extremely astute, especially Lauren, but Cydney wanted to protect them as much as possible. They had been through so much without their dad being around and she wanted their daily lives to be normal and without anxiety. Also, she had heard that Sophie's fiancé's tour had been extended and he wouldn't be home after all, so Lauren would be particularly upset, not to mention their nanny herself.

Cydney felt exhausted, as if every ounce of energy had been sucked out of her body, but she had to keep up the pretence that nothing was wrong as far as the twins were concerned. The intention was to indulge herself by taking a long hot bath with a large glass of wine. However, her mind was distracted and when she went into her room she decided to get down the family albums and have a nostalgic look through them.

There were over a dozen books piled high inside the top of her wardrobe. Despite her height, she needed to stand on a chair to reach them and when she'd lifted them all down she spread them over her bed. She had started the albums as a teenager, shortly after losing her dad, and had collected lots of photos of her parents growing up and then getting married, and with her and Claire as babies, and carefully stuck them onto each page, writing a little sentence under each as a reminder of the date and event. She kept the hobby up throughout her school life and into university, through her European travels with friends and with various boyfriends, until she had finally met Steve. There were many more albums showcasing their life together, both before and after the twins arrived.

As Cydney turned each page she realised how many memories the pictures evoked, and she wondered why she hadn't looked at them for so long. She laughed to herself at the clothes she used to wear, not believing some of the styles that were fashionable at the time: blouses and jackets with thick shoulder pads, jeans with ankle zippers, tight leggings and oversized shirts cinched at the hips by wide belts. In some of them she was standing next to young men who thought they were so cool copying the 'Miami Vice' look in their snowy white t-shirts and bright jackets, with the sleeves turned up to reveal their muscled arms.

Then she found her wedding album and turned the white pages carefully in order not to tear the waxed paper between each photograph. After about six pages, she noticed one of the pictures of her and Steve was missing. She shook the album to check if anything had got caught on another page, looked in the large box where it was kept, and then stood up on the chair again to peer into the cupboard space to see if anything had fallen out.

"How strange," she said aloud, then dismissed the thought on the basis it must have got lost somewhere before continuing to flick through the album. Steve looked so handsome in his uniform with his best man, another officer in the army, and Sean looked so happy to have been invited. Her mum, smiling directly at the camera in her beautiful turquoise suit, looked so young. What a difference to how she is now, Cydney thought.

After reminiscing for nearly two hours, she stacked the albums up but kept them by the side of her bed for the twins to look through. She knew it would be interesting to Lauren and hoped even Jake might want to see them.

It was gone midnight when she finally got undressed and slid into bed, but she couldn't sleep. Her mind, so full of thoughts, refused to give up the battle and she tossed and turned under the duvet, unable to settle at all. The more she stayed awake, the more frustrated she became. She knew she had a huge amount of work to get through later that day, including a briefing from Richard and Jenny on various matters, and George would be arriving back into town for their dinner which they had arranged for the weekend. The clock read two-thirty when she eventually fell into a restless sleep.

CHAPTER TWELVE

"**D**O you trust me?"

Trust? That really was a gigantic and momentous word in Cydney's vocabulary. To her it meant giving in and that was not part of her make-up. Now she was being asked not only to trust George, but to leave Steve behind and she didn't know if she was ready to do that.

"Cydney, this isn't a difficult question. I want to spend some quality time with you. Is it really so complicated?"

They were sitting in The Freckled Hen, one of those new gastro pub slash hotels that had suddenly popped up everywhere, in a small village just outside of Aylesbury. It was a charming thatched inn with only twelve rooms, merging modern touches with period features in the most perfect English setting. The bar was lively but with a quieter conservatory-restaurant and large garden area bordering the local cricket pitch, which was currently being blasted with rain. The chef was well renowned for his Italian cuisine, Cydney's favourite type of food, and she was relishing the sardines marinated in red wine vinegar, olive oil and oregano, accompanied by a perfect, crisp Chablis. Now George was taking her hand in his, but how did she feel? So far Cydney had managed to swerve his advances, apart from a relatively informal kiss on the cheek. But now he was talking about something completely different.

"I just don't know... I understand what you're saying, but..."

"Listen to me, please. I want you. I have from the moment I saw you. There are no buts here. It's time. I'm not telling you what you need to do, or how to live your life, but Steve is dead and you're still young. That may sound harsh, and it's not meant to be. Do you not think he would want you to be happy? I promise I will never try to take his place, but surely there is another place in your heart where you could make room for me?"

Cydney sat and stared at the man in front of her. She couldn't even begin to make an argument against what he had just said. He was right. Steve was lost to her, it had been nearly four years, so why shouldn't she make a life for herself now? Her ammunition was the kids.

"I have Lauren and Jake to think about."

"That sounded lame even to you. Once again, I would never try and replace their dad, but I'd like to meet them, and be their friend. I'm quite a nice guy when you get to know me."

Cydney smiled in spite of herself. She did like George, more than like even, if she was truthful. He was open with her, extremely attractive, and he made her laugh, more to the point.

"What did you have in mind?"

"This is not a torture, you know." He laughed. "However, I need to know you trust me first. Answer me. Please Cydney." He still had not let go of her hand.

"Okay. Yes I trust you. Yes, I would like to spend quality time with you. Yes, I like you too. Happy now? Can we eat?"

"Good to hear. In that case, I'm taking you away next weekend. Just the two of us. Now kiss me properly and no more talking."

Cydney stared George in the eyes and watched him intently as he moved towards her. Just as their lips were about to touch, she hesitated. The look he gave her encouraged her to carry on, telling her with his eyes that it was okay to continue. As their lips touched, the feelings she had repressed gave way to a delicious sensation that reached the depths of her body.

George cupped her face in his hands.

"See? That wasn't so bad."

"No." She smiled. "Perhaps we could try it again."

Cydney's face remained close to his. She knew she wanted more from him and she feared losing the moment.

"What? In front of the whole restaurant, when I haven't even had my escargots?"

"Don't joke with me."

"Will you come with me now? Right now."

Without waiting for an answer he called the waiter over, asked for the bill, paid it immediately in cash, grabbed Cydney's hand and dragged her off to the hotel reception of the inn, requesting a room. She stood slightly in the background, behaving like some young virgin protecting her maidenhood, but still feeling the excitement left from his mouth on hers. With the key in his hand, he pulled her up the one flight of stairs and opened the door to reveal a four poster bed. No words were spoken as they kissed again, falling through the door as one, George slamming it shut as he pushed Cydney up against it, both pulling at each other's clothes.

"No. Stop," George said, his breath short.

"What? You want to stop? Now?"

"No. I want to do this properly. I want to make love to you, my darling, not treat you like a harlot."

He drew Cydney over to the bed and sat down, leaving her standing vulnerably in front of him.

"Turn around."

She did as she was told. This was no time for putting up an argument. Her defences were down. She felt a thrill as he unzipped her dress and let it fall to the ground.

"Now back to me."

She turned to face him, standing in just her underwear. She heard his intake of breath as he looked at her, up and down, saw him taking in the moment.

"My God. You're beautiful."

Cydney knelt down in front of him and bent forward to kiss him, the sensation of his hand trailing over her shoulders and back sending shivers through her body. He found the clasp to her bra, letting it loose in one movement. She moaned aloud, encouraging him.

"I had no idea," he said, as he gently took her breasts in his hands and kissed each one in turn.

She unbuttoned his shirt and he removed it to reveal his honed body and the chest she had refused to acknowledge the first time she'd met him. Her fingers moved through his hair and he pulled her to him and onto the bed until they were lying side by side. George gazed at her intently.

"I love you, Cydney Granger, with all my heart."

She said nothing as their kissing became more intense and soon there were no clothes between them. She shivered, not from the cold, but the expectation of what was to come. As he moved over her body and entered her, slowly and then with more purpose, all the pent up feelings of the last four years broke free.

CHAPTER THIRTEEN

S EAN lay in his cottage staring at the ceiling. He couldn't shake the feeling that something momentous was about to happen, again. Call it intuition, sixth sense even, but not like Cydney's, of course. This was something he had always had in his army days, just before going out on a reconnaissance or into the field. The army called it being alert. Call it what you will, all of Sean's senses were on edge and he was waiting for the something, whatever that would be. He knew it could be today, tomorrow, or even the next day, but it would happen. He didn't feel there was anything wrong with his feelings and it was better to have them than not, to be cavalier about everything. He was concerned about Cydney and her mum, this business with Charles Gordon was getting more interesting by the day, and for some reason he kept thinking about Steve more than he had done for many months.

Richard called Sean a little before eight in the morning and reported on the previous day's events with William Harper. They were going to meet that night and have a nosey around the office; it seemed churlish not to use the keys that had conveniently fallen into Richard's hands. They knew it was not quite above board, to put it mildly, but need's must. It wouldn't be the first time they had put their joint skills to good use. Harper was not quite legitimate, that was for sure. Richard had already detected there was no alarm system on the office premises and Jenny had noticed during her foray to the ladies' that there was a back door that they could access via the fire escape. Hopefully, they would find what they were looking for and get out without anyone being any the wiser.

During the journey to Cydney's office, Sheila rang, sounding quite agitated. Cydney hit the loudspeaker.

"Cydney, Charles has called round. It was so early and I wasn't up yet. I came downstairs thinking he was coming for a coffee to discuss the estate but instead he started shouting at me, accusing me of all sorts of things. I just don't know what's happening. I feel so frightened, it was awful."

"Sheila, please calm down. What exactly did he say? Is he still there?"

"No. Thankfully, he left. He said all the money was his, the company, the insurance, everything, and I wouldn't get a penny, and it was no good trying to get my hands on anything. It was all tied up. He accused Ray of being stupid, he laughed at him and called him an idiot. I feel so shaken up. He woke up the kids. They heard everything. I don't know what to do at all."

"Look, Sheila, I'm almost at work but Sean will be with you within the hour. Please don't worry. You can trust him."

"But Cydney, this all makes no sense. Charlotte is in tears, the boys won't leave the house. I just don't understand what's happening here. I hate all this and want to be left in peace." Cydney heard the sound of Sheila's sobbing down the phone. "Isn't it enough my husband is dead? Charles was shaking his fist at me and I thought he was going to hit me. Then he left in a temper, slamming the door behind him and throwing down one of my vases at the front of the house. He drove away like a madman."

"Sean will take the kids to school for you. Just sit tight and wait for him."

Cydney ended the call and slipped the phone in her bag.

"He knows someone's on to him," Sean said.

"So it would seem. But I wonder how he knows? We've been so careful."

"Personally, I think he's running scared and quite desperate now. He knows he's about to get a deal in place with Prestons and everything rests on that. He's so near he can smell the money. But you know what they say, 'Desperate men do desperate things and take desperate measures'. His temper will be the ruin of him."

"Sean, please be careful."

"I have faced the Taliban, Mrs Granger. I think I can face Charles Gordon."

Turning into the cul-de-sac by Sheila's house, Sean noticed the same British Telecom van was there. As he drove past, the man looked up and then immediately away, as if he was trying to hide. Sean felt the hairs rise on the back of his neck, recognising that something wasn't quite right. Sheila was waiting at the door for him.

"Thank goodness you're here. Sean isn't it? Please come in."

Sean made his way through the hallway and into a very spacious kitchen spread across the whole width of the back of the bungalow. The three children were sitting around a table, looking very upset.

"Why does our uncle want to hurt us?" Charlotte asked.

"That's what I'm here to find out. I think he just got a bit angry. Anyway, what do you say I get you all to school?"

"I suppose we'd better go," Harry, the oldest boy said. "Will you be okay, Mum?"

"Yes, darling. Sean will come back after he drops you off."

The three of them went upstairs to collect their bags and Sheila made Sean sit down across from her. He noticed what an attractive woman she was, despite her agitated state. She was slightly older than him, but definitely a fine figure of a woman.

"I do appreciate your help. I can't think what that was all about, apart from what Cydney has told me."

"We're trying to get to the bottom of things but it's going to

117

take a bit of time. Mrs Granger is very efficient, you know. I've worked for her for quite a few years."

Suddenly they heard running down the stairs and Freddie came pounding in.

"Mum, there's a man in the front garden!"

Sean sprang to his feet and raced out the front door to see a man jump into the van and drive off down the road. So his intuition was right after all.

After a minute of chasing down the road after the van, Sean realised he wasn't as fit as he used to be in his army days and gave up. He stood at the end of the road with his hands on his legs and his head bent down, trying to catch his breath as the van disappeared around the corner. Sheila and the kids were a few yards behind him.

"Who was that, Sean?"

"That was our friendly British Telecom man who, for some reason, wasn't here to fix your telephones."

"I got the number plate," Charlotte said helpfully, and recited the number for him. "I have a photographic memory."

"Good girl. Right, let's get you all off to school and then I'll come back and see to your mum."

Richard discovered the van registration was a fake, which didn't get them very far at all.

"I don't suppose you got a look at the man, Sean?"

"Well, only the back of his head. Probably not a lot of help."

"Maybe you should try and take more regular exercise."

"Very helpful, Richard."

"Just saying. Anyway, it seems Charles isn't as stupid as we first thought but he's certainly scared and starting to show his hand. He must have been keeping an eye on Sheila. You said the BT van was there the other week when you went with Cydney. That means he knows about us, or has done some checking into

118

Granger Associates, even. We need to get into Harper's as soon as possible."

"I agree. When I went back to Sheila she was in a right state. She thinks she'll have to sell the bungalow, move away, and she has nowhere to go if Charles takes everything. It just can't happen. Surely she has rights?"

"Well she does, but we can't do anything until we know the whole situation."

"I'll meet you tonight at eleven, as we said. There's an old farmhouse about a mile before you get into town from the motorway. We can park up there and move in together."

Richard put down the phone and headed down the corridor into Cydney's office where he found her briefing Jenny and Ash on Benton and Crossley.

"Ash, could you tell Richard what you've discovered, please?"

"Okay. Centurion has mortgages with cross guarantees in place over the properties owned here in the UK, through a private bank called Sigmunds Bank and Trust."

"Is that the one owned by Eric Sigmund?" Richard asked.

"Exactly," Ash confirmed. "Sigmunds' portfolio under management is vast and they have thousands of millions invested. If you look in the Financial Times, they have really good world funds showing a rate of interest above most of the other funders."

"So, I presume if they are crossed, the original loan was to Pegasus Group and then the UK company was the guarantor. Pegasus is the ultimate offshore holding entity which owns the UK one. They bought the properties. But what's their position now?" Cydney questioned.

"As it happens, I have a contact there, sort of in the family. He owes me a favour but it may cost us a bit in commission. The word is that Sigmunds are going to call in the loan. They are owed so much in unpaid interest that even if the portfolio is sold, it will just about manage to wipe its face."

"When is this likely to happen?"

"I'm told any day."

"What are the chances you could get me in front of the CEO? I may be able to broker a deal with them and pull the rug from under Crossley and Benton." Cydney was trying to think ahead of the game. "Sigmunds may do something knowing they would get their money back on the turn. Ash, I'm not worried about the commission. Rupert is my concern. I think if we can put this together he will be very happy and there'll be enough to go round."

"What about our two friends?" Richard asked.

"That will be in the hands of the police and Her Majesty's Revenue, don't you think? If we can help them along the way, well…"

"Sounds like a plan then," Richard said. "I suggest we keep this very close because I don't trust Benton or Crossley. Rupert warned us already; a desperate man can be very dangerous and there are two of them, and possibly huge repercussions. Anyway, I'm off. Cydney, I'll take you home on the way as I'm meeting Sean later. Just give me five minutes."

Left alone in her office, Cydney switched off her computer to pack up for the day and as she bent down to grab her handbag a huge pain ripped through the back of her head causing her to go off balance and fall against the side of her desk. She stood still for a few moments to try to get herself together and wait for the pain to subside. She had never felt anything like it before.

"Please watch what you're doing."

"Oh Ray, it's you. I'm okay. Just wonder where on earth that came from."

"Cydney, you really need to tread carefully. I'm not happy with the way things are going. You are getting too involved."

"I'm fine. I can look after myself, and I have Richard and Sean around me."

"You are getting messed up in things way beyond your control, and mine.

120

I can only guide you. You have to make your own decisions but please watch out. That pain you felt was a warning. Please take heed."

As Ray faded away, Cydney shook her head to check she was feeling better. She had no idea what had caused the pain and what Ray had meant but she chose to ignore it, or rather put it to one side, and followed Richard down to the underground garage where he was waiting for her in his Land Rover Discovery. She had to admit that she did feel uneasy but didn't know why, and as Richard pulled out into the road towards the motorway, the feeling remained with her.

Neither Richard nor Cydney saw the black Range Rover pull out after them until they had been travelling for a couple of miles. Richard was the first to notice it as it reared up behind them in the middle lane.

"Idiot," he mumbled.

Cydney laughed and looked in the side mirror to see the car.

"It's okay, they're over-taking us."

"What, in the inside lane?"

The driver drew up to their side but fell back again, as if he had changed his mind.

"Bloody hell," Richard swore. "Doesn't anyone know how to drive anymore?"

"Good job you can then, with all your police training."

"No need to be sarcastic," he laughed.

They carried on for a few more miles and Richard could still see the Range Rover within his rear view mirror. He started to feel uneasy now. He didn't want to concern his boss unduly, but the awful feeling they were being followed was very real.

"The driver's acting very strange. Comes up close, seems about to overtake, then falls back. I think someone's trying to frighten us."

Cydney twisted round to look.

"Who would want to follow us? I think you're being paranoid

121

and in any case we're coming off at the next junction so we'll know then," she said.

Richard put his foot down on the accelerator and the car surged forward. He saw the sign for the junction and as he was about to go past the exit, he turned the steering wheel violently to the left at the last moment, catching the wheel arch and tearing the bumper from the back of the car.

"Richard!" Cydney screamed out. "What the fuck are you doing? Trying to get us killed?"

The other driver took the same exit, anticipating Richard's moves. They seemed to know where he was heading.

"Cydney, we're being followed. Get as low as you can in the seat and hold on. I'm gonna try and lose them." *If I can*, he whispered to himself.

Richard slammed the car into a lower gear, weaving in and out of other cars for another mile. He knew there was a right turning shortly and just as it was within his sight in the road, he tore across the dual carriageway, tyres fighting the tarmac for their grip, narrowly missing a van coming towards them. The driver had to swerve to avoid them and behind him Richard was confronted with angry hand gestures, which for once in his life he chose to ignore. He turned down the narrow country road that he knew he could navigate at speed. Cydney, speechless with fear, was grasping the side of the car seat with all her might. Richard glanced in the mirror again and saw the Range Rover looming menacingly closer. He couldn't shake it off.

"Hold tight, Cydney," he yelled, as the car careered down the narrow lane at full speed. There was only room for one vehicle and Richard prayed nothing was coming from the other direction. Either side of them were dense trees, beyond which were fields, and he knew there was no escape across country so the only choice available was to try and out-run them. Suddenly they felt the full force of the impact from behind as the Range Rover hurtled into them at top speed, made worse without the protection of the bumper. Thrown forward, the seat belt tightened like a python around his chest, and Richard almost lost control of the car and just avoided a ditch. The action threw Cydney around and pushed her sideways. Her knee crashed painfully on the glove compartment and her head hit the side window before she was flung back against the seat, jarring her back. Richard managed to straighten the car and put his foot heavily down on the accelerator to escape when there was another almighty crash as the other driver rammed into them again, this time pushing the Land Rover towards the trees. The car scraped along Cydney's passenger side, causing it to zigzag dangerously.

"What the hell?" he shouted.

Cydney screamed in panic. "What's happening? Oh my God! Richard, do something!"

Richard reckoned he was safer whilst they were on the narrow lane but ahead of him the road widened and, looking in his side mirror, he watched as the Range Rover came up towards them again. Were they going to slam into them or overtake? He could see the two men smiling as if they were enjoying watching their victims' terror and this game of pursuit they had started. Richard accelerated again, surprising them with his driving skills, hopefully, but it was not enough. Suddenly, with a roar of their engine, they came right up next to Richard, as if to hit him from the right side but then overtook. At the same time, the side window opened and the passenger aimed a gun straight at them. Richard yelled at Cydney as he slammed on the brakes to try to get out of their sight and to avoid being hit, and they both ducked as the bullet whistled through the air, struck the windscreen and then the rear window, shattering both completely. Glass fell everywhere as Richard tried to escape and get ahead of them again but there was no let up. He grabbed Cydney's shoulder, pushing and screaming at her to stay down.

The pursuers slowed down, taking control of the road to

prevent Richard moving away. However, the passenger had a clear view of his prey as he aimed another bullet through the now open windscreen, which caught Richard's left arm. He felt nothing with the adrenalin coursing through his veins, but turning, he saw the blood seeping through his sleeve. At the same time he looked at Cydney to find her covered in blood. Her eyes were closed and she wasn't moving.

"Don't fucking die on me!" he yelled.

As the nerve endings in his arm became aware of the bullet, the pain hit Richard and tore through him. His left arm was now useless. Dizziness came over him and he almost passed out. He shook his head to clear it. All his senses told him he had to stay fully conscious and alert, to get away, and although he accelerated, his car was no match for theirs. They came tearing into him from the right, their intent obvious, and this time it was with such force that their car hurtled through the air, somersaulting into a ditch.

Richard's last thoughts were of his wife and kids.

CHAPTER FOURTEEN

SEAN drummed his fingers on the steering wheel. It was so unlike Richard to be late. His thoughts turned to the feeling he'd had earlier that morning, the feeling that something wasn't right. Although he'd called Richard and Cydney countless times over the past two hours, he reached for his phone. Again, there was no answer from either of them. Had everyone deserted him? It was past midnight, and even though all his training told him he should abandon the night's activities, he knew Cydney wanted answers and there was no way he was going to let her down. Richard must have got delayed somewhere and wasn't able to get in touch, he thought. Feeling more impatient by the minute, he decided he would give him another half an hour and then set off on his own.

It was at moments like this he had time to think back to when he was more or less detained at Her Majesty's pleasure the year before, after the initial meeting with General Ian Bowles-Smith. He recalled the temporary enforced quarters for his overnight stay. It was a basic square room with the walls painted in a lack-of-imagination cream with a single bed, wardrobe and chest of drawers – matching in serviceable wood, and a separate bathroom. The room smelt musty and unlived in and it brought back memories of when he was first enlisted at eighteen and stayed in barracks, which never failed to smell of old socks and unwashed male bodies. With not even a TV or newspaper to occupy him, he could do nothing but wait. They delivered his evening meal at six o'clock and, after he had eaten, he tried to leave the room and explore his surroundings but they had locked the door. He was more or less a prisoner of the British Army. What did they think he was going to do?

He knew nothing about this so-called Dragonfly who had suddenly appeared from nowhere. He recognised the codename as belonging to Captain Steve Granger but why had the name reared up now? Unless it really was him. And if it wasn't, why was he being questioned so thoroughly - did they think he was party to this?

He stayed awake for most of the night, recalling the recce three years earlier – and everything that had happened before, during and after he had got back from Syria. Sean's debriefing in Tel Aviv had lasted for two weeks before they had allowed him to head back to the UK and he'd been unable to comprehend the fact that he was still alive, thanks to Steve, while the captain he looked up to, along with four of their colleagues, were dead. Furthermore, the captain had saved his life. The Americans, then the British, and finally the Israelis had interviewed Sean repeatedly about their activities and the role of Salim, who had worked for the combined governments in Syria. After writing the report and presenting it to them, they had torn each sentence apart and went through everything with a fine-tooth comb until they'd been satisfied.

His information had been invaluable and proved what they had known more or less already, that the Syrians were clearly building up secret supplies and weapons for some sort of military operation. The question as to who would be their target was yet to be determined but it was not going to be Sean's job to find out. After such a tiring debrief it was mutually agreed that, to the outside world, Steve and the others had been killed in an explosion in Afghanistan. The secret of their time in Syria was, to all intents and purposes, dead and buried – like the captain, Sean had thought.

The last year had passed too quickly but he remembered every single moment of the interview with his commanding officer. He was woken up at eight in the morning, when the same army guys collected him. He hated the idea of being held a prisoner and thoughts of trying to break away from them momentarily crossed his mind, but he realised there was no point. It would not accomplish anything at all. In any case, he wanted to find out for himself about Dragonfly. So, he went along with the game being played out by General Bowles-Smith and acted out the good soldier that he was, determined to get to the bottom of everything. He could not keep thoughts of Cydney out of his mind though, or the twins. She would be worried about where he was, especially if he didn't turn up later that day. The fact that her husband could be alive was not something he wanted to confront her with now, the shock would be too much to contemplate. However, first he had to verify if it really was Steve, or an impostor.

Sean's escort took him down to the car in which he had originally arrived and drove him back to HQ in complete silence. This time he was taken by lift to a secure communications room situated three floors underground. They knew Dragonfly would be calling early morning. They, and two other men with earphones attached to high-tech tracing equipment, sat waiting in the semi-darkened room. Every so often Sean looked at the clock on the wall. The general paced backwards and forwards, muttering to himself.

An hour passed and nothing. The general's constant movements were unnerving Sean but he would not dare mention it. He looked over at the clock again. The second hand ticked round slowly. If this was Steve then he would only phone if he knew it was safe to do so, although Sean had so many doubts in his mind about the fact he could be alive that his thoughts were scrambling his brain. Thankfully, the general decided to sit down but started drumming his fingers on the table in front of him. Another hour passed. No one talked. Everyone was on edge now, staring at the phone and willing it to ring.

The eventual ringing of the phone startled everyone and the general jumped to his feet to answer it. Sean followed, his heart racing.

"Hello," he answered simply, hitting the loudspeaker.

"This is Dragonfly. I say again. This is Dragonfly. I am ready to come home to roost."

"Yes, so I believe. Where are you?"

"Where you left me."

"And where would that be?"

"I only have a few minutes, stop wasting my time."

Sean moved closer to the speaker, not quite believing this was happening.

"I can hear somebody there. Are you listening to me?"

Sean again heard the voice he'd believed dead to him. He almost swayed with the sound he thought he would never hear again.

"Hello Dragonfly. I am receiving you, loud and clear."

"Sergeant, I have our word. Walnut tree."

Sean nodded, and mouthed, "It's him! Not a shadow of a doubt."

"Dragonfly," the general said, "we understand who you are but we can't simply bring you out. Call me in twenty-four hours and we'll put together a plan in the meantime."

The phone went dead and Sean sat there not actually knowing what had happened.

"You understand, Sergeant, we can't just bring Captain Granger home, don't you? If it is really him, and it appears it is, he's more use to the British Government where he is. We need him in the field. This could be absolutely crucial to us and our fight against the insurgents in Syria."

Sean looked at General Bowles-Smith with absolute incredulity.

"Are you insane?" The insubordinate words came out before Sean had had time to think about them.

"Sergeant, please remember your place. This is my decision and I would appreciate some degree of respect. Even in these most unusual circumstances."

"Please excuse me, Sir, but we can't possibly think of leaving him there. He'll be in constant danger. What about his life here, and his wife and kids?"

"Now this is very difficult to say, but she believes he is dead, as does the rest of the world. He is invaluable to us. I won't hear another word. When he calls back, I will tell him myself and don't forget you are still sworn under the Official Secrets Act. I will give him his orders and you will abide by my decision. Final. This has come from the very top, Sergeant. I fully understand and appreciate how you feel and how hard this is."

"Then let me go out to him. I'll act as his liaison."

"No. You'll stay here and carry on your life as if nothing has happened. This is now ours to deal with. I know you are looking after Mrs Granger, you must continue to do so and not let her suspect anything. Can you do that, Sergeant O'Connell? Can I rely on you?"

"Yes, Sir," Sean agreed reluctantly, but he had no idea whatsoever how he was going to live with this and make out that nothing at all was wrong.

Since then Sean had been living a lie, and it didn't sit easily with him. But now he had to concentrate and he forced himself to focus on the task ahead, which was to gain access to William Harper's office, undisturbed, and find out as much as he could regarding Charles Gordon and his nefarious business affairs.

The street was quiet and dimly lit from the few lamps that shone sporadic light onto the pavements. He drove to the back of the building, checking the road for any signs of life, parked up and looked around him. When he was certain the place was deserted he climbed the iron fire escape leading up to Harper's office. Unfortunately, Richard still had the keys but Sean had brought with him sufficient means as a precaution. He crouched down outside the door and pulled from his inside jacket pocket a small cigarette-type case that opened up to reveal a mini set of tools. He felt around the keyhole with his hands, not wanting to use a torch then, satisfied he had identified the right tool to use, he fiddled around to try to open the door. The first attempt failed but after changing one of the screw tops he felt the lock click and the door opened. Will people never learn? he thought. He glanced around and finding it safe to enter, moved through into the corridor and silently closed the door behind him.

He made his way towards the secretary's desk, feeling with his hands until he got used to the dark, but then decided to chance using his torch as the blinds to the windows in the front office were shut. The room was exactly as Jenny had described with files everywhere. As he moved around the desk, his foot caught in a raised seam of the carpet causing him to trip and catch the top of his leg. He clutched at the corner of the desk to stop himself falling, at the same time righting a pile of papers which were about to hit the floor. He uttered an expletive under his breath and shone the light around so he could avoid any potential damage to the rest of his body. Jenny had told him she had seen a file on top of the safe but of course, now there was nothing. The safe was an old Liberty one with a combination lock and Sean really wanted to get into it.

He had a feeling Harper was a little bit naive when it came to security, similarly his secretary, and he wondered whether she had the combination written down somewhere on her desk. He searched through the drawers, pulling each one out separately, and moved his hands through even more papers, tissues, and hundreds of loose paper clips and other assorted items. There were no keys or anything useful.

The secretary's shorthand note pad was open next to the computer. He thumbed through the pages and then turned to the final page to see there were quite a few numbers written on the inside hard cover. Some were telephone numbers and one was headed 'bank account' but he thought he would try that anyway. He clicked the combination round but nothing opened. He shone the torch down a bit further on the pad and scrawled at the bottom were a series of numbers. Worth a try, he thought. He dialled the combination again. This time the lever shifted and the safe opened with a groan.

Inside the safe he found various rolled up papers tied with green ribbon, a small black money box, and huge wads of money tied up with elastic bands. There must have been many thousands of pounds there. Very interesting, but not what he wanted. He flicked the torch around some more and saw a file on the bottom shelf, which he pulled out. Just as Jenny had told him, the label read 'Industrial Estate'.

He stood up and placed the file on the desk. As he turned each page, he saw there were various Agreements for Sale for each of the five units where the Gordons had their factory. A company called Intervest Holdings had purchased the units for a pittance. The next section revealed the bank facility documents, but Cydney knew about these already. The final section held the original stock forms transferring Sheila's shares in Rayshel to Charles, and copies of the remaining company documents showed the shareholdings in the company. Sean shook his head. He knelt back down to the safe again and pulled out a pile of the rolled up documents. He shone his torch on the front of each so he could read the typing on the front and they seemed to be the title deeds to the five units and Rayshel's own.

The last documents he pulled out were two similar looking Wills, allegedly drawn up for Ray Gordon. One was dated fifteen years previously, which was more or less what Cydney had advised him, but the second was more recent. This was strange in itself, particularly as the signatures were different on each document, but Harper had apparently witnessed both. Sean photographed all the documents on the basis his boss would sort out the legalities, and returned everything to the safe, ensuring it was firmly locked.

As he walked along the short corridor to Harper's office, avoiding various cardboard boxes that lined the route, he wondered how anybody could work in such disorder. He manoeuvred himself to the front of Harper's desk but stopped when he thought he heard a car outside. He peered out between the blinds but saw nothing. The drawers were all unlocked except for the middle one. Now what did the guy possibly have to hide? He pulled out his tool kit again and easily opened the drawer that, unsurprisingly, was full of papers. Sean rifled through them quickly. He reached his hand to the back of the drawer and felt a large thick envelope that he pulled out and opened. What he saw astounded him; this Harper certainly was a guy. There were a series of coloured photographs featuring Harper with a young blonde woman in various stages of undress, in the most compromising of positions. He turned one of the pictures upside down and leaned his head to the left, questioning the ability of a man of Harper's weight to have managed such a position. Other photos showed Harper handcuffed to a brass bedpost wearing only black leather briefs, whilst the blonde stood over him with a whip in her hand. Blackmail? So who had this on Harper? This case was becoming more and more interesting with twists and turns at every corner. He photographed everything but, as he was finishing, his phone vibrated in his trouser pocket. It was a message from Jenny.

Richard and Cydney in accident. Serious! Meet you at St George's A&E.

Sean's thoughts of earlier flooded back to haunt him. He couldn't believe he had let his guard down where Cydney was concerned. He had promised to look after her. What the hell had happened? After making sure everything was precisely as he had found it, he rushed out of the building and sped to the North London hospital as if his life depended on it. He raced up the corridor to Accident and Emergency and found Jenny holding hands with Richard's wife, Christine, both of them in tears. There were two uniformed police officers with them.

"Oh, Sean! Thank goodness you're here!" Jenny said, scrambling to her feet.

"Where's Mrs Granger? What happened? Where's Richard?"

"Sean, she's okay. Concussion, dislocated knee that they put back. Her leg's in plaster. Whiplash. Very bruised and battered. It could have been worse."

"And Richard? Can we see them?"

Jenny shook her head. "He's in surgery. Head injury and some broken bones we've been told, but not sure of the extent or anything. We're just waiting. They've sedated Cydney and won't let us in yet."

"How did it happen?"

"No idea. We got the call and made our way here. Richard's kids should be arriving any time."

Sean nodded and sat down, leaning forward, his elbows on his knees, his hands resting on his chin. He had known something was going to happen and had felt it since this morning. It was going to be a long night. He felt helpless, but all they could do was hope and pray.

The doctor came to see them a few hours later. He was still in scrubs and looked as exhausted as they felt. Sean and Jenny stood up.

"We've managed to set all his broken bones. The bullet, thankfully..."

"Bullet? He was shot?" Sean called out.

"Unfortunately, yes," the doctor went on. The bullet passed through his arm but there was some damage to one of the muscles. We're confident the nerve damage, if any, will be minimal. But that isn't our main concern, I'm afraid. The next forty-eight hours will be crucial because of his head injury. There is severe swelling and bruising." He turned to Christine. "I've moved your husband to the ICU. You can go and see him shortly but he's heavily sedated. Please try not to be too shocked when you see him – he's connected to a lot of equipment at the moment which is monitoring how he's doing. It looks frightening but really, it should be a comfort to you. We're doing all we can."

"What are his chances, Doctor?" Christine asked, a sob breaking through her words.

"As I explained, the next couple of days will be crucial. I'm sorry I can't give you anything more."

When Christine and her sons had left to go to ICU, Jenny turned to Sean. "I can't believe it," she said. "He was shot, for Christ's sake!"

"We're getting into something here that I'm not happy with at all. Someone knows we're getting too close to something."

"Do you think it's Charles Gordon?"

"I have no idea, but I intend to find out. Personally, I think he's a chancer and a petty criminal. But this is big stuff, Jenny, and I think someone's trying to stop us finding out more about them."

Sean told Jenny everything he had found during his foray into Harper's office, as they headed towards Cydney's room. They entered tentatively, first peeking around the door, anxious not to wake her and fearing the sight that would confront them. Cydney's head was heavily bandaged and there was a support brace around her neck. She had bruising around her face and an angry gash along the side of her cheek. They approached her bedside and sat down either side of her. Jenny reached for her hand and Cydney groaned in her sleep. She turned her head towards them, opened her eyes momentarily, saw them sitting there, smiled, and then fell back to sleep again.

"I'm going to stay with her tonight, Sean. Go home. Be there for the twins in the morning. You'll know what to say."

"Sure, but call me if there's any change and I mean *any* change. Promise?"

As Sean left the hospital, he knew he now had to send the one message he hoped he would never have to send, but the choice was no longer his to make. Cydney was in danger and Steve needed to know. He had to contact General Bowles-Smith immediately and make sure the man understood what was happening to the captain's wife and get him out. They had had a year of his time now and enough was surely enough. However, it was not going to be easy dealing with his return. Of that he had no doubt.

CHAPTER FIFTEEN

THE sun was starting to set over the mountains west of Damascus as Steve sat on his haunches in the village he called home, contemplating his life. It was another of those oppressively hot and windy days, with the sand blowing around him and into every conceivable orifice. He pulled the cloth of his red and white keffiyeh further around his head to protect his eyes, and looked around him.

The village consisted of nearly ninety stone houses set out at angles in no orderly fashion and in varying states of disrepair, with no doors or windows to hide from the elements. Renegade soldiers had ravaged the village many times and eventually it was bombed a year before his arrival, yet the rubble remained. Now it was a place for kids to play and hide since they no longer had a school to attend. A couple of stray dogs roamed around and foraged in the dust to try to find something to eat. He knew how they felt. He'd been living on a diet of bread, beans, goat meat and very little else for the past few years.

Everything was grey dust and sand. What he wouldn't do to see a bit of greenery. Even the people were grey and old before their time. He watched a pregnant woman walk past him wearily, her face bearing her misery and the weight she was carrying, her three small children running around her. She was probably only about twenty. What future could she possibly have, could any of them have?

He scratched at his beard, tearing at the growth as if to pull the hairs from their roots, and ran his hand over the scar down his cheek that still bothered him. After nearly four years he looked like a local with his skin turned olive by the sun. What was he doing still in this isolated pit of the world? He wanted out now. He had done his duty for a year longer than he should have done, all for Queen and country, and he felt so weary. He wasn't well and knew that the toll of his injuries and the strain he was under were having a serious effect on his health. In truth, he felt as if his body was giving up on him. He needed to get himself fit but couldn't summon the strength, which he knew he would need to get out of the place and back home.

It was nearly time to meet the local village chief, Mohammad Ahmad Bin Amadi, who had been his protector since his arrival. He lifted himself up and made his way to the house at the top of the street. There was a dusty blanket acting as a makeshift door, and he pulled it aside to enter the room where Bin Amadi was propped up on an array of coloured cushions with a tea urn and a plate of sweet biscuits in front of him. The smell of humans and animals cohabiting had no effect on Steve now. The elderly man looked every inch of his seventy-five years, tired and weary of life, his gnarled arthritic hands resting on his knees, his long beard completely white. Steve's heart sank to see him this way.

"Come in, my son. Please join me."

"Greetings. How are you, Father?" He used the term of endearment wholeheartedly, as he had grown to love and respect this man over the years. He leaned towards him to greet him with a kiss on both cheeks.

"I am good today. The pain has lifted slightly but I am old and dying. I won't be long for this world and will shortly be with Allah."

"Please don't speak like that. I can't bear for you to leave."

The old man's eyes creased to see better the one he had come to look on as a son.

Bin Amadi recalled the day Salim had half carried, half dragged the man into the village from his truck with blood pouring from an open chest wound and his face and head torn and bleeding. One of his legs was clearly broken and mangled and his breathing was barely perceptible. He'd believed this man would not live to see another week but Salim was a trainee doctor in the big hospital in Damascus and, together with one of his daughters, they nursed the man back to health. All day they would sit with him in his delirium, changing his bedding as he sweated and tossed and turned, giving him sips of their precious water, as he called out in a language they did not understand. As he slowly recovered, they helped him to walk again and caught him as he fell into their arms, screaming out in pain, but more importantly they hid him away from the soldiers patrolling their village. They waited until the day when he might remember his previous existence and come out of the amnesia that had torn his life away from him. It was a long journey for all of them and Bin Amadi knew that he and the villagers had risked their lives protecting him. At any moment the militia could have found him and they would all have been shot without a moment's thought.

The man was not an Arab, despite the fact he spoke their language fluently and with hardly an accent, but they accepted him amongst their people and he became accustomed to their way of life. Bin Amadi had questioned his nephew about the man. Salim was living a double life working in the hospital. He was a qualified surgeon but secretly waged war against the regime with his band of revolutionaries. Salim had refused to answer Bin Amadi's questions, perhaps believing it was better for him not to know anything so, if anybody ever questioned him, he could state with his hand on his heart that he knew nothing. He respected Salim for that decision and never asked him again.

Bin Amadi quietened his thoughts and turned to Steve.

"I am afraid to give you this news. One of Salim's men visited me earlier. Salim has been arrested. It was bound to happen. He takes so many chances and now I am afraid for you. We are getting more and more patrols here all the time. I think it is time for you to leave. If Salim is tortured, I have no doubt it will not be long before you are discovered."

"But..."

"Hush. There is something else. We got a coded message via Al Jazeera. It seems you have no choice. I don't know what this means but I have been told to tell you that the walnut tree is hurt. We believe your position has been compromised and you need to get out now. They are on to you, and we could all be in danger too."

Steve, unable to find the words to voice his thoughts, merely nodded, his eyes not leaving Bin Amadi's for a second. *Was Cyd hurt? What about the children?*

"I have sent Mira and her sister to the north to stay with my cousins. I thought it was best. We are strong in this family but we have gone through so much. They could not bear to see you taken, or die. I always thought you would remain here but I understand you have a life somewhere else – and Mira would rather you lived in another country, with someone other than her, than risk your life. Your work is done here. Go with Allah, my son," Bin Amadi said with tears in his eyes, and gave his blessing, a father to a son.

Steve walked wearily out of the village for the last time, without a backward glance. Now he had to return home and somehow get back into Cydney's and his children's lives. How they would accept his return after believing him dead for so many years was not something he was going to contemplate. His main objective was to get out of the country now, unscathed and un-noticed, and he needed every part of his mind focused. Dragonfly was coming home to roost, whether they liked it or not.

As he walked, Steve thought back to his arrival in the village that seemed so many years ago. He and his troops had arrived from Israel in the dead of night with the help of Salim and his compatriots. It had been a treacherous journey for them over the Golan Heights, a wild mountainous elevated plateau with little or no protection from the bitter cold, where temperatures could drop as low as minus twenty even in summer. The Heights extended like a finger between the borders of Israel and Syria, overlooking the Sea of Galilee and the Jordan River, with Mount Hermon rising nine thousand feet high above them.

The men had covered the distance to Damascus, some two hundred kilometres, in less than five days. They'd moved quickly through the dark using their night vision binoculars and found hiding places in small caves or abandoned bunkers built by both sides in the conflicts between the two countries, where they were able to rest up in daylight hours. They were used to this from their training and Steve never had to chivvy the guys along. Everyone knew their role and the work they were there to do and any orders they were given were carried through to the letter without question. Any man who did question was not fit to be part of the tight-knit team, as they had to work as a unit, completely unified and reliant on each other for their very survival.

In one of the caves not far from the outskirts of Damascus, they met with Salim and established their lying up point for stowing their personal kit, supplies and ammunition that they could easily reach on their way out. They entered the city invisibly, dressed as locals, their 9mm Brownings and other essentials hidden beneath their robes. Salim split them up into twos and took them to various safe houses owned by men he could trust, who were part of his group. They all wanted to see the end of the current regime. Steve's orders were to be in and out of the country within no more than a month. They were there to observe, to listen, to photograph unusual military activity and to report to the respective governments and nothing else.

They spent the first week or two mixing with the locals, sitting around in the cafes and listening to local gossip to try to pick up useful information, but without any luck. It was dangerous as they were strangers to the area and had to be careful how they went about their business. However, Salim and his friends were doing everything in their power to protect them. Then one day Salim met up with Steve and advised that one of his friends in the military had reported that his entire regiment, accompanied by lorry loads of equipment, was moving out to the outskirts of Homs, situated about one hundred kilometres north of the capital. To the east lay the Syrian Desert, renowned for being the centre of operations for Iraqi insurgents. This was not an ordinary movement of troops and Salim thought the captain and his men might like to witness the exercise first hand. It was the opportunity they had been waiting for and Steve knew he had no choice but to follow this up.

At midnight, Salim collected them under the guise of a baker and in his delivery truck they headed north, praying no one would stop them. There was no reason they should as it was normal for bread to be baked and delivered through the night. They wanted to do nothing that would arouse the suspicion of locals. However, this time the bread trays concealed rounds of ammunition and large amounts of plastic explosive detonators.

As they moved further away from the town, the road and surrounding area changed and the truck bumped its way over the bad rocky terrain in complete darkness. The men were impervious to this; their minds were set on the task ahead of them - to get in, and get out without any loss of lives. However, they were taking no chances and each man held his AK47 tightly in his grip. The troops trusted their captain and he had never let them down in the past. They remained silent for the journey and let Salim drive, peering out from the dusty windows to the back and sides of the truck to check for lights in the distance in case anyone was following them.

After a couple of hours the truck came to a grinding halt and Salim signalled for them all to get out. They would be going the rest of the way on foot. The men jumped out of the van, took off their robes to reveal their desert camouflage that would make it easier for them to do their work, grabbed their supplies and put on their night visuals. Salim led the way with two of his men, leaving one behind to guard the van and remain ready to drive off in a hurry. They set off at a fast pace, anxious to get to their destination, take photos of the military activity and get straight out. The plan was for Salim to take them back to their lying up point after the recce, from where they would trek back over the border into Israel.

They moved fast, maintaining complete silence, the captain leading and signalling to his men via hand movements, each one understood and learned as rote in advance. Every man focused on the task ahead. This was no time for lagging behind, despite the cold and biting wind that would penetrate the very bones of lesser men.

They travelled in this way for over an hour until they reached a plateau of rock and stopped. They had arrived at their destination and Salim signalled for them to spread out. The captain looked down at the land below, almost like a hollow, leading into which a crude road had been built. This was not a new site. It was evident how much work had been going on there, and now he could see a few hundred men or more in uniform, moving around and focused on their tasks. Large spotlights erected on metal poles lit the ground, and the men spied several soldiers heaving massive containers from trucks into various large windowless warehouses, whilst others were standing around, seemingly counting and counter-checking the transport. Over to one side the captain saw a dozen or so helicopters sitting like huge birds of prey, some undergoing maintenance checks. There were barrels stacked up, one on top of the other, which he surmised must contain some type of liquid, possibly fuel. Armed guards were based in a high tower and the searchlights they were using circled beams sporadically around the camp perimeter, overlooking the many tents and every activity. So much was going on in the middle of nowhere. This was not normal and the task for Steve and his men was not going to be easy. He made a mental note of the layout in case he needed to get out quick via an alternative route. He had to be ready for all eventualities.

He signalled he was moving in closer. His sergeant, who was second in command, plus four of his men and Salim, were to come with him and the others were to keep watch and wait. He knew he needed to get down behind one of the buildings, avoiding the lights and the tower, so he started to make his way down the purpose built road, holding up his left hand and opening and closing it twice so his men knew they had to follow at ten foot intervals. The route was not at all easy as the path down was narrow, pitted and covered in rocks, with a sheer drop down to inevitable death. One slip and it would be over.

They advanced quickly despite everything, their training second to none and everything they learnt coming to the fore. After several minutes they reached the bottom. Steve gave the hand signal to stop. He pointed at his sergeant and motioned his arm, signalling for him to move around to the left with one of the men.

Their purpose was to cover him from the other side. The sergeant acknowledged by touching his nose and pointed his thumb in the right direction. He took the right with another and dropped his hand down for the other troops to hold the ground, machine guns at the ready. He needed a few seconds to move around the building that was about twenty-five yards away to discover exactly what was going on, take the requisite pictures and get his men out in one piece and away. That was the plan.

As he reached his target, however, the ground shook and he looked upwards to see a huge explosion coming from the top of the rock. The sky lit up as he heard repetitive gunfire quickly followed by shouts and screams of men. The sergeant ran to his side and they sprang into action as hundreds of the Syrian troops seized their weapons on the order to attack. Quickly taking in the situation, he made the decision to escape in the opposite direction, while everyone was in panic mode and running towards the explosion.

What had happened? He had no choice but to leave his men at the top of the rock to defend themselves and to face their own fate. He had to deal with his own situation and get himself, Salim and his other men out and away into darkness. They ran along behind the buildings and he saw ahead of him another crude and rocky track, which they now had to navigate upwards. It would be hard going. Steve stopped, waiting for his men to go ahead whilst he took up the rear - checking behind him and below for anyone coming close.

He heard the sound of the helicopters before he saw them rising to eye level, their searchlights fully focused. He dropped to the ground, their gunfire just missing him. He was never going to be able to avoid this, he thought to himself.

Looking into the distance, his men were running still and he knew he had to catch them. He dragged himself up with some difficulty and carried on behind them, his eyes fully focused in all directions. The gunfire came again, hitting the rock face and sending splinters all around him. He felt something crack against his face and put his hand up to feel warm liquid dripping through his fingers. Painful, but not deadly. He fired his AK47 into the night in retaliation, directed at one of the helicopters. He missed as it turned into a dive to avoid his fire. This gave him some valuable minutes before it came at him again.

He reached the top of the promontory behind his men and saw they were in fighting position, their machine guns ready and aimed. He caught up with them as the helicopter came into sight again. The men fired, this time hitting one of the rotor arms. The aircraft fell to the ground, bursting into flames and crashing into the hollow. He shouted at them to move on - this was no time for silent orders.

Steve doubted they could reach the baker's van on the other side of the hollow, so it was going to be a long night's journey to get out of harm's way. The second helicopter landed at the top and a dozen troops jumped out and rushed after them. One of his men lobbed a grenade and it exploded amongst them, taking out at least two men. They had to find some sort of cover but there was nowhere at all they could hide. It was now a matter of who could outrun whom; which troops were the fittest. It wasn't just about weaponry.

The sergeant led them along now as he was undoubtedly the strongest and fittest, and Steve followed, but it was every man for himself. He watched as one of his men got hit in the leg and fell to the ground, crying out in pain. He clutched at his calf as the blood spurted from his wound. Two of his comrades dragged him; they were never going to leave a man down if there was a chance he was only slightly injured, and they ran with him, holding him up under each arm. Steve had the feeling he'd lost a few men. He felt the regret but knew he could not go back for them.

His sergeant was in front of him when suddenly the ground shook like an earthquake and there was a huge flash of light in the darkness. The noise was deafening as a grenade exploded almost on top of them. He pushed the sergeant out the way to avoid the hit and Steve felt the full force in his chest, and then nothing more.

CHAPTER SIXTEEN

C YDNEY felt as if every bone in her body was broken. Attempts at opening her eyes made her feel dizzy, as if the walls of the room she didn't recognise were spinning around her in a white fuzzy haze. She tried to move, but the slightest motion caused pain to shoot up every limb. She tentatively wriggled her toes and then her fingers to check everything was in working order. Trying to lift her head from the pillow, she cried out in agony.

Jenny reached for Cydney's hand and gently held it.

"Where am I? What happened?" The words were little more than a whisper so Jenny had to lean forward to hear.

"Don't worry. You're in hospital. You've had an accident but you're fine. Please don't move. I'm going to get a nurse...I'll be right back."

Cydney felt herself falling into the murkiness of unconsciousness. She tried to fight it with all her being but it was too late and she drifted away from the pain that was too much to bear, vaguely aware of voices in the background. Dreams followed her as they always did, nightmares of Steve just before he died, and a premonition that left her paralysed with fear. Always the same one, and just as real as if had happened yesterday.

Cydney was in the wrong place. Gunfire erupted in the distance, a rolling thunder in the night. The sky was pitch black but at intervals rockets streaked into the sky, creating sporadic strips of light. The sound of engines came nearer, the smell of fuel in the air overpowering her senses. The sight of a dozen or more army tanks, with their guns pointed down at her, caused her legs to give way. There was no escape; no hiding place.

The tanks had created a barrier through which it was impossible to penetrate. The top of the sand dunes was her only way out, away from danger, but as soon as she climbed even a few feet, the sand slipped away under her feet making it impossible. Panic overtook her. She could hardly breathe. The sky was alight now from the beams of several helicopters approaching the hollow. With her hands over her ears to deaden the deafening sound, Cydney prayed for deliverance, for anything and anyone to rescue her. The tanks surrounded her on all sides and began firing in her direction, and she ran around wildly in her desperation to avoid being hit.

"Help! Help me, please!" she screamed. "For God's sake, help me..."

Then as suddenly as it had begun, the firing stopped, as if her prayers had been answered. The helicopters were silent and now she was not alone. Steve was standing in front of her, dressed in his uniform, but there was a big red stain on the front of his jacket, slowly spreading. She looked at the face she loved so much and saw the tears in his eyes. The tanks started to reverse, the helicopters flew away, until only the couple were left. He reached for her hands, shaking his head in regret, but now he was out of uniform and wearing a white robe. Slowly he let her go as he walked backwards away from her, his arms outstretched and beyond her reach forever.

The sound of screaming pierced the air, waking her. Her hand automatically reached out across the hospital bed expecting Steve to be there but there was nothing except an empty space. She had forgotten momentarily that he was dead and the feeling of loss invaded her soul. The worst was knowing that his life had been endangered and she had been powerless to do anything about it those few years before. Now it was too late.

The darkness of the night felt like a heavy cloak around her with so little light breaking through under the door to the corridor. She wondered how long she had been asleep. The button for the light switch was just within her grasp and as the room lit up, she adjusted her eyes to the sudden change. The pounding of her heart echoed in her ears and there was silence now, but Cydney waited for the sound to penetrate the dark again. It was as if the world held its breath. She put her one free hand to her chest and breathed in and out deeply, attempting to lower her heart rate, waiting for a nurse to come running in. She knew it was the same dream as always but everything had felt so real and the same fear engulfed her.

She would never forget the days after the army had come to report Steve's death. She had spent weeks in complete shock, unaware of what she was doing, saying, or to whom. People surrounded her, coming and going day and night, yet all she wanted was to be alone. The twins stood around, staring at her in silent anguish. There were no words for them.

It was important for her to say goodbye properly, to see him one last time, but it wasn't possible. There had been a bombing, they explained. Cydney knew what they were trying to tell her and the implication made everything worse. Forcing down the tranquilisers prescribed by her doctor made her feel giddy and out of control and, although it helped in some ways, she needed to retain power over her life, something she had been unable to do when she had lost her dad.

Since her father's death, everything she had done centred around being in control of her life and the situations she faced. But now her children were in the same position as she had been and life was repeating itself in the worst possible way.

Then they all had to go through the memorial service two weeks afterwards. The entire battalion were there, giving Captain Granger the full honours he deserved, but there was no body, nowhere to visit afterwards. Cydney had held her head proudly high with the twins by her side as they huddled together. She had allowed herself some momentary lapses of weakness but that would not happen again, ever. She had to be strong in front of everyone.

Now she was in a hospital room, all alone, injured and in

pain, and nobody knew why, least of all her. Steve should be here looking after her. Where was he now when she needed him?

Oh yes, he was dead.

The next time Cydney woke up she opened her eyes to see the familiar faces of Claire and Sean next to her. She was expecting pain so knew not to move too much this time.

"Hey, you. Welcome back to the world," Claire said quietly, leaning over her.

"Where are Lauren and Jake?"

"They're waiting outside to come and see you," Sean said.

Cydney's lips were dry and sore and she moved her tongue over them.

"Here, take a sip of this." Claire passed her a cup with a straw attached.

"I dreamt of Steve again. The same. He was here."

Sean and Claire looked at each other.

"I felt him in the room with me but he was dressed differently. Wearing some sort of white robe. And he had a full beard. But I recognised his eyes. I would know them anywhere."

"Just a dream, Mrs Granger."

"Of course. I know that Sean. But it felt so real. Can I sit up? Help me move, please."

Sean gently aided her into a better sitting position, then propped more pillows behind her. He froze each time she winced with the pain.

"How long have I been here?"

"Nearly a week. Don't you remember anything at all?"

"Nothing. A week, really?" She touched her head with her free arm as the other one was still attached to a drip. She felt the bandage.

"Christ, that hurts."

"You had concussion and a severe whiplash so don't try to

149

move your neck. Also, the ligaments in your right knee are torn. That's why your leg's in plaster. You can probably come home in a couple of days."

"Was I driving? I have a vague recollection of leaving the office with Richard."

"He was driving and taking you home. He..." Sean paused, unsure if he should continue. "I'm sorry, but he was shot."

"Shot?" A dagger of pain shot through her head as she attempted to move. "Is he...?"

"He's in intensive care," Sean interrupted. "The car turned over. The bullet didn't make too much of an impact but he has swelling on the brain. He hasn't woken up yet and now it's a waiting game."

Cydney sank back against the pillows. It made no sense at all. Who would want to shoot him, or her come to that?

"Christ, if only I could remember what happened."

"The police are outside waiting to interview you."

"But I have no idea what to say to them. I just can't get my head around this at all. Sean, I'm really scared."

"It may have something to do with Richard and by chance you were in the car, or it could be about one of your investigations. I suggest we look through all your files, once you are up and about. But don't be scared, you're safe here."

"Can I see the twins please?" Cydney wasn't up to this and could think of nothing but Lauren and Jake.

"I'll get them," Claire said, and walked to the door to call them in.

Cydney held back the sharpness of the pain as her sobbing daughter flew at her, but the feeling of having Lauren in her arms was indescribable. Jake stood at the foot of the bed, his face white and staring at her as if he was too scared to move.

"We thought you'd gone, like Dad."

Sean looked away.

"No darling, I'm here. Come and give me a cuddle."

As Cydney held the twins, she mouthed to Claire, "How's Mum?"

"Fine. You get yourself well, please. She's being looked after. Quite enjoying the fuss, to be honest."

There was a tap at the door and a familiar face peeked around the door. George. He walked in, his face rather sombre, carrying a basket of fruit in his hands. The twins stared at him as Sean and Claire passed a curious look between them.

"Rupert told me what happened. Thank God you're okay." He laid the fruit on her bedside table and bent down to kiss her cheek, lingering there for a moment. "I can't leave you alone for a moment, can I?"

"Let me introduce you to everyone. My sister, Claire, the twins, Lauren and Jake, and this is my right-hand man, Sean." She had momentarily forgotten about George as all her thoughts were of Steve. This wasn't the way she'd expected to introduce him to her family.

George greeted everyone and Cydney watched as the two men looked each other over. She shifted herself on the bed, struggling to sit up, and Sean was by her side in an instant, adjusting her pillows. George took a step back, his eyes flicking briefly to the window and then back to Cydney.

"I brought some flowers but the sister took them. Not allowed it seems, even in a private ward." He shrugged his shoulders and gave Cydney a half smile. "Jenny told me about Richard. Any news?"

"Nothing yet. We're waiting. I really don't know what happened. Do you think this has anything to do with Benton and Crossley?"

George's face showed an emotion difficult to fathom, then it changed to one of concern, almost fear. But what could he be frightened of? Cydney watched the two men. She saw Sean's eyes narrow and knew instantly he'd been transported back to his army days, intent on prying information from a suspect.

"Well, I don't know, but I will do my damnedest to find out for you."

"Perhaps we could pool resources?" Sean said, and Cydney knew immediately he had an ulterior motive. She wasn't stupid... Sean wanted a chance to get to know the guy who was making a move on her. She hadn't told anyone how far their relationship had actually moved on.

"Sure," George said, and reached into his inside jacket pocket. "Call me anytime." He handed over a business card and Sean took it with a nod.

"Mrs. Granger..."

She turned her head on her pillow and looked at the doctor in the doorway.

"The police would like to interview you now. I think it's best if..."

Sean got to his feet. "Sure. We were just leaving."

When everyone had said their goodbyes, Cydney took a deep breath as the two detectives walked in to greet her.

Left alone finally, Cydney attempted to gather her thoughts. She had been absolutely no help to the police, as she had no recollection of events whatsoever. They'd asked her about her business and clients, her current cases and whether she had any enemies. She had to retain client confidentiality and, in any case, nothing was happening with Rupert's matter as they were simply gathering information. The matter with Ray was not something she wanted to talk about either and she didn't think she had any enemies. She'd told them she was a widow and that her husband had died in Afghanistan several years before. They'd taken notes of everything she'd said but had left empty-handed and somewhat frustrated, requesting that she call them if anything came to mind.

She thought back to the previous week in her office and suddenly remembered the pain she had felt in her head, which had come from nowhere. It was a warning to her to watch out but at the time she didn't know what to watch out for. Now she knew someone was after her. The thought made her shiver. "Why couldn't you tell me? Why did I have to find out the hard way?"

"I tried to warn you and I told you to watch out. I can't prevent what's going to happen in the future. You make your own choices."

"Thanks Ray. That's helpful. So is this your brother fighting back?"

"No, I don't believe it is. This is too refined for him."

"So who is it then? Who's trying to kill me? Someone is trying to stop me finding out something. It must be that as I can't think of anything else, although I think your brother is on to us."

"Charles is an idiot, always has been. He sees an opportunity but won't do things the correct way. He's always on the wrong side and then he wonders why it never goes right."

"So tell me then."

"All I can say is you should keep your friends close and your enemies even closer."

"Steve came to me for the first time. I'm sure of it, or was I dreaming? Did you see him? I don't understand why I can't speak to him though, like I can to you."

Tears filled her eyes now and started to roll down her bruised face.

"Cydney, it's not for me to say."

"You know something and you're not telling me. It's been years. I don't care how he comes through to me. I just want him and need him so badly. Can't you help me?"

"You have to understand. This is my path I am trying to sort. I can't move on until I know Sheila and the kids are okay. I'm sorry you are getting caught up so much in my mess but I still need you. I have to focus on this and then maybe afterwards I can help you."

"I do understand and I'll do my utmost to help you once I get out of here."

"You have lots of people watching over you. That's why you survived."

Ray left her as she lay in bed crying over the loss of her

husband, but now over Richard too, who may or may not pull through. As the pain that started to penetrate through her body took over, she pushed the morphine pump and floated into oblivion once more, the thoughts of Steve still with her. She dreamed of him in the desert, wandering endlessly around like a nomad, dressed in white flowing robes. She wanted to touch him and to hold him but he was always that little bit beyond her reach.

CHAPTER SEVENTEEN

CYDNEY was getting ready for the reception to which she had been invited a couple of months ago, despite remonstrations from all those around her not to go. Managing with a walking stick now the plaster had been removed wasn't easy, but she was determined. She wanted to see who was there, especially as Robert Crossley was the guest speaker, as this would be her opportunity to see him up close. Richard was still in a coma in the hospital and in any case her relationship with George was moving forward so it was natural for him to accompany her.

She had visited the hospital several times and held Christine's hand as she'd sat by Richard's side throughout. Cydney couldn't believe that the man who always acted as her protector was lying helpless in a hospital bed. Nobody knew if he would wake up now, or even at any time in the future. Her words of comfort to Christine and her two boys were platitudes and meant nothing at all, but it was all she had to give.

Her dreams of Richard standing by her side but saying nothing were vivid. She hoped they would expose something and that even in his coma he would reveal what had happened to them, and more importantly why, as she had no clues at all. Cydney remembered nothing of the accident but a few times had woken up as if from a nightmare, her heart beating fast, her mind cast back to the fear.

Her recovery had been slow and painful, made more so by the knowledge that she had no way of finding out who was behind the action that had felled her and Richard. It was the most frustrating

155

of times and she hated relying on everyone for her mobility. After coming out of hospital she was forced to endure bed rest, which was not something she was used to. Cydney had tried to rule her company from the bedroom, but the Sean she thought of as her ally became her commander in chief and he'd refused to let her move an inch, no matter how many orders she'd given.

The twins had been brilliant and even Jake had spent less time in his bedroom, talking to her and sometimes playing the guitar or singing one of his new songs. Lauren had been the quieter and more worried of the pair, not wanting to leave her for a second in case something else happened to her. Lauren had confided her fears to her new friend, George, who had attempted to put her at her ease on the basis that he and Sean were there to look after her mum and not let her out of their sight. That had seemed to pacify her but Cydney saw the light in her daughter's bedroom going on and off all night because hers was doing just the same. It felt as if her family was falling apart. Everything was out of control and her thoughts of Steve, despite George's love and care, constantly haunted her.

After a few weeks her frustration of being at home, where she hated everyone fussing over her, had felt as if it were going to erupt. She needed to work for her sanity, so with Sean's help and despite his remonstrations, she had returned to work on a part-time basis. George had remained in London all this time at Rupert's insistence and had continued to visit her at home. He got on really well with the twins and thoroughly spoiled them by never arriving empty-handed. It was more than evident that Lauren had secretly fallen in love with him . Cydney knew Sean was wary of him and she laughed at the looks he gave George behind his back. Sean had told her that he was making himself too much at home. Well, she was entitled to have male company, whether he liked it or not, and she wanted George around now and maybe in the future too.

Lauren helped her mum into the silver sequined dress. Cydney had lost some weight over the last few weeks but she knew she looked good, albeit a bit pained around the eyes. She made her way carefully downstairs where George was waiting for her and almost gasped at the sight of him in his dinner suit, looking as if he'd just stepped out of a Vogue magazine. Smiling at her, he walked up a few stairs to guide her down. Sean was driving them to Claridges and she understood the two men had forged some kind of mutual bond of acceptance, for the time being anyway. It seemed they both had her best interests at heart, which was gratifying.

The reception was crowded when they arrived. Three hundred people or more milled around, chatting in small groups as they sipped from champagne flutes and ate the canapés passed around by waiters. A string quartet played in the corner. Cydney felt good to be out in company and it didn't hinder her either having a good looking man at her side. She recognised one of her clients, the Chief Executive Officer of a large engineering group, and wandered over to speak to him, dragging George with her and passing a few people on the way who asked after her. They all commiserated on the situation with Richard and gave their good wishes for his recovery. The speed at which word got around within the internal intrigues of the London business world was akin to wildfire spreading through the Australian bush.

They spent some time talking to the CEO until the Group Director of one of the large city banks approached her, and then dragged her away to introduce her to one of his clients. Without even a backwards glance, George wandered off, advising her curtly that he would return shortly, as he had to make a quick call. There was no time for her to respond.

"Cydney, I would like you to meet Robert Crossley. I don't believe you two have met before."

Cydney was completely taken aback at the suddenness of seeing the man before her. She knew Crossley was speaking later but her intention had been to work her way slowly to him and view him from afar, not to be confronted with him so early on. They looked at each other. Cydney gave no indication she knew about him from her investigations and, if he was aware of them, he didn't let on. He wasn't how she'd expected him to be from the information she'd received. He was a tall impressive man, slightly overweight and expensively dressed from head to toe, but he was certainly not good looking. The ravages of time hadn't been kind to him and, in his early sixties, his face, although tanned, was wrinkled by the sun, the benefits of his spoils no doubt.

"Good evening, Mrs Granger. I have heard so much about you." Crossley looked directly at her, his piercing blue eyes boring into her. Amazing that just a few words could evoke so much feeling in her and generate such a sense of power.

"Really? How interesting to hear that. I could easily say the same."

Sean leant against Cydney's car, which was parked amongst a long line of Rolls Royces and Mercedes by the hotel's entrance. He took the time to relax and chat to the other drivers, some of whom he recognised from previous occasions. A couple of them were ex-army, so there was an immediate bond, but the conversation mostly centred around upcoming horse races and dire football referee decisions. Not that he minded, it was good to be away from the constant worry over Cydney.

He glanced up and saw George walk out of the main hotel reception, talking on his phone. There was something about the man he just didn't trust. At the hospital he'd watched George as he'd sauntered down the corridor to the lift, checking his phone as he went. He was a tall, good-looking man and a few of the nurses had looked up from their station and checked him out, up and down. George had smiled and winked at one of them. And this was the man who was wooing Mrs Granger? The guy worked for Rupert, whom Cydney had known for years, so perhaps he was being a tad over-protective, he'd thought at the time, but possibly not without good cause. He'd followed George through the main door of the hospital and into the car park where George had ended his telephone call, slammed the cover of his phone shut, almost in anger, then strode to his car and had driven off. Sean's suspicions had made the hairs on his arm stand on end, but it was part of his army background to be on the lookout for signs, good or bad.

Sean left his fellow chauffeurs at the front of the hotel with the excuse he was going for a smoke and wandered after George, until he reached a corner where he could just about hear him talking.

"Yes, she's fine… I agree. I will look out. No, I don't want to see him. I told you years ago, I never wanted to see him again. How could you put me in this situation? Uncle, no! Please don't ever ask me to do this again. He's dead to me."

In the silence that followed, Sean rested his head against the wall and closed his eyes, waiting for George to speak again. Distant sounds of laughter from the reception drifted through the air and he cocked his head to the side, trying to tune them out. When he opened his eyes again, George was suddenly in front of him.

"Everything all right, sir?" Sean asked, without the slightest hint of surprise in his voice at being discovered.

"Yes, Sean. No problems. Just getting some fresh air. You know how it is going around with the ever-energetic Cydney. I hate these affairs, you never know anybody and I feel like a spare part really."

"Yes, sir. I understand."

Sean looked at George, sizing him up. Something was going on here, the man looked rattled. The argument with the person on the other end of the phone, his uncle, had clearly disturbed him and it was apparent how hard he was trying to hide his feelings. All Sean needed to do was find out who this 'uncle' was and exactly what was going on.

Sean had not been sure about George from the beginning. It was not only because of Cydney and the way he always protected her. This went further. Sean was no less than a dog with a bone when his senses were on fire. And they were now. Every instinct in his body screamed out at him, and there was no way he was letting this one go.

"Shall we walk back?" George asked.

"Sir, if you don't mind my saying, you don't look too good. Is there *anything* at all I can do to help?" He emphasised the word, implying that George could trust him.

George stared at Sean for a good few seconds. "If only..." he whispered under his breath.

"Sorry?"

George shook his head. "Forget it. Everything's fine. Just a bit of a headache coming on. Let me go back to Cydney now."

Returning to his car, Sean wondered what they were all tangled up in. His mind went back over everything that had happened in the last month, starting with the accident that had left his closest friend in a coma. Who *was* behind all of this? Richard had still not woken up. The doctors were trying to bring him slowly out of the coma by reducing the medication, but so far there had been no sign of life and he remained in the ICU. Richard's family and Sean all took it in turns to sit with him, Sean especially through the night shift, allowing Christine to go home for much needed sleep. Sean was used to staying awake and surviving with little or no sleep. He regaled Richard with army stories, not knowing if he was heard or not, smiling to himself in the knowledge that his friend couldn't ask him to shut up even if he wanted to. Watching the comatose man for long periods, wanting to shake him out of this deep unconsciousness and willing him to acknowledge life, occupied him. But there was nothing, not even a flicker of his eyelids. Furthermore, the more concerned he became about Cydney and no matter how hard she tried to hide it and get on with her every day existence, the shadows behind her smile, and the fact she was so distraught, concerned him. Thankfully, apart from her knee, outwardly she had no visible signs of the accident. The internal machinations worried him though.

Cydney had started back at the office, slowly and part-time, and Sean had joined her, taking over some of Richard's role. He had to admit he loved the busy environment, being at the heart of everything, and began to understand what drove his boss. But he constantly watched her and, together with Jenny, begged her to slow down. They might just as well have been talking to a brick wall as Cydney, back at the helm, was ferocious in her quest to discover what had happened. Only earlier that week during their internal meetings she'd vented her despair and frustration on them, starting with Ash, firing questions and orders without waiting for any responses.

"Have you got that meeting set up for me with Sigmunds Bank? I recall you have a contact there."

"Well, I was waiting, for obvious reasons, but I will organise it for you."

"Great. I don't want to hang around any longer. My brain's working, even if my knee isn't. Have they pulled in the loan yet on Centurion? I don't want Rupert to think we aren't concentrating our efforts on his matter."

"I'll check that also."

"Ok. So, you can go and do that now while I catch up with Jenny and Sean. I mean now, don't just sit there… and you two can stop looking at each other like that. I'm fine. Everything is perfect and I have work to do. So you can pull faces or we can get on with the job in hand."

"Right boss," they said, almost together.

"What the hell have you got to smile about?"

Neither Jenny nor Sean would dare to answer that one but she knew it was all about how much they loved having her back.

"Richard isn't around to help us, and God knows I miss him, but it doesn't mean we can't carry on. So Sean, first of all, where are we with the Gordons?"

During Cydney's period of recovery, Sean had not let up on his investigations into the activities of the slippery Mr Charles Gordon and proceeded to brief his boss. He thought back to his successful foray into the office of the solicitor, William Harper, before he got the call from Jenny about the accident. Those photos... Charles was obviously blackmailing the man but he was curious as to how Harper had found himself in such a situation. What hold did Charles have over him, apart from the images? What would make a solicitor forge a Will, act as an accomplice to illegal share transfers, and fraudulently buy and sell properties for money – fully knowing the possible consequences of his actions? Sean decided he needed to know more about Harper's wife and her involvement. He had seen them both at the funeral of Ray Gordon and they certainly didn't act like a loving married couple; far from it. She had accosted her husband and berated him in front of Charles Gordon who had looked blindly on, almost as if he was involved in the tirade.

Sean had also been spending some time with Sheila and her children while George was with Cydney on the pretext, in his own mind, that he was ensuring her safety. The time with her was relaxing and she always put him at his ease, fussing around him, cooking him his favourite chocolate cake made especially for his visits. He told himself he shouldn't get too comfortable in her company especially as he had a job to do, which was to investigate Charles Gordon, her brother-in-law and to get back what she was no doubt going to lose unless he took some action. Furthermore, she was newly widowed and in mourning. The word 'however' slipped into his mind from time to time, and he couldn't help thinking what an attractive lady she was, for sure.

"Sheila, you've known the Harpers for many years. How do you actually see this marriage? We know William is involved in the potential fraud in a huge way but I don't get it."

"I've never trusted William, and there was talk of him having an affair. But you've seen him – he just hasn't got the charm or wherewithal to go looking for another woman. His wife always retained the purse strings and had him in the palm of her hand. He's a weak man. The problems he had before, which were actually never proven, really hit him and that's why he set up his provincial practice, to get out of the limelight. He then put on weight, started drinking, and if I were a betting woman I would say she was the one having an affair, if anyone."

"That's what I tend to think," Sean added, but he hadn't told Sheila about the photos. "You know we'll do our best to get you what is rightfully yours."

"Yes, I trust you both. I only hope I haven't got Cydney into a lot of trouble."

"We can't prove the accident was down to Charles, and to be honest I don't think he would get involved in that kind of thing."

"So who do you think is?"

"I wish I knew."

Sean reported to Cydney the conversation he'd had with Sheila.

"So, we are no further forward. Fantastic! Meanwhile, we have potential killers at large, the police doing nothing, and we're sitting on our backsides. Just great." Her frustration was overwhelming her and spilling out to her employees.

"I don't think that's strictly correct. Actually, I have news," Sean continued. "I haven't let up following Charles. He's been a very busy boy, and I don't mean at the factory. I wondered what was happening for him to leave work so early so I followed him home. He was there for about half an hour and came out carrying an overnight bag. He then drove for about a mile or two and picked up this woman who was waiting for him at the side of the road."

"Well, who was it, Sherlock?"

"I'll give you one guess."

Everyone stared at him blankly. Cydney drummed her long fingernails on the desk.

"The lovely Patricia Harper."

"What? They're having an affair?"

"So it would seem. I followed them to a country hotel in a village a few miles from Reading. I waited until they'd checked in then went along to chat to the receptionist, who just happened to be from the old country."

"Sean, you could schmooze the birds from the trees," Jenny said. "And, don't tell me, they were signed in as Mr and Mrs Gordon."

"They certainly were, and obviously not trying to hide anything."

"So then what did you do? Come on, Sean, for Christ's sake, you're really dragging this out." Cydney's impatience was becoming more apparent.

"Well, there was no point hanging around, I saw what I needed. I wonder if William Harper knows about this? Mrs Granger, I really think we should have a meeting with Harper and confront him. I'm sure he's not the brains behind any of this. Maybe his wife and Charles are the ones blackmailing him. But there's only one way to find out, isn't there? Are you behind me with this?"

"Well if you go, I'm going too," Cydney said.

Jenny stood up. "I'll make the appointment. He knows me now."

CHAPTER EIGHTEEN

G EORGE stared aimlessly into Cydney's garden attempting, but not actually succeeding, to take stock of everything. Life was getting too complicated, he thought. He imagined running away to hide on some deserted island for the rest of his life and wished he could just snap his fingers and make everything and everyone go away. But not Cydney, whom he had now fallen in love with, along with the children. No, they'd be coming with him. He'd even take Sean, he thought, with a sardonic smile.

The night before he had been confronted with the man he hoped he would never have to see again, his older half-brother, Robert Crossley. Thankfully, they had not met for many years after George had left New York to go to work in South Africa. His mother had married John Crossley and George was the result. There were some eighteen years age difference between them. George hated Robert with a passion because of the way he'd been treated by him as a child. Far from being a caring older brother, Robert had bullied him, often with violence, all of which had been hidden from his mother. The only escape was when George left to study law at Harvard and joined the law firm that would give him the career he wanted. He spent many hours working through the night to avoid going home. Then, when his father died suddenly, he and his mother found themselves at the mercy of the Crossleys. His father had always protected him from Robert, as far as he was able, but now the funds were in Robert's hands who did everything he could to keep monies from George – which he said were all tied up in a Trust Fund.

George felt terrible. He knew all about the trusts and the offshore companies because, with huge pangs of guilt, he had set them up for Robert and Craig Benton, their brother-in-law, albeit under pressure. Christ, what an absolute mess! George leant forward and buried his face in his hands, every fibre of his body wanting to scream out. He'd believed nobody would ever find out about the part he had played but now Cydney was in the process of discovering everything and Rupert would know soon enough about his involvement. It was probably only days away from the whole sorry business being out in the open.

George had thought at the time he was doing something for the family, that this was something to put him in Robert's good books for once. All he'd wanted to do was to try and mend the bridges between them. He'd had no idea how underhand everything was or that it was their intention to bring them in even more millions and to try to cover up their insider dealing over American Securities and the monies they had made. Once he'd found out, he had left for South Africa, adopted his mother's maiden name of Edwards, and it was purely by coincidence that he'd met Rupert after he had been admitted to the Bar. He thought Rupert a genuine man, despite everything he had heard from his brother, and there was an immediate rapport between them. When he offered George a job as Chief Counsel in his organisation, George had felt he could make amends for everything he had done, and had prayed Rupert would never find out about him.

Over the years he truly considered he had compensated for Rupert's loss when he'd tried to buy Caxton Trust Bank, by working hard and being loyal. When he'd joined him in London and met Cydney for the first time, and she'd launched into her findings on Crossley and Benton and all their companies, he'd thought he would have a heart attack as the life from which he'd hoped he had escaped forever came back to haunt him with a vengeance. He had flown back to New York for the first time in many years, giving Rupert some pretext for his trip and a conference he had to attend, but he had never got to see Crossley, despite all his attempts. The man was travelling, tied up in meetings, on his yacht; every excuse was given to him. Clearly George wasn't going to be allowed to see the man he hated. So he'd returned to London empty-handed.

But were his half-brother and Benton really capable of attempted murder? Were they the ones who had tried to kill Richard and Cydney? He could not imagine they were capable but maybe it was possible if they thought everything was about to fall apart around them and they would get found out. Now he was involved, he had fallen for Cydney, and everything he had done would be revealed. When she found out, as he knew she most certainly would, it would be the end. He had to leave before this happened. What a complete and utter mess.

Arriving at the reception, George knew he was not going to be able to avoid his half-brother but he was going to do his utmost. He had seen him from afar, which was why he had gone outside to call his uncle, but when he walked back inside Cydney was deep in conversation with Crossley, of all people. He tried to turn around and walk away but as he did, he heard his name called out and he had no choice but to sidle up next to Cydney.

"Let me introduce you, this is Robert Crossley."

"Hello," Crossley said, holding out his hand. George reluctantly took it and his hand was held just that extra bit too long. As the two men locked eyes, Crossley almost smiled, but not in a friendly way.

"Oh, do you two know each other?" Cydney asked.

"No Cydney. We don't," he responded quite emphatically.

"I was asking Mr Crossley about his business affairs, before he speaks of course. What an extremely exciting life he's led."

"Indeed."

Crossley looked down at her.

"I understand you had an accident. Sorry to hear about that. I'm glad you're up and about now."

"I was wondering whether we could meet up in the next week. I'd love to know more about your business activities."

"Well, Mrs Granger, my thoughts exactly. I understand you've built up a huge reputation in forensics. Perhaps we *could* meet up. I'm staying at the Ritz. Yes, I know all Americans stay there. We just like a bit of old fashioned English hospitality, I guess. How about dinner with me, next Wednesday? Say seven-thirty, for drinks beforehand?" He looked at George, "you're welcome to join us."

"No, thanks all the same. I'll be back in South Africa."

Cydney spun round to face him. "I didn't know that."

George saw the glaze of confusion in Cydney's eyes and sensed her irritation, or pain even. But, like a true professional, she didn't allow the moment to linger and, thankfully, allowed no time for his response.

"Thank you," she said, turning back to Crossley. I'll look forward to it."

"Well, I have to go and speak now. Good to meet you both." He nodded at George and then made his way to the top table where he was guest of honour.

"Why didn't you tell me you were returning to Johannesburg? And what was all that about with Crossley? Is there something I should know?"

"No, stop nagging me. I'm under no obligation to stay here; you're not my keeper. Let's just go and sit down, shall we?" George stormed off to the table, hating himself for being so cruel. But what other choice did he have?

"I love this room, don't you?" Cydney said, sidling up to George on the sofa. "Always so peaceful, looking out into the garden."

"You built all this with Steve?"

"Yes, although the walnut tree was always there. Unfortunately, he never got a chance to see the house finished." She turned to him. "Are you okay? You seem to be in a world of your own."

"I can never replace him, can I? In your eyes he was a hero, and always will be."

Cydney took George's hand in hers and stroked his fingers, meeting his gaze. She had slowly connected to this man in her mind and now in her heart. Her husband was no longer with her in life but would always be there in her thoughts, and that was enough for her. She felt ready to move on at last.

"I can never let go of Steve fully, you know that, but…"

He stood up and turned to face her.

"I should leave."

"But George, I was going to say…"

"No, Cydney. It's better I leave now before anyone gets hurt. I can't replace Steve and I doubt I should even try. I'm not the man you think I am. I've done things I'm ashamed of."

"What? Tell me. I'm sure it's not as bad as all that. I can help."

"No, you'll no doubt find out soon enough. But I need to go away, from everyone and everything. I'm going to Johannesburg to hand in my notice, and then I'll probably head for Australia."

Cydney stared at this man in front of her. She felt the beginnings of cold air moving along the side of her right arm. Not now, she thought. I can't deal with spirit. I need to keep this man with me.

"I thought you loved me, that we had a future together. You asked me to trust you. Did you forget that? And I put my trust in you completely. Whatever you've done, it can't be that bad. Can't you at least tell me?"

"No Cydney.. I can't stay, no matter what you say. I have to go."

George left the room without a backwards glance, leaving Cydney open-mouthed on the sofa.

"But … I love you George," she whispered, and watched as another man walked out of her life.

Lauren came bounding into the room and Cydney wiped away her tears with the back of her hand.

"Mum, are we going to Nan's now? I really want to see her! Auntie Claire said she was going to be there, too. Can we leave now? I'm ready. Where's George going? I thought he was coming with us." The questions bombarded Cydney, not giving her any time to think at all. "You alright, Mum?"

"I'm fine. Something in my eye. Yes, let's go and see Nan. She'll be pleased. Anyway," she added, trying to change the subject, "George had to leave."

"When will he be back? He is coming back, isn't he?"

"I don't know, darling. Let's get ready. Can you call Jake?"

Lauren sloped off, leaving Cydney alone with her thoughts.

"You couldn't have stopped him."

"Ray, not now, please. Is nothing private?"

"I'm only trying to help."

"So tell me, why couldn't I? What have I done that's so bad he couldn't stay with me? Am I really so bad a person?"

"Nothing to do with that, and please stop crying."

"But he's left me. First Steve, now George. I just don't know who I am anymore."

"Well, let me tell you. You are a person I've come to trust, and I would say with my life but that doesn't work anymore. With my death then."

"Stop trying to make me smile."

"Let's keep things on track, can we? He will come back if he thinks it's right for him and for you. You can't control another person's destiny. I have come to realise that, but what we can do is right some wrongs."

"Okay, Ray, so where are we exactly? You know what has been going on, I'm sure."

"Charles is ready to run. You have to stop him signing the contract with the supermarket. Once he does that, Sheila has no chance of getting the money."

"How are we supposed to do that, kidnap him and tie him down?"

"Even I can appreciate sarcasm. No, William Harper is ready to help you. He's at his wits end. You know my wonderful brother is blackmailing him. Harper's wife will leave also. I don't think Harper is in a position to argue now. He's completely alone and needs someone on his side. That could be you. Go see him, and send him my regards."

"You think so? Families are really something, aren't they? Okay, I'll go with Sean in that case. Send your regards? Would he appreciate that?"

"No, that was me being sarcastic this time. Anyway, talking of Sean, he is spending a lot of time with my Sheila."

"He's a good man. Do you mind?"

"As long as he looks after her I am okay, and there's nothing I can do anyway. I want her to be looked after and cherished, like I always did for her."

"I don't quite think it's like that, Ray. Sean is only looking out for her, nothing else."

"We shall see."

"Can you help me any more on the accident? I so miss Richard and need him back."

"Now, I have told you before. I need to sort out my own wrongs first. All I would say is that nothing is yet cut and dried. You still have to watch your back."

Cydney felt a shiver down her spine and images of Steve crept into her mind.

"Why did I think of Steve when you said that?"

"I can't say. No reason, I'm sure. Just be careful."

With those last words resounding in Cydney's mind, Ray left her side. Always back to her husband. After four years, he was as much a part of her life now as he was when he left to go to Afghanistan. No wonder George left her. Why should she be surprised? Steve was always there with her, as if he hadn't died at all, and there was no place left for another man. She felt the shadows creeping around her again. Such was her fate, she thought to herself. Well, she had the children and Sean, but what if he left her for Sheila? No one stayed with her. She was simply not a good enough person, obviously.

Cydney dragged herself up, collected her walking stick and limped out of the room to go to her mum, who wouldn't be around much longer either. Cydney Granger was a woman who had everything on the outside, but deep down, what did she have around her but her children?

When George left the house he was distraught, and painfully aware that he had nowhere to go and nobody to whom he could turn. He was not a weak man who would usually seek to escape from his problems but this situation was insurmountable. He thought of telling Rupert everything but doubted his boss would believe him. Why should he? His belief would be that George had infiltrated his organisation purely to gain information to share with the Crossley family. He would not understand there was no family and never had been. It had always been him and his mother against the Crossley family, and when she'd died he was on his own. George had really believed all that previous life was behind him, yet now it had reared its ugly head.

George had never wanted to go to the reception the previous day but Cydney had insisted on him accompanying her; she'd needed him. He'd thought he could have avoided seeing his half-brother but Robert Crossley would have made a beeline for George whatever the circumstances, just to show him up. George had managed to avoid an initial confrontation and had sneaked out before Cydney could gauge his reaction at meeting the man. He'd called his uncle, his father's brother, when he was outside the hotel to try to get him to reason with Robert, to get him to keep quiet about their family connection. The only suggestion given was for him to try to reconcile with Robert, and that was never going to happen. Now he knew he had to disappear, to walk away from everything he held dear, including the potential of the family life he'd always wanted. Everything was disintegrating before his eyes.

As George strode towards his car, Sean appeared on the driveway.

"Here we are again, then. Can I assume you're leaving?"

"I have to. Please look after Cydney for me."

"Are you not coming back, sir?"

He shook his head. "If only I could."

"You know, sir, I couldn't quite help over-hearing your conversation with your uncle. I don't mean to pry, but if there's anything I can do, you only have to ask."

"I wish I could tell you what's going on because I could do with a friend right now, but I can't. I just can't."

"Surely it can't be that bad?" Sean asked.

"It is." George took a deep breath in and looked towards the horizon, blowing out slowly.

"Why don't you cool off a bit, eh? Call me in a couple of days. Don't do anything hasty."

"Thank you, Sean," he said, climbing into the car. "I'll think about it." And with those final words he revved the engine, closed the door and drove away, glancing back at Sean who stood there and watched him go.

CHAPTER NINETEEN

CYDNEY made her way gingerly up the stairs to Harper's office, her arm linked in Sean's. The narrow, high steps didn't help at all and by the time she reached the top, her knee was pounding with a heartbeat of its own.

"Are you sure you're okay, Mrs Granger?"

"Yes, Sean. Let's just get this over with. Though how I'm going to get down is another matter." She turned to look at the stairwell, which looked almost impossible to descend. It might as well have been Everest. "We'll sort that one out later."

Sean recognised the office from his night excursion a few weeks before. This time, however, there were fewer files sitting on top of the filing cabinets and around the secretary's desk. Although the surfaces looked tidier, there was hardly enough room to stand for all the storage boxes that were taking up most of the floor space and almost reaching the ceiling.

"Moving?" he enquired of the secretary who was sitting at her desk looking quite upset.

"Yes," she said tearfully. "Mr Harper is closing up the practice and retiring. I really don't know what I shall do."

"We have an appointment," Cydney interrupted, as Harper came out of his office.

"You're not the Fothergills!" he said. "I was expecting them."

"No, but you'll see us," Sean said, moving towards him. Harper backed up and knocked his huge frame against the door.

"This is totally out of order. You can't just barge your way into my office!"

"Oh yes we can," Cydney replied, following behind Sean. "You have no choice."

"Mr Harper, shall I call the police?" the secretary shouted after them.

"Yes, Mr Harper, shall we call the police?" Cydney asked. "I think we should, don't you? Shall we give Charles Gordon a call to help you decide?"

Harper looked defeated. He called through, "No, it's okay, I know this couple. Everything's fine, Mrs Taylor. "

The man walked backwards towards his desk and sat down hard on his once black leather chair.

"What do you want?"

Cydney took in her surroundings. It was messy and disorganised, exactly as Jenny and Sean had described to her. Piles of paper were in every corner but now there were numerous black bin bags everywhere, all overflowing. They sat down without waiting to be asked.

"I see you're packing up."

"I'm retiring, as if that is any business of yours. Who are you? What do you want?" Beads of perspiration fell down from his forehead. He wiped them away with a rather grey-looking handkerchief, which he took from the inside pocket of his jacket. His face started to redden. "Where are the Fothergills? They had this appointment."

"Ah yes, the Fothergills. Friends of mine, nice couple. Unfortunately Mr Fothergill is in a coma in intensive care."

"Nothing to do with me."

"Really? Were we asking that?" questioned Sean. "There was no mention of blame. Now why would you say that?"

"Please state why you are here, then go. I've no time for this, or your games. I knew the Fothergills' story didn't ring true."

"So, Mr Harper, let's get to the point. You do recognise the name Ray Gordon, of course? Yes, I see by your face you do. Complete tragedy that he died. Such a shame about his wife,

Sheila. Why, Mr Harper, you look guilty. Sean, do you think Mr Harper's looking guilty?"

"Why yes. A solicitor like him looking guilty, you would think he had something to hide. *Do* you have something to hide, Mr Harper?"

"I don't know what you're talking about. All these questions you're asking me. I know Ray and Sheila, they're old friends of mine – in fact I went to his funeral. I don't know what you mean, I've nothing to be guilty about," Harper blustered, wiping further beads from his face and around his neck. He moved his tie around to loosen his collar and reached out to take a sip of water from a glass sitting on his desk.

"Are you feeling uncomfortable, Mr Harper?" Sean asked.

"I think we should get down to the reason we're here." Cydney was beginning to enjoy Harper's discomfort. He deserved to squirm. "Let's start at the beginning then," she continued, "and see what we know so far. We'd like to help you, Harper." Cydney started to feel Ray's presence around her. This was good and she knew he would help her fill in some of the gaps if necessary.

"And if you comply, we can do so much more for you," Sean added.

"I'm listening, get on with it!" Harper snapped. "And can we stop the good cop, bad cop routine? I'm far too weary for all this, just cut to the chase. You obviously want something from me, whoever you are."

"Please feel free to correct me or interject at any time. Ray Gordon and his wife are, or should I say, *were* the owners of Rayshel Plastics, until Charles Gordon turned up. I see you know Charles. Would you like some more water? Apparently not. So, to continue. Now, we know that somehow Sheila's shares in the company were transferred to Charles without Ray's knowledge. Charles also became the sole beneficiary of Ray's Will when he died, and that in fact there are two Wills but the signatures seem to be different, although according to Ray himself, he doesn't recall finalising anything. There is also a life insurance policy that names Charles, while cutting out Sheila and the kids. We discovered you managed to obtain the leases from all the other properties on the site where the factories are situated, and put them in the name of Intervest Holdings, owned by Charles and with your lovely wife, Patricia as company secretary. The main Rayshel factory and land is also owned by Intervest, coincidentally. Finally we've discovered Prestons are about to sign a purchase agreement for the land, which should bring in quite a bit of money, although putting many out of work, but I doubt you're concerned about that. Oh, and of course, Sheila and her children will get nothing."

"You're doing well, Cydney. Look at the man. Amazed he can live with himself. Keep up the good work."

"Are you sure I can't get you some water now?"

Harper's face turned ashen. He got up from his chair and walked slowly around his desk to the office door. Both Cydney and Sean watched his every move but doubted he would do anything drastic. He called out to his secretary.

"Mrs Taylor, you can leave for the day."

"But Mr Harper, the packing... Is everything alright?"

"Yes, please just go, we can finish tomorrow."

Harper came back in and sat down.

"So what are you going to do?" he said.

"I haven't quite finished. There's the question of the blackmail."

Harper seemed to shrink as he slumped even further back in his chair. He clutched at his chest.

"You know about that?" he whispered, as if he couldn't even bring himself to say the words out loud. "And about...?" He left the sentence hanging in the air.

"Yes, the pictures. Harper, we know everything," Sean said.

"But how? I thought we had everything tied up. It was going

to be so easy, Charles told me. I was led on. All I wanted was a life for me and my wife."

"Oh, yes. I hate to break the news but Patricia..."

"Yes I know," he interrupted, "she's having an affair with Charles. I've always known... I thought she would come back to me when we had money. But look at me. Why would she, what have I got to offer someone like her?"

Don't feel sorry for him. He's not the man I knew. Pretending to be sorry for himself. It was all his doing. He could, and should, have stopped my brother."

"What about the money from your old practice, where's that now?"

"Do you have to rake up the past? It's all over and done with. Patricia spent everything years ago. She likes to live a lifestyle I could never give her, though I tried."

"Well, if you'd confronted and fought for her, it wouldn't have got to this."

"You don't understand. With those pictures, Charles had everything. The law practice, my wife, my life. I had nowhere to go and no one to help me. He held my future in his dirty little palms. The bastard. I knew it would all come out eventually."

"As it should," Ray added.

"So what are you going to do, go to the police? I have nothing to hide now. I know I'll end my days courtesy of Her Majesty, but it will be worth it to see Charles go under and my wife too. They can stew in their juices for all I care."

"You know that Charles has been watching Sheila and scaring the kids," Cydney said.

"I had no idea. The man is insane. Out of control."

"Well, the question now is whether you're going to work with us and help get Sheila what's rightfully hers."

"I have no choice. I'll take my punishment but I want to see that bastard strung up and left to rot. What do you want me to do?"

"Ultimately, we need to make sure the correct Will is restored so that Sheila is the sole beneficiary. I presume you still have both Wills?" Harper nodded. "This will be done the *legal* way, and the Courts will need to reinstate the original one, with your full cooperation," she added, emphasising the word 'legal' to ensure he would be in no doubt. "It's unlikely we can do anything about the companies that have gone from the site but if Prestons want to continue with the purchase of the land, we need to ensure that Sheila gets everything that's rightfully hers. Are you with me so far?"

Harper nodded in agreement. "Again, I have no choice, do I?"

"No, you don't. I'm not quite sure what to do about Charles as yet, but I'll work out a plan. We know the result and now need to get Charles out of the picture. What about Patricia?"

"I have no feelings for her after all of this. I'll be locked up anyway and she can go to hell for all I care."

"I suppose it goes without saying that you're not going to reveal anything about our meeting and what we know. If Charles gets wind of this, everyone will lose. We need to catch him red-handed."

"You have my word, for what it's worth. I have nowhere to go now."

"Cydney, is this really going to happen now? Are we nearly there?"

"Yes Ray, we are nearly there. But I need to know from you that once we've sorted this mess out, you will help me."

"You know I will. I can't thank you enough. I will always be in your debt. To think Sheila and the kids will be ok..."

"Everything alright Mrs Granger?" Sean asked.

"Yes, I'm fine, thank you." She turned to Harper. "We need you to hand over all your files on Ray to us. We need everything so we can go through the whole lot."

Harper walked over to the boxes piled up in his office and placed the first of them on the desk.

"Would you believe me if I told you I've wanted to do this for a very long time? Everything is in there that you need. I thought I might burn the lot, but I see now that would have been stupid and maybe I will come out of this a bit better."

"What about the pictures?" Sean asked. He knew they were in Harper's desk drawer.

"Well, they don't show me in the best light but you can have those too." He bent down to his drawer and pulled out the large brown envelope. "You realise that Charles has the originals. These are merely copies to keep me in my place."

"Of course."

"So tell me. Who are you, and how come you know all about this? There's no point not telling me now."

"We're friends of Ray. He told me everything," Cydney answered.

"But how did he know?"

Cydney felt Ray move closer to her. She shivered.

"He knows. Let's leave it at that."

"Can I say how sorry I am about everything? It was not supposed to be like this, any of it. Charles got carried away."

"Yeah, everyone is innocent. It wasn't me, it was the other man," Sean said. "Meanwhile, our friend is lying in a hospital bed, having been shot, and we don't know whether he's going to live or die. Some innocence."

"I don't know what you're talking about. Charles is a bad apple, guilty of many things, lying, cheating, adultery, but I don't have him down as a murderer. I don't think he would have the guts for it. He thinks he can get away with fraud – but murder, that's totally different."

"Well if he didn't do it, then who did?" Cydney asked.

CHAPTER TWENTY

I T surprised Cydney that she felt George's loss from her life so intensely. She hadn't realised how much a part of her existence he'd become. Wasn't that always the way? It reminded her of the line from the song about not knowing what you've got until it's gone. Well now she knew.

Lauren nagged at her, asking where George was and when he would be back. Her daughter was so young and Cydney hated to tell her he wasn't coming back at all. If she could have explained she would have, but it was unclear, even to her. She even called Rupert to see if George had returned to Johannesburg but he was equally in the dark.

Despite all that was going on around her, Cydney, her sister Claire and the twins had spent a lovely day at the nursing home. It was the annual garden fete and they had brought their mum out in a wheelchair to watch all the events and sing along to the old songs, led by the entertainer. Cydney still required her walking stick, but it was more a case of when she needed it rather than having to use it all the time. Claire had picked them all up in a new white Cayenne her husband had bought for her.

"Just a little something to keep me happy," she'd said.

"You must be delirious then," piped up Jake.

Cydney had clipped him playfully around the ear. She did love his humour, although sometimes he went a little too far. Laughing at his remark, she'd realised how she and Claire were getting on so much better these days, but maybe it was because they were united in looking after their mother. Cydney was delighted at this turnaround from her once selfish sibling. Ever since her accident, Claire had more than pulled her weight.

"Can I have an ice-cream, Pam?"

"Mum, it's Cydney, your daughter. Pam's your sister and I'm sorry but she isn't here."

"Well, where is she then? Call her and tell her she's late."

Cydney hadn't the heart to tell her that Auntie Pam had died many years ago. There was no point in any case, if she reminded her it would only cause upset and then she would only forget about it afterwards.

"Auntie Pam can't make it today, she sends her love."

"Oh, okay. Then who are you?"

"Cydney," she said again. "Claire's here too."

"Let me give you some money. Will you make sure you pay all my bills? I don't want to have my gas cut off."

"It's okay, everything's paid."

"Good. I want to see my solicitor."

"Why, Mum?" asked Claire, with a sigh.

"Because I'm going to die soon and I want to make sure my girls get everything."

Claire and Cydney passed a look between them. They couldn't fathom where their mum's thoughts would go from one second to the next, one day to the other. Sometimes she was extremely agitated and at others she was completely off the scale when it came to making sense. They now took things in their stride but this last sentence threw them completely off guard.

"Mum, why would you say such a thing?" Cydney asked.

"Because it's true. That nice man, Ron came to visit me again last night, I think I'll probably go on a date with him. He wants to take me dancing."

"Ron's your husband, our dad. You remember don't you?"

"No, he's not. He's the man in the room next to me. Now where's my ice cream? Can I have strawberry?"

Their mum's condition since the cancer diagnosis a couple of months ago had not actually deteriorated as much as they'd thought it would. She was terminal, they knew that, but strong, and she wasn't going anywhere without a fight. The lump was still visible on her neck since they'd decided there would be no surgical intervention, but the dementia was worsening, and her moments of lucidity were getting fewer and farther apart. Anyway, today Cydney was determined for the whole family to enjoy themselves and not think too much of a future without their mum. The twins were having a great time, with Lauren entering various competitions and spending all her money on absolute rubbish at the tombola stall. Jake sat chatting to a few of the elderly male residents, pouring them tea, passing cakes and being generally useful. She was very proud of them both.

After a couple of hours their mum started to doze and they thought it was time to take her back to her room for an afternoon sleep. Tucking her up in bed, they kissed her before leaving. She smiled gently at them, and they crept out quietly, closing the door behind them.

"She didn't look well, Cydney."

"Well, that's not surprising, is it? Anyway, the doctor is due tomorrow so we'll get an update from him."

"I think we have to face the fact that she isn't going to be with us for much longer."

"Can we not talk about this? I'm not ready to let her go yet," Cydney snapped.

"Just saying. No good burying your head, you've got to face up to things."

"I'm the only one who does." Tears welled up in Cydney's eyes as Claire put her arm around her.

"Let's not argue today, eh? Let's wait and see," Claire said, taking the initiative. Cydney had a feeling Claire was stronger than she made out, and more responsible, but had a laziness of character that simply forced her elder sister to take the lead in everything – ever since childhood.

Back at home, and while the twins were in their rooms, Cydney gave herself the luxury of some alone time. She sat in her usual chair in the sitting room and pondered her life. This was not what she had planned for herself at all. A sense of loneliness swept over her in a wave and nothing could shake it, not even the third glass of wine she held in her hand. She stared out at the walnut tree, the house's protector. It had stood for centuries, branches spreading in a constant embrace. She was sure it had seen many changes, people coming and going, and yet it carried on and would do so long after Cydney and her family had gone. It had a life about it, a presence that normally gave her peace, but not tonight.

She shivered as someone came up close. She tried to focus, to work out who was there, when the image of a lady materialised in front of her. It took Cydney a moment or two and then, as the focus changed, she recognised the person and felt a huge warmth as a sense of love descended over her.

"Hello Cydney," the lady said with a soft, Irish lilt. *"I've been meaning to come to see you."*

"You only come through when there's a problem in my life, Grandma."

"I know. You look so sad, my darling. I want to help you."

"I wish you could, but having you here is enough. So many things are happening now. I don't know what to do or think first. Especially with Mum."

"You don't need to worry about your mum; she's at peace within herself. You know she sees your dad now. That's because she's preparing to leave this world for spirit. I know I can talk to you like this, and that you won't be upset about where she's going because you understand there is a better place for her to be - with me, your dad and all her family."

"But I'll miss her so much. She's all I have left, apart from the twins, and Claire of course. I do understand, and I know I'll be able to talk to her still, but it won't be the same not being able to touch her or hold her hand. I'm not ready to come to terms with this yet."

"The main thing is for your mum to pass peacefully. The rest will take care of itself. Anyway, I'm not here for that."

Cydney paused for a moment and wondered why her grandma had come through. She had always been so straightforward and direct in life, and nothing had changed since she had passed over into the spirit world. Cydney understood there would be no barriers to the purpose of her visit. They had been so close when Cydney was growing up, more like best friends, as they understood each other so well. It had been a while since her grandma had come through, but whenever she did it was always with a particular purpose in mind.

"I want you to take more care of yourself. I'm not happy with what you're involved in. Sometimes you can't see things clearly for yourself and you need to watch out."

"I can take care of myself. I always have and I always will. You know that."

"I recognise the confidence in your abilities. You're strong, and determined, but please be careful how you go about things."

"I really want Steve to come through to me. If I can talk to you and Dad, why can't I talk to him? Please tell me as I really don't understand," she begged.

"Cydney, nothing is ever straightforward. I can't bring Steve to you. He was hovering between you and spirit for a long time. I can't say more. You need to concentrate on what is around you, not always searching for what you can't have. Try to be satisfied, my darling. I know you feel like things are going wrong for you at the moment, but what did I always tell you? You make your own life. Wake up to this and be aware of what you do have."

Cydney thought for a moment. Talk about a lecture and tough love, but her grandma was actually giving her a good lesson and she ought to listen. If she couldn't advise, having her best interests at heart, then who could? How ridiculous for her to feel so downtrodden. She needed to pull herself together. Her business was good, close friends were supportive, and so what if there wasn't a man around? She had no control over her mum and when she would leave but she would make the best of the time she had with her. Cydney straightened up in her chair, her senses fully alert.

"I'll think about what you've said and put things into perspective, I promise."

"Good, don't forget. Anyway, I've been around you for some time."

"So you know about everything going on? What about Richard?"

"He's slowly healing and has a lot of love surrounding him. I'm more interested in this other business, a certain lady called Patricia. She's the one to watch."

"What do you mean? She's married to a solicitor we're investigating for Ray. I presume you know about him?"

"Of course I do. I told you I've been around for a while now. I feel she's going to run. You need to act quickly."

"But she's just the wife. Although her name is on the documents, we assumed she was just a figurehead for them. I know she's having an affair with Ray's brother but does that mean they're both going to try and get away with all the money?"

"She's not being straight with anyone. She has her own agenda and it doesn't involve anyone else at all."

Very quietly and almost un-noticed, Cydney felt Ray around her, as if on cue.

"Well you didn't think I was going to miss out on this one, did you?"

"Ray, your presence is most welcome, as always. You two know each other of course?"

"Don't ask silly questions, darling," said her grandma, *"I brought him with me."*

"I've known Patricia for many years. I can't say I warmed to her and she has never been a good wife to William but she stayed with him, more for appearances sake than anything else. He's such a soft touch, which left her to do whatever she wanted and whenever - as long as she had money, which was her main priority. She may be fooling Charles, who's an idiot and can't see the wood from the trees, but she's no fool herself," Ray said.

"Well that puts an interesting slant on everything. So is she responsible for the accident?"

"She's mixing with people who don't have the best reputation in the world."

"I think I should spend some time watching her, or rather get Sean to when he eventually turns up."

"Oh yes, the lovely Sean. I'm happy he's around. Someone from the old country," said Cydney's grandma.

"He's a good guy. Ray, you shouldn't be concerned about him and Sheila. He won't do her any harm."

"Yes, I'm sure. I'm around her a lot and there's nothing I can do but watch her crying, standing in front of our wedding photo, full of regret about my not being there. I only want her to be happy, back to the old Sheila I know and love with all my heart."

Cydney felt the love from him and knew that was what she wanted again, too. She knew it couldn't be with Steve but she was determined to find George and sort matters out. *Carpe diem.* Seize the day. That was her mantra now. She would call Rupert again, and get Sean on the case.

"Anyway, we are going now and we will leave our love with you. Just think about what I said, and be careful."

Her grandma and Ray moved away and left Cydney even more perplexed about everything than she was before. What was she supposed to be careful about? Robert Crossley and Craig Benton? Charles Gordon? George? The list seemed endless. That aside, there was still the little matter of her husband's avoidance to work out. Why hadn't he come through to her? This constant ignoring by everyone about why she couldn't speak to Steve was really frustrating. Anyone would think he was still alive.

CHAPTER TWENTY-ONE

"**D**RAGONFLY, can you safely make your way to the reconnaissance point? I'll be there. Five days, is that enough?" The phone went dead. Sean took the receiver away from his ear and stared down at it.

"He heard me, I'm sure. Can you get me as near to the border as you can?" he said to the general. "The captain will be there. He knows where we would meet if there was ever a problem and he has the navigational points. We've supplies already in place. Even after four years they'll still be there, though in what state is anyone's guess."

"Sergeant, this is most irregular. Look, I have no doubt you know what you are doing…"

"Sir, he'll want me there," Sean interrupted. "We both know that. He trusts me to get him out and now we don't have a choice in the matter. I'm here. I know him and none of your troops do. Don't you think we have to be sure it's him, even if there's a small chance we're being led into a trap?"

"He's given us information on the land, the politics, how the tribes are building up their arms and where they are strongest. I doubt he would do that if it was a trap."

"I agree, but he may be followed, you don't know. You've had him for longer than he wanted and we don't know what's happening there. His mission has been highly dangerous and his position could be compromised."

"We don't have long to get a team together," the general said.

"Just get me into Israel. I need four men plus supplies, and medics on standby. And make one of those guys Corporal Dave Smith. He was in my unit on one of my tours before. I need him. I'll do the rest. The captain must be in trouble, so we have to get him out, and now."

A few weeks previously Sean had left the hospital where Cydney was recovering and made the call to General Bowles-Smith's office immediately. He had no idea if it was the right thing to do or not, but if Cydney was in danger Steve needed to know, never mind that he had been forced to remain under cover in the field a year longer than necessary. It had been the wrong decision, in his opinion. They should have allowed the man to come home to his family. He knew his heart was ruling him in this but his army head understood, nevertheless, that the combined Governments were doing the right thing by gaining more information that Steve could feed them on the rising situation in Syria. What better plant could they have than someone who had been there for nearly four years, was known and had fully integrated into the community and could come and go without anyone questioning him? Invaluable, but the captain was being used and was potentially a target for the insurgents. His luck couldn't run for ever.

Now all Sean had to do was try to extricate himself from Cydney for a few days, which was going to be difficult, especially when he knew she needed him more than ever. Everything was falling apart around her. Her mother was ill, George had gone, the case with Rayshel was hopefully about to reach a climax and there was the possibility somebody was after her.

Sean wished George was still around. The guy was troubled, clearly, but he had Cydney and the kids' best interests at heart - which was the most important thing. Hang on...what on earth was he thinking? He was about to go and get Cydney's husband! And then what? *Oh, by the way, look who's come back from the dead!* How was he supposed to deal with that one?

He certainly needed the luck of the Irish to get him through the next few weeks.

Steve had heard a strange *click* on the phone, which is why he'd put the receiver down so quickly. Was somebody else listening to the conversation? Was he being watched? He hoped Sean and the general had heard him. He had five days to get to the reconnaissance point at the border near to Israel. In fact, he probably needed double that as he doubted there was enough strength left in him to reach that point.

He stood in the hallway of the hostel that had cost him yet another week's wages in bribes to the manager and looked outside for several minutes. Everything looked normal as far as he could see, people still going about their business. There were no unusual cars parked nearby, nor people lurking about on the street corners or potentially watching him. He needed to get to a position where he could wait out until nightfall, then make his way to the lying up point that had taken him originally a few hours on foot, but he guessed was going to take him slightly longer now.

His mind and all his senses were alert as he left the hostel and made his way down the street and towards the north east corner and out via Bab Tuma gate to get away from the town. Every so often he stopped on the pretext of attending to the laces on his old white plimsolls, and took a moment to look over his shoulder to make sure he wasn't being followed. All he had on him was a knife given to him by Bin Amadi, as some form of protection, but it would be useless against a team of soldiers. Perhaps he was being paranoid, but as he turned a corner of the street he kept his back to the wall and looked around carefully, just in case.

Walking further along the road, he was beginning to feel less on edge when there was a sudden loud bang from behind him like a gun firing. He sprung into action, pulled the knife from inside his jacket and took cover in a doorway, ready to fight, ready to stay alive. The second gunfire was even louder and seemed to echo down the street. Fearing for his life, he remained hidden but fully expected a platoon of soldiers to descend upon him; he knew the risk of capture was imminent. He waited where he was, not wanting to reveal his position, but after a few moments there was silence. He peered round the corner and saw a somewhat battered truck and realised, with a sigh of relief, that the noise had come from its backfiring exhaust. Christ almighty! His nerves really were on edge. He crept out from his hiding place and approached the car but when he saw the driver and his wife staring at him, wide-eyed with fear, he realised the knife was still firmly gripped in his hand.

"Please don't kill us, leave us alone!" the woman yelled.

He withdrew the knife and hid it away, then stood up straight and signalled for them to drive off. The truck came towards him, stopped, and the man wound down the window.

"Get in cousin, I can take you out of town."

Steve looked at the man and recognised him as one of Salim's older cousins who lived in a nearby village. They had met on several occasions socially and during secret meetings regarding the Syrian regime. Relief washed over him as he looked into the cousin's weatherworn face.

"Quickly. Hide down at the back and throw the blanket over you."

A quick-fire string of words followed him into the truck.

"You can't do this! He is mad, he'll kill us! We'll be found out, tortured, and killed. Leave him to his chances, think of our children!"

"Wife, be quiet. I will do exactly what I want. He's family."

Steve crawled down behind the front seats. The blanket roughly covered him but it smelt like goat's pee and he could just about breathe through it. As the truck drove on, with the exhaust banging out noisily every so often, he felt every single bump. The roads were not built well and there were pits every foot or so, which caused his body to be tossed around as the truck manoeuvred over them, moving its way precariously from side to side and flinging Steve up from his position. At six feet tall he was not made to crouch, and after half an hour his muscles were aching so badly that it felt as if he had banged each and every bone in his body. He tried to ignore the discomfort, and the wife who was still making noises at her husband in front of him. Instead, he concentrated his mind on what was ahead of him and what he had to do to get home.

His thoughts lingered every so often on his life for the last four years. He had so many regrets – that he'd been injured and had lost his memory, that he hadn't been strong enough to say no when the Government had asked him, or rather ordered him to stay longer. His biggest regret concerned Cydney and the fact he wasn't home with her and the twins now, especially following the message that the 'walnut tree was hurt'. They were his chosen, pre-arranged words to be used to verify his identify if a situation arose, and if his wife's life was ever in danger. Impatience was not one of his better traits. Now he wanted to get home, and in the least possible time in case Cydney really was hurt, or worse. He feared his life would be over before he even had a chance to return, unless of course he could pull himself together and actually concentrate on what he was supposed to be doing. He was an officer in the Special Forces and it was about time he remembered that. His mind was alert without any doubt, but he hoped and prayed his body wouldn't let him down.

After about an hour of travelling the car stopped and the man got out, releasing Steve from his numbed position. As he stood up the blood rushed back to his limbs and he felt the intensity of the pins and needles tingling all over his body. He shook his arms and legs, stamped his feet for several seconds and tried to walk around until he felt able to go on. The wife sat in the passenger seat staring at him, still mumbling obscenities under her breath. He didn't feel anger towards her, only pity she felt so frightened to help him and was being forced to do something by her husband against her will. The face of the woman staring at him was not only full of disillusionment and fear, but red-faced with anger. The fact she was clearly overweight made her look old beyond her years, but living in dire circumstances and having many babies did that to the local women. Steve had seen it so many times, when once slim and attractive girls lost their femininity upon marriage, especially when faced with abject poverty.

The man handed him some water and a cloth containing some bread and goat's cheese and after thanking him profusely, Steve set off on his own. He knew the terrain well and prayed to every god imaginable he'd be able to find all the equipment they had packed away some four years earlier, which would enable him to get out of this hell-hole: night vision goggles, warmer clothes suitable for the freezing nights, food to sustain him for a day or two until he reached the next point, but more importantly, guns and ammunition – in case he needed them. He had a strange feeling he would.

CHAPTER TWENTY-TWO

CYDNEY strode into the Ritz the following week for the dinner planned with Robert Crossley, the first time without her walking stick. She adored the hotel that spoke of wealth of days gone by; it always brought out the romantic in her with its grandiose décor and elegance. She and Steve had often come here for afternoon tea in The Palm Court where famous people used to go to see and be seen. She loved the dramatic design with the high walls of mirrors, the wonderful golden trellised ceiling, and the resident pianist playing tunes in the background. Everything was so quintessentially British. She stood in the reception area and looked around her, breathing in the history.

"Mrs Granger, good evening."

She turned at the mention of her name and found herself in front of Robert Crossley, who had obviously been waiting for her to arrive. Meeting him for the second time created feelings in her she couldn't disregard. It wasn't exactly hatred, but he made her skin crawl, which she couldn't ignore. She wanted to know this man, what made him tick, and this innate curiosity in her was not going to disappear until it was satisfied.

"Ah, you also admire the Ritz," he went on. "I can see from the way you stood when you came in. It always amazes me as an American in London how they get away with the mix of French Louis XVI furnishings but still remain so very English."

So, he had been watching her.

"It dates back to the early 1900s, an Anglo-French design

project. Yes, I do love this place. Thank you for inviting me here," Cydney said, remaining polite.

Crossley took her arm in such a way that she was unable to break free without appearing rude. So, was he of the old school or just trying to take the upper hand and tell her directly who was in charge of this meeting? When Steve or George had taken her arm, it was done out of love, courtesy, a way of protecting her. This felt completely the opposite, but if he thought she was going to be intimidated he was clearly underestimating her.

"Shall we go into dinner? I've booked a private room for us and asked them to put the Dom Perignon on ice."

That was presumptuous, Cydney thought. Again, controlling the evening. Why weren't they in the main dining room? What did he have to say to her that was so private he couldn't risk being overheard?

"How lovely of you, Mr Crossley, or can I call you Robert?"

"Bob is fine - all my friends call me that. Robert seems so formal, don't you think? And I do intend for us to be friends."

Why would she want to be friends? He didn't even know her. Being friends was the furthest thought from her mind.

One of the staff led them down the corridor towards the left, Crossley's arm never leaving her, and into the Queen Elizabeth private dining room. It was sumptuously laid with pure-white tablecloths, matching napkins placed in silver rings, and silver chargers on which sat three bone china white plates in various sizes. The centrepiece was a massive floral display of summer flowers in golds, reds and yellows, which emitted the most amazing perfume. The champagne was there, as advised, and the immaculately presented sommelier was ready and waiting to serve it into tall, gold-rimmed flutes. Cydney couldn't help but be impressed at this show of wealth. She took the flute and sipped at the champagne, feeling the cold liquid slip down her throat.

"This is beautiful, Bob." She couldn't lie, despite all her misgivings.

"Glad you like it. You must try some of this caviar. They have it especially flown in for me from Moscow. My favourite in the world. Here..." and he scooped a large helping onto one of the small crackers presented on a tray by another waiter.

"You've stayed here before then?" Cydney questioned with a slight smile.

Crossley laughed at the comment.

"Oh yes, I'm well known here. I have a few business interests in London, some properties I'm involved in. I often come here and always stay in the Prince of Wales suite."

Cydney was surprised at the fact he mentioned his business interests. She looked him up and down. He was dressed well again, in a beautifully tailored navy suit with his striped tie fashionably knotted. She looked down at his wrist. A good watch was always a giveaway and, predictably, he was wearing a Rolex, but not a design she recognised so it must have been custom made. Cydney was not usually one to make assumptions about someone's worth but he was clearly giving off an impression of tremendous wealth.

"Anyway, Cydney, I assume I can call you that now, please tell me all about yourself, although of course I know quite a lot about your company as you're well known in the corporate world."

"You've done your homework."

"Of course, my dear. Why wouldn't I want to know beforehand about a beautiful lady whom I've invited to dine with me? I've no doubt you have done the same."

Cydney and Crossley chatted generally whilst the waiters flitted unobtrusively around them, serving hors d'oeuvres. Cydney, despite everything, found herself talking about her children but every time she asked a question about him or his interests, he skirted the subject and turned it around.

They had almost finished eating the most exquisite lamb, which melted into Cydney's mouth, when he asked the one question that floored her.

"So tell me, Cydney, how do you know George? I saw he was with you at the reception when we met."

Cydney looked out of the room and across at Green Park, trying to regain her composure for a few seconds, without giving away that she was doing so.

"George? Why do you ask, do you know him?"

"Oh yes, Cydney, I do. And extremely well. He is my half-brother, much younger of course."

Crossley's voice didn't change at all. He carried on eating as if he had said nothing at all out of the ordinary, whereas Cydney nearly choked. She grabbed hold of the red wine and took a mouthful.

"Ah, I see I have surprised you, my dear. So you didn't know, clearly. He has been a mysterious boy, hasn't he?"

"I'm sorry but I don't understand. He's your half-brother?"

"My father had the misfortune to marry his mother and he was the result. Awful woman, after my father's money from the start. Came from nothing. She was his secretary and latched on when my mother died. I tried to break it up, of course, but father was having none of it. Unfortunately, he died but left everything in a trust fund for both of us. I put him through Harvard Law. His mother was a complete waste of space. I got her out of the house as soon as I could, so I wouldn't have to see her anymore. George has been after my money for years now and did all he could to break me. In fact, I got him his first job in the New York law firm to try to help him out, as I knew he was never going to make it on his own. Then he disappeared, after his mother thankfully died. I didn't even bother to look for him, no point as we didn't get on and I was better off without him. Now he's turned up with you. My goodness, dear, you look quite pale. I thought you were unshockable."

Cydney stood up and pushed her chair back, glaring at him. She picked up her handbag and as she headed towards the door that familiar feeling arrived, sending cold shivers down her right arm.

"My name is Angela. I'm George's mother."

Cydney stopped in her tracks and the image came through to her of a quite beautiful woman, with shoulder length dark hair, dressed in a simple blue suit.

"Now, don't be so dramatic. Sit down and finish your meal," Crossley pressed. "At least tell me what this brother of mine has been up to."

"I can't believe you got me here on this pretence! So much for talking about business. All this, for what? To put down a friend of mine and play with me? Why? I doubt it's because you care about me, or him for that matter. You just admitted you don't. So what good could it possibly do?"

"Do calm down, Cydney. You must really love this brother of mine, or half-brother should I say. I can't possibly see why, or what redeeming features he may have."

"Well, we can't all be like you, can we?" Cydney made a mental note to be careful what she said in anger.

"I'm sure you have done your homework, as I said earlier, and the meal was so pleasant. Oh, do just sit. I hate to get indigestion."

Cydney stared at him. His facial expression hadn't changed one iota. His demeanour was extremely calm, although his face was turning slightly pale and his eyes looked pained. She watched him as he popped a pill and swallowed it with some water. What was all that about? The spirit of George's mother came nearer to the table and stood to the side of Crossley, watching and listening.

"Do excuse me," he said. "Obviously the matter's distasteful. I really did all I could for George. For years after our father died I tried to do the best for him but he threw it back in my face. In fact, he stole many thousands from the Trust Fund. The trustees were part of the law firm where he worked. We had no idea, until the annual audit, and by that time he'd flown the nest. I couldn't be bothered to find him, it would have been a waste of time. He'd probably spent the money anyway, so what would be the point?"

"Don't believe him. This isn't the truth, he's bending everything! My husband and I loved each other very much. George was born out of that but my stepson couldn't take it. George never took the money. Robert gave it to him. He hated both of us, and the fact I'd replaced his mother. My husband and his first wife didn't get on for years, I saw it all every day when I was working in the office. Robert was a taker, selfish and thoroughly spoilt. Please believe me."

Cydney tried to picture the young George in her mind. If the truth be told, apart from a few general things, she actually knew nothing about him, such as where he was born or how he grew up. It was hard to digest what Crossley was saying to her. Was it true about George being a thief, a fraudster, a liar? It was questionable why Angela would come through and give Cydney information, as she had nothing to gain. The worst thing was knowing that he may have deceived her and the twins, and that Sean had been right all along. Cydney's world was about to fall even further apart and the urgency of wanting to get away from the smug man in front of her was uppermost in her thoughts. She needed time to filter everything, put it straight in her mind. Her thoughts went back to the reception when she had first met Crossley. It was true George had walked out on the pretext of a headache, and he was in a strange mood, especially when he'd returned and was introduced to Crossley. That must have been a trauma in itself, and then there was all the work she and the team had been doing for Rupert on Crossley's companies. George must have known all about it and said nothing but, on the other hand, here was George's mother telling her Crossley was lying through his teeth.

"Bob," the name grated on her even as she spoke it aloud. "I should go. Thank you for the most enlightening evening. I don't know what you have gained from it, but I hope you have enjoyed yourself." The sarcasm wasn't lost on the man.

As she once again tried to leave the room, Crossley made his last passing shot.

"Oh, by the way, tell your friend Rupert he can have my company. He doesn't have to get you to go to so many lengths to find out about me and everything else. I'm willing to talk at the right price. Actually, my health isn't good and I've been given only a few months to live. My preference would be to sell it to Rupert rather than let it fall into someone else's hands. I know he thinks I did him wrong, but in fact it wasn't me at all."

You could have knocked Cydney over with a feather.

"Cydney, let's not play games, we're both adults. I know about your relationship with Rupert and I know you have been delving into my various companies and their background. Perhaps it would be much easier if you actually got the information from the horse's mouth, so to speak. I do hate people going behind my back, it feels so nasty."

"Please watch him carefully. He wants something from you. He always did get his way however it was possible and with whatever the consequences."

Cydney returned to her chair and sat down, crossing her legs to face up to Crossley. She was now determined to hear more.

"Please proceed. I can't wait to hear all about this."

"You of course know of my brother-in-law, Craig Benton. We started on very good terms. We were at Harvard Business together and that's how I met his sister. She's nothing like him. We got on immediately, fell in love, and eventually married a few years later. By that time I was very much involved with Craig and we set up a business together with a view to floating companies on the New York stock exchange, in return for which we would take a position, normally a percentage of the shares, sometimes as high as twenty-five percent. We helped raise the capital for the flotation and sold the idea to various media firms who brought in the investors. It was quite easy, really, and goes on all the time. These companies were involved in mining in Canada, mineral extraction in various parts of the world, property development. You name it, we were able to do it. Sometimes the companies floated, got their investment but never really did anything else."

"So the investors lost out. But you got your money?" Cydney questioned.

"Oh yes, within a couple of years we were making millions. Built up a reputation and the money kept rolling in. You see, we always got our return quite quickly as part of the deal we made. After that, we had no interest in the companies, or what they did. Nothing to do with us and we made it clear at the beginning. We helped the shares to rise once the companies were floated and then we sold out quickly."

"Was that legal?"

"At the time we were young and these sorts of things were never investigated. However, as time went on, I didn't like what Benton was doing. I felt we were taking investors' monies, and then letting them get on with it, not caring whether they lost their savings or not."

"That's not true at all. He took money wherever he could. He made some of the investors' lives a misery as many lost their entire savings. It was awful. I watched and could do nothing about it. George tried but we had no money without Robert. We were reliant on the trustees and Robert had them firmly under his control."

"So what about American Securities?"

"Yes, I will come to that. I decided to break loose from our company and when I told Benton he was livid, saying we were in it together for life. With what he knew, he'd make sure I ended up in jail, and wouldn't his sister love that? Well, I had no option. I had a wife and three children to support, so we carried on and diversified along the way, but in the background. At the same time, Benton was asked to head up American Securities. He had the experience and he was the right man for the job. However, we didn't know it was about to go into Chapter 11, or at least I didn't."

"So what were you doing at the time?"

"I was involved with Caxton Trust Bank. Benton got me a non-exec Chairman role for a huge fee."

"So it was all about the money?"

"Well, I can't say it didn't matter but I was nervous at the time and worried I would lose everything, including my wife, so I kept quiet."

"But it was that bank which bought out American Securities when it was in Chapter 11."

"Yes, I know – Benton was behind it all."

"See how he moves the blame from himself and doesn't take responsibility? Ask him how and why he was so beholden to Benton."

"You were in business together, so you must have known what was happening and what he was up to. As far as I understand things, you did some devious deal to get the bank out of Rupert's grasp."

"Well, I admit it was a very nice deal for us, but it was my brother-in-law who negotiated everything. I went along on the face of things, hoping the IRS wouldn't look too closely at things, as I knew if they did I would be the scapegoat."

"So you were clearly involved in insider dealing."

"Not nice words, Cydney. I did nothing wrong, I held the position at the bank and got on with things."

"How can he say this? He used my son!"

"So how does George come into this?" Cydney asked.

"Ah yes, the wonderful George who can do no wrong. Good looking isn't he? Takes after his mother. She was certainly a looker, but then whores often are."

Cydney glanced across at the woman next to her. She looked so sad.

"He tried it on with me but I rejected him, which is why he's so bitter. He was jealous of the love I had with his father and of how we treated George. Then he got involved with Benton. The only good thing to come out of it was his wife and children, who I must say he adores."

"Why whore? Did she reject you?"

"Stupid woman preferred an older man to me, when I could have given her so much more."

"Then you met your wife?"

Crossley's eyes softened momentarily.

"Yes, she's supported me throughout but sees her brother through rose-tinted glasses. Anyway, back to George. He was working at the law firm. Benton got him to set up a structure under the family trust, to protect us from the potential fall out of the American Securities deal."

"But why did he do it, knowing it was wrong?"

"His mother was dead by then and we promised to pay him a good sum to get out of the country, away from all of us. We only needed him to do one thing and that was to keep our names out of it."

"They held him to ransom, he had no choice. My darling George was innocent. He was given the money, he didn't steal it."

"So you blackmailed him. I see a familiar pattern emerging here."

"I was trying to protect myself. It wasn't blackmail from me, although Benton probably had a little more to say to George."

"What happened then? Was that when you bought this portfolio of properties in London?"

"With some financing help."

"Which is now disappearing," Cydney commented.

"Ah, more homework I see."

"So why did George steal monies from the trust fund? You say you gave him money to escape from your clutches."

"I wouldn't put it that way - more to help him get away. It obviously wasn't enough as he took beyond what he was entitled to."

"No he did not. They put more in his bank account to make it look like it was stolen. Then George suddenly and tellingly left New York."

"I don't believe he'd do that, I know George."

"Well, why did he run away, answer me that?"

"Perhaps he wanted to escape from you."

"As I said earlier, tell Rupert he can have whatever he wants

203

now. I've sorted out my wife and children financially, and Benton can rot in hell for all I care."

"You need to warn George, tell him all you know. I can see him and he's very sad now. He needs you in his life. He'll tell you the truth and will guide you as to what to do about Robert and his brother-in-law. But do be careful. Robert will shortly have to prove himself to someone higher than you, and Benton is dangerous. He's got nothing to lose now." With that said, she faded out of Cydney's sight.

"I'm leaving now but I'll be back in touch. I have to think through what you've told me. I'll speak to Rupert as you suggest, but I need to be clear on everything. To be honest, I think you're just trying to protect yourself, although what good it will do is anyone's guess."

Without a further word, Cydney once again stood and walked towards the door. At the last minute she turned round and looked at Crossley. He simply raised his glass of champagne to her and waved her away dismissively with the back of his hand.

CHAPTER TWENTY-THREE

THE clack of Cydney's stilettos as she made her way towards Richard's room echoed down the hospital corridor. He'd been waking up on and off for the last week and was slowly coming out of his coma. She was still reeling from the events of the evening with Crossley but now turned her attention to her friend, and with all her being willed him to get better. Despite feeling completely alone, especially as Sean had asked for a few days off to visit an ailing aunt in Ireland and she'd reluctantly agreed to let him go, she would deal with those feelings later. Now was the time to concentrate on Richard.

Entering the room, she was shocked to see him lying there, several of the tubes gone and a smile growing on his face when he saw who it was.

"So you decided to re-join the land of the living then?" she joked.

"You can't keep a good man down."

Cydney sat down next to him and took hold of his hand.

"We were so worried about you," she said gently, looking into his eyes for any signs of pain. "How are you feeling, if that's not a stupid question?"

"Like I've been battered by a tornado. For the life of me, I can't remember the accident. You have a mark on your head, was that anything to do with it?"

"Richard, I don't think we should go into that now. I just want you to get better, for all of us."

"I do get flashbacks, Cydney. If only I could piece it all together. Anyway, I'm glad you're here." He squeezed her hand.

"Don't look so worried, I'm fine now. Be up and about in no time, once they get this plaster thing off me." He tentatively moved his arm. "Be glad to get back to work."

"I don't think we should rush that, do you? As much as I want you back, I'd prefer you to concentrate on getting better, take one step at a time – and you have your wife and sons to think about. Where is Christine, by the way?"

"Oh, she's been with me all night and only left a short while ago. I sent her home for some sleep. I feel so awful causing all this grief for everyone, you know how I hate fuss."

"Sean sends his best wishes. He's gone back to Ireland for a few days but he's been worried about you. We all have."

"That old reprobate. By the way, what's happening with our friend, that solicitor? Can't remember his name, but I know we were working on something or other."

"Harper. Yes, that's progressing," and Cydney slowly brought Richard up to date on the case.

"Cydney, I'm going to be out of action for a while now, you know that. I have a very good friend, Tom Patterson. He was working for me in the Fraud Squad before I left and has now set up a private security firm. I think you should call him and let him help you on this. With Sean away, and me laid up, you need somebody you can rely on, and Tom's that guy."

"That's a good idea. Give me his number and I'll call him later. You're definitely looking tired now, Richard. I'm going to let you get some peace and quiet. I'll be back tomorrow," and she leant over and planted a kiss on his forehead.

"Well it was worth being in hospital just for that," he laughed, and Cydney joined in, pleased he was showing signs of being on the road to recovery.

She met with Tom later that day in her office. He was younger than Richard, shorter and fitter with his blond hair worn slightly longer, although there were early signs of baldness to the front of his head. She noted to herself that he had the bearing of a police officer that he would most likely never lose, whether in uniform or out. Bit like the army.

"Thank you so much for coming in at short notice. Richard's highly recommended you."

"He was a great chief. Anythin' I can do to help, I will."

"I'd appreciate your assistance on a case I'm working on. To be honest, I really don't know whether we should involve the police in this now, or see it through and then present it to them as a fait accompli. I don't think we can avoid bringing them in sooner or later and I could do with your advice."

"Well, why don't ya tell me what ya know and I'll see what I can do? I never used to condone members of the public doin' things on their own when I was in the force, but I look at things a bit different now."

Cydney appreciated Tom's pragmatic attitude and she began to explain where they were with Charles Gordon, William Harper and his wife.

"Mrs Granger, how come you're involved in this in the first place? From what I gather, this ain't your normal line of work. I thought you were more international, bigger clients."

Cydney wondered if she could be honest and tell him that Ray Gordon had come to her in spirit while she was in a taxi going to a meeting. It was not something anyone would easily accept and she decided not to let that one out of the bag.

"Ray Gordon and his wife are old friends of the family. He died suddenly of a heart attack a few months ago and Sheila asked me to help. She was desperate and had nowhere else to turn. Since then we've discovered their solicitor is being blackmailed by Charles Gordon, and he fraudulently prepared a second Will, maybe even the first one, allegedly signed by Ray, in favour of Charles and bypassing Sheila and their three kids."

"So they get nothin'?"

"Exactly, and it gets worse. It seems the shares in their

company, Rayshel Plastics, and all their property and land are now in the hands of Charles and not Sheila."

"How did that 'appen?"

"Charles got Ray to sign papers giving him rights on his death. Ray never understood what was happening and thought he could trust his brother. Yes, it was naïve but he thought he was doing the right thing for his family and believed Charles would look after his wife and children."

"Which clearly he ain't gonna do, right?"

"Correct. From what I've learned so far, he's a nasty piece of work and we need to watch our step. He's been having his brother's family house watched. Now, with his ownership, albeit fraudulently obtained, he's trying to sell the land to Prestons."

"The supermarket company?"

"Yep. They're ready to bite any day now, but wouldn't if they knew what was happening. One further thing, Harper's wife's also involved. She's having an affair with Charles. They have a company, Intervest Holdings, which owns the land that used to belong to Rayshel."

"When ya say 'used to', what d'ya mean exactly?"

"Again, Charles must have signed over the land to Intervest without Ray knowing. That's the only explanation."

"Audacious, ain't he? How could he possibly believe what he's doin' wouldn't be found out?"

"Well, he probably thought with Harper in on it, being a solicitor, that everything was safe, and then once the money was in his pocket he could escape overseas with Patricia Harper and that would be the end of it."

"He's a bit clueless then. You've done good to uncover all this so far. Anythin' else? By the look on your face, I get the feelin' you're not telling me everythin'. Why's Harper bein' blackmailed? What's Charles got on the man?"

Cydney was beginning to feel very comfortable with Tom and, what's more, appreciated his pragmatic approach. He took everything in she was telling him and made simple but apt observations, which she liked.

"Charles took photos of a very drunk Harper in the most compromising of positions and threatened to tell Patricia."

"What, even though they're 'avin' an affair?"

"Yes. Harper's obviously still in love with his wife, oddly, although he denies it quite vehemently. He thinks that if he keeps to the plan Charles has set up, he will see him off and away and Harper can get on with his life. Maybe even with Patricia."

"That's never gonna 'appen, is it?"

"Not in a million years."

"What's this Patricia like then? D'ya think she knows about the pictures?"

"Personally, I think she and Charles set everything up, but we're working on proving that theory. She clearly wears the trousers and, having met Harper, I can understand why she's gone for the younger and better looking Charles."

"So what's our next move?"

Cydney liked the way he'd said 'our' next move.

"We've confronted Harper and he's now working with us, realising he has little choice. He knows he's going to end up in jail but isn't going to go down alone. He'll take Charles and Patricia with him."

"So, do we approach Prestons and see if they're willin' to help?"

"Might be a good idea," Cydney said. "My goal is to ensure Sheila gets everything Ray wanted her to have."

"And the police?"

"Well, that's where you come in, Tom. You must know people in the Fraud Squad. If we all work together, we could catch them before they get away with everything. What do you reckon?"

"I've got a mate who's a Detective Sergeant at Edgware Road. I'll speak to 'im but I've a feelin' there's even more you're keepin' from me."

"Tom, I need to know who tried to kill me and Richard."

CHAPTER TWENTY-FOUR

THE plane taxied to a standstill at Ben Gurion International Airport and Sean gazed out at the blue skies and perfect August sunshine of Tel Aviv. He disembarked and made his way along the moving walkways and escalators and down to passport control on the ground level. He hadn't been there for four years and had forgotten how far it was to get out of the place. As he reached security, two uniformed officers of the Israeli forces met him so he was able to bypass the normal luggage checks.

Walking to the waiting car from the air-conditioned building, Sean was hit by the sheer force of the heat descending over him. The sun was at its highest now and he shrugged off his leather jacket to reveal bands of sweat that were already appearing on his t-shirt. One of the officers informed him they would be going to the military base on the border of the Golan Heights where he would join his troops.

The journey was over one hundred miles from the airport to the north of Israel, during which Sean had plenty of time to think, since his companions remained silent throughout. However, he couldn't help but admire the views of the ancient and ruined settlements on the way. He passed the sacred baptismal site on the banks of the River Jordan and continued towards Hammat Gader, the hot springs on the edge of the Syrian and Jordanian border. As they approached Mount Avital Military Base he could see Mount Bental in the distance, towering above the Golan plateau. Despite the magnificent scenery, Sean needed to turn to the task in hand, knowing this was no time to let his mind wander.

On arrival, Sean was taken through Base security and into a room where he met the four British serving Special Forces men who would be working with him. They were a typical bunch, large and brawny and dressed in desert fatigues, but more importantly young and fit, as he once was. But his work was not to play soldier so much as to ensure it really was Steve they were bringing out. The advantage he had was that he knew the terrain and where the captain would be heading. The plan was to allow him five days to reach the rendezvous point, and to get the helicopter there at the allotted time. Once there, they'd wait the agreed ten minutes, then leave and return the next day, and keep doing so for a reasonable amount of time until the captain turned up. Sean knew Steve would understand and that if he missed the RP he'd return if he was able - that was the key. It sounded easy but in practice it was going to be hell, and he doubted the Syrians would appreciate a helicopter flying into their airspace.

The border with Syria was well supported by Hezbollah and there were constant attacks on Israel on the once-quiet frontier. It was a dangerous mission, no getting away from it, but the four guys in front of him had been chosen for their experience. Now all they had to do was plan for every eventuality. Despite the danger, Sean was in his element and couldn't believe how much he'd missed being in the field. Everything he'd learned in the forces came back to him as he briefed the guys as to what to expect on this mission - get in, get their guy, and get the bloody hell out.

"Corporal, can we have a private word please." Sean walked Dave out to another room.

"How are you lad? Sophie's missing you but I'm pleased you're here. I need someone around me like you on this mission."

"I miss her too. I was hoping to get home until this came up. You weren't thinking of her when you requested me." He laughed but Sean could tell he wasn't that happy. "So tell me, what's it all about. I've not really been briefed – just told to get my arse out here."

211

"Okay. So what exactly do you know?"

"All we were told is that we were here to 'collect' one of our guys out of Syria, and stat."

"Absolutely true. Except that the person in question is Captain Steve Granger. The others don't know so keep it quiet between us."

"What the fuck! You're kidding me, right? Mrs Granger's husband. The one who died a few years ago?"

"You said it. I'm still in shock, and that's the truth."

"Well, if it is him, you know there's no room for failure here."

"Exactly, Dave. So from now on, this is strictly business. But I'm glad you're on board, son."

"Talking of which, how is my Sophie? Christ I miss her."

"She's fine. When are you getting married? She desperately wants that ring on her finger. And I want my girl happy."

"As soon as I can get home. And you're not helping matters."

"I'll buy you a Guinness tonight and we can chat a bit more. Now let's go prepare the guys."

Steve found the going more than hard and the rugged terrain he thought he knew wasn't at all as he remembered. He'd set off around nightfall after the man and his wife had dropped him off and six hours later, exhausted, freezing and hungry, he eventually arrived at his lying up point, just before the sun was about to rise.

The cave was carved out of a sheer rock face surrounded by dark volcanic boulders and everywhere had looked the same to him. The memory of it being near a waterfall had vaguely come back to him but as it was summer he knew it would be dried up and, after four years, hidden behind overgrown bushes, which would make the search so much more difficult. He had been going around in circles all night and was cross and frustrated with himself for losing his way, along with precious time. The idea was to rest up and be ready to move again when the sun

212

went down and there was some doubt in his mind whether he would be able to make the time up.

Once he'd found the place, locating the gear was another obstacle to overcome, mainly due to his memory. He had some recollection that everything was a few yards in and buried just below the surface. However, animal droppings covered the ground and it smelt like death itself. It was extremely difficult to breathe even, especially as there was little air, and he had to crawl on all fours.

When he eventually found the area he wanted, it took some time to dig into the solid ground. His hands were bleeding and sore and his knees scraped beneath his thin cotton trousers, but he almost screamed with joy to find everything. He grabbed the sealed packets of food stock but after opening them tossed each one away in anger. They had all perished. Thankfully, the sleeping roll was still unharmed so he unravelled it and threw it around himself to ward off the cold.

Although there was still a cooking stove there was nothing to cook on it, and even if there had been it was far too dangerous. He could not leave any evidence of his being there, not even of his basic bodily functions. He had to move on without trace.

The hunger was getting to him. He found a pack of cigarettes and a disposable lighter, but he hadn't smoked for years. Regardless of the fact, he knew this would kill his appetite so he lit one up, careful to cover the lit tip that could possibly be seen from miles around. He dragged deeply, feeling the smoke hit his lungs. The resultant violent coughing lasted for several seconds. Christ, and people enjoy this, he thought. He stubbed out the cigarette, placed it in his backpack and reached for the 9mm Browning, pleased to note he had two clips with about twenty rounds in each. That should be enough if he needed it, plus he had the larger Heckler and Koch MP5 with plenty of ammo. The guns needed to be loaded in readiness and he managed this by feeling around in the semi- darkness. The torch and batteries that had been in the bag were rusted away and useless, as he'd half expected. Everything else could wait until he was ready to move off again. Now he needed to bed down for a few hours and regain his strength, so he curled up with the sleeping roll around him and drifted off into dreamless unconsciousness.

The sun woke him later, finding its way into the cave in shafts of light, after what must have been several hours of sleep. It took a while for him to remember where he was and he tried to take in his surroundings, expecting to be in the village still. Then just as it hit him, the sound of rustling from outside the cave alerted him to possible danger. Shedding off the sleeping roll, he reached for the nearest weapon and ran back to crouch down behind a boulder and waited, ready to fire at any moment. The darkness of the cave prevented him from working out who was there. The noise continued and seemed to come closer but he remained hidden. He was not ready to die after everything that had happened and if someone was after him he was not going without a bloody good fight.

A twig snapped, and then another. The bushes outside the cave rustled and Steve's heart raced. Was there more than one of them after him? For a moment he questioned his strength and whether he was capable of fending anyone off. However, he did have the upper hand having adjusted to the darkness of his surroundings, whereas anyone coming in from the light would need a few moments to get their bearings.

When a shadow cast itself over the entrance Steve aimed his gun, ready to fire, his finger poised, every sense alert. The shadow came into focus. He was ready, but with an audible sigh of relief he saw it was only a very old dog, obviously foraging for food. Steve sat back and lowered his gun. The animal was small and extremely thin and for a moment he contemplated giving it the spoiled food as there was no way he could consume it, even though he would need anything he could get his hands on to reach Sean. He hoped the dog was simply lost and there were no villagers nearby who would be prepared to give him up to any local patrols for the mere price of a day's food supply in exchange.

For the past year, he had been living in danger and putting his new-found family and the entire village at risk. By working as a baker he was able to move around from village to town without attracting suspicion, chatting with the locals, ingratiating himself into their lives and finding out what was going on within the various tribes. All the information was collated in his mind and sent back to the general's staff via the ancient wireless set that he had been given, but which took him some time to master with its hand-cranked dynamo.

The call sign given to him when the mission had begun remained unchanged – G8BLW. That, plus his identity, provided the proof HQ needed, but he hated what he did because his mind was set on returning home. The only comfort was the belief he was supplying invaluable information to the various governments. Everything was about the get-out plan and each night he would return to the village and, from time to time, see Mira.

The looks she gave him portrayed fear in her eyes, betrayal almost, because he recognised the love she had for him and the knowledge he would leave her and return to his normal life. Steve could do nothing about that love as every one of his thoughts was about Cydney.

Sitting in the cave and chewing the old dogmeat, because the provisions had been inedible, he thought of Mira, who was without a doubt his saviour. She'd nursed him back to health when everyone had given him up for dead, kept his secret with risk to herself, and now he had left as she'd expected and without a goodbye. Whatever she was doing now with her sister, it was his greatest wish that she was happy and safe. He did love her in a way, not passionately as with Cydney, more as a protector than a lover. She was a light in his life that would always be there no matter what, never extinguishing, and he would be grateful to her every single day for the rest of his life, however long that may be.

Steve readied himself for the long few days ahead. He had his rucksack prepared with as much as he could carry without causing him to slow down. Thankfully, the map that had been left had not disintegrated over time and he had his compass. He remembered clearly the six digit coordinates for the rendezvous point where Sean would pick him up. He needed to plan how to get there, take the route least expected and the most difficult possible, over the top of the mountain, avoiding roads and checkpoints. His best bet was to move fast across the terrain at night, navigating by the stars and his compass, and bed down during the day somewhere safe to get what rest he could, conserving his energy. At least he had some food now, but water was always going to be the most difficult to obtain, unless he came across a stream. He was limiting his supplies to a few sips each hour but that was hardly going to sustain him and, furthermore, his leg was already giving him pain. Despite Salim's best efforts, he had never fully recovered from his injury. Well, he was here now, and he had no choice but to move on. However, he was worried about the task ahead of him.

The Golan Heights was occupied by Israel under an armistice with Syria, who not only wanted it back but wanted to control the borders. There were thousands of settlers in the area, both Israelis and Syrians, with settlement outposts everywhere, and he didn't want to bump into either of them. He looked like an Arab so the Israelis would probably shoot first and ask questions later, before he'd have a chance to convince them he was a British officer. The Syrians would question what he was doing in the area and then shoot. He was damned if he did and damned if he didn't. It was going to be tough and he needed every ounce of energy to get to his rendezvous point.

Three days passed and Sean was becoming increasingly impatient and worried. The helicopter was commissioned to go out on a recce every so often, testing the skies. The Syrians were either ignoring them or watching very carefully to see what they were going to do. The question was whether they knew about Steve and were waiting until the last moment to catch him. They weren't taking prisoners, especially one of the captain's calibre, and if he was caught he would be put to death without a shadow of a doubt, considering what he had been up to in the last year.

Sean spent his time poring over maps, discussing with the four Special Forces men all the alternative routes, and going through different scenarios in an attempt to take his mind off the fact that Steve's position was maybe compromised. He considered the possibility that someone would not allow the captain to get all the way to the pick-up point, that something would happen, that he would be taken or killed out of spite to teach him, or rather them, a lesson.

Another day passed. Sean was at the end of his patience and took out his frustration on the men around him. All this sitting around was grating on his nerves. He wanted to know where Steve was now, not in twenty-four or forty-eight hours. Furthermore, Cydney needed him at home and he could only push the lie about his ailing aunt so far. He looked in his wallet from time to time, looking at the picture of the couple on their wedding day. He had borrowed it from her album to give to Steve when he reached him, something to sustain him until Sean could get him home to his rightful place.

On the fifth day, with sufficient time before the appointed pick up, Sean at last went into top gear.

"Guys, let's roll."

On that command the team grabbed their kit and ran for the pad. The rotors of the helicopter were already turning and after a few seconds it took off to the east of the Golan Heights and headed towards the rendezvous point. Sean was on full alert, looking out below for sightings of someone who could be Captain Granger, although he silently admitted to himself that he was not one hundred percent convinced he would see him.

After fifteen minutes one of the men called out, "Below. Look, man down!"

Sean pulled out his binoculars and there on the ground was someone lying face down, not moving.

"Can you winch me down?" Sean shouted through his headphones to the pilot.

"You stay just where you are, Sergeant. I think we can land. Terrain looks flat. I'm gonna give it a shot."

The helicopter moved to a few metres away from the body and hovered before it landed. Sean and two of the soldiers remained inside with machine guns at the ready, while Dave and one of the others jumped out and ran towards their target. Sean followed every move anxiously until Dave signalled with a thumbs-up that they had arrived successfully. He watched as his future son-in-law turned the body over and felt for a pulse but then made a cut-throat signal.

Sean's heart was in his mouth as they lifted the lifeless body and brought it into the helicopter. After everything they'd gone through, could the unimaginable have happened? They laid the body onto the floor and Sean knelt down to look at the man he had admired for so many years and wanted so much to bring home.

It wasn't Steve.

CHAPTER TWENTY-FIVE

"OF course I know about George, Cyd. Do you really think I would employ someone without checking their background in minute detail?"

"Sorry, Rupert, I don't understand. You know Crossley is George's half-brother, and about his involvement with American Securities?"

"Yes, I never let on because I wanted George to feel secure in his job. I think he's been the fall guy for everything that's gone on with Crossley and Benton. I didn't believe George would get involved with anything like you've just told me, although I have to say I discovered most of it during my investigations. I saw it differently and, as you know, I like to take people at face value. Those two guys are crooks and I want to see their downfall."

"You're not blaming George?"

"He's been with me for some years now and is invaluable to my business. Everything that happened to him was when he was very young and I'm pretty sure he and his mother were treated badly after his father died. He was certainly held to ransom and I can't blame him for leaving the States."

"Where is he now?"

"I have no idea. He may have come back to Jo'burg but he's not been in touch. If I were you I'd just wait it out. I know it's been a shock but rest assured I have people looking for him and he will show up. He'll be feeling extremely sorry for himself and once he comes to the conclusion that he wants to do something about the situation, I have no doubt he will come to me."

"Okay, Rupert. I trust your instincts. But I…"

"I do know, Cyd. I have come to realise your relationship with him and if you do love him and he loves you then he will come back. Give him time, that's my advice."

"One more thing, which did come as a bit of a shock, when I met with Crossley he told me he was dying. Cancer, three months to live. He says you can have the property company, at a price no doubt."

"Well, well, well. So he gets to have the last word it would appear."

"He blamed everything on Benton."

"I don't believe that for a minute, do you?"

"You know, Rupert, this may sound strange and I know Bob Crossley is not a nice man but I felt a bit sorry for him for some reason. I think he's under Benton's spell."

"You're getting soft in your old age."

Cydney laughed. "Not so much of the old, although these days… Anyway, I don't believe everything he said. I think he's bent the truth to suit himself and I doubt very much he's completely the innocent party. So, what action do you want to take? Do you want this company or not?"

"If we can get all the necessary due diligence and it stacks up and there's nothing sitting there that's going to come up and bite us, then I'm willing to look."

"Why don't we get solicitors involved? Let them do their work and see what emerges. We're under no obligation."

"I agree. Deal with it Cydney and please don't forget George, he needs your forgiveness."

Cydney hung up and stared at the receiver for several moments. She felt relieved he knew about George. It gave her some comfort that George wasn't the man Crossley had made him out to be, but she wished she knew where he'd gone. Typical male, hiding out somewhere. Retreating to his cave to lick his wounds. She could scream with the frustration of it all. If only

George had opened up to her. She would have understood, but instead he'd sat there listening through all the information that she'd found out about the set-up for Rupert, and had gone with her to the dinner where his half-brother was speaking and disappeared on the pretext of a headache. Maybe Sean was right after all, and the man wasn't right for her. Did she want someone with such a chequered past, with secrets to hide from the woman he allegedly loved, who didn't deal with his responsibilities and hid away rather than facing up to everything? She was really in turmoil. Where the hell was Sean anyway, and who was this aunt that she'd never heard about? She should quiz his daughter, Sophie, and see what she knew. And she needed to know where Richard's friend, Tom was in his investigations.

There were so many unanswered questions.

Tom Patterson sat in the Metropole Hotel in Edgware Road, London, with one of his oldest friends, Jim Donaldson, who was himself now a Detective Sergeant in the Fraud Squad. They went back years to when Tom was the DS himself at Harrow Road and Jim had joined the team, straight out of Hendon training as a young police constable.

"I have some information, Tom, but this is strictly off the record. I shouldn't even be having this conversation with you. You know as well as I do what the form is on this."

"Yeah, but I'm callin' in that favour."

"I'm well aware, but this is the first and last time. After this we're quits."

"Fair enough, but I'm doin' this for my old boss," Tom reminded him.

"I know, and that's why I'm helping you. Anyway, it appears your friend's entirely correct about Charles Gordon. I checked back on his records and he's been in trouble over the years but fairly quiet for the last few. This Patricia Harper, well there's a story in itself. She was a working girl in her teens. Bad family background and taken into care when she was seven, then ran away at thirteen. Known around the clubs in London, you know the score. Originally Patty Brown. She was arrested a few times for soliciting, but then married her lawyer."

"William Harper?"

"Yep. She certainly came from the wrong side of the tracks."

"Workin' girl made good, eh? What did he defend her for?"

"For running a house."

"Was he a punter?"

"May have been. It was a good get-out for her though, away from the business, and all I can say is that if Patty, as she used to be called, and Charles are together then there's a pretty good reason why."

"They knew each other before, then?"

"I would think so. He was working around the London clubs himself when he was younger, mostly as a runner for some of the big boys. I have no doubt they did, and it wouldn't surprise me if she just married Harper simply to gain some respectability."

"So, what d'ya think about things now? I've told you what he's been doin' with his brother's Will, and the sale of everythin' to Prestons. He stands to make a packet and then get out with this Patty," Tom said, reminding his friend why they were meeting today.

"I'm glad you brought this to our attention. Gordon is certainly involved in something dodgy."

"Jim, I want to hook this guy, get him before he does anythin'. But I'd like you on board."

"'How? This isn't how we do things, you know that."

"We can speak to Prestons. Together. The deal can still go ahead, from what I've been told, just not with this Gordon bloke but with the wife."

"You mean Sheila, his widow?"

"Yeah. I'll call the Chairman, and set up a meetin', you in your official capacity, obviously. If we can get 'im together with

Gordon, we can get everythin' on record and nail him before anythin' happens. And ya know William Harper's ready to make a statement."

"That sounds like a plan, and if the means justifies the end..." Jim added.

"Glad to have you on side. You won't regret it."

"Now, where have I heard that before?" He laughed. "But one more thing, I've been looking at this accident Richard was involved in. A shooting, I understand. Do you think these are connected?"

"No idea. Rich called me in cos Cydney Granger, his boss, was also in the accident. She got off lightly but hardly remembers anythin', although apparently she's started to recall they were being followed for a bit."

"Who is this Mrs Granger? What's her involvement?"

"All I know is that Rich has been workin' for her for a couple years since he left the job and she's some kind of expert in corporate forensics. Her husband died a few years back in Afghanistan. Army captain. She was the one who brought this business with Harper and Gordon to our attention. I think she needs to be involved in this. Her company has all of Harper's documents."

"I'll go and see her. What's she like?"

"Bit of a sort. Straight-talking, knows her stuff. Surprised you've not come across her before."

"Not as far as I know."

"Don't be fooled by the looks. She won't be flutterin' her eyelashes at you. Cydney gets what she wants in other ways." He tapped his finger on the side of his head.

"I'll remember that. Does your friend think the shooter was after her? What do you think?"

"I didn't really quiz him much on that, the guy's just come out of a coma. He asked me to help on this one matter and is probably leavin' everythin' else to the police."

"I'll check with my colleagues on this. Won't do any harm to see if there's any connection. We can't have people going around shooting at anyone they like."

"I think we should establish whether this Patty and Charles are capable of murder. Are they desperate enough, d'ya think, from what you know of 'em?"

"Leave it with me. It doesn't really fit their background. We may be looking at another scenario altogether. Was any of this with Harper and Gordon reported at the time?"

"Doubt it, from what Rich says. I don't reckon they connected the two."

"Well, I'll look into it. It just doesn't ring true."

Tom got up to leave.

"I'll call when I've set the meetin' up with Prestons. Later this week, eh? I think we should do this sharpish, before anythin' else happens, and before they suss we're onto 'em."

"Agreed. Meanwhile, I'm going to go and speak to Richard and Mrs Granger."

CHAPTER TWENTY-SIX

"WE need a plan."

"What are you talking about? We have one. You met with the woman and you told her exactly what we agreed you would say. Blame everything on that half-brother of yours. Now what's the problem, unless of course you changed things?"

"I don't feel comfortable, Craig. She's too clever for her own good. What's more, she has Van der Hausen with her. He's out to get us and has been since that American Securities deal."

"Oh, for goodness sake. Do I have to do everything myself?"

Robert Crossley and his brother-in-law, Craig Benton, were sitting on the terrace of Benton's penthouse apartment in midtown Manhattan, New York, overlooking the evening skyline. The sun had just set and below them the city was ablaze with lights and flashing multi-coloured neon signs, with a whole life of its own. The air was oppressively hot still when Benton's English butler came through and brought them their normal scotch on the rocks, which Crossley refused.

"Sorry, not today."

"Have you got that stomach thing of yours sorted yet? You're of absolutely no use to anyone at all at the moment."

"I need to tell you something."

"What?" Benton was extremely impatient, more so today, and he unleashed his anger only in one direction.

"I'm ill. Got three months. Cancer."

Benton chuckled. "Why the hell didn't you tell me before?" He heaved his huge frame up from his chair and poured himself another drink. "Well that's bloody inconvenient."

"Thanks for the sympathy vote."

"You get nothing from me. All of this is your doing. You should have listened to me in the first place."

"And look where that got us. We were under investigation by the IRS, for God's sake. And probably still are."

"I told you to stick to the story. We knew nothing about anything. Everything was done to preserve the investors' money; we were pawns in the game. And how the hell did this Granger woman get all the information on Centurion? I thought you had those guys in the BVI and Jersey in our pockets. Well?"

"Yes of course I did. But maybe I missed someone. Anyway, it's too late now. She has everything. I'm sure of it."

"May have missed someone? I think that may be a slight exaggeration. You told me the set up was fool proof and nobody could find out."

"It was… it is. Anyway, I told her that Van der Hausen could have Centurion. We need to get rid of it quickly. The bank is going to call in the loan and we don't have the funds anymore to service it. This could be our way out."

"Christ, you're bloody useless! All that money we made from American Securities and Caxton, yet we can't service the fucking loan."

"You know what the market has been like. We put all our money into this, not expecting it to crash like it has. You kept telling me buy, buy, and borrow as much as you can. So I did, and now you can't complain when it's all gone wrong for us."

"You've always had no back-bone, Bob. If it wasn't for the fact you married my sister I wouldn't have helped you out all these years and without any thanks in return."

Crossley got out his pills and popped two, washing them down with a glass of water. The pain was getting more regular and sharper now. He looked across at his brother-in-law and realised, not for the first time, what the man was really like. He hated him now, with a vengeance, for all he had put him through. Crossley knew he himself was no innocent and he'd certainly played a part in the game, but it was over for him and he wanted out now. He wanted to live out the rest of his life in peace. Benton was overweight, a heart attack waiting to happen. He used to be such a good-looking man. Had all the girls after him, unlike Crossley, but now the excesses of food and too much drink had caught up. His face was permanently red from high blood pressure and he could see he had difficulty breathing when sitting down. Oh yes, the man was rich, very rich still, but what good was money when you were six feet under, as he himself was going to be pretty soon, he reckoned. His main concern now was to get as much money in as he could so his wife and kids were cared for, forget about Benton and leave him to the IRS or HMRC, or whoever got to him first.

"So, how much can we get from Van Der Hausen? That portfolio is worth hundreds of millions," Benton said.

"It was. Not much I reckon now, after payment of the bank loan, but hopefully we should have something left in the Trust Fund."

"Fantastic," he said with more than a little sarcasm. "Now you leave this to me, you've done enough damage."

"What are you going to do?"

"Don't you worry your head about that, I have everything under control."

"Tell me you weren't behind that incident with Cydney Granger. Fraud is one thing, but attempted murder..."

"Now, Bobby boy, you know me better than that. Would I stoop to such a level? No, I have something much grander in mind to get her off our backs."

"Is it worth it? Just leave her alone," Crossley said wearily, not believing Benton one bit. The man protested that one little bit too much.

"I would do, but you know me. I like to play my little games. We can't have her running around telling all sorts of tales about us now, can we? She needs to be stopped and I know precisely the right way to do that."

"Please don't do anything stupid." He took a sip of water. "Oh, by the way, my half-brother has emerged out of the woodwork."

"George? Christ, I thought we'd got rid of him once and for all. Where is he?"

"I found out he's working for Van Der Hausen." Crossley could hardly bear to tell his brother-in-law and sat there waiting for his reaction.

"Oh, this just gets better and better. How do you know?"

"I saw him with Cydney Granger at that reception last month in London."

"They were together? What's their relationship?"

"I think they're lovers or were, anyway. In fact I have no doubt, but she wouldn't admit to anything."

"And where is he now? In the UK?"

"No idea, and I don't think she knows either."

"So, do we have a problem here, Bob? Because if we do, I need to know now. That brother of yours knows far too much about our business. I thought he had disappeared."

"Trust me, so did I," said Crossley.

"Well then, that's another thing I'll have to deal with. You stay out of things and get on with your dying. For once, I'm going to do things my way."

CHAPTER TWENTY-SEVEN

O N so many levels, George regretted walking out on Cydney and not telling her the truth. By nature he was not a coward but he believed that she would never forgive him for lying to her, for not acknowledging anything about his past and what he had done. Even though his intentions were honourable, his actions certainly were not, and all because of his bloody half-brother and Crossley's brother-in-law. He loved Cydney and he knew she was beginning to love him too, but that was not enough for anybody. Love does not conquer all, especially when someone is dishonest, he thought. Cydney needed so much more than he could give.

He was hiding out at his friend's game reserve in Kruger Park, wonderfully named 'The White Rhino', set in the heart of Africa's bushveld. He had returned to the country he now called home, as where else in the world could he have gone?

His eyes swept across the idyllic and tranquil setting. He was staying in one of the private luxury lodges in the Park, set amongst five hundred year-old ebony trees. The lodge was modern and sophisticated with floor to ceiling glass panels, which framed the magnificent views of vast landscapes and spectacular wildlife. He intended for his surroundings to help him think through his problems and reflect on his life, to enable him to work out how to put things right, and he hoped the warm and balmy days would give him that sense of peace he sought. It was such a beautiful setting and he had visions of eating wonderful meals under the stars with Cydney, listening to the sounds of the African bush and the music of the thousands of cicadas, while making love with the woman he adored. But here he was alone and the whole setting was wasted on him. All he saw was the sinking sun, as the black night approached and engulfed him, time and again.

Occasionally, after eating another glorious meal his friend had brought to him, he would get up and go for a swim or a walk around, and then sit down and reflect on everything for hours at a time, breathing in deeply the sweet and earthy African aroma. He didn't know where the time went and the days fell into weeks. He was a lost soul but he knew that something had to happen. He couldn't stay where he was, no matter how accommodating his friend was, and at some stage he had to emerge from his monastic existence. So he called the one person he knew would help him - Rupert, who arrived by helicopter the next day without question.

"Before we start, I have to ask how Cydney and the kids are. Is everything okay with them?" George had hardly let Rupert through the door before he bombarded him with the one question uppermost in his mind.

"Cydney is well. Still recovering from the accident. But I do believe she's missing you, and certainly the kids are. Oh, and Richard is out of his coma, thankfully."

George let out a breath he hadn't realised he'd been holding. "Rupert, I really need to talk to you. There's something that's been preying on my mind."

"I think I should tell you something first."

"But I need to tell you things about me. You won't like them; I haven't been totally honest with you."

"George, I know. Why would you be working for me if I didn't? I know about everybody who works for me. I make it my business."

"You know? Everything?" George could not believe it. He thought he had kept his life so nicely covered but he also knew he should never underestimate his boss.

"Yes. Your life in the US before you came to South Africa, your wonderful half-brother and how he affected your departure. George, listen to me. I've become very fond of you over the years. I was never going to let the whole story with American Securities lie there."

"And so you blame me? Not without just cause, I would add."

"I think you were naïve and let your brother pull you into his schemes. But I know it wasn't your fault at all."

"And you said nothing at all when this came out in your meetings."

"As I just told you. You were young at the time. He took advantage of you."

"What about Cydney? Please tell me she knows nothing."

"Well, to tell you the truth she had the misfortune to have dinner with Robert Crossley and he told her everything, although it's not the version I know but one slightly distorted, from his point of view."

George rose from the couch and walked across the room towards the fully stocked drinks cabinet. He needed a stiff scotch.

"You want?" He indicated the bottle as he poured himself a large double.

"Why not? Seems like we both need this."

"How did she take it?"

"Angry at first but once she calmed down, and we spoke, she just felt very sad. You realise she loves you?"

"Yes, and I love her too. Very much. But what chance do I have now?"

"In my considered opinion, and knowing her as I do, I think a phone call may help the situation. She understands you were very young and doesn't believe what Crossley told her entirely. I think you need to put her right about a few things. She has not had it easy in life, and you could be the lifeline she needs."

Christ, I even miss Sean, he said, almost aloud, as he downed the scotch in one. "So, I should make the call then?"

"I'll talk to Cydney first."

"Will she listen to you, Rupert?"

"I can but try. I'll let you know what she says and then it's in your hands."

Cydney was having one of those days when she couldn't settle to anything. Tom had called her earlier in the day to report that the Fraud Squad were fully informed of Charles Gordon's and Patricia Harper's activities and were willing to work with them. He briefed her on the next steps and she heard with great pleasure that Sheila was now likely to get what was rightfully hers. She was certain her lack of concentration was due to the fact she was impatient to get this case sorted so she could turn her thoughts to George.

Jenny called through to announce Detective Sergeant Jim Donaldson's arrival and showed him into Cydney's office.

"Do come in and have a seat. Can I get you anything to drink?"

"No thanks, I'm fine. I've just had an interesting meeting with Tom Patterson. I understand he's a friend of one of your employees, Richard Barrett?"

"Yes, they worked together. Well, Tom was in Richard's team when he was the Detective Superintendent. But I'm sure you know that, Sergeant."

"I do. Tom briefed me on this matter regarding Rayshel Plastics. I wonder if you could put me in the picture, if you wouldn't mind, about your involvement, that is."

Cydney proceeded to explain everything to the sergeant, taking great care to leave out the bit about how Ray Gordon had approached her in the first place, and certain other parts that were not quite within the realms of the law, although nothing illegal – unless you could call Sean's late night foray into Harper's office illegal, of course. The ends justifying the means, as always.

"How do you know the Gordons?"

"They're old friends of mine. I was asked to look into the

matter when Ray suddenly died as Sheila Gordon was very anxious about what was going to happen to her and their children. She had no idea she was no longer a beneficiary under the Will, or that Charles, her brother-in-law, owned the business and land around her. It all came as such a shock to her, so she turned to me."

"And you approached William Harper?"

"Well, yes. I looked into Mrs Gordon's affairs, did some digging on the land registry and went to see him to try and get to the bottom of his position in the whole matter. With his background, and what we discovered, he didn't come well out of this and I suspected fraud. I don't believe either Ray or Sheila Gordon intended for Charles Gordon to get his hands on all the assets they'd worked so hard to accumulate. And now Charles is planning to sell everything to Prestons, then take the money and run, so I thought it was time to take appropriate action."

"That's when you went to the police?"

"No. Again, as you're well aware."

"You tried to do it your way…so why come to us now?"

Cydney sat forward in her chair and put her hands on the desk, confronting him.

"Sergeant, these are friends of mine. I do have certain means at my disposal, and very well trained staff with professional backgrounds in forensics, or rather discovering information not readily available to the general public. I came to you via Tom when it came to the point I couldn't go any further without your help."

"And?"

"What do you want me to say? I'd suggest it doesn't matter how we got to this point, just that we have, and we now do something about it. What do you think?"

"I'm very interested or I wouldn't be sitting here now."

"So can we try and work together? I believe that will be much better for everybody. I've done nothing that I'm ashamed of and am fully prepared to give you all the information I've accumulated and what's more, hand over William Harper's files which he gave to us. Plus some very interesting photographs of him."

"Please don't get me wrong, Mrs Granger. I'm grateful for all you've done, but now it's a police matter."

Cydney put her hand to her head and sighed. She was not used to her actions being scrutinised so intensely and was tired of his attitude.

"I'm well aware of that. However, I was involved from the beginning. Tom tells me you're going to be wiring the meeting with Charles Gordon and the Chairman of Prestons."

"He shouldn't have told you that."

"Well he has, and I want to be there."

"Sorry, but the answer is no."

"I can help. I think you should put aside your police rules for the moment and look at the situation itself. I know more than is down on paper, or in the files, and that could be useful if something is said, or not said, at the meeting."

The sergeant pondered for a while.

"Look, if I get the okay from my boss, and if he says its fine, then you can come along, but as a witness only."

Cydney gave him one of her all-engaging smiles that totally changed her demeanour and hoped made her look more approachable.

"Thank you. I'm most grateful."

"Actually, there is one more thing. The shooting and car incident. I understand you were injured and Richard Barrett was shot and has been in a coma from head injuries, although I hear he's now out of the woods and waking up."

"I honestly wish I could help but I don't remember a thing," she said, as her smile faded.

"Do you have any enemies at all who would want you killed? Are you undertaking any other investigations of anyone who would want to harm you, or Richard?"

She met his gaze. "You need to understand that my world is very much one at high board level, and extremely confidential. The wrong word said at the wrong time or to the wrong person and who knows the repercussions? I have no idea who'd want to harm me or any of my staff." Cydney decided not to mention her investigations into the world of Robert Crossley and Craig Benton. She felt a duty of professionalism and care to Rupert, rightly or wrongly.

"Okay, we'll leave it at that then. Let me know if anything else comes to mind please. Meanwhile, perhaps we can go through all the boxes from Harper's office."

"Gladly." She came around from behind her desk to walk the sergeant through to the boardroom where Jenny had laid everything out. She knew this was going to take another couple of hours.

Cydney managed to leave the office eventually and went via the nursing home to check on her mother who, surprisingly, was still holding strong. More so than her daughter, it seemed. Cydney couldn't pinpoint why she felt an unease today, as if something was about to happen but she didn't know what. Her mother was fine, and the twins were their normal selves. Sean was somewhere in Ireland with his aunt and hadn't been in touch at all, which was most unlike him. But if his aunt was dying then he would be surrounded by relatives who would be unlikely to leave him alone, and anyway he needed some solitary time rather than occupying himself with her matters all the time.

Moments before leaving the office, she had called Sheila.

"I need to ask you something and I want you to think very carefully about this."

"Whatever's the matter? It sounds so serious."

"You know what your brother-in-law has been up to with this Patricia. I went through everything with you."

"Yes, Cydney. I'm so shocked about William Harper though,

and all those photographs. What was he thinking of, a man of his age?"

"I think we're nearly there to catching them at their game. The Fraud Squad are now involved and Harper has agreed to work with us."

"So what's the problem?"

"Prestons still want to buy the land, once it's reverted to you and the correct Will reinstated."

"Oh, I couldn't possibly sell it. What about all the people who have worked for my husband for years? No, I just couldn't put them out of their jobs."

"Sheila, you know you'll make millions from this."

"Yes, but it's not the money. Ray wouldn't want that. It was never about the money. He gave everything to the business and his staff were loyal throughout the bad times. Cydney, please don't even mention selling again."

"You have to convince her Cydney. I want her to have the money now. She can't run the business. I want her to enjoy her retirement, to look after the kids and give them everything I couldn't. It was always a struggle, making ends meet."

"I hear you Sheila, but suppose it was what Ray wanted now? For you and the kids to have a good life, and forget all that's been going on?"

"But suppose he doesn't?"

"Suggest to her she gives all the workers a bonus from the proceeds. Then she can't possibly feel guilty."

"You know there's going to be enough money to go around for everyone, even the guys on the shop floor."

"What are you saying? I make them redundant?"

"We could set up a good pension scheme for the ones near retirement, and give them a bonus too. Or help them with a buy-out. New premises. There are many things you could do, and I'll be here to guide you, Sheila."

"That's it Cydney. I can see she is wavering."

236

"Can I think about it please? I don't want to do anything in a hurry at all."

"Ray isn't here and you have to make the decisions, I understand, but you don't have much time. The police have already seen Prestons and the chairman is working with them. Next week is when it's all going to come to a climax and once Charles and the Harpers are behind bars, you'll need to decide what you're going to do."

"Cydney, are you sure this is what Ray would want?"

"Remind her of when we bought the land all those years ago and our discussions. It took ages pondering whether to make this enormous step and I hated the thought of bank financing but she persuaded me. We were sitting in The Blue Peacock near Witherington. This was going to be our pension, our retirement to do anything we wanted to do once the kids had left university and set up on their own. Now I am not there, it just means everything is brought forward. Think of what she can do with the money, I want her to enjoy life."

"Do you remember, Sheila, when you and Ray bought the site and built up your business? What did he say to you? Think about your conversation in The Blue Peacock."

There was a pause. "Oh my, yes I remember. We were sitting outside in the sunshine. Beautiful day, it was. He hated the thought of borrowing. I made him think about it. It was going to be our pension."

"Exactly. So?"

"Yes, I hear you. Has Ray just said that to you?"

"Yes, he has. He wants you to do the right thing but this is an opportunity for you. He wants you to take it."

"I'll think about it. Thank you Cydney, I'll get back to you tomorrow. If I do agree, would you sort it all out for me? I don't have the head for this kind of thing."

"You know I will."

"That's all I needed to hear," Ray said, as he drifted away.

CHAPTER TWENTY-EIGHT

PRESTONS' Chairman, Christopher Harris, who had called Charles Gordon on the pretext of wanting to finalise the deal, set up the meeting. The man could hardly retain his excitement, Harris thought to himself. Tom Patterson and Jim Donaldson with his team from the Fraud Squad had fully briefed him and, actually, he quite liked the idea of being part of a sting. Just like in the movies except this was for real, he reminded himself with a laugh. On behalf of the company, he wanted the land belonging to Rayshel. Developing the site would be of great value to the community. He had visions of a hypermarket and cinema complex with restaurants and play areas and, with a large donation to the charity of the moment, this could very well get him his long desired knighthood.

He fully understood Charles Gordon had played him during their few meetings and now he knew the background he wanted the guy to get whatever was coming to him. He didn't like being made a fool of in front of his board of directors. When he had informed them of this deal they were happy to proceed on the basis he'd outlined, and the monies were set aside for the project. Now he wanted redemption for himself and he would help the police in any way he could, and better still if he could buy the land from the widow and go ahead with his plans. This could work out very well in his favour.

Christopher Harris's office was wired and so was he in more ways than one, and there were cameras installed at various strategic points. He felt extremely self-conscious of the fact and wasn't quite sure how to behave, especially with the policemen from the Fraud

Squad listening and watching him from his secretary's office. It had all sounded like a great adventure when they had come to see him previously, but now it was actually happening he hoped he wouldn't put his foot in it and either say or do the wrong thing to alert Charles Gordon. His secretary had been primed to show Gordon up to the fifth floor executive suite and then the office security guards would secure the floor and lifts on the pretence his secretary had gone out. Again, he hoped Gordon wouldn't suspect anything and would take it as a gesture of his own importance that he was being shown up to see the chairman personally. Harris's heart was beating quickly and the palms of his hands were sweating profusely, as well as his armpits. He looked at one of the cameras sitting on his desk. Christ, he thought, they must think I'm a complete idiot.

The constant haranguing of his partner in crime, Patty Harper, was marring the excitement Charles felt as he made his way to the head office of Prestons. That woman could certainly nag. He almost felt sympathy for that idiot husband of hers, William, the so-called solicitor whom they'd managed to twist around their little fingers. Gullible didn't even cut it - and those pictures! What was the man thinking of when that pro picked him up at the bar in town and took him back to her house? Did he really believe a young, nubile girl of half his age would fancy a fat, balding and ageing excuse of a man? It was so easy to set up that it was almost laughable, and it hadn't cost them much either. A few hundred to her and the guy who set up the video camera on the book shelf to film everything, and they had him.

Charles had laughed aloud in William's face when he'd showed him the stills of his antics and threatened to tell his loving wife. It was a picture, in many ways. He and Patty had watched the video and it was quite enlightening – who would have thought he could be that athletic at his age and size? Once they had him hook, line and sinker, the constant threat of Patty finding out that he had been unfaithful with a prostitute…well, he was like putty. But now Patty was driving him insane. When will we get the money? When are we leaving? Do you have everything tied up? Charles was not going to take her anywhere. Why would he want to be saddled with an old slag like Patty when he could have any woman he wanted, once he had the money and was living the life of luxury in some South American country? No, he had kept her satisfied for the last few weeks, literally, but he was leaving her behind with that ridiculous husband of hers. Charles knew he was smarter than anybody else. Look what he'd done to that half-wit brother of his. He was another one. Sign here, and he did. Agree to this, and he did. The man didn't have a brain between his ears. His up and dying was the most intelligent thing he had ever done, and convenient for all concerned.

Charles parked his BMW once again in the car park of Prestons and made his way to reception. He felt satisfied that all his plans were coming to fruition and even gave a patronising smile to the old security guard on the front desk, who sat there with his medals from some prehistoric war nobody could give a damn about. Christ, the man should have been retired a century ago to some old people's home.

Taking a seat on a rather comfortable beige settee, he glanced around at the well-decorated surroundings and waited for the chairman's secretary to come and get him. Damn right, he should get respect. Look what he was offering them. They were going to make billions from what he had to sell, but he wasn't going to be greedy. Oh no, he simply wanted a just reward for his effort. A few million - or ten - and he would be happy. Then he could get out of this place for the last time and never have to set foot in England again.

He didn't want to think of Sheila, nor his nephews and niece, though he did wonder what all that business was with the guy seen visiting her when he sent someone round to watch her house, under the guise of a British Telecom engineer, to take photos of everyone coming and going. The man he used was stupid and gave the game away so easily. You just couldn't trust anyone. However, with his goal firmly in sight, he'd dismissed the visitor as a mourner who wanted to pay respects to the grieving widow and her offspring and he hoped he'd been right. Nothing was going to spoil his day now. He was going to sign the sale agreement drafted jointly by Harper and Prestons' lawyers that he'd approved already. In his mind's eye, he saw all the money floating down and piling up around him. Nothing or nobody could touch him now. He was invincible.

William Harper walked into reception and over to his client.

"I presume you have all the papers with you and there's no cause for me to be concerned about your possible ineptitude?"

Harper almost winced at this derogatory remark about his professionalism, even though he knew Charles Gordon was about to get his comeuppance, finally. The Fraud Squad had interviewed him several times in detail, and he was hoping that by turning in Charles, any sentence he'd get would be little more than community service. He didn't think he could face prison at his time of life, although he realised it was a distinct possibility and that being struck off by the Law Society was inevitable. He was more than happy to move somewhere far away, where nobody knew him, and spend his time in quiet solitude and anonymity. Without Patty, of course, whom he believed was being picked up by the police at this precise moment.

Her not being in his life was something he was going to have to get used to. He still loved her, for some odd reason that even now he couldn't fathom. Certainly, he felt flattered she had even considered marrying him all those years ago, but he wasn't stupid and he now knew that she'd been playing him - along with Charles.

"Yes, I have everything ready for you." He patted his battered old brown briefcase on which one of the metal fastenings was hanging loose. "This should be a doddle. Nothing can go wrong."

"Well, let's make sure it doesn't shall we? Because if it does, I'm not going to be responsible for my actions, if you understand me."

"You don't have to keep referring to that, Charles. I'm fully aware of what you have on me."

"Just you remember that and we'll do fine. I'll pay you off and then I'm away to pastures new - and I hope never to see your fat, ugly face again."

Harper looked at the man sitting opposite him and wondered, not for the first time, how Charles could have come from the same parents as his once good friend Ray. A sense of shame overwhelmed him that he'd treated his friend so badly and let him down, all because of one stupid night with the hooker. Charles had him after that and he did everything asked of him: forged papers, Ray's Will, signatures. Now he vowed to do everything in his power to make things right for Ray's widow and kids. For the moment he would ignore the comments thrown at him, maybe deservedly, and instead wait without rising to the bait thrown by Charles for the meeting with the chairman, when all would be revealed. Sergeant Donaldson had fully briefed him and he knew what his role was and what to say. It was planned out to the minute detail and as long as he kept his cool and played his part, then there would be no more Charles Gordon and, once again, he could breathe easily.

At the designated time, the chairman's secretary collected the two men and showed them into the lift and up to the executive suite on the fifth floor, where they strode along the thick-piled carpeted floor to Christopher Harris' office. The secretary opened the door and signalled for them to enter. Harris was at the board table together with another man, who Harper assumed was his lawyer. Both men got up to shake hands with them and Harper sat down and waited for Charles, who he could see was attempting to chat up the secretary within earshot of everyone. The man was incorrigible. Harper could not have hated anyone more than he did at that moment. After a few seconds, Charles came through and sat down. He had no niceties.

"Well gentlemen, are we ready to sign?"

"Thank you both for coming, Mr Gordon, Mr Harper. I have a few things to go through still in our Sales Purchase Agreement. Shall we do that first?"

"I thought everything had been gone through. What else is there? We agreed the amount and I'm happy with the terms. Let's just sign." Charles was already on edge.

"Now, Mr Gordon, we must make sure all the legalities and due diligence are in place, for everybody's sake, wouldn't you agree?" said the lawyer. Charles let out a huge impatient sigh.

"If you insist. But I have to say, I'm not happy. I'm paying my lawyer here to deal with these things and assumed he's been earning his money over the last few weeks."

Harper moved his hand around his over-tight shirt collar and, as normal, felt the sweat pouring down him. If they weren't careful, Charles was going to ruin all the plans so carefully put in place. He spoke to his client quietly.

"Charles, this won't take long. Let's just do it and then we can move on. I've gone through every clause in the Agreement and I can't believe there's anything much we need to discuss."

"Whatever!" Charles responded. He pushed himself back in the chair, causing the legs to creak loudly under his weight.

The lawyer pulled out the Agreement.

"Now, I want to double check the site itself. Can you all please turn to the plans in Schedule 1. I've outlined the area in red, as you will see. Mr Harper, can you just confirm you agree? I've taken this from the land registry details but there seems to be a question over the various plot numbers, which I need to tie into the plans. I note they were put into the name of Intervest Holdings Limited not too long ago, together with the main unit belonging to Charles Gordon's brother, I believe, Ray Gordon."

Charles sat up straight. "And your point?"

"Well, we need to get the facts straight here before I can advise my client to sign."

Charles glared at William Harper. "I'm sure if my brother wanted to put everything into my name, he had every entitlement, wouldn't you agree?"

Harper placed a restraining hand on his client's shoulder, which he instantly shrugged off. "I don't believe that's what we're being asked, Charles."

"Of course, I am not suggesting otherwise, Mr Gordon. However, the numbers do not match. I had asked Mr Harper to provide details of these, but he hadn't got back to me."

"William, is there a problem here we don't know about?" Charles seethed through his teeth.

"Uh, no Charles. I did look into this. They are simply land registry anomalies. When the plot numbers were assigned, and then the land was carved into separate units, the numbers changed." Harper looked at the solicitor opposite him. "Are you happy now?"

"Yes, I think we can carry on. Now let's turn to page two of the Agreement."

An hour and a half later Charles was practically tearing his hair out.

"Can we all get to the point here and sign? I cannot see what we are doing discussing every bloody clause. I have a life, even if you lot don't."

Christopher Harris was doing everything they had told him to do and was now quite enjoying himself. He found he had almost forgotten the wire on his lapel and the fact they were watching and recording every one of his actions. He felt quite the consummate actor. He also loved seeing this man in front of him becoming more and more angry and frustrated. That was the plan. Go into every clause and pull it apart and, by the end of it, Charles Gordon would be so irate he would say something he shouldn't and dig himself a hole from which he had no chance of ever getting out.

Cydney was in the secretary's office with DS Jim Donaldson and Tom Patterson, plus a few other members of the Fraud Squad, sitting at small computer screens and watching the scene unfold. It had been a couple of hours now and she thought they were nearly reaching their goal. Charles Gordon was beside himself at this point. He was not even pretending to be nice to anyone and was openly berating William Harper and the other solicitor at every opportunity. It was going well. Not too long now and they would have him.

Ray came through to her and she felt comforted in the knowledge he was about to see an end to his problems, which would enable him to move on.

"I told you what he was like - I'm so glad you're seeing this for yourself."

"Don't worry, Ray. He doesn't need any help from us. He seems extremely capable of screwing himself."

"He never was a bright boy... his temper was always going to be his ruin."

"So I see. Hold on a minute, things seem to be moving."

Cydney watched as Charles Gordon scrambled up from his seat, pushed his chair back so hard it hurtled across the floor, and grabbed William Harper by the lapels. He shoved him so forcefully up against the wall that one of the pictures came crashing down, shattering glass all around him. The men behind her stood up, readying themselves to charge into the boardroom.

"What the fuck d'ya think you're doing to me, you arsehole? We should have signed and been out of this fucking place two hours ago, with the money in my hands."

"Sit down, Charles, you're behaving like an idiot. We're nearly at the end. Just behave for a change, will you?"

"Please sit down, Mr Gordon. We must clear these points," said the other solicitor. "I have to prove you have just title to these lands so my client can purchase everything from you."

"Just title? You load of pricks. Course I have just title! I signed the bloody documents myself..."

The words hung in the air around them.

"I'm sorry, Mr Gordon," Christopher Harris said. "Did you just say you signed them yourself? Do you mean to say that your brother didn't sign the asset over to you at all?"

The world suddenly stopped for Charles Gordon as he realised what he'd said. There was a commotion behind him as four guys catapulted out from the adjoining room. He shoved the board table away from him so it fell over on its side, papers falling everywhere. Harris and his solicitor moved out of the way just in time and stood with their backs against the wall to avoid the affray. Charles ran for the door, turned the handle and stopped still in his tracks. He couldn't believe the door was locked, and he knew there was no escape. He turned towards Harper, who was standing stock-still.

"You bastard, Harper! You screwed me! You did this!"

"You did it yourself, Charles. Greed, simply greed."

"And you think Patty loved you? She despised everything, you complete lump of shit. She won't wait around."

"Patty's in custody, Charles. She's told them everything. I knew it wouldn't take long for you to shoot yourself in the foot. That temper of yours was always going to get you into trouble. I said to keep it in check, but no. It was so easy."

"I'll have you!" Charles spat, and rushed at Harper, grabbing him by the neck, until the four police officers tore them apart and got hold of Charles, pinning him to the ground. Jim Donaldson stood over the man.

"Charles Geoffrey Gordon, I am arresting you on suspicion of fraud…"

"So, it's over Ray. They have him. Sheila will have everything she wants now. I will see to that."

"I can't thank you enough Cydney. You've been my saviour."

"I did what I thought was best, that's all. I helped you because it was the right thing to do for everyone. And I have to say, I've grown very fond of Sheila and the kids."

"You will look after them for me then, always?"

"Yes Ray. I will."

"I know you want my help too, and I think I know how I can give you that."

CHAPTER TWENTY-NINE

"So who the hell is this?" Sean said, staring at the body lying on the slab in the hospital morgue, "because it certainly isn't Captain Steve Granger."

"Are you sure?" asked one of the medics.

"Of course I'm bloody sure. I'd know the man anywhere. What have we got on this guy here?"

"I've examined the body and there's no obvious sign how he came to be where you found him. There are no gunshot or stab wounds. I found some bruising to the abdomen as if he'd been kicked repeatedly, his right shoulder is broken and there are scratches and abrasions on his legs, probably caused by being dragged along. At the moment we're waiting for lab results to come back."

Sean looked down, totally mystified. The man before him was younger than Steve but with the same dark hair and eye colouring, and a full-grown beard.

"Do you think he's Israeli, or Arab?"

"We may know when the results come back but we could make a guess after we examine the contents of his stomach," the Chief Medical Examiner explained.

"Stomach?"

"Yes. Certain types of food eaten would indicate where he came from," answered one of the other medics.

"I see." Sean looked up and down the body for signs of anything else they may have missed. There was nothing apparent that he could make out.

So where the hell is Steve? he thought.

He left the group of men and made his way back to his room. He was at a loss as to what to do now. He had called the general and reported everything that had happened and his commanding officer had ordered him home on the next available flight. Sean was loathe to leave without an answer but he couldn't stay in Israel indefinitely. If Steve hadn't made it to the rendezvous point there was a valid reason. He was either dead or had been taken alive and would be dead soon. There was a possibility, he supposed, that he was in hiding somewhere but that was extremely unlikely, given the circumstances of the body they'd found. Was there a connection? Who would be playing games and perhaps plant a body in Steve's place? Was it some sort of warning to the Israelis to keep off? If so, that could mean someone was holding the captain and might intend to use him as a bargaining tool. If that was the case, then whoever it was would be aware that Steve had been collecting information over the past year and would know he was trying to exit. The situation was unthinkable as it meant he was unlikely ever to be released.

Sean had to head home and be with Cydney now. He wasn't giving up on Steve but how long could he remain in Israel? She would need him more than ever but, then again, he was never going to tell her about this. He would keep up the pretence of his sick aunt for all intents and purposes and do what the general had ordered, but it was going to be the hardest act for him to pull off.

He'd be on the next flight home and wait there for news. With any luck, the capturers, if there were any, would play their hand and try to bargain for the man's life. If, of course, he was still alive. That would remain to be seen.

Sean stared at the wedding photo he had brought with him. He left it with the medics. There was no other option.

It was the morning of day four of the most arduous journey Steve had ever endured, made all the worse by the changeable conditions in the Golan Heights. He'd spent the nights since he left his lying up point shivering under the stars with little to protect him from the elements. He couldn't always reach the safe haven of a cave to rest up during the day, and it was too dangerous for him to light a fire. The covering he had was thin and gave little comfort. His one consolation was that he lived in hope of reaching Sean the next day and that he would be picked up from his hell and taken home to Cydney and the kids. He'd hardly eaten anything, apart from a few plant leaves and roots found on the way, as the meat from the dog he had killed had barely lasted. He could feel his ribs through his shirt and his water supply was almost depleted, despite his attempts at rationing. He had found a small stream two days ago and filled his water bottle but he didn't have the time or the energy to return and still reach the designated meeting point. Now he was seriously beginning to feel the effects of dehydration. His mouth was dry since he was producing no saliva and his heart was beating rapidly. At this stage he was ready to drink his urine, if only he could produce some of that also.

He had been pushing himself all night so he could rest up during the daylight hours but the thought of stopping scared him. If he didn't reach the pick-up point he knew it would be the end for him and he doubted he could hold on another day. They had an agreement that Sean would wait for him no longer than ten minutes and thereafter return in twenty-four hours. Furthermore, he knew he was behind schedule. His health was a burden to him and his body was in danger of letting him down. With his leg so swollen and sore he was dragging it behind him, impeding his progress. His heart physically ached in his chest and not just from the lack of water. The recognition that it had been damaged a few years ago was always in his mind and therefore the decision to chance the journey during daylight hours was one that he took being fully aware of the consequences. All he had learned from being on active duty came to the fore, but he knew it may not be enough.

After so many hours of walking, he was beyond weary. From time to time he saw movement out of the corner of his eyes and crouched down with his rifle, aiming and ready to shoot. Each time he moved the weapon around frantically in all directions but there was nothing there. It was obviously all in his mind and that scared him. It was the early part of the afternoon when the sun was at its highest. He was hardly in control of his mind or his body and there were signs he was beginning to hallucinate. The temperature was reaching well over one hundred degrees Fahrenheit but his entire body was freezing cold and shivering.

He walked to the top of another rock formation and gave a cry as one hundred yards ahead of him he saw a waterfall. Running with all the strength he could muster, over boulders and indents in the terrain, and forgetting the potential of further damage to his leg, he almost fell down the hill. He rolled the last few yards and lost his rifle on the way. He crawled forward, ready to drown his head in the water but the waterfall had disappeared. Turning over onto his back, he looked up at the sky and the sun blazing down on him. The temptation to close his eyes and sleep for an eternity was too great. A picture of Lauren came to him, and he imagined himself sitting on her bed and tucking her in at night, as he used to do. Then his beautiful wife knelt down beside him. His hand reached out to caress her face. It felt soft to the touch and he could smell her perfume. "Cydney," he whispered, "my darling. I've come back to you."

Cydney was so pleased to get through her front door at last, after such an eventful day. As usual, Lauren talked twenty to the dozen about everything - her day, her friends, the latest fashion, the boy band she'd been crazy about for weeks.

"Give me a chance to catch my breath, darling. Where's Jake?"

"He had music practice for this competition thing. He'll be back late. Told me his friend's dad would give him a lift home."

"So just the two of us. Shall we go out…fancy a pizza?"

"No. Can we have a girlie night? We could do nails and hair and watch a DVD! That would be awesome!"

"Okay. But let's be pyjama girls. Go and get changed and I'll get Sophie to put the dinner on."

"Thank you!" Lauren said, racing into the hallway. "Oh, and Mum…" Cydney looked up at her daughter's face peering around the door. "I saw Daddy last night."

Cydney went cold. What? She saw Steve? Her husband who had never come through to her in four years, and was now making himself available to Lauren?

"Sorry. What did you say?"

"I saw Daddy. He came and sat on my bed and stroked my face. It was lovely. Just like he did when I was little. Don't look at me like that! I wasn't scared."

"It's just that…"

"I know. It does sound funny. But it was really nice. Can we go upstairs now?"

"Did he say anything to you?"

"Only that everything would be all right. He promised he would always look after us."

"You really weren't frightened?" asked Cydney.

"No! It was Daddy!"

"And he said nothing else? Gave you no other message?"

"No, Mum. We didn't sit there having a long chat, you know."

"What did he look like?"

"Oh, I don't know. Different. He had a long beard. Come on, let's get changed."

And with that, the conversation was closed. Lauren simply dismissed the fact she had seen her dad as if it was an everyday occurrence; she accepted everything as normal and who was

Cydney to question her? But a jealousy swept over. She'd tried so hard to reach Steve over the years but there'd been nothing, and yet he'd come to Lauren. The question was *why*? Why after all this time would he not reach out to his wife? Lauren was young and yes, seemed to have the same gift as her, but he was her husband! Why was he avoiding her?

Cydney wondered if spirit had a choice as to whom they could contact. It sounded so ridiculous but, if they did, why hadn't he contacted her?

"I'll be up in a minute. I need to speak to Sophie," she shouted after Lauren, and walked through to the kitchen, desperate for answers. For some reason she had a feeling Sean would have them and the nearest person to him at this precise moment was his daughter.

"Do you know where your dad is?" Her direct question caught Sophie off guard and she stopped stirring the soup she had made and turned round to face her. "There's something going on here that I don't know about. And stop looking so sheepish. I know your dad is up to something. This 'ailing aunt' business never did ring true to me."

"I don't know what you're talking about, Mrs Granger. Dad's in Waterford now."

"Well if that's the case, what's the aunt's name? Let me have the number."

"I don't think I have it. He didn't leave it with me."

"And have your heard from your dad at all?"

"No... He doesn't always ring me."

"Now we both know that's not true. So you're not going to tell me. But you know something. I can see it on your face."

"I'm sure I don't. There's nothing to tell."

Cydney gave up, knowing she would get no answers.

"And what about Dave? He was supposed to be here, and all of a sudden his leave is cancelled. This is just too much of a coincidence. It's all about the army again," Cydney muttered as she strode out the kitchen. "And when you hear from you dad, tell him I want to speak to him. Don't you forget." She didn't wait for a response.

She made her way upstairs determined to think it through later, when she stopped in her tracks. It had been there in the back of her memory all along but now the recollection knocked her sideways and she reached out for the banister. Steve had actually come through to her when she was unconscious after the accident and he'd had a beard, just as Lauren had said. What the hell did that mean? There was no doubt in her mind it had been him. She recalled him leaning over and kissing her but he'd said nothing. After all these years! Cydney needed time to assimilate everything but it was not going to happen now as she was about to spend quality time with her daughter and would wait until she was alone later to think everything through.

By nine o'clock, Cydney and Lauren were watching The Princess Bride for the twentieth time when the phone rang. It was Jake.

"Mum, I'm staying over at Ben's tonight. Tell Dad he can pick me up in the morning would you?" and the phone went dead.

"Who was that?" Lauren mumbled.

"Jake."

"What did he want?"

"He's staying at his friend's tonight. Who's this Ben? Do you know him?"

"No. You know Jake, he keeps everything secret. He's a law unto himself."

Cydney thought Lauren was a law unto herself if the truth were told. Where did she pick up such an expression anyway, for goodness sake?

"You must know something," Cydney said. "Where does he live?"

"Somewhere around. Mum! Can we watch the film? I love this bit when she falls into the fountain."

"No, Lauren. I need to know about Jake. He said something really funny about Dad."

"Oh," she said, still staring at the screen. "Did he speak to him too?"

"What? No. I don't know. I'm calling his music teacher. His number's here somewhere."

"Then can we watch the film?"

"Yes, Lauren."

Cydney went to fetch her phone book. She had this awful, horrible, sinking feeling in the pit of her stomach. Something just wasn't right. Why would Jake mention his dad? Was he trying to warn her about something or had he been mixed up and meant Sean by accident? Although, Jake knew Sean was away in Ireland. Or was she being stupid and Jake was simply being his normal self? A teenager, evasive, non-committal, not thinking his mum would be worried. No, it felt wrong to her, and she would check it out to be sure and then get back to her evening with Lauren.

There was no answer from the music teacher or the school, only a voice message giving opening times and asking the caller to leave a message. Cydney called every number in her book of Jake's friends, but without success. Nobody knew who this Ben was, or where he lived.

Panic took over and Cydney started to feel physically ill. What was she to do now? She really needed Sean, Richard and even George. She couldn't cope with these things on her own, it was just too much after the day's events with Charles Gordon, but nobody was around. Maybe she was overreacting, getting fearful over nothing, but the fact that Jake had clearly said 'Dad' was very strange. She needed some reassurance and the first person she thought of was Claire. They were getting on much better these days.

"Hi. Everything ok? It's a bit late for you to call, you're normally in bed by now."

"Yes, I know. I'm a bit worried about Jake. He had music

practice after school but he's not home yet. Then he called and said he was staying with a friend called Ben. But nobody knows a boy with that name."

"Oh, you know your son and his music, he gets lost in things. What does Lauren think?"

"She doesn't know anything. Something odd happened though. Jake asked if Steve could pick him up in the morning."

There was a pause. "Perhaps he meant Sean. Kids get mixed up sometimes."

"I know, but I'm sure he was warning me about something....or he's in trouble."

"Do you not think you're over-reacting somewhat? What could have happened to him? Come on, Cyd. Your imagination may be running away with you just a little bit, don't you think?"

"No, Claire. It really doesn't seem right to me." A cold shiver rushed through her as she spoke the words. "I'm really frightened."

"Are you having one of your moments? Do you want me to come over? I can be there in an hour."

"Yes, would you?"

"Mum! Quick!"

Cydney dropped the phone and, without a second's thought, hurtled down the stairs. "Lauren!" she cried out, rushing into the room. "What's the matter?" She gripped her daughter's shoulders and shook her gently, then cupped her palm under her chin, lifting it to her face. "Stop crying, darling. What's happened?"

"I saw Jake."

She flicked her head around. "What here, he's home? Where is he?"

"No. I saw him in a cellar of a house."

"What? Doing what, Lauren? Speak to me! What do you mean, you *saw* him?"

"He was lying in the corner of a cellar. It was all dark and dirty, he was asleep with some old blanket over him."

"What are you talking about?"

"I saw him! I'm not sure where he is but he's not well. Please believe me, Mum. I just know he's not well."

Cydney stared at her daughter who was standing, openly distressed, in front of her. All the feelings she'd had before came up to meet her again. She believed Lauren. Something really was terribly wrong. The twins had always had this silent understanding, something particular to them. When one was hurt, the other felt the pain. If one was ill with a high temperature, the other had a similar one. As toddlers they'd had their own private language, a way of communicating that was beyond anything she and Steve could comprehend. And Cydney knew that her daughter had the same sixth sense that she had.

"I'm going to ask you to calm down, and think clearly, okay? I know you said Jake was in a cellar, but where is it? Please try and be as precise as you can, sweetheart."

Lauren sat down on the couch and closed her eyes. A few seconds passed.

"There's a large garden and a long road leading up to it, a bit like ours, but the grounds are more overgrown. Oh, Mum. I really can't think like this. I need Jake," and Lauren started to cry even louder, despite Cydney's arm around her.

"Lauren, I need you to concentrate. Pretend you're talking to Daddy again. You can do this, for Jake. We have to find him."

"There are some men outside in big black cars. But I don't know where it is. Jake's sleeping. Maybe when he wakes up he can tell me."

"Is he hurt? You always felt things when you were little. Daddy and I always wondered about this."

"He's sleeping. I feel sleepy, Mum. I need to lie down. Can I lay down here?"

Cydney watched her beautiful daughter as she curled up on the couch and closed her eyes. This was so strange. One minute she was fine yet the next drowsy, as if she had taken a sleeping pill. So if Jake was asleep, did that mean he'd been drugged and Lauren was feeling the same effects? And who on earth had taken her son and why? The temptation to call the police was strong. She turned to pick up the phone and call the one person she knew, Jim Donaldson, when the handle of the lounge door turned. She froze, her heart in her mouth, and felt her legs giving way under her. Someone had broken into the house.

"Hi Mrs Granger, I'm home!"

Sean ran to her side, catching her in his arms as she fell.

"What's wrong?" he said, easing her onto the nearest chair.

"They've got Jake! You have to do something!" she cried.

"What? Who has Jake? Mrs Granger, talk to me!"

"I don't know...today. Lauren saw him in a cellar." Cydney stood up and began to pace, trying to breathe through her tears.

"Lauren was in a cellar?"

"No! She saw him in her mind...you know they've always had this telepathy thing. Sean, we haven't got time for this! Do something!"

"Okay...okay. Tell me everything. Have you called the police?"

"I was just about to when you walked through the door, and where the bloody hell have you been? Oh God. I think Jake's fine because Lauren is but when she wakes up, who knows? If something's happening to him she'll tell me. If they do something to him, she'll know. What should we do?"

"Let's call the police first and let them deal with it. Cydney, you have to keep calm."

"That's the first time you've called me Cydney," she said, almost smiling through her tears.

"Well times are changing."

When the phone rang, Sean jumped out of his seat and reached the receiver before Cydney even had a chance to move.

"Where is he? We know you have him. If anything happens to him I'll kill every last one of you."

Cydney froze. *Oh God. Please let him be alright. Please let him be alright...*

"Yes I understand. We'll get him here."

Sean slammed the phone down. He looked angrier than Cydney had ever seen him in her life.

"What is it, where's Jake? I want my son. Why have they taken him?"

"They want Rupert here tomorrow. No police."

"Rupert? So this is about Benton and Crossley?" Cydney collapsed in a heap on the chair. "I knew they were desperate, but I didn't think they were capable of this."

"I doubt they're going to do him any harm. They want out of their situation and they know Rupert will bail them. That's clear from what you told me," Sean reasoned.

"But they didn't have to do it this way. Why take Jake to get to Rupert?"

"I don't know. But Cydney, you can be sure I won't rest until Jake comes back to us," he said, and Cydney knew he meant it.

CHAPTER THIRTY

THE light, filtering through a small metal-barred window above him, woke Jake. He had no idea how long he'd been asleep but he was cold, hungry and wanted to pee. Pushing a smelly old blanket off him, he tried to stand. His head hurt like hell, waves of dizziness washed over him and he felt sick. He promptly plonked down again on the cold tiled floor, propping himself up against the wall. Where was he and, more to the point, why was he here? Two men had literally picked him up yesterday when he was in the school music room practicing for the competition and told him they were taking him to a friend. His mum would have been proud of him as he put up a fight, kicking one of the men where it would hurt the most, but he'd had no choice but to give in. They were far stronger than he was. They'd ordered him to call his mum, telling him what to say. At the last minute he'd added in the bit about his dad coming to pick him up, hoping the men wouldn't understand. Nobody had said anything at all.

They'd bundled him into the back of a big black car with the two men either side so he couldn't escape. He'd never felt so frightened in his life. They drove for what he thought was nearly three hours as he was counting the minutes in his mind but he couldn't really see where he was going as they told him to keep his eyes closed, which wasn't easy, and he kept trying to peek. When they eventually stopped they walked him through a hallway of some derelict house that was dark and smelt damp. They let him to go to the loo, and gave him a sandwich and a lemonade, which had a funny taste to it. Then the next thing he knew he was awake in this room with no idea about anything apart from having a very sore head. He guessed it was some time during the day because of the sun coming through, but that was about all.

Jake decided to make some noise and see who came. He started shouting out as loud as he could, despite the fact it hurt his head and his mouth was dry. Nobody came. Perhaps there was nobody here and he had been left all alone. He decided to try to stand up again and this time made it to the door, about ten paces away. He tried the handle once but nothing happened. Trying again, he shook at it violently but the door was obviously locked from the outside. He bent down to peer through the keyhole, but someone had blocked it. He banged on the door with his fists, but again nothing. He decided this wasn't going to achieve anything and he didn't want to hurt his hands; he was a musician after all and his hands were very important. There was also no point kicking at the door as they'd taken his trainers away. He turned around and walked back to the window but couldn't see through as it was too high. It was throwing some light into one corner though, and he could see the room was completely bare – nothing to sit on, nothing to stand on. All he had was the skanky blanket and the clothes he stood up in. Not much help at all. Perhaps if he lay down and had another sleep, someone would come to him.

The message he'd given to his mum had been a bit cryptic but he hoped she would understand, being so clever and knowing about these things. He wished his dad was around. He often thought of him, as he was his absolute hero. He died helping people in Afghanistan and got a medal for it. He wanted to be like his dad but not as a soldier like he and Sean were. No. He wanted to help people through his music. That was his aim in life.

He thought of Lauren. She was such an annoying sister but he loved her to bits and would always look after her. He decided there and then that he would try to be a better brother to her.

He wanted to pee badly still but there was no toilet. He had no choice, he would have to do it in the corner of the room away from where he slept, but it felt awful.

He was beginning to feel very sleepy again for some reason. He never slept in the day. He wondered why he felt like this and thought back to the lemonade. Did they put drugs in it? He was always watching this sort of thing on TV and he decided that was the reason. Possibly they would come back soon as he was so hungry and his stomach was rumbling non-stop. He was used to eating when he wanted to so this lack of food was making him feel quite sick. Or maybe it was the drugs. What a story he'd have to tell his friends, if he ever got out of here.

He lay back down on the makeshift bed on the floor in the corner of the room and a sudden image of Lauren came to him. It was so vivid he almost passed out. She was sitting on their couch in the living room with mum and she was asking him where he was. In his mind he answered back that he didn't know, and then went through everything he did know and what had happened to him.

He and Lauren had this thing between them that he found quite funny but nobody else understood. She knew what he was going to say before he said it, and vice versa. It was the twin thing, people had said. Anyway, he tried to communicate with her, just in case she could hear him. 'Never underestimate the power of the mind', his mum always told him. He missed his mum. Although he always told her he was too old for cuddles, he wasn't, and he wanted her now so much. He felt tears prickling his eyes. No, he wouldn't cry, he was fourteen and a man nearly, and men didn't cry. But the tears came anyway and fell down his cheeks. He didn't know whether he was ever going to see his mum or Lauren ever again.

"You've done what? Are you completely out of your mind? If we weren't in trouble before, we certainly are now."

"Oh, calm down, Bob. You'll give yourself a heart attack, unless the cancer gets you first. I'm not going to harm him."

"He's a young boy. You can't go kidnapping someone just to get your way! Money laundering and insider dealing is one thing, but this? I can't believe you've done this to me!" Robert Crossley was beside himself with an anger that was at explosion point.

"You? I've done nothing to you, except make sure you had a very nice roof over your head to keep my sister in the style to which she's become accustomed. Now who's insane? You're just as much a part of this as me. You seem to have a very short memory. Must be the drugs you're on."

Robert Crossley was sitting with Craig Benton in his suite at the Ritz in London. They had arrived the day before. Crossley had felt too ill to travel but Benton had practically ordered him, or rather persuaded him in his inimitable way, as they had a few things to sort out apparently, and his presence was required. Frankly, he hadn't had the energy or willpower to argue so he'd taken as many strong painkillers as he could and boarded the plane. Now he felt at death's door and wished he was back in New York with his wife and kids around him. However, it was doubtful he could actually get back. Now he was petrified as to what his brother-in-law had done.

"But why? What can you hope to gain?"

"I need Rupert Van der Hausen here. The only reason he would come here is if the Granger woman asked him and if she was in trouble. What better way than having some hold over him, and her of course, by looking after her son for a few days?"

"But to what end?" He shook his head in absolute horror and dismay. "Sometimes I just don't know you."

"Well think about it. We have not quite played cricket, as the English might say, for the last few years. We have earned plenty of money but not as kosher as one would want. We have this problem now with Centurion and we know Van der Hausen wants to buy it. We also know that the lovely Cydney Granger, somehow down to you and your ineptitude, knows everything about us and our little games."

"How can you be sure?" Crossley said. A sharp pain tore through him and he thought he would pass out. He clasped his stomach in agony, his whole body bent over double to get some relief. Oh, for that escape from pain, he thought to himself. But that wasn't going to happen yet.

"Don't be stupid, as well as everything else. Of course she knows. I spoke to the agents in the British Virgin Islands and in Jersey. One of their guys told her everything. Must have cost her, or rather Rupert. Shame he's not going to get the chance to spend his ill-gotten gains."

"Where's the guy now? What have you done with him?"

"Oh, he's just gone on a little journey to Australia for his health. I believe he's working on some distant sheep farm now." Benton sounded so matter of fact.

"So what now, where's the boy?"

"Nowhere you need to know about but he's safe, for now anyway, as long as Van der Hausen and the lovely Cydney Granger play ball. My intention is that we come to some very amicable agreement and in return she lets us off the hook and tells no-one about our past and all she's discovered. Then we sell our portfolio for a very nice sum, more than we would have got before. He will also make a tidy packet, so everybody will be happy. Then you can go off and die under some stone or whatever, and I can continue with my very nice lifestyle."

"I never wanted to get involved in kidnapping. I wanted nobody harmed," Crossley said, finding it even harder to concentrate on anything Benton said to him.

"You have quite a short memory, brother-in-law. It was you who screwed your young half-brother out of his inheritance, I do believe. And no harm involved with him or his mother? I don't think so."

"I didn't get involved in anything like this. Yes, it was all about the money, but nobody got hurt physically. I've done some bad things in my life but nothing compares to this. Just tell me one more thing. Was it you who tried to kill Cydney Granger and her associate? Are you really capable of murder?"

Benton looked at him and laughed.

"Well nobody died, did they? I'd hardly call it murder. Just a little frightener I would say." He sipped slowly at his drink.

"So it *was* you! I can't believe you would do that and involve me in it."

"Oh, do give it a rest. She's alive, and so is the guy she was with. We're about to get our fortune back, so stop whinging like an old man. Do as you're told and we'll come out of this smelling of roses."

Smelling of something, Robert Crossley thought to himself, but he doubted it was going to be floral.

CHAPTER THIRTY-ONE

CYDNEY had not slept all night. Sometimes she paced the room, but mostly she sat beside Lauren, holding her hand and stroking her face. Occasionally Lauren would stir, moaning slightly, turning over but going back to sleep again. Sean and Claire helplessly watched on. Sophie was in tears but kept herself busy making coffee and bringing sandwiches every so often, which she laid out on the table and kept replacing as they were mainly left untouched. Cydney was beside herself with worry and fearful for her son. She wanted desperately to phone the police but knew this might put Jake's life in danger. It wasn't worth the risk so instead she and everyone waited for more news, for the phone to ring telling them the next steps to take.

"Cydney, please sit down. You need to rest," Claire said.

"Rest! How can I rest when my son has been taken by goodness knows who? I can't believe I let this happen. It's all my fault. Sean, what should we do? Should we call the police anyway?"

"I think we should sit and wait it out until we know their game plan. We have no idea why he's been kidnapped. We know it's to do with Rupert. They want him here."

"Who are 'they', exactly?" Claire asked. "Is this anything to do with your accident?"

"I'm sure of it, Claire. I just can't think who else has anything to gain from Rupert."

"But what have you been working on? Who are these people?"

Cydney started to explain, leaving nothing out. There was no

265

reason to keep anything secret any more. There was too much at risk and she needed all the help she could muster.

"Well, they sound like a nice bunch of guys. I can't believe what the hell you've got yourself involved in," Claire said.

"Well, I *am* trying to earn a living. It's all right for you, swanning off whenever the mood takes you. You have everything you want, including a rich husband to keep you. I have nobody to keep me." Cydney was near to tears again. As usual, her sister had got to her, had pushed the wrong buttons.

"Ladies please," Sean interrupted. "Really, this is doing nobody any good. Cydney, why don't you go upstairs and lie down? We'll watch Lauren and call you when she wakes up."

Claire stood up. "I'm sorry, Cyd. I'm just so upset about Jake. I didn't mean to say what I did. You know me, always putting my foot in things. I'll come up with you."

"No, it's okay. I'm fine. I didn't mean to yell but it's all this waiting around that I hate. I'll go and take a shower. You sit with Lauren, I won't be long."

Cydney climbed wearily up the stairs. She didn't go straight to her room but to Jake's, and sat on his bed, looking at the guitar he had left there. She stroked her fingers down the fret and strummed softly across the strings. All his things were there, untidy as always. Posters on the wall of his favourite singers, the keyboard set up with his hand-written scores in front of it. He had his own mixer next to the desk and on the floor scattered around were a dozen CDs and a few percussion instruments. She pushed her foot forward and touched the closest one, a tambourine, and the bells made a tinkling noise. Everything about him was his music. She sat there quietly, the tears cascading down her face. Suppose he never came back? What if his talent was for nothing and all his music was wasted and never heard? What if she never saw him again? It was all too unthinkable.

"I hate seeing you cry."

"Oh Ray, it's you. Sorry." She tried to wipe her eyes with the back of her hand.

"I know about Jake. Lauren was right."

"You know? Where is he? Is he ok? Can you see him?"

"He's fine for the moment."

"What does that mean, for the moment? What's going to happen to him?"

"Try and keep calm. I can see him in the house that Lauren mentioned. They are not trying to hurt him; this is a warning to you."

"Oh my God, what have I done? My work is supposed to support us, not harm my children!"

"Cydney, there's more to this than meets the eye."

"Please explain, Ray. Can you cast any light on my accident at all? I know it's all connected. You told me just before it happened to keep my enemies close. I should have listened. You said you couldn't help me then. Can you help me now?"

"I know there are these two Americans around you. One of them is very ill, but it's the one called Benton you need to watch out for."

"You mean to say Robert Crossley was telling the truth when he said it wasn't his fault? Is he not the enemy to keep close?"

"No. He was, for sure, but he's not directly involved in this. He wants to make peace, whilst he's here. Benton is the one who organised the kidnapping. He's in a real financial mess and he's desperate. He will try to force your hand, or rather that of your friend. He's mixed up with some not very nice lenders, who are after him."

"Sorry, Ray, let me get this straight. You're telling me that Benton's borrowed from somewhere or someone other than a bank? So what are we talking? Mafia money?"

"Well, something like that. He needs to pay them back, and quickly."

"So he needs Rupert to move quickly. Which means I have to get him here without delay, and he's using Jake as a means to do so?"

The realisation of this hit Cydney as she leant forward in her chair, her hands covering her face, in total disbelief that the situation had come to this. Claire was right in what she had said. She needed to get Jake back and then totally rethink her life. She couldn't go on like this, endangering her kids. She tried to think rationally. What would Steve do in the circumstances? Then again, he wouldn't have got them into this mess in the first place. What had she done? It was all her fault. Everything.

"Yes, Cydney. That's exactly as I see things. I am trying to help you but you need to impress upon Rupert the urgency."

"I understand. Thank you. We'll find Jake, there's no *if* about it. Can't you tell me where he is?"

"We need to rely on Lauren for this. When she wakes up, I'll be there and we can help each other. I need her too."

"What does that mean?"

"She can tune in to her brother better than either you or me, you know that. I'll be back later."

Cydney was left alone as Ray moved away. She sighed deeply, got up and left Jake's room to take a shower, to try to wash all the hurt away. Some chance though. As the water splashed over her, she put a hand to her mouth to stifle a sob, then let go completely, the tears falling down her face and mixing with the soap. The twins were her life. An enormous surge of love rose up in her as she felt Jake's loss as keenly as she felt Steve's, even though her son was not dead. She shook the thought away – that was not going to happen. Cydney craved normality but most of all she yearned to know her family was safe. A sense of foreboding grew like a cloud over her, and the feeling she could not protect her loved ones invaded her.

An hour later she was getting dressed when she heard a car in the driveway. She ran to the window and saw a chauffeur climbing out of a car and moving around to the back to help somebody out. Rupert! Thank the stars and everything else, she thought, as she rushed to finish dressing and raced downstairs to greet him. He must have taken his private jet from

Johannesburg for the eleven-hour trip. Cydney had called him soon after Sean had put the phone down to the kidnappers, and more or less summoned him to the UK, giving no reason, explaining she couldn't talk over the phone. But she'd sounded so desperate, which was most unlike her.

Cydney ran out of the house and rushed straight towards Rupert, crying into his arms, nearly knocking him over.

"My, what's all this about?" He took hold of her shoulders and stood her upright. Tears were pouring down her face.

"They have Jake!"

"What do you mean? Who has Jake?"

"It's those two, Craig Benton and Robert Crossley. They want you and the only way to get to you was via me and my family."

Rupert put his arm around Cydney's shoulders and led her back into the house and into the living room where Sean and Claire were waiting.

"You'd better tell me everything then. When did this happen?"

"Last night. I knew you would come but I couldn't tell you why then. I was told not to. I didn't want to jeopardise my son's life. Oh my God! We must get Jake back. Please, you have to get him back for me!" Cydney was more desperate than she had ever felt in her life. She would never forgive herself if anything happened to her son. Steve would never forgive her either.

"Sean, perhaps you could put me totally in the picture, please," Rupert said.

"They called me. Told me to get you here no matter what or they would harm Jake. From what Cydney tells me, they want to do a deal with you for the company but also come out of it unscathed, fully protected against any potential police or tax action that could put them in jail, and no doubt keep as much of their money as possible."

"So that's their form of ransom, then. I buy the company, give them what they want, and they will release Jake?"

"Yes, sir. I believe that is entirely the picture," Sean said.

"And that's the type of people I have to do business with?"

"Rupert, I don't know what to say," Cydney responded. "I met with Crossley and he assured me you could have the company, for the right money. I don't understand why he and his brother-in-law would go to such extreme lengths to get what they want, when they could do it the nice way. However, I was told Benton borrowed money from a certain, shall we call it syndicate? And they want their money back immediately."

"I see. Then they're really desperate and will go to any means? Or rather, have gone already"

"Rupert, I think this is more Benton. Crossley's very ill, and I don't think he has the energy or strength for any of this. He may not even know what his brother-in-law has been up to. To be honest I think he would have told me when we met before. He had no reason to hide anything once he told me he was dying."

"Are you getting soft on him?" He gave her a weak smile. "Anyway, I'm glad you're beginning to think clearly now."

"I have no choice. And no, I'm not getting soft. It's important to keep things together to get Jake back, and look after Lauren, but there's something vulnerable about Robert Crossley."

"Mum?"

Cydney flicked her eyes towards Lauren, who was beginning to stir, and went to her side.

"Are you okay darling? Here, let me help you up."

"Oh, Uncle Rupert, you're here. Are you going to get Jake back for us?" Lauren rubbed at her eyes. Her face was red and her eyes swollen from crying, even though she had been asleep for so long.

"Yes, Lauren, I am." He turned to Sean. "Can you and I go and have a quiet word, please? I think we need to get a plan of action together."

The two men sat in the library, drinks poured. They needed every resource now and for everyone to pull together.

"Sean, I doubt their threat of harming Jake if we call the police will be carried out. We know the last thing they want is for the police to be involved. No, they have Jake and they think they hold all the winning cards. Well, they have some of them but we're holding many ourselves. I'm the only one who can give them money and what's more, immunity. From what Cydney was telling me, they need me to save their skin and while Jake is with them they think they can hold out until they get what they want. What we need to do is get to Jake first somehow, and the way to do that is to play them at their own game."

"I agree, sir. They're obviously desperate and they've taken wild measures, but they may not be thinking clearly. That's where we have the upper hand. What Cydney said makes sense, but we need to move quickly. So what do you think their next step will be?"

"You haven't heard from them again then?"

"No."

"I take it we can't make contact with them. So we wait, or do you have another suggestion?"

"I'm reluctant to ask Cydney too much, as her mind is on Lauren and Jake, but how about we call in Ash and Jenny? And I'd suggest sooner rather than later. I doubt Jake is being held in salubrious settings."

Cydney opened the door into the library. "Jake is somewhere in Sussex."

Rupert looked at her. "How do you know that?"

"Lauren told me. He's in an old derelict mansion house set in acres of grounds, near a lake. She doesn't know where, though. We have to find the location. Ash and Jenny are on their way."

"Great minds," Rupert agreed. "We were just going to call them in. But you need to tell me a bit more about what Lauren said."

"That's it, everything. Sophie's taken her upstairs to freshen up now. I don't want to involve her in any more unless we have to. If she gets anything else from Jake, then she'll tell us. Rupert, don't look at me like that, it's a twin thing."

"At this stage, I'll take whatever we have."

"Sir, I have an ex-army mate who lives down there. I'll give him a ring and see if he recognises the description of the house. There can't be many like that in the area."

"Good idea. Cydney and I will try and put together a game plan."

"You know, Rupert?" Cydney said. "This is all about timing. This thing with the syndicate has forced Benton's hands."

"Does Crossley know about this other lender?"

"I'm not sure. Maybe he's in the dark about it but when I met with him, he was very open, especially about letting you have the company for the right price. About everything, in fact."

"You told me the bank was about to call in the loan. If they do that then they'll get nothing out of it. No, they need me and they know it."

"They also need to pay off these people, it would appear. Rupert, I have to ask you, do you still want the company after all this? I know it started off as a very good idea and you had plans for re-development and so forth, but now?"

"No, Cyd, I'm not going to part with a penny of my money. How could I, when everything about this is tainted by fraud, corruption and goodness knows what else? But Benton and Crossley don't need to know that."

"I'm pleased. It's the right thing to do. So now what?"

"My aim is to get Jake back as soon as possible, and then deal with these two reprobates. Let's wait and see how Sean gets on with his friend, and your two employees should be here soon. The most important thing is Jake now. Please don't cry again, Cydney. We'll get him back, if it's the last thing we do."

CHAPTER THIRTY-TWO

EVERYONE was poring over a large map of Sussex and the surrounding areas, which was spread out across Cydney's dining room table. Sean's ex-army friend had suggested a couple of areas to check as a possible location for the mansion.

"This is like looking for a needle in a haystack," Claire said. "Sean, did your friend not have any idea?"

"He mentioned a few places, but Sussex is huge - a few thousand square miles - and he couldn't specify which part. It goes all the way down to the coast."

"Ash," Cydney called out, "are you getting anywhere on the computer?"

"Nope. Still looking through the search engines. I found a lake called Bewl Water, on the borders with Kent. There's also Ardingly Reservoir."

Sean pinpointed them on the map.

"Yes, I can see those. They're man-made. Didn't Lauren say it was a house with its own lake?"

"Yes she did," Cydney said. "How about looking for some empty heritage houses?"

"Are they normally empty?" Claire asked.

"How do I know?" She was feeling far too weary to even think about being nice.

The ringing of the phone made everyone jump. Cydney rushed to answer it.

"Where's my son? What have you done with him? I swear I'll kill you if anything happens to him!"

Ash had set up a loud speaker from the phone so everyone could hear the conversation on the other end. He pushed a button to record it all.

"Is Van der Hausen there?" a clear American and well-spoken voice asked.

"Yes, he is. Who is this? What do you want?"

"Please, don't play games with me. You know exactly who I am and what I want. A meeting first, though."

"Where and when?" Cydney asked.

"This afternoon, three o'clock. Heathrow Airport. Shall we say the Radisson?"

"Where's Jake, how do I know he's okay?"

"Your son's fine, and will remain so as long as you play ball. Be at the meeting. No police. I want you, Van der Hausen and no one else. Certainly not your little Irish hound, is that clear?"

Sean made a fist with his right hand and punched it into his left palm, grinding his knuckles with rage. Jenny put a hand on his shoulder to calm him.

"How can I trust you?"

"You have little choice, if you want your son back," and the phone went dead.

Cydney stared at the receiver for some time then replaced it in its cradle.

"Rupert, let's get ready. We have to do what he says."

"Yes. I know. Sean, you need to continue searching for Jake with Ash and Jenny."

"Surely you aren't going on your own, Cyd?" Claire asked.

"I trust that was rhetorical? We have to do what Benton wants. You know there's no choice. Please stay and look after Lauren. Sophie will be here too. Call if the phone goes again."

"Cydney," Sean said, walking towards her, "I'm coming with you. I'm not going to let you go with just Mr Van der Hausen. Irish Hound indeed!"

"No, he knows you. Call Tom Patterson, Richard's friend.

Tell him to get to the hotel as soon as possible and watch out for Benton. Tell him whatever you need to. He's a good back-up, if we need one. Meanwhile, you need to find where Jake is."

Jenny and Claire stood at the door, grabbing each other's hands while they watched Cydney and Rupert leave.

"I feel so helpless."

"Me too, Jenny. Come on, let's have another cup of Sophie's tea."

"I'm knee deep in it already. Not sure I can drink anymore, but it does seem to take your mind off things."

They closed the door and walked back towards the dining room.

"Sean, I think I've found something," Ash called out. "A small lake in Southwick."

"What, where's that?"

"Just outside Brighton. Look, about five miles from the main town."

Sean went back to the map and located the area.

"Ok, I've got it. Now what?"

"I've been looking on the land registry sites and planning department. There's an old mansion that used to belong to Lady Gillinghall and her family. When she died she bequeathed the house to a local nursing home but they couldn't get planning permission so it was left empty."

Sean walked behind Ash and leant over his shoulder.

"Can you find any pictures at all?"

Ash clicked onto another site.

"Yes, look. It's set in twenty acres with a long driveway coming up to the main house. And there's the small lake with the summer house next to it."

"It looks lovely," Claire said.

"The pictures are old, and on a 'Famous Houses' site. It may not look like that now, if it's been left to go to wrack and ruin. What do you think, Sean?"

"I think it's the best lead we have, the only one in fact. It's going to take me a couple of hours at least to get down there. I'll call my mate and a few other friends. I suggest I set off now," and he practically ran out the room, shouting on his way, "Call me if you get anything else, or if anyone phones."

Finally, Sean thought to himself, some action. He hated the hanging around, waiting for something to happen. He couldn't bear the thought of Jake being locked up somewhere and if anyone was going to find him, he would. He ran to get a few specialised items from his cottage and within ten minutes roared off in the Mercedes, calling his ex-army pal, explaining the situation and asking him to muster whomever he could. Sean was unsure if this was going to be a wild goose chase or not but he was not going to take the chance. If it turned out Jake wasn't there, well at least he had tried, for the sake of Steve and Cydney - and Lauren of course. He loved that little girl, and Jake, as if they were his own.

Driving down towards Brighton, thoughts of the captain tore through his mind. Where was he? And, more to the point, was he still alive? Whose body was it that they'd found in the desert? He'd still had no news from General Bowles-Smith on that, and the man had promised to keep him in the picture. Sean knew the person he'd spoken to on the phone when he was at HQ was definitely his commanding officer but over time he had started to doubt himself. Since his return, he had tried with some difficulty to hide his anguish from Cydney. It was probably the most difficult thing he had ever had to do in all his life, especially knowing that the captain had been almost within his grasp, and yet he had lost him. In some ways, Sean thought it would be better for Steve not to return. How could he explain where he had been for the last four years? Cydney would never forgive her husband for not coming back to her, no matter what, and she would blame Sean for lying to her. All would be completely lost.

Cydney and Rupert stepped into the modern and very busy lobby of the hotel and looked around them. A coach load of guests were just alighting, and in between the people coming and going with their multitudes of luggage and the hotel staff and bellboys racing around, she glimpsed Tom Patterson reading his newspaper by the lounge area, drinking a coffee. He flicked his eyes up as he saw her but made no sign of recognition.

Two heavy set men in black suits approached them and indicated with a flick of their heads that they should follow them down the corridor. Cydney glanced over her shoulder and Tom nodded that he understood she was moving away from the reception area. It was comforting that someone like Tom was watching her back, and Rupert's. She didn't know who else was there with Tom around the hotel, but she doubted he was on his own. His job was to mingle with the people around him, to be there, watching and waiting, protecting whoever it was he and his team of men and women needed to protect. This time it was her and Rupert.

"Cydney," Rupert said in a whisper, as they were escorted away. "Try and leave the talking to Benton. Let's see what he has to say. I don't want us to play our hand too early. My intention is to agree to his demands, whatever they are. I'm thinking here of Jake. Benton has to know, and believe, that I'll pay whatever he wants."

"I know, I'm with you on this. He has no reason to believe you'd pull out of this, especially while he has my son." Cydney said the last word with a break in her voice.

"Be strong, Cyd. I'm with you." He took her arm and held on to it.

"Sean will find Jake, I know it. I have every trust in him. He's never let me down."

The two suits took them into a small room off one of the many conference centres that were dotted around the hotel and then stepped outside, closing the door behind them. There was a click as the door was locked from the outside.

The room looked like any other boardroom, laid out with pads and pens for about twenty people, empty glasses in front of each place and bottles of water in the centre. Benton was sitting at the head of the table and drinking a small glass of what looked like whisky, despite the hour. A smartly dressed middle-aged man was next to him with his laptop open and various papers laid out neatly in front of it.

"My signature drink, in case you were wondering. Sometimes you just need this, don't you agree?" Benton raised the glass to them.

"Where's Jake?" Cydney demanded. "Stop playing games and give me my son back."

Rupert touched Cydney's arm, indicating for her to quieten.

"Please, both of you, come and take a seat. I do hate to stand on ceremony. May I introduce myself? Craig Benton, but of course you know that, although we've never met. Van der Hausen, I believe we crossed paths once over a little matter in the States. Sorry you didn't win, such a shame."

Rupert stood there, maintaining an air of calm, and said nothing at all.

"Seems I have the silent treatment. So be it. Mrs Granger, you have of course had the pleasure of meeting my brother-in-law, Bob Crossley. Sorry he couldn't be here. The man has taken himself off to hospital to die, probably dead by now, in fact."

"You're all heart," Cydney said.

"Yes, I know. Anyway, please don't worry about your son. He is being well looked after and he will be home with you before you know it. Hopefully today, if we can sort out this little deal of ours. Oh, by the way, I see you have your handbag with you. I'm sure you don't mind handing over the cell phone you have in there. We don't want any uninvited guests arriving at our private gathering."

"What do you want, Benton? Why go to such extremes?" Rupert asked.

"I had to be sure you would come."

"Well, I'm here now. You've got what you wanted."

"Oh, do please sit down, both of you. It makes me feel so uncomfortable with people standing around me. Sorry we had to meet in such surroundings but I'm about to jet off back to the States and this was more convenient for me. I have my lawyer with me, Stephen Frost, who has drawn up our Agreements. I knew you wouldn't want to wait around."

"Surely you can't expect me to sign anything now, without my lawyers present? Don't be ridiculous. I haven't looked at anything in detail and you want, how much?"

"I do find talking about money distasteful. But yes, I do expect you to sign now. I'm sure the lovely Mrs Granger has briefed you on everything. After all, she's so efficient, which is why we are all sitting around the table right now."

"This is blackmail. You can't do this," Cydney snapped.

"Well, actually I can. Because I have your son and if you want him back then I want this sale to go through. Today."

"I need time to read through everything," Rupert said. "I'm not handing over anything without that."

"I tell you what, you can have an hour. Just bear in mind the longer you take, the longer Master Granger is in my hands." Benton looked at his watch. "It's now three twenty-five. I'll return at four-thirty with Mr Frost, and if the papers are not signed at that stage then you'll suffer the consequences. Oh, one more thing for you to consider. Once signed, I want the money within twenty-four hours in a bank of my choosing."

"What about the loan from Sigmunds Bank? Oh yes, and let's not forget the private loan."

"You really have done your homework, Mrs Granger. How

unusual for a woman to have looks as well as brains. Oh, don't look so hurt, take it as a compliment. Anyway, Sigmunds is all sorted. I have the chairman neatly in my hands."

On that passing shot, Benton and his lawyer left the room, ignoring her second comment, and left Rupert and Cydney surrounded by documents they had little time to read through.

"What a lovely man," Cydney said. "So what did he mean about the chairman? He must be blackmailing him too. He's really desperate... if he let the bank call in the loan he would have lost everything, and we know he's borrowed heavily from elsewhere. So now he has to pay back whoever he's borrowed from before they come after him, and by all accounts they're not going to wait around. It all rests with you, Rupert."

"My main concern is Jake. We need to stretch this out as long as we can. He thinks he holds us in the palms of his hands, but he doesn't. If I don't sign then he doesn't get his money, so he believes, but he's getting nothing from me anyway. This isn't the way to do business, especially not with me. We need to give Sean enough time to locate Jake."

"But you know, even if Sean finds Jake, there's no way Benton is going to let it rest at that. You think he's going to let us walk out of here?"

"No, I don't, but he can't do anything in such a public place. Don't forget we have Tom outside, and whoever he's brought with him. You know, we might as well look at what he's given us here," and Rupert picked up a set of the bound papers in front of him. He passed a second to Cydney. "It'll take your mind off Jake for a moment."

Poring over the documents, Rupert came to realise what a vast range of excellent investments Benton and Crossley had made, despite everything.

"You didn't tell me they were part owners of the Sphere, that new building in Docklands."

"They must have kept it out of their main structure. It's an amazing building. I don't know how the glass bends like that, to give it the shape."

"Cyd, I'd love to get my hands on this portfolio. Just think what I could do! They bought wisely, especially in areas ripe for regeneration in East London, going out towards the south to Battersea - and there are a couple of hotels in Central London."

"I know, but think how they got their money. If you give Benton what he wants, you can't guarantee he will pay back Sigmunds and hand over the money to these so-called other lenders. Are you really changing your mind?"

"I am not condoning what they did at all, far from it, but in some ways they took advantage of people's greed and the system. They made money hand over fist, taking a high percentage of shares in companies they managed to float on the stock exchange, then walked away leaving the shareholders to run on their own. They offered mortgages to people who couldn't really afford them, and knew that after a couple of years their bank would foreclose on the loans. It was easy for them to increase their property portfolio and nobody stopped them."

"But, what about the way they dealt with you over American Securities? That was clearly insider dealing."

"I agree, but that's water under the bridge. I haven't always been so clean, you know, although I've never gone in for attempted murder or kidnapping."

"So you think it was Benton who tried to kill me and Richard? But why?"

"Actually, I think they were trying to frighten you more than anything, which they certainly did."

"To put it mildly."

"As I said, I am not excusing their actions. However, if we play this right, we could get Benton in custody and then deal directly with Sigmunds, who I'm sure will be pleased to get out of bed with Benton, and I'll be left with the portfolio, which is what I want."

"Well, okay. As long as we do everything legally - completely straight, Rupert - then I'm with you on this."

"We need George here. No good nodding your head or looking aghast at the thought. He has the legal mind we need. I met with him recently and he's completely cut up over the situation. He really does love you and the kids, you know. There's a story behind everything. Anyway, it's not for me to tell, you need to hear it from him directly. All I can see is that he was wronged and you should let him tell you."

"Then get him on the phone."

"Well, as soon as we have one..."

Cydney reached inside the top of her trousers to reveal a small device. "Always pays to be prepared."

Rupert smiled. "You never cease to amaze me, my dear."

The phone vibrated just as Rupert began to punch in the numbers for George and he passed the phone over to Cydney with a questioning glance.

"Hello?"

"Please don't put the phone down. I was hoping I could reach you." She could barely hear the voice on the other end.

"Who is this?"

"Bob Crossley. Please, I need to speak to you."

"How did you get my number? And what can *you* possibly want?" Cydney pulled the phone away from her ear and whispered to Rupert, "It's Crossley."

"Mrs Granger, Cydney, you must believe me. I had no hand in this. I'm not innocent, but I have never got involved in murder or kidnapping."

"So, what do you want?"

"Your son is held in a house near Brighton. Place called Southwick, I believe. My brother-in-law bought the house some time ago but it's been empty for years." Cydney heard the sound of Crossley coughing and gasping for breath. "I'm sorry, I can't speak any more. I wanted to tell you before I died."

282

"I'm not your confessor!"

"I'm not asking you to be. I just wanted to apologise for everything." Crossley's voice was getting weaker. "Also, I've called the police and told them everything. They should be in Brighton soon, and with you too. Please forgive me." The phone went dead, leaving it cold in Cydney's hand.

"Good Lord!"

"What? Tell me what he said."

Cydney repeated everything Bob Crossley had told her. "The hour's nearly up," she said, looking at her watch. "I don't think we should tell Benton anything about this call. Let's string him along until the police get here, see if he'll let down his guard."

"And what about George?"

"I'm ready to face him."

CHAPTER THIRTY-THREE

THE sound of crashing doors and people shouting woke Jake from another drug-induced sleep. The same horrible taste remained in his mouth. Moving his tongue over his dry lips made no difference, it was still there and he craved water. He sniffed at the disgusting smell of vomit in the room. Trying to stand, he only made it to a sitting position with a tremendous effort, then flopped heavily back down again onto his makeshift bed. His brain was incapable of engaging his limbs. Helplessly he lay there waiting, wondering about the noises, while trying to stop his eyes from closing - but he could feel himself sinking into the murkiness from where he had come. He didn't even care. The effort was too much. He couldn't think straight. Everything was a muddle and he couldn't reach the real world, so it was pointless even trying. His only thought was of his mum and Lauren, as he closed his eyes and met the darkness, the background noises fading into the distance.

"Jake, wake up. Jake! Come on, it's Sean! I'm here. You're safe."

Someone with very strong arms lifted him and nestled his head against their shoulder. Inwardly he knew this was a safe place and he gave in to the feeling of security but was incapable of anything but a groan. The smell of cigarettes on the person leaning over him was familiar, though.

"Jake. Can you hear me? You're safe. I'm taking you home."

"Dad?"

"No Jake, it's Sean. Come on lad, let's get you out of here."

"Going home?"

"Yes, we're going home."

The relief Sean had felt as he'd held Jake in his arms was indescribable. Thank goodness for this telepathy, or whatever it was, between the twins. Someone must have called the police to tell them after all, despite the orders not to. They'd arrived at more or less the same time as Sean and his crew, surprising the three men guarding the boy, who found themselves surrounded and gave themselves up without so much as a fight.

The house was vast, set out over three floors, and they found the doors to every room locked. Some of the men took on the outbuildings whilst others made a start on breaking down the doors, but Sean headed straight to the cellar, recalling what Lauren had told him.

The door down to the cellar was off the kitchen. Sean tried to kick it open but it was solid and wouldn't budge. He searched around and feeling under the bell board found a large ring of keys. He tried each one in turn, becoming increasingly frustrated until he found one that finally worked. Yanking back the door, he peered down at a steep stone staircase, the majority of which was in darkness. Reaching out, he flicked the light switch to his left but there was nothing. He fumbled his way down the steps, counting each one as he went, and held on to the rickety banister that felt as if it would break away from him at any moment.

There were scuttling noises from below, his favourite ... rats, and he saw a dim light as he reached the bottom. There was a small window with a grill over it, which was letting a little light through, and his eyes were drawn to a bundle of blankets in the corner. He flew across the floor and the smell that rose up made him heave. He put his hand over his nose but the mixture of urine, vomit and an unwashed body was still there. Please let Jake be alive! He dragged the blanket away, grabbing the boy, and lifted him into his arms.

One hundred miles away Lauren woke up from a deep sleep. "Thanks, Daddy."

Steve shook himself awake. There was no way he was going to die out here in the Golan Heights on his own but how easy it would be to give in. Pushing himself up slowly into a sitting position, he surveyed the terrain around him and not for the first time wondered how the hell he was going to reach Sean within twenty-four hours, the allotted time. It was just too far to go; it was too difficult.

The dream he had just had of his beautiful daughter came flooding back to him. He was sitting on her bed saying goodnight to her as he used to do but the scene didn't seem right to him. There was someone missing. Where was Jake? For some inexplicable reason he felt anxious. Frightened. But not about his own situation. Something was happening to his son. The dream seemed real and the feeling that Jake was somehow in danger was overwhelming. The worst part was that Steve was completely powerless to do anything about it. It was as if Lauren was trying to tell him something, but what? The emotion was just too much and tears of frustration fell uncontrollably. He didn't even bother to wipe them away from his face. He was simply too weak.

"Pull yourself together man," he shouted. "What the fuck do you think you're doing?"

He scrambled to his feet, with some difficulty, careful not to move his leg in the wrong way. The ground beneath him shifted as a wave of dizziness and nausea washed over him. He noticed his rifle not too far away up the hill from where he had fallen and he knew how important it was to retrieve it. He was going nowhere without that, but it was out of reach. The sun was beginning to go down now and he realised he must have been out for a couple of hours or more. There was not a person in sight thank goodness, which was all to his advantage. The last thing he wanted was settlers in the area to approach him or, worse still, troops.

Now there was no other choice, he had to go on. He hoped Sean would not give up and would keep coming back for him - the next day and the one after that. But Christ, he was in pain and the thirst he'd had previously was nothing compared to what he felt now. The sleep may have given him a bit of energy and his worry for Jake would push him along, but his leg was bleeding profusely through his trousers and he doubted he could manage to go too far.

He tore a piece of cloth from his shirt and wound it around his leg as a tourniquet to try to stem the flow of blood. The pain took his breath away. Perhaps Sean would guess he was in trouble and not give up on him. He could only pray. The main thing was that he was still alive, and whilst there was breath in his body he vowed to keep it that way. It was amazing what the body could sustain when it had to.

About an hour later, Steve had journeyed no further than a few hundred yards due to having to drag his leg along. The sun was setting and the temperature was falling rapidly. He desperately needed to rest through the night but there was no shelter. Thoughts of Jake were still with him but there was nothing he could do. Falling down to the ground, he rolled himself up into a tight ball to keep as warm as he could until the morning, and then he would decide what to do for the best.

The sound of a helicopter approaching woke him from his sleep. It was still dark and the lights beamed down onto him from above. He covered his eyes to protect them. Thank God! Sean had come to rescue him. Pulling himself up with as much strength as he could muster, Steve watched as a ladder was released and slowly descended. Two men in desert fatigues climbed down and ran towards him.

"Captain Granger?" asked one with a strong Israeli accent. "Here, take this," and he handed him a container of water. He grasped it in both hands and threw the water down his throat, hardly taking a breath. He responded when he could finally speak, his voice barely a whisper.

"Yes. How did you know where I was?"

They ignored his question.

"Can you stand, Sir?"

"My leg's no good. You'll have to help me."

The two men nodded at each other and one ran back to the helicopter and shouted up an order, whereupon someone lowered a basket. They lifted Steve and one held on to him as he was winched up into the craft. He was hardly conscious. They laid him on the floor and a medic was waiting with an intravenous drip. Steve looked up and as he drifted away, he heard a familiar voice,

"So, Dragonfly, you really are alive."

It was General Bowles-Smith.

CHAPTER THIRTY-FOUR

"I PRESUME you've had time to go through the bundles, and I feel sure you've come to the right decision. For everyone's sake, if you know what I mean. Shall we proceed?"

Rupert and Cydney watched as Benton and the lawyer strolled casually back into the room. They really needed to create more time without giving anything away.

"I have a few questions." Rupert was the first to speak. "How can we trust you? You could just take the money and run. How do I know you will pay off Sigmunds Bank, and anyone else you owe, and not leave me with the debt?"

"You don't, I suppose. But that would be very mean of me, don't you think? You have no choice in the matter. Pay the money and take your chances, and there is the matter of Master Granger of course, unless you've forgotten."

The hairs on Cydney's right side started to bristle as she knew Ray was by her side.

"Jake is safe."

"What do you mean?"

"Sean has him. He's okay, although a little drowsy. He's been taken to hospital to be checked out but will be fine."

Tears started to prickle behind Cydney's eyes but she couldn't betray what she knew to Benton, and did her best to stop them falling down her face.

"However," Benton continued, "it's all in the written Agreement which, I can assure you, is perfectly legal."

"Why are you doing this? Yes, I know you need the money,

but why go down this route? We could have sat around the table with our lawyers and drawn up the Agreement together, without resorting to attempted murder and kidnapping."

Benton sat there for a moment.

"You may be right, and yes, that might have been nice, but time isn't on my side. I had to be sure you'd do this. And you, or rather Mrs Granger, know too much about my activities."

"What about your brother-in-law? Where does he come into all this?" Cydney asked. The situation with Crossley bothered her. She felt sorry for him, against all her better judgement.

"We were in this together, all the way, until he fell ill. Then he went soft on me and wanted out."

"And he was involved in your little schemes with my family?"

"Reluctantly, I have to say he knew nothing about that. Anyway, we're wasting time and I have a plane to catch." Benton took out a Mont Blanc pen from his inside pocket and passed it to Rupert. "Shall we?"

"You need to stall him a bit longer."

"I have another question."

Benton stood up, pushing his chair away from him and sending it crashing to the ground.

"You have no more questions! Here's my pen, sign or suffer the consequences!"

The lawyer pushed the Agreement for Sale towards Rupert, already open at the signature page.

"This is not acceptable!" Rupert yelled, unable to contain his anger any longer. Cydney put a restraining hand on his arm.

"I would strongly urge you to do as you're asked, the lawyer said."

"I want to speak to Sigmund."

"All in good time. Now just sign," Benton ordered once again.

Rupert picked up the pen and leaned over the document. He looked up at Benton. Slowly, he removed the lid of the pen and hovered the nib over the paper. Then he pulled the pen back and started to flip through the pages again.

"For God's sake man, what are you doing now?"

"I want to check the list of assets. Make sure everything is there."

Benton snatched his mobile from the desk and held it up.

"In five seconds I am going to call my men and then it's goodbye to your son. Don't play with me. I'm deadly serious. Fuck the consequences."

"The police are here, Cydney. It's ok."

The sound of the door crashing open startled everyone. Benton looked at Rupert and Cydney quite calmly.

"I might have known. You think you're so clever."

"Actually, it was Bob who called them. He told us where Jake was too," Cydney said, "and yes, I think we've been *very* clever."

Nobody saw Benton take a small pistol out of his jacket pocket until it was too late. He placed it in his mouth and pulled the trigger, and a mixture of blood, bone and brains splattered onto the wall behind him.

A veil like pure gossamer drifted down over Cydney as, in the distance, she was vaguely aware of someone screaming.

CHAPTER THIRTY-FIVE

"I'M sorry to break this news to you, O'Connell. Israeli reconnaissance troops have found a second body they believe to be that of Captain Steve Granger. I know how much he meant to you. I wanted to tell you personally."

"Do we know what happened?"

"Not really. He was located outside a small settlement in the Golan Heights. From the autopsy, it would appear he died of heat and exhaustion. However, he was also suffering from heart disease which wouldn't have helped."

"So he nearly made it?"

"Yes. I think you should now try and get on with your life and not dwell on what might have been. He gave us a lot of invaluable information over the last year and we're all very grateful to him."

"Thank you for telling me, Sir. What plans do you have for the captain?"

"Arrangements have been made for his burial in Israel. In the circumstances, I think you'd probably agree this is the best course of action. I can't believe repatriating him will do any good, and I think it best not to tell his wife."

"I agree, Sir. It will do more harm in my opinion."

"Good. Well that concludes the matter."

Sean replaced the receiver and stood beside the telephone, staring down at it. Something didn't feel right to him. It was far too easy and compact. Steve was found dead and now he was being buried in Israel? Although he'd half expected it and resigned himself to the fact that the captain might not be alive, there were thoughts lurking in the back of his mind that he couldn't quite put his finger on. Sean had been back from the Golan Heights for a few weeks now, without any contact from HQ. The fact that Steve had only just been found didn't ring true. The captain would never have given up on reaching the meeting point, no matter what state he was in, unless he had actually died, of course. But why hadn't they found him sooner? The general might think the matter was concluded but Sean wanted to know more and he was going to do his utmost to find out what had happened. He didn't trust what he'd just been told. If there was a chance Steve was still alive, he knew that the general would keep him and use him for his own devices in whatever capacity he chose.

For now he would remain quiet and keep his thoughts to himself for the sake of Cydney, but if it took him forever, he would get to the bottom of it. If he *was* still alive, Sean knew that Steve would make contact by whatever means possible.

Dragonfly may not be coming home to roost now, but he bloody well would in the future, if he had anything to do with it.

"My two favourite girls. You really do look beautiful."

"Thank you, darling," Cydney said to George. "You don't look so bad yourself."

George smiled. "Is everybody ready?"

"Yes, Sean's in the car with Sophie, Sheila and her kids. I'm so pleased they could come. Sean seems to be getting on so well with her. We'll follow them. Claire and her husband are picking up mum with the carer and meeting us there. Rupert was due in an hour ago and should be making his way directly to the concert hall."

"Do you think he's happy with the offer from Sigmunds Bank?"

"He should be. I think he's done very well, actually. He gets the properties he's after at the price he wants to pay and Sigmunds have agreed to continue the financing, so everybody makes out of it – including us."

"Well, we could hardly say no to the percentage commission he

293

was offering," George said. "That should make you feel secure now."

"All the better for having you with me." Cydney turned and wrapped her arms around the man she now accepted in her life and kissed him on the lips, savouring the moment.

"Mum, is that absolutely necessary?" Lauren laughed. "Can't you do that when I'm not around?"

"Get used to it. It'll be happening every day if I have anything to do with it," George said, with a wink.

"I can't believe Jake won the competition," Cydney said, pulling away from George and checking herself in the mirror. It's amazing...getting to perform on his own in front of all those people."

"I know! Three or four hundred, he reckons. Is he playing all his songs, Mum? Even that annoying one?"

"Yes, Lauren, even that one."

"I'm taking my earplugs then."

George laughed.

Cydney flicked a loose curl behind her ear. "You two go on. I'll just grab my bag, I'll be out in a minute."

She stood for a moment in the hallway, looking around her, thankful for everything in her life. The door into her sitting room was open and she smiled at the sight of her walnut tree that was now in blossom. Steve would love it, she thought to herself, but now she had George by her side and she needed to let go of her husband and concentrate on what was around her. She smiled in the knowledge that the shadows that had followed her all her life would dim into the background and she'd be able to lay them finally to rest. She wiped a tear from her eye at the thought of the life they once had together.

"I still love that walnut tree, my darling."

Cydney heard his voice as if for the first time. The essence of him washed over her and her body went cold. She felt her knees buckle under her as she turned round to face him.

"Steve?" The shock was palpable and the blood drained from her face. "This can't be happening."

"Please don't cry. And please don't be angry with me."

"I've wanted to contact you for such a long time! Why haven't I been able to speak to you?"

"I'm here now and what went before doesn't matter."

Cydney looked at him. It was certainly his image and his voice, but something about him wasn't quite clear. His body kept drifting in and out of focus.

"Steve, I don't understand. You've spoken to Lauren. Why not me?"

"Yes. She's no longer a child. She's the image of you!"

"I want to know what happened to you."

"I wish I could explain, but I can't. I tried to get back to you but everything was against me. It wasn't my fault."

"That's not good enough," she snapped.

His image disappeared again.

"Come back! Where have you gone? I didn't mean to say that, I'm sorry! It was the shock!"

Cydney closed her eyes and willed Steve to return to her, but instead her mind was taken to a white room, empty apart from a bed. On it lay a man covered in white sheets. He was hooked up to several machines. She was aware of their whirring sound and the occasional bleep of the monitor as it recorded his heartbeat. The face of the man was very pale and she watched as his body rose above the room and floated in the air. It was apparent that he was on the brink of death, as if between two worlds. It was her husband's face, it had to be. However, that meant that he hadn't died four years ago. He was still alive.

The realisation hit her like a bomb had exploded in front of her. She shook her head to break the image. No! She fell forward and clung to the sideboard in the hall. She turned round to look at the front door, hoping that neither Lauren nor George would come in, wondering why she was not with them and ready to leave for the concert. That her husband was not dead was impossible, but it was so clear to her now why she could never make contact with him before.

"I'm sorry my darling. Please forgive me."

"Then help me understand!"

"I wish I could," he said, as the tears slipped down Cydney's face.

"You helped save Jake."

"I helped Lauren save our son, yes. It was easier for me to come to her."

"But I wanted you! I miss you so much. Where are you?"

Again his image disappeared and Ray came into her vision.

"You knew, didn't you?"

"I told you I would help you. I brought your husband to you, as you wanted. You have to be careful what you wish for."

"But he's not dead! All these years I've grieved for him, every single night of my life! I've been on my own. We all needed him, and all this time..."

Ray was silent as she glared at him, her words lost.

"So tell me," she said. "Where is he? I have to go to him!"

"Cydney, that's out of my hands. You'll have to wait. And if he wants you to find him he'll tell you when, and if, he recovers."

"Wait? How the hell do I wait? Ray, for God's sake, you have to help me!"

Cydney felt her strength evaporate as Ray melted away, leaving her alone again, her plea unanswered.

"Darling, are you coming?" George called.

Oh my God. George! What was she going to do now? How could she even...

"Are you joining us today?" George pushed through the door and walked back into the hallway. He tugged at her hand. "You look beautiful," he said, pulling her towards him and into his arms. "I love you, Cydney Granger. So very much."

Cydney, with her head against George's shoulder, stared into the empty space where Steve had been standing. "I love you," she whispered.

TO BE CONTINUED